TARGET

**Center Point
Large Print**

**This Large Print Book carries the
Seal of Approval of N.A.V.H.**

TARGET

Stella Cameron

CENTER POINT PUBLISHING
THORNDIKE, MAINE

This Center Point Large Print edition
is published in the year 2007 by arrangement with
Harlequin Enterprises, Ltd.

The text of this Large Print edition is unabridged. In other
aspects, this book may vary from the original edition.
Printed in the United States of America.
Set in 16-point Times New Roman type.

ISBN-10: 1-58547-992-6
ISBN-13: 978-1-58547-992-4

Library of Congress Cataloging-in-Publication Data

Cameron, Stella.
    Target / Stella Cameron.--Center Point large print ed.
    p. cm.
    ISBN-13: 978-1-58547-992-4 (lib. bdg. : alk. paper)
    1. Large type books. I. Title.

PS3553.A4345T37 2007
813'.54--dc22

2007000178

In memory of Julian Savoy.

TARGET

Prologue

The Refuge, California. 1990

"Take the girls and go."

"Now?" Nicholas asked. "Go where, Mom?"

"Wait here," she told Muriel and Ena and beckoned for Nicholas to follow her to the back of the trailer where she and Colin slept. "I'll leave first. Then you take Muriel and Ena and get on the bus."

Colin Fox was leader of the thirty-four-member north California commune where Nicholas had lived most of his life.

He thought of the old school bus Colin had brought back to the group a long time ago. Colin and the other men had taken out many of the seats and painted the vehicle green. Nicholas knew what it drove to "market" and it wasn't vegetables. Colin was his mother's partner, but not Nicholas's father.

"You'll get to the bus first?" Nicholas said. "Why can't we all go together?"

"I won't be there at all. I have to be somewhere else."

Nicholas breathed through his mouth. "No," he said. His hands tingled and he made fists. "Tell me what's going on. When will you catch up with us?"

"I've told you this is the only way I can keep you safe until we're past the dangerous time."

"What *is* the dangerous—"

9

"Please, Nicholas." She reached beneath the bed. "There isn't time for discussion."

He crossed his arms tightly and waited until his mother got to her feet again.

She stood quietly before him, looking into his face, with a regular-size envelope and a larger, padded one in her hands. "When you're on the bus, read this." She showed him the smaller envelope with his name written in her big, round hand. "You must keep these safe. Don't show them to anyone but Delia Board in Savannah."

"Savannah, Georgia?" Nicholas said, struggling not to panic. He had only seen the place on a map and it was a long way from California. "You want me to drive the bus to Georgia, to a woman I've never even heard of before?"

Mary Chance stared, and then she blinked. "No. I'm sorry, I'm not explaining this well enough. Put this money in your pocket." She gave him a roll of bills. "Take your bikes and make sure you're not seen. Get to town. You know the way well enough. Find the Greyhound bus station. Don't speak to anyone. Nick, give the girls the money, and each of you buy your tickets separately. Don't stand together. Get on the bus as if you don't know each other and sit separately. Do not travel as a threesome."

"I'm sixteen, Mom," Nicholas said. "You don't have to worry."

"You don't know how it is in the world." She glanced toward a window. "It's starting to get dark.

We're running out of time. Just listen and do as I tell you. There's a map in your envelope. It's of Savannah and I've marked the way you're to get to Delia. Her address and telephone number are there. She will know what to do. You have nothing to fear, but watch over those girls carefully. They've already had enough bad luck. If I can, I'll write to you. There's food in your packs."

He felt sick and confused. "Please tell me what's happening," he said. "Why send us now?"

"I can't tell you anything." His mother turned to the window again. "It's time. Muriel and Ena will have no one to turn to but you. Remember that."

The thirteen- and fourteen-year-olds had been runaways when a member of Colin's group had brought them to the commune. Colin had insisted on keeping them in the trailer he shared with Mary and Nicholas "Until I decide if there's a way to reunite them with their own," he'd said. Colin often sent a couple to San Francisco to look for a runaway child to befriend. He told the group this was their mission, to befriend the lost and help them go home, or at least find them a safe place to live.

Again, Nicholas had learned to doubt if Colin had the welfare of these kids in mind. Each time one of them left, Nicholas became desperate to learn their destinations.

He had never been able to find out a thing for certain.

His mother took one of his hands in both of hers.

She trembled. Tears glossed her blue eyes. Left alone to curl around her face and shoulders, her black hair showed no strands of gray. He had been born when she was younger than he was now and she could still pass for being in her early twenties.

Fear gripped Nicholas.

"Listen to me," she said. "And keep your voice down. I don't want Muriel and Ena frightened. I've been worried about them—we've got to get them out of here. Once you're away from the bus in Savannah I want you three to stay together. Delia will help you make your way."

"What will Colin do to me when I come back? How will I explain what I've done?"

"You will never, ever come to this place again."

Colin's followers left their trailer homes, taking with them anything that identified them. The group moved slowly, higher up the foothills. They knew the forested country well, that's where they worked over the crop each day, but were unfamiliar with other areas since Colin preferred that they not risk wandering away.

Darkness didn't help their progress.

With Mary at his side, Colin led the way. She completely lost her bearings but his long legs, his tall, strong body moved with the quick assurance of one who had been that way before—more than once.

He spoke to her in a whisper, "Are you certain those girls are waiting in the trailer?"

"Yes." Her heart pounded while she prayed all three young ones were safely away by now. "Why do they have to wait?"

Colin took his time to answer. "You know I prefer that you not question me. I have made contact with Muriel and Ena's family. They want them home again. I'll go back and take them to safety before the police come. I wanted to make sure our people were tucked in first."

"The police?" Mary said. "Why—"

Colin interrupted her, "Why do you think? Someone has spoken carelessly about our crops. That's why we must leave like this."

Crops? He had been calling the marijuana they grew "crops," as if he were talking about strawberries, or peaches, since the first plants went into the ground years earlier.

They scrambled over rocks for some distance before Colin stopped again and turned to wait for the others. When they drew close he said, "Hold up while I explain what's happening," in his quiet, authoritative voice. "There's going to be a police raid tonight."

After a short, heavy silence, muttering started. "How did they find out what we've been doing?" one man asked. "We have always been so careful."

"I'm not sure," Colin said. "We're lucky it hasn't happened before. But I promised you I'd take care of you if trouble ever came our way. We're going to a place where they won't find us—just until it's okay to come out again."

"How long will we have to stay away?" a woman asked.

"Until I'm sure it's safe," Colin responded. "Leave it to me. But we'll have to move on afterward and find somewhere else to live."

Sounds of sadness went up.

"Hush," Colin said. "You know I will always do what's best for you. I already have a place in mind and it's a good place where the land is fine and irrigation will be no problem."

Higher they climbed. Colin didn't use a flashlight, only the faint light of a weak moon. They all bunched closer to stay together.

Eventually Mary lost track of how long they had traveled but she thought it was perhaps two hours. Her nails were broken from grasping rocks and she'd stumbled once and skinned her knees.

Colin moved confidently. "We're almost there," he said at last. "There is food and water. The place is an old gold mine and absolutely solid."

No happy chatter followed.

"Blankets, sleeping bags, I tried to think of everything. No one will ever find us."

Nausea squeezed Mary's stomach. As she'd suspected since Colin told her to get ready for tonight, something was very wrong. If this raid was a fact, there would have been a meeting and decisions would have been made. That was the way things always went with the group. Colin had the final say and they all accepted that, but they talked first. "How can you be so sure the police are coming?" she asked.

"I'm sure they're coming," Colin said. "I have an inside contact who warned me. I trust him." He raised his voice. "We've arrived. Each of you brought a flashlight?"

A murmur of assent went up.

"Don't switch them on until you have all climbed down the shaft. I'll go first and help you find your way."

He cleared a place in an area strewn with boulders and felt around with his foot. "There's a rope ladder," he said. "It's strong and well anchored at both ends. I made sure of it. But don't all crowd in at once."

Colin gradually disappeared into the shaft and Mary followed him at once.

The shaft was fairly deep and she rested from time to time to ease her torn hands. She felt one of the others put a foot on the ladder. Little was said while they concentrated on finding each rung.

When Colin had told her to leave the girls behind and join him when it grew dark, Mary had feared for them. But perhaps she had been mistaken in sending them away with Nicholas.

There were no handholds to grab in the walls, nothing to stop the feeling that she swung in blackness with no beginning and no end.

She reached the bottom where Colin stood, his flashlight on and aimed at the ground. "This must have been a sort of chimney," she said to him. "For air. They couldn't have come in and out of the mine this way, could they?"

"I don't know about that. If there was another way in at some time, it's gone now."

One by one the others arrived and they clustered together. Mary's friend Belinda pressed close and whispered, "I don't like this. Closed-in spaces make me feel ill."

"Me, too," Mary said.

"This way," Colin said and led them along a rough-sided passage where they had to bend almost double. The passage opened out into what seemed to be a place where men had worked, hacking away at the rock in search of their fortunes.

The supplies Colin had mentioned were stacked along one wall.

"How did you get that lot down then, Colin?" One of the men, Zack, asked. "Wouldn't like to go up and down that ladder more'n a time or two, I can tell you."

Colin's smile, not often seen and always fleeting, came and went. "I lowered everything," he said. "Make yourself comfortable. We'll hope they come tonight as planned. If they do, we'll get away tomorrow."

He met Mary's eyes, then looked around, a heavy frown pulling down his pale brows. "Where are the girls?" he asked, loudly enough for all to hear.

Mary followed his example and pretended to search for them. "They knew we were leaving," she said. Being dishonest with her friends upset her.

Colin's silver-blond hair shone in the gloom. His

light green eyes roamed over everyone present and he appeared to hesitate.

He would ask where Nicholas was. He would see he was missing and be suspicious.

Then he moved. "I'll have to get them. William, watch over everyone until I get back."

He hadn't noticed. "I'll come with you," Mary said. She'd talk and make sure he didn't realize her boy hadn't been there.

"No. I'll be quicker on my own." And Colin went into the passageway again.

Mary listened until she couldn't hear his movements anymore. No one spoke but eventually the women started spreading sleeping bags on the rocky ground. She thought of Nicholas's concern about what Colin might do if he discovered he had been crossed. How would he react when he found out she had lied to him?

He had to hurry, Colin thought. Getting up here and leading the group into the mine had taken longer than he'd expected. He burst into the fresh air and pulled himself from the shaft.

The knife he took from an ankle sheath glinted. He paused, looking at the handle in his hand.

The blade sliced through the heavy rope ladder where he had fastened it to strong stakes driven into the ground a short distance away. For a moment or two more, he thought, then he dropped the useless ladder down into the blackness and removed the stakes.

He had already handpicked a rounded boulder that stood a little uphill. He braced his back against it, his feet firmly wedged against a rocky outcropping, and strained until the stone first rocked, then rolled over the entrance to the shaft. He used smaller rocks and gravel to seal any gaps.

1

In the Pointe Judah News *seventeen years later:*

MASS GRAVE UNCOVERED IN CALIFORNIA
Skeletons of thirty-three recovered:
Workers stumble on abandoned gold mine.

In one of the most horrific mass-death discoveries in California history, a sudden ground collapse during installation of a new cell tower has revealed multiple human remains.

Tangled skeletons suggest a desperate struggle to escape asphyxia in an abandoned gold mine.

Workers drilling at the site report that they became aware that they had broken into an existing cavity when surrounding earth began to cave in. The drill had pierced what is believed to have been a large vent intended to bring air into the mine. Most of the victims were heaped at the bottom of this hundred-foot-deep vent and are presumed to have been trying to claw their way up.

Officials have already tied the deceased to members of a northern California commune known as

"The Refuge." Seventeen years ago, people in the nearby town of Grove noticed the sudden absence of commune members. Until then, people from The Refuge had frequented shops and other businesses in Grove. At that time, police visited the settlement and found trailers still filled with possessions, but the owners had left.

It appeared that these people had supported themselves with extensive marijuana cultivation.

All efforts to track down members of the commune failed until the recent discovery.

Officials have announced that pieces of identification for thirty-three people were found with the remains. Longtime residents in Grove recall some of the people whose photographs are on these documents as commune members.

The public is asked to contact their local police departments with any tips, and to be advised that intensive efforts are under way to complete positive identifications.

If you think one of your friends or relatives may have been among the dead, the police would like to hear from you as soon as possible.

Pointe Judah, Louisiana

This was it. Decisions had to be made.

Nick Board didn't want to admit, even to himself, that he was afraid, but he'd be a fool if he wasn't. He had to protect the lives of the people he loved, and his own.

He turned his Audi from Main Street into the forecourt of Ona's Out Front, the bar and diner side of Ona's business. In the same building, Ona's Out Back, an unlikely tea shop, lay directly behind the diner. He parked next to a familiar, bright yellow Miata that reflected dazzling sunbursts off its spotless paint.

Inside, her elbows propped on the stainless-steel counter that spanned the windows, sat Sarah Board, one of his supposed sisters and the owner of the Miata. From the direction of her glance, she couldn't see him for the glare.

Nick got out of the car and faced Main Street, just to give himself a little time to settle down. Vehicles and people passed through the white-hot haze of midafternoon. He poked at the nosepiece of his sunglasses.

Two weeks ago the headline and lead article in the *Pointe Judah News* had stunned Nick, stunned Aurelie and Sarah and thrust them back where they'd learned not to go: to the day when Mary Chance had sent them to Georgia. He could not get past the conviction that she had suspected they were all in deadly danger. She had stayed to make sure he and the two girls got away. Nick had no proof, would never have proof, but he knew what he knew. While they escaped, she covered for their absence.

Today, after a relentless national media feast since the grave was discovered, a new story twist had come out. He had read about it on the Internet a couple of hours earlier.

He thought back to when he, Muriel and Ena set off for Savannah. By the time they arrived, the sisters had chosen new names, Sarah and Aurelie. In their fabricated lives, all but four people thought they were his sisters. The fourth was Delia Board, Mary's old friend, the CEO and primary shareholder of Wilkes and Board Cosmetics. Delia had taken in three teenagers and raised them as if they were her own children.

Even members of the Board clan—all retired now—accepted the story that Delia had quietly adopted the three children of an old friend. Delia was the "whippersnapper" of the family and the old brigade didn't question anything she did as long as they didn't have to become actively involved in the business. The Boards had bought out the Wilkes, but the name of the company was too famous to change.

He couldn't have guessed then how grateful he would become that although they had taken the Board name, adoption was automatically out of the question. They had continued to hope his mother was alive, and to this day he and Delia didn't know whether Sarah and Aurelie had a family somewhere. They had steadfastly recoiled from the subject.

Aurelie was never far from his thoughts. He'd made up his mind he had to do something about his feelings for her. At least test the waters. But he would wait until this nightmare passed.

Delia had insisted on moving the teenagers away from Savannah soon after they arrived. She was too much of a public figure there, she said.

First they'd gone to Portland, Oregon, where Delia's cosmetic company had offices. Again, she decided her profile was too high and they'd moved on, this time to settle in Pointe Judah. Delia continued to run the business from there and built a small research and development lab outside the town.

The second move had worked. After initial curiosity, the community accepted and mostly ignored the quiet folks who lived in antebellum Place Lafource, a mansion on a lush estate backing onto Bayou Nezpique.

"Nick Board, how much longer are you going to stand out here gaping at nothing?" Sarah, almost six feet of her, was already raising her voice at him when she came through the doors of the diner. "I believe you think I'm the least important person around. You said to meet you and Aurelie in Ona's half an hour hour ago but I find you wandering around outside with no concern for my feelings."

"I didn't see you coming," he said. "I'm enslaved to your feelings, Sarah, my love. I was sort of waiting for Aurelie to get here. I'm glad she decided to come home and stay until we figure out how big a problem we've got." Aurelie was a New Orleans insurance lawyer.

"Nick! You're really scaring me."

When he turned his head, Sarah put her face so close to his that her eyes distorted into one fuzzy blue thing between her eyebrows. He drew back to see her properly. She wore her short, bleached hair in spikes and used dramatic makeup on a face composed of upswept lines and sharp bones. A fascinating face and a build like a tall dancer attracted a lot of attention.

They were both chemists and worked at the Wilkes and Board labs just east of Pointe Judah. Nick's position had expanded into taking over direct administration of the facility and being Delia's right hand whenever she wanted it.

Sarah crossed her arms and tweaked at her hair, signs that her temper was about to reach gale force.

He look a step backward. "Okay, okay, settle down. We probably don't have a thing to worry about." Sometimes even the peace-at-any-price guy ended up on the battlefront.

"I'm so mad at you." Sarah landed a fist on his shoulder and he jumped.

"Now what?" he asked. Scrubbing at his face didn't help calm him down.

"You dither around, lost in who knows what, while I worry myself to skin and bone. You are a thought-less, self-centered bastard."

"It's not nice to remind me about the circumstances of my birth," Nick said, but his humor was thinning rapidly.

"You told us to meet you here because we've got to talk. I don't want to stand around imagining the worst. Tell me the latest."

"I'm not saying it twice," he told her. "As soon as Aurelie gets here we'll go somewhere private and decide what to do next."

"You love controlling things."

"You don't get it, do you?" Nick said. "I want out of all this intrigue we've lived with as much as you do. Maybe more."

A black Hummer, the giant kind they'd stopped making, cut across Main Street in front of oncoming traffic and howled into the parking lot. "Shit," Nick said.

"Look at that," Sara said, clearly grabbing for a diversion. "Dangerous driving."

The driver's door opened slowly and Aurelie Board slid her feet into blurry waves of heat rising from the ground. Nick said, "Shit."

Sarah elbowed him. "You already said that. Why are you so late?" she called to her sister.

"Go easy," Nick said. "Aurelie's usually prompt. Something she couldn't get out of must have kept her."

"Sometimes I think you get sucked in because she's little and looks helpless. You're always making excuses for her." Sarah pinched up her mouth.

Aurelie had the same pointy nose as Sarah, that's where the similarities almost ended. "There you are," she said loudly. "Don't start on me. Just don't start."

Half a foot shorter than her sister, Aurelie's hair was as dark as Sarah's would be if she didn't use bleach.

Aurelie leaned back into the car and called, "Hoover, get out here." A Bouvier, around 120 pounds, black with a white blaze on his chest, lumbered to the ground like a small bear. He definitely outweighed his boss.

Nick tried not to grimace at Aurelie's straw hat, the brim tipped up all the way around. He loved looking at her and had to make sure he wasn't too obvious. She had a wide, soft mouth that looked as if a smile was never far away. Her eyebrows were upswept like Sarah's and very dark. She sparkled. She melted people just with her presence. And Aurelie might be short but she wasn't exactly "little," not entirely.

He pulled himself together. "Let's get on with it, shall we?"

"I've been at Poke Around," she said. "I came as fast as I could." A passing truck honked and she put her fingers in her ears.

A gift boutique, Poke Around occupied the conservatory in the original Oakdale Mansion at what was now the Oakdale Mansion Center. Some of Nick's condo windows, in a complex built to blend with the older buildings, overlooked the shop.

"We're waiting, Nick," Sarah said, raising her voice again to overcome a noisy truck that was passing by.

"Do we have to yell this conversation?" Nick said, exasperated.

"It's not my fault it's so loud," Aurelie said and pulled her dog onto a shorter leash. "I mean, it's not like, well, it's just not my fault it's hot and noisy out here."

"My sister, the big—make that small lawyer," Sarah muttered.

Aurelie's mouth turned sharply down. "What does that mean?"

"Nothing," Nick said.

"It means that for a smart woman you wear a good disguise. The hat doesn't help. You had the thing when you were in high school and the kids laughed at it then." Sarah gave one of her, "top that," looks.

Nick said, *"Sarah."*

"Could we keep this on topic, please?" Aurelie said. "I believe in wearing my clothes out. This hat is fine. Hoover needs water." She led him to the big enamel bowl Ona kept filled for the purpose.

"What does it cost to feed that dog?" Sarah asked.

"I don't trust people who don't love animals," Aurelie responded, finding a wad of tissues in a pocket and wiping her pet's dripping mustache. Her thick hair reached her shoulders and fanned out in tight curls beneath the brim of her hat. "Neither of you even has the decency to give him a kiss and you know how he looks forward to that."

"You've had him at my place ever since you came home. Doesn't that make me an animal lover?" Sarah said. She lived in the guesthouse at Place Lafource. "He's been there for ten days and I can prove it."

"Don't be silly," Aurelie said. "How?"

"By the number of nose prints on my windows."

Nick grinned and gave Sucker, as he preferred to call this admittedly fantastic floor sweeper, a good rub. "I don't kiss dogs," he said.

"Oh, don't make my dog an excuse to admit you

only get heated up around good-looking women," Aurelie said. "Why remind us how shallow you are?"

Sarah snorted.

"Look, Rellie," Nick said to her, resorting to the nickname he used for chummy moments. "I'll pretend you didn't say that. You both know we're dancing around the only reason we're here, so let's quit stalling."

"I don't even want to think about it anymore," Aurelie said, winding the dog's leash back and forth between her fingers. "If something awful's happened, how come I haven't heard about it?"

"Did you see or hear any news today? Or read the paper?" He'd already decided Sarah hadn't.

"I've been busy at Poke Around," Aurelie said.

Nick pointed at her. *"Poke Around?* You wouldn't buy birdhouses with chimneys and straw roofs, or anything else they're likely to have."

"Eileen Moggeridge is my friend. She manages the shop, remember?"

"Of course," Nick said, too uptight to pursue to topic. "Let's get somewhere private. We'll go to Delia's later."

"Aurelie was on a job interview at Poke Around today," Sarah said and her eyes were too bright, too pleased. "She got the position and started right away."

"I don't want to practice law anymore," Aurelie said at once, leaving Nick with his mouth open, ready to ask a question. "You wouldn't, either, if people

27

hated you for what you do. And they've got a right, some of them. It's not the same with all insurance companies, but mine is still scrambling for reasons not to help Katrina victims and I've had it."

"But you'll practice somewhere else," Nick said, and felt his voice rise.

"Ask me in a few years. Maybe I'll think about it then. For now I'm going to make espresso and sell birdhouses at Poke Around."

This was a nightmare. "Have you told Delia?"

Aurelie didn't answer. She looked overheated in her black linen suit with wide crop pants and flat shoes.

"How long before you've got to get back to work?" Sarah asked, apparently happy to have the youngest Board big-brain hanging out among the butterfly barrettes, ant colony kits and the glass aardvarks for which the shop was particularly known.

"Eileen's really glad I could start today at all. She doesn't mind me being gone for a couple of hours," Aurelie said. "Look, why don't we save time by talking right here. Nobody thinks anything about seeing us together and we can't be overheard."

Nick looked at Sarah, who nodded, yes.

"When the thing in California broke we knew we had to decide if I should go back there," Nick said.

"We wanted to go, too," Aurelie said.

"Just let me spit this out. Today they announced there weren't enough bones in that mine."

Both women stared at him. "Not enough for what?" Sarah said.

"For thirty-three people. Not enough. One adult human skeleton has 206 bones, 300 until some early-childhood bones fuse together. They recovered most of the bones for thirty-two people and none—with the exception of some small animal contributions—that didn't belong to those thirty-two."

Aurelie's blue eyes turned glossy. "Why aren't all of the bones there—for the thirty-two, I mean?"

"Do we have to go into this?" Sarah moved closer to Nick and rubbed his arm. "This is so hard on you."

He gave her a quick smile. "Thanks." All his efforts not to think of his mother as a "tangled skeleton" hadn't worked, but he appreciated Sarah's empathy. "Some of the bones would be dragged off and gnawed—by rats and such. More pieces may be found."

Neither woman spoke.

"They listed all the names they've got on pieces of ID. I recognized them all."

Aurelie made a small noise.

"My mother's was there and so was Colin Fox's."

"How awful," Sarah said. "Poor Mary."

"I ought to get in touch with Billy Meche about this," Nick said, referring to the local police chief. "That's what the California cops would want."

"They would," Sarah agreed.

"Yes." Aurelie studied his face. "But would it help anything? I mean, really help? Or just mean we say goodbye to having any peace again? Sheesh, I feel selfish for even thinking about that."

"Why?" Nick said. "All three of us are thinking it. And what about Delia? You know how she felt when she read that piece in the *News*. She felt terrible, and sad, but I don't think it crossed her mind that we'd consider blowing our lives apart in public."

Sara slipped a hand under his arm. "This isn't our biggest problem."

"No," Nick said. "But we know what is."

"If you want to go, you go," Aurelie said. She tipped her hat forward to shade her face. "You have the right to take care of . . . of Mary. We'll stay here with Delia."

"I'm not going," Nick said. "Not now and maybe never. If I did, I could be putting targets on our backs."

"I know I'm a coward," Sarah said. "But I feel sick, I'm so frightened. I ought to do better than that."

He felt her tremble.

"Well, you're not doing any worse than I am," Aurelie said, reaching for their hands and joining the three of them in a tight bunch. "Do you really think the missing person is . . . I don't even want to say the name." Never ruddy, she had paled, including her lips.

Nick squeezed her fingers. "I know it's Colin Fox who may still be alive."

Aurelie pressed her eyes shut. "He could have left his ID behind to throw the police off if they ever found the grave."

"The pig," Sarah said. She still trembled. "He had

big plans for Aurelie and me. Disgusting man."

"They've found remnants of a rope ladder at the bottom of that vent," Nick said quietly. "Still attached to deep stakes. There weren't any stakes at the top, but they think the rope was cut up there and dropped down."

Tears squeezed from beneath Aurelie's eyelids and slid down her cheeks. "We didn't come right out with it, but we already guessed Colin killed them. *All of them*. They were so nice to us, especially the women and the other kids." Her eyes flew open. "He murdered the kids, too."

"Probably. And if he did all that, he's not going to want anyone around who could connect him to The Refuge." Hoover bumped against Nick's hip, looking for attention, but there wasn't any to spare right now. "He would have had a new life to walk into, with a new name. But we could still identify him."

"His eyes," Sarah said. "They were like green glass. I know he was good-looking but I can't understand why Mary . . ."

"No," Nick said. "But there must have been a reason. I only asked Delia about my mother once and she didn't tell me much. When I wanted to know why both my mother and Delia decided to keep us hidden, all she said was that someone dangerous could come looking for us."

"So you've definitely decided not to go to the police here—or to California?" Sarah said. "Not even to Matt Boudreaux? He's just about your best friend."

Matt was also deputy chief of police, Billy Meche's second-in-command. "No, not even Matt," Nick said. "I'm not going to do anything official. And we'd better be watching our backs in case Colin decides he'd seriously prefer us dead."

"Oh, God." Aurelie knelt beside Hoover and buried her face in his fur. She held him around the neck and looked up again. "Nothing official?"

Nick considered his words carefully and said, "If the opportunity comes to deal with Colin, I'll take it."

2

Baily Morris slipped off her earphones and listened. She worked as a chemist on the lowest of four floors at Wilkes and Board's Pointe Judah lab and, faintly, she'd heard what could have been a thud from the room above.

There shouldn't be anyone upstairs and there should be nothing likely to fall on the floor without help.

Concentrating hard, she strained to hear any other sounds. There were none.

Open vertical blinds made stripes through purple-pink evening light beyond the windows. Baily glanced at the still fronds on shadowy palm trees outside, then at the ground fog starting to gather. She'd arrived earlier than usual this evening, waiting only long enough to be certain all those who worked by day had left. In the future she might make a habit of stretching her hours at the lab.

Night was her preference, night and solitude. She liked the peace, and not having to deal directly with any of the Boards. Sarah was jealous of Baily's abilities. Nick didn't spend a lot of time there, but when he did show up, he pretended not to notice her. For a few weeks that had been very different, until he decided she wasn't what he wanted anymore.

His loss. Baily intended Nick to pay for the way he had treated her.

Each evening, for as long as she dared to put off her Wilkes and Board assignments, Baily worked on a project of her own. In weeks or months or however long it took, she would show the Boards who was the superior chemist. A product guaranteed to fill and keep deep wrinkles invisible for hours would be Baily Morris's ticket to freedom and fame, or at least to being her own boss. Her cream would come out before Wilkes and Board's planned the release of something very similar—she would make sure of that. Baily smiled.

When Nick had first asked her out for dinner, she had been happier than she ever remembered being. For months she'd spent her time at the lab waiting for a glimpse of him. She'd let him know, subtly of course, that she was interested. And then it happened, the first date.

Baily pushed her chair back. Nick had taken her to Damalis's, the ritziest place for miles around, and by candlelight he'd concentrated on her—only her. Afterward he'd taken her home and kissed her on the doorstep. What a kiss. But he'd gently turned down her offer to come in.

Tears prickled in her eyes. There had been more dates, over several weeks, but increasingly she'd done most of the talking. But he was so masculine, so sexy, and just being with him made her feel all she'd ever hoped to feel with a man.

He never invited her to his place, and never came inside hers. She liked sex and she knew she would more than like it with Nick. At last she'd come right out and asked, "What weird rules are you playing by, Nick? Is there something that's stopping you from sleeping with me?"

That had been their last date. He'd gone on being kind, but became steadily more distant. No arrangements were ever made to get together outside work again. When she did find the courage to ask him what happened he had told her, "I'm not a rules kind of guy. That makes you and me different. You see a certain progression for a relationship, I like things loose. You're lovely, Baily, and I like you, but we're not a match in the way we tried to be."

So kind, so general—and so embarrassing for her to be told, if not in so many words, that he didn't want a romantic setup with her if it included sex.

Baily scooted her chair back in and concentrated.

The sound she had heard still hadn't been repeated.

Naturally, the formula she was working on for the company, the result of Nick's research, stayed at the lab. Her own, slightly different and much better version, she carried back and forth in her briefcase. It took up so little room—just a few small containers in the bottom of the bag.

She finished assembling everything she needed on the counter before her, including fresh tubes.

Another heavy impact came from overhead. This time she hadn't replaced her earphones and the vibrations made her flinch.

The cleaners. It had to be. Sarah Board occasionally worked at night but she would have popped her head in to say hello before she went upstairs.

One thing she didn't need was an interruption from people working earlier than scheduled. The cleaners usually came after midnight.

Baily fumbled in her pocket for her keys, then remembered they were in her briefcase. She found them, hurried from the room and locked it behind her.

She would tell the cleaners to leave and come back when they were supposed to. Some people didn't understand they had to follow the rules. The elevator stood open and she ran inside.

Baily twirled, already reaching for the second-floor button. She pulled back, stuffed down a scream, glanced at the door. It slid shut.

In front of the control panel stood a man with his arms crossed. He didn't look at her but pressed the button for the fourth floor. In his other hand, he held a gun.

3

"**M**ight as well take a bath," Aurelie said. She dropped a lumpy canvas bag and her hat on the hall floor in Sarah's place. A wall had been removed and the hall opened up to the living room where Sarah had been waiting and watching for Nick to come so that they could continue talking.

"Enjoy," Sarah said. Avoiding the subject, the most important subject that was on their minds, appealed to her. Sarah admitted to herself that she was more likely to pretend there was no big problem than Aurelie was.

Aurelie, with Hoover ambling behind, came into the living room. "Are you okay? I mean, apart from the obvious, are you okay?" She fell into a chair and hooked both of her legs over one striped damask arm.

"You don't have to worry about me. I'm fine."

Aurelie didn't look at her. "That's a lie. Just like it'd be a lie if I said I was fine. Neither of us is okay and this is likely to get worse."

Sarah listened hard for a moment, hoping to hear Nick's car.

"Sis," Aurelie said, "we're in major trouble, aren't we?"

"Not for the first time." Sarah waited for Aurelie to lift her face and make eye contact. "We've been in tight spots before. True, this could turn out to be the tightest, but we all have to hang together."

"We can't be together all the time. What if Colin finds us? What if he already has? He could be out there waiting to get one of us alone, then pick us off one by one."

Sarah couldn't swallow. "Don't say those things. Colin wouldn't have any way of knowing where we are."

"He could," Aurelie said. "He could have known almost all along but while we weren't a threat—because he was safe and didn't want to draw attention to himself anyway—he let it go."

"I wish Nick would get here," Sarah said. She collected herself. If she and Nick ever got together, that would be a hard adjustment for Aurelie to make. She'd have to tell her about the change when it happened—if it happened.

It had to happen, Sarah thought. She couldn't bear wanting but not having him for much longer.

Hoover gave a single rumbling bark, reminiscent of a low-pitched foghorn, and flopped down on Sarah's pride and joy: an antique Chinese silk rug that sparkled when light settled on the pale outlines of leaves.

"He's drooling," she said. She loved animals but there were limits.

Aurelie glared at her. "He's had a bad day. He ate a pot of chrysanthemums outside the shop. We stopped on the way back but he still didn't make it completely out of the Hummer before he threw up."

"That's too bad," Sarah said. *She would not grin.*

The day was winding up with a pale purple flourish. If she hadn't dealt with the heat since morning she might be fooled by the soft drama of it all and think it was balmy outside. "Delia had some business in New Orleans. She should be back anytime. There's a message to both of us from her to go to the house."

"We won't go until Nick gets here," Aurelie said. "I don't want to worry Delia. It's not fair to her after all she's done."

Sarah spread her fingertips on the windowsill and leaned even closer to open the jalousies. "They should both be along any moment."

"I'm worried about Nick," Aurelie said.

So was Sarah. She narrowed her eyes. Her stomach rolled—again. "He's making decisions based on our feelings—I'm sure of it. I know him too well. If he didn't feel responsible for us, he'd go to California. His mother's . . . Mary's there and he'd want to take care of her."

"Bury her," Aurelie said. "Of course he would."

Sarah looked over her shoulder at Aurelie. "I love you because you care about us all so much. You understand us. And you put yourself last."

"You give me too much credit. I put us all first would be more accurate. You're solid, so is Nick. How much luckier could we get than to know we can go to him anytime we need to?"

Comments like that showed the difference in their feelings for Nick. To Aurelie he would remain her big brother. But not to Sarah. "You're right." Making the first move with him was so dangerous, she'd put it off for a long time. For years. She blinked, momentarily shocked to think of how long she had loved Nick Board, and not as a brother. He wasn't their brother.

"Are you sure you feel all right?" Aurelie asked, getting out of the chair. "Do you feel ill or something?"

Or something. "I'm okay."

The firmness of Aurelie's touch on her arm comforted Sarah. She covered her sister's hand.

Aurelie cleared her throat. "It would be a good thing if Nick found a woman he could really care about. He needs the balance. He hasn't been lucky with women in the past."

Shut up. Sarah couldn't think about Nick with someone else. "It was bizarre when he dated Baily. When they started going out he seemed really interested. He never gave any hint of what happened, but he didn't feel good about it. We helped him through that fiasco and he knows we would with anyone else." She could not, must not wait any longer. Nick wouldn't make the first move.

"He likes women," Aurelie said.

"Sis, take your bath."

4

"I don't know," Baily said. She had given him the same answer a hundred times. "I don't know anything."

The wind blew hard across the exposed roof. A burning wind. How could she be so cold? Her muscles locked.

Hysteria wouldn't help.

He walked around her. "Sure you know. I'm getting tired, honey. Be a good girl and gimme a break."

Baily didn't answer. Each breath reached the top of her lungs and puffed out in little gasps.

It wouldn't matter what she told him, the roof of the building would be the last place she felt beneath her feet. A gust filled with raindrops wetted her face and she licked dry lips. She hadn't cried. Her eyes were dry; they stung.

Baily didn't want him to see her cry.

"You and him are real close. He had to tell you. You gonna let him keep it all for himself?"

"I don't know what you're talking about." But she did know that a man who didn't bother to cover his face when he broke the law also didn't intend to leave any witnesses around when he had finished. And he knew the Wilkes and Board Pointe Judah lab was isolated enough for him to be sure their movements through the shadows on the roof wouldn't catch anyone's attention.

Unless someone got lost and drove through the entrance and into the grounds by mistake. Or the security company made their two-hourly check of the perimeter. They weren't due for another hour and were never regular anyway.

Miracles happened.

A grimy light in a metal cage shone from the side of the elevator shaft. Baily looked past the man and over the trees toward the driveway from the road.

"What?" He leveled the gun at her head and looked quickly over his shoulder. Just as fast he turned back to her. The hand that held the weapon never wavered. "You're a nice-looking woman. It would be a pity to spoil that face. Don't bother watching for the marines—or the so-called security guys. No one's coming here tonight. Not anytime soon."

Her intestines contracted and she clutched at her lower belly.

He didn't comment.

From the moment she turned around in the elevator and saw him, she had known the man had murder in mind. When he pushed her from the fourth floor, up the stairs to the roof, Baily had felt as if she'd already left the world behind.

He kept his hands off her. The muzzle of the gun, twitched this way or that, told her where to go and when to stop. She'd been told not to speak unless spoken to.

She couldn't see his eyes through glasses with dark gray lenses.

The muzzle twitched.

Baily took a step forward.

Another twitch.

Another step.

"I haven't done anything to you," she yelled, and heard her voice hitting inside her skull.

He flicked the gun again. Baily ran at him, fingers spread, aimed for his eyes. She collided with him and he didn't give, any more than a concrete buttress would give. The knee she aimed at his crotch never reached its target.

"Just let me go!"

One of his feet came down on the very end of the toes on her right foot—just enough to make her fall forward. And with one firm shove he pushed her back.

She screamed, heard bones in her ankle snap. His foot still held her toe down, held it while she slammed into the tar on the roof with its scatter of small, sharp rocks. Gravity and her whole weight drove her head against the ground.

"Stupid bitch."

The words came from a distance. Fire consumed her leg, shot through her thigh, her groin. She writhed, and vomited. Consciousness slithered.

"Get up," he shouted. "Don't you choke on me. *Get up.*"

Baily couldn't see anything but bright lights, blinding lights.

His hands were on her now, dragging at her. "Stand up," he said.

She fought him but her fists bounced off his body. And she cried.

As soon as he released her she crumpled. Before she could go all the way down, he supported her. Held her and hauled her, the right leg useless and dragging behind, toward the parapet around the roof.

"The cleaners are coming," she said through splitting torment, trying to stand on her left leg. "They always come now. It's a rule here. You came at the right time."

His laughter shuddered into Baily's brain. Sweat filled her eyes, soaked her clothes. The pain tore at her, ripped her apart.

"You've made this harder for me but I'll give you one more chance. What did Nick bring with him when he ran from California all those years ago? And where is it now?"

Nothing she said would matter. "Kill me. I don't know anything. Kill me now, I don't care anymore. The cleaners will walk in before you get out."

"Keep your mouth shut."

She screamed again. "I don't know anything."

"Too bad. You're gonna help me anyway."

Baily waited for the click of the hammer pulling back.

"Walk," he said, a hand under her arm, and she hopped, her knee all but doubling each time. "There you go."

The front of her leg banged into the parapet.

Below, a white vapor rose so very far away.

Swirling, clinging to things she couldn't see. She swayed forward, scraped her knee, felt the pull of the soft, white mist spread out below. Soft, white, like foamy water.

"All you have to do is tell me where it's hidden."

"At Place Lafource," she said. Whatever it was, if it belonged to the Boards, why wouldn't it be there, and why wouldn't that seem logical? And why was he asking her?

"Where at Place Lafource?"

Consciousness slipped. "The house."

He shook her. "*Where* in the house?"

She shook her head slowly and couldn't keep her eyes open.

"It'll do," he whispered and let her go. "Very nice, Sarah."

He was going to let her live. She panted and told him, "Baily, not Sarah."

His face came very close. "What are you saying?"

"I'm Baily Morris. You don't want me anyway. You want Sarah Board, don't you?"

"You're lying."

"No. My badge is in my pocket. I don't like wearing it. Baily Morris." She moved a hand toward her pocket.

"Shit," he said. "I believe you. And you just gave away any chance you had. I've got to do this now."

A gentle push at the back of her left knee and the exhausted leg buckled. She tipped forward, her scream clotted in her throat.

Baily flew, so slowly, her arms spread wide; she twisted in the air. Currents tossed her, buffeted her head. Faster, faster, she flew, a dive to the soft white foam.

5

Headlights swung across the windows in Sarah's living room. Aurelie peered outside, saw a familiar Audi and stepped back. "It's Nick's car," she called. "Delia's with him."

Sarah hurried from the kitchen, wiping her hands on a towel.

The engine noise died away.

"Let's try to look as if we're not scared out of our minds," Aurelie said.

Sarah disappeared for a moment and returned without the towel. "You're right. We can help the most by being calm."

"Right," Aurelie said, and slid to the floor beside Hoover, who was dreaming. He blew loudly through his quivering mustache and gave little whines.

Delia used her key and came in just ahead of Nick. "It's started raining," she said.

"Nick!" Sarah said, and looked as if she might run to him. But she held her ground, "And you, too, Delia. You both look so tired."

"Save the drama," Delia said and Aurelie smiled at her favorite woman's choice of words. Delia didn't believe in tiptoeing around people's feelings, particularly if she decided they were unworthy; besides, she owned the family drama crown herself. "Nick and I are just dandy."

"Come in and get comfy," Aurelie said, smiling at Nick who did look pretty exhausted.

He didn't return her smile. The front of his dark curly hair stuck up, a sign he was agitated.

Delia, auburn-haired, above-average height and with just enough ballast to lend authority to her presence and her theatrical stride, went to the center of the room and shook back her hair. "Sit down, Sarah. Nick already filled me in on some of what you all learned today."

Sarah sat at once and kept her eyes downcast. Her manner puzzled Aurelie. Sarah seemed abruptly deflated yet she didn't usually let Delia's take-charge manner bother her.

Delia put a hand on Sarah's head and stroked her mussed hair. "Let's settle in. There's a lot to cover. But regardless, there's nothing to get overly excited about. I'll take care of everything."

She left for the kitchen and returned with a bottle of white wine, four glasses and an opener. The bottle and the opener she handed over to Nick. Then she stood beside him until he had poured.

"Nick picked me up at the airport and we had a meal," Delia said, passing out glasses. She stiffened her back and tugged on the short jacket of her figure-hugging, white silk suit. Delia was a walking advertisement for her company's products. Her soft skin and perfect makeup looked the same regardless of the time of day. Her age was something they had guessed at many times and she couldn't be younger than fifty-five or so, but forty was a number unlikely to be questioned.

Sarah said to Delia, "So you know about—"

"My friend Mary?" Delia cut in and her throat moved sharply. "Yes, I know. She could have been dead by the time you got to Savannah. Poor Mary. Poor Nick."

Nick had sat down. His slate-blue eyes became unfocused.

Goose bumps shot up Aurelie's arms. She hopped up from the floor and went to kneel beside Nick's chair. She hugged him and rested a cheek on his arm. When she knew what she should say, she'd say it. He hadn't had nearly enough time to absorb the shock. None of them had.

He freed an arm and touched her back, then left his big, hard hand there. Aurelie felt his fingers curl into a fist. "I'm really sad about Mary," she said. "When we were at The Refuge, we prayed every night that we'd be able to stay with her. Nick, I'm so sorry."

Delia sat with her forearms crossed over her knees and her head bowed.

Sarah cried quietly.

"Did you ever stop hoping she'd find you?" Aurelie asked Nick. She got up and pulled a chair close to his.

"No," he said.

She studied his face, the whiteness of the bone in

his straight nose, the flare of his nostrils—and the bleak distance in his eyes. "I stopped watching for her," she said. "But I never stopped hoping."

"We didn't know what a real mother was like until we shared yours for a while," Sarah said. "But then we got Delia. That was because Mary knew what we needed even if she couldn't be with us."

"Ooh." Aurelie scrubbed at her face. "I'm really going to bawl in a minute. What I don't understand is why all those people went into the mine. There were too many of them for Colin to have forced them."

"I don't understand, either," Nick said. He put his hands behind his head and stretched, his chest expanding inside his black T-shirt. "We probably never will."

"Couldn't there have been an accident?" Sarah said. "They went inside and there was some sort of slide that moved the rocks?"

Delia, her eyes bright and moist, said, "The police don't think it was an accident, but I do. It probably happened exactly the way Sarah thinks. An unexpected rock slide."

This woman's gift for sailing through difficult times by glossing them over had often been a blessing. Aurelie worried that on this occasion, Delia was afraid of the truth and what it could mean to all of them. "It wasn't an accident," Aurelie said. "There was a rope ladder and it was cut at the top of the shaft and thrown down so they couldn't get out. Someone had to have cut it."

"Remember my mother's hair?" Nick asked, rushing out the words.

Nodding, Aurelie closed her eyes. "It was beautiful. Long and thick—and black like yours, Nick."

"And the same blue eyes," Sarah added. "Almost. Yours are darker."

"Can we stop this?" Delia said quickly. Gone was the breeziness. She sounded badly shaken.

"Let's cut to the basic facts," Nick said. He told Delia his theory about Colin and what it might mean to all of them if he still lived, and decided they could be a threat to him.

Sarah got up. She paced back and forth and Hoover woke up to give one of his barks. "Can't you stop him from doing that?" Sarah said, slapping her hands to her cheeks. "It shocks me every time and I hate it when he barks in the night."

"Sarah—"

"He doesn't bark at night. Not very often," Aurelie said, stopping Delia from jumping into the fray.

"He barks, and he slobbers on my rugs."

"You're just upset," Nick said. "We understand. Come on over here, Hoover."

"He can come up to the house with me," Delia said. "Shall I get some rooms ready for you, Rellie?"

Aurelie shook her head. "No. Don't worry, I've been thinking about going into one of the condos at the Oakdale Mansion Center. The cheaper ones, not in Nick's swanky compound."

Sarah closed her eyes. "I sound selfish. I'm sorry. I

49

don't do very well with stress. I'm not proud of that."

"There's a town house available in the new complex at Oakdale," Nick said. "Several, I think. You know them, Rellie? The Quarters, they're called. Come back with me this evening and look at them tomorrow."

"I can't believe we're having this discussion *now*," Delia said. "*Inappropriate* is the first word that comes to mind. Thanks, Nick. I know you three hate the idea of ever coming back into the house to live. Not that it would have been for long."

"Will that work for you?" Nick asked Aurelie. "You know I've got nothing but room."

"Yes, thanks." Great, Aurelie thought, so now Sarah was eyeing her as if she'd grown fangs.

"You're fine here," Sarah said. "Let it go."

"She'll be closer to Poke Around staying over there," Nick said with the stubborn toughness they recognized the instant his square jaw rose and his normally humorous mouth settled in a straight line.

"Why does Aurelie have to be closer to Poke Around?" Delia asked.

Aurelie had been dreading this. "I've started working there. I got the job today." She had even hoped Nick might have broken the news to Delia. Too bad that hadn't happened.

Delia looked from one face to another. "You've got a job in New Orleans," she told Aurelie.

"I quit."

"You quit? You didn't tell me that when you came home."

"I should have," Aurelie said. "Look, let's not get into this too much now. I've had it with the law. I may change my mind, but I need a break. And I need to be here with all of you."

Delia's lips parted, then Aurelie saw her take a moment more before responding. "It'll be nice to have you here," she said. "It's good to go home when you're tired."

Aurelie smiled at her but knew she would hear more about using her law degree, a lot more.

Nick fidgeted. Conversations like this one made him uncomfortable and it showed. "Get a night's uninterrupted sleep, Sarah," he said. "I want us to be aware of what's going on around us until it's safe to relax."

"It's probably already safe," Delia said, sounding like the take-care-of-everything mother she did her best to be for them.

"True," Aurelie said. "Let's not get ahead of ourselves. There's a good chance Colin won't find us. If he did survive—and he's responsible for what happened—wouldn't he get out of the country? He could be dead by now, you know. He was a lot older than Mary."

"Not so much," Nick said. "He'd be in his fifties."

"He's not going to come looking for us and drawing attention to himself," Aurelie said. "Think about it. Would you take the risk of connecting yourself to those murders?"

"Always the logical one," Nick said.

Sarah got up and went to Nick. "What if the press finds out something? They do all that investigative reporting and they turn up things you'd never expect them to. Someone in Grove could remember you and go to the police to take another look at the photos, then say you couldn't have been there that night. If the police don't find us, the press might."

"I won't have that," Delia said, standing abruptly. Her three-inch heels showed off a great pair of legs. She looked around, then made an awkward little gesture with one hand, "I mean, that's silly. It's not going to happen. And there're three of you, they wouldn't know to look for three of you, would they?"

"Aurelie and Sarah never went into the town—not until the night we left. I don't think anyone there would remember them."

Delia grinned. "There, I told you. This will all work out just fine. Hasn't everything else we've had to deal with worked out?"

They chorused that it had. Aurelie let in a fleeting thought that wealthy Delia tended to believe that she could buy whatever she couldn't get by other means. Her generosity saved her from seeming spoiled or too unworldly. No one questioned her intelligence or her business savvy.

"This is different though, Delia," Sarah said. She stood behind Nick and held his shoulders. "It could be really dangerous. Nick doesn't want to, but do you think we should call Chief Meche? He might know what we should do."

"Like hell," Delia said explosively. "All Billy Meche wants is to be retired. We don't need to make this public. We don't *want* to make this public. Keeping things to ourselves works for us."

Sarah kneaded the muscles in the sides of Nick's neck. "Matt Boudreaux, then. He'd want to help."

"Matt's a good friend," Nick said. "But like I said this afternoon, if we do go to the police here, they'll contact the people in California. I think that's a bad idea, and this isn't Pointe Judah police business."

"No, it isn't," Delia said.

"It will be if someone comes here and kills us all," Sarah said.

6

Hoover stood on the backseat of the Audi with his head on Aurelie's shoulder. The dog looked straight ahead, panting loudly, and snuffling from time to time.

Nick drove back through town, passing through a typical wispy blanket of ground fog coming in the wake of a boiling day. What Delia had called rain was more mist. "When we get there, just drop everything and get to bed. I'll take Hoover out back." He had better not give in to any more selfish urges, like trying to find a way to do more than give Aurelie a bed for the night—on her own—unless he was prepared to ruin the family Delia Board had so successfully put together.

"I'll take him," Aurelie said. "He likes to be out for a bit."

He had never wondered how she took care of her dog. "I'll go with you." He knew better than to say she shouldn't be out alone at night, even with a big dog.

Aurelie scratched the dog's neck, then gently pushed him back. "Lie down," she said and the animal surprised Nick by doing just that.

More or less forcing her to spend the night at his place had been one dumb move. Sure, she would be fine there, but it wouldn't help him.

He felt her look at him and glanced back.

She smiled.

Smiling at her was easy.

Funny how a face you'd known as well as your own for years could seem mysterious. Each time he looked at Aurelie he got a jolt. And the jolts were getting harder to brush off. For months now he'd fluctuated between longing to be around her and trying to stay away. Well, hell, maybe he would hate having her in his space. That would solve the problem.

"Tough times," she said in a small, tight voice. "I hope the way I left hasn't upset Sarah."

Always saying the right thing could wear on a guy. "You dealt with her fine. And she needs to be on her own to think. She's used to that." They all were, but it could be nice to have someone around to be quiet with sometimes. Or could it?

"I'm glad I came home," she said. "At first I

thought I was being a chicken and turning the bad news into an excuse for giving up my job. Everyone else was managing just fine, or so I thought. Only they weren't—aren't. Not all of them."

"Who are *they?*"

"All kinds of people working in New Orleans. Could be I need a break and then I'll go back, just not as a lawyer."

He cast her another grin. "You could change your mind about that."

"I guess. Can't imagine it, though."

"Delia's pissed." He chuckled, but knew it would have been kinder not to bring up the subject.

"She'll be okay," Aurelie said. "She's an over-achiever and she wouldn't understand what I'm doing or why."

Being with her was comfortable, and like balancing on the edge of the Grand Canyon at the same time. What the hell was he going to do with his fantasies about Aurelie? What would she say right now if he told her he never went anywhere without her photo, that he couldn't remember the last time he'd seen her mouth and not thought about kissing her?

They reached the middle of town and he drove slowly past familiar shops, Sadie and Sam's, Kay's Handicrafts, the butcher with the neon pig, missing a few of its pulsing bulbs. A single spotlight shone on a bouquet of giant yellow daisies in the window of Fabulous Flowers. Buzzard's Wet Bar came up on their right. Lights shone inside but the place looked sleepy.

Wet droplets became heavy enough to coat the windshield and Nick turned on the wipers.

"I know I can't stay at Poke Around for long," Aurelie said. "But it's fun and I've got to do something while I try to plan my life."

She had never given him even a tiny hope that she had other than sisterly thoughts toward him. "You don't have to feel rushed about it," he said. "We've all been lucky enough to have choices. Delia did that for us."

"Uh-huh. The best thing we can do is forget we knew any other lives. Not easy at the moment, but it will be again."

He didn't remind her that as long as he'd known them, she and Sarah had behaved as if they were born at ages thirteen and fourteen. They had never opened up about their beginnings, their parents, why they had run away from home, nothing, and whenever he had tried to press them for information they both responded with prolonged silences.

His cell rang. He picked it up to check the readout. "Private number. Maybe I won't answer it."

"Half the people I know show up as private numbers," Aurelie said.

Nick put the phone to his ear, "Hello?"

"You'd better get out to the lab."

He frowned. "Who is this?"

"Sorry. It's Matt. I called your place first."

"Matt," Nick said. "What's wrong at the lab? Is it a break-in?"

Wherever Matt was, and Nick assumed it must be the Wilkes and Board labs, a siren sounded, growing closer.

"Just get over here," Matt Bordeaux said. "There's been an accident."

Nick steered to the side of the road, beneath a trailing willow, and put the car in Neutral. Branches slithered across the roof. "What kind of accident?"

Aurelie's hand on his leg startled him. She met his eyes, questioning silently. He shook his head, but he squeezed her hand.

"It's a bad accident, Nick?"

Twenty minutes away from downtown Pointe Judah, the land Delia had bought twelve years earlier couldn't be seen from the road. Delia had cleared as few trees as possible and the light on top of the four-story building didn't come into view until at least a quarter of a mile along the curving driveway.

"Why didn't you ask Matt who had the accident?" Aurelie asked, knowing she was repeating herself.

Nick shook his head and drove faster than he should.

He had tried to drop her off at his condo before coming out here but she'd insisted on coming.

"You shouldn't be here," he said, also repeating himself. "Please stay in the car while I deal with things."

Sometimes it was best not to argue.

They broke out of the trees and Nick slowed to a

crawl. "Jeez, they must have called in every available emergency respondent from miles around."

That meant a big white van with no windows, two fire trucks, an ambulance and three police cars. Another car, this one unmarked, passed the Audi and went ahead to park next to the cop cars. The shapes of men and women moved purposefully among the raised beds of mist-wreathed roses in front of the building.

Aurelie noticed a green van, this one small, its rear pulled up to the front doors. Lights shone on each floor of the building. And, as a shock of white light had suddenly flooded the top of the building, she noticed people on the roof.

"Don't call Delia or Sarah," Nick said. He braked and turned off the engine without pulling all the way into a parking space. "Give me enough time to check this out. When I get back we'll call them if we have to."

He leaped from the car and slammed the door hard enough to make Aurelie flinch. "The damsel will cower until your return," she said under her breath.

True to his suspicious nature, Nick hadn't gone twenty yards before he checked his stride to take a look back at the Audi. He leaned forward to stare at the windshield and Aurelie laughed. He couldn't possibly see her so she rolled down the window, stuck out a hand and wiggled her fingers at him. "I'm still here," she murmured.

Immediately he jogged away among the roses.

"Hoover, stay." She slithered from the car and flattened herself against its damp side. When she set off, taking a wider angle to get to the same place Nick was going, her heart thumped hard enough to shorten her breath.

She heard another car behind her and pulled back to make sure she didn't get caught in its headlights.

Delia took an interest in the roses, so the grass that edged up to the stone retaining walls around the raised beds was kept manicured.

More lights were trained on one area and Aurelie knew she was about to discover who the accident victim was. Did she knew the person?

Matt Bordeaux, a big, rangy Cajun who looked as if he'd been born to wear his dark blue uniform, stood with one booted foot braced on what looked like a toolbox. He spoke into a collar mike but Aurelie couldn't hear a word.

Nick approached from the opposite side and his sudden exclamation startled her. He wasn't looking at Aurelie but at a twisted female figure lying mostly on her face amid smashed rosebushes.

Nick's shocked expression unnerved Aurelie. She made herself move closer until she could see the victim.

She opened her mouth and swallowed air, gasped to steady her breathing.

A scream rose, unbidden, into her throat and blasted loud enough to grab the attention of everyone present. She ran forward but Matt caught her around the waist and her feet left the ground.

"You don't need to see this," Matt said. "How about you go back to your car and wait? I'll send someone to sit with you."

"Put me down," she whispered. "Or I'll kick where it'll hurt."

"Aure-lie," he said, dividing her name as he frequently did. "Let the professionals do their job. Stirrin' up a ruckus isn't what we need."

"Put her down, Matt." Nick's voice roared through the silence that had fallen in the wake of Aurelie's arrival.

Her feet touched the ground again, she watched Nick move in and crouch beside the body. He shook his head slowly and made to touch the woman.

"Don't touch the body," a female officer said sharply.

Aurelie wrenched free of Matt and joined Nick. They knelt side by side, looking down at a face marred by multiple contusions. Trickles of blood from the nose and ear had dried on her skin. More blood turned the whites of her eyes purple and her neck should never have been able to twist as it had. One foot was bare and again, turned at a sickening angle. Bone projected through the skin just above the ankle. A considerable quantity of blood caked the leg.

"My God," Nick muttered.

Aurelie squeezed his arm. "Baily," she said. "She never was happy. I feel awful, but I'm relieved."

"Because you thought it was Sarah?" Nick asked very quietly. "That's why you screamed. There was no way she could have got here but I thought the same thing. I'm so used to the two of them, I forget how alike they are."

"Only the coloring and height," Aurelie said. She turned her face up to the roof of the building. "Did she jump?"

"Looks like it," Nick said.

"I hope she did." Her eyes never left his.

7

Delia walked into Matt Boudreaux's dreary office at the station. She surveyed the scene, gave long, cold stares to Matt, Nick and Aurelie, in turn. "What *incident?*" she asked, returning her attention to young Boudreaux. "What could possibly make you have someone I don't even know call and say I had to come here? Now? And don't repeat any nonsense about Nick and Aurelie being involved in some invented *incident.*"

He sighed and gave her a pleading look with deceptively sleepy-looking eyes that were so dark they seemed black. "Miz Board—"

"Did you two do something?" The idea had to be unthinkable.

They looked at her as if she were the one with a problem. "Did you call Sam? You know better than to say anything in a place like this without a lawyer."

"With respect, ma'am," Matt said. "Your cart is runnin' away with your horse."

"I should have squelched that rumor years ago," she said. People liked to suggest she jumped to conclusions, which was ridiculous.

"Ma'am," Matt said. "Why don't you take a seat." A tall, strong-looking Cajun, he had those lovely manners such men tended to have. It was past time some energetic woman snapped him up.

Delia kept her voice even and said, "Nick Board, how long are you going to sit there and say nothing?"

He had the grace to shift in his scratched-up folding chair.

"Sit here," Aurelie said. She hopped up and beckoned to Delia. "I think Nick's brain has disengaged."

Nick snorted. "Nick's brain is very busy, thanks. When everyone settles down, we'll get to what happened tonight."

"Yo, people," Matt said. "Can we keep on track here? Kindly take a seat, Miz Board."

"When did I stop being Delia?"

"Delia," Matt amended. "There's been an incident at the lab. Nick didn't want us to contact you—he took care of as much as he could."

Delia breathed through her nose. She still felt threatened by the new bombshell in their lives. "You should have come straight to me with anything to do with Wilkes and Board." At least this wasn't anything to do with the California mess.

"I asked him not to," Nick said. "You and I have an

agreement that I help shoulder the weight of the company locally. At least with things like this. You agreed that Matt or Billy could always contact me for security issues."

She didn't recall arrangements exactly like the ones he mentioned. Her black warm-ups were suddenly too hot and she sat in the chair Aurelie had vacated. "I'm waiting," she said. The flip in her stomach was becoming familiar and she resented it.

"It was a shock," Aurelie said. "When I saw—"

"You were told to stay in the car," Nick said.

Aurelie drew herself up. "You are not my father. What I do is up to me . . . dammit."

Delia was well aware of Aurelie's spirit but didn't recall seeing her get quite so mad at Nick.

"Delia," Matt said. He took a bottle of pills from a drawer, shook four on the top of his metal desk and swallowed them, one at a time, with coffee that looked cold. His grimace affirmed the suspicion.

"You were saying?" Delia prompted him.

"We have a sticky problem and it's attracted more attention than I like to see. The word got out too wide and we got help from all over, whether we wanted it or not. I reckon they think the law in little places like this is still wet behind the ears. Makes it hard for us folks if we get tromped on by the big boys—they think they're big, anyways—so I want to get to the bottom of all this right here, in this department."

He spoke slowly and Delia took a moment to gather

everything he'd said together. "*All* this?" she asked faintly.

"Yes, ma'am. We've got a dead woman and it looks like a suicide."

"Oh, God," Delia said. She held the neck of her jacket.

Nick rested his chin on his chest. "It was Baily Morris. I know she didn't always fire on all cylinders, but she had a lot of good in her and I sure never expected her to do this."

Delia sat sideways on her chair. She looked at a wall where notices tacked to a board flapped faintly in the current from a fan. "Silly girl. Excellent chemist, too. She never seemed happy." She glanced at Nick but didn't add that the one time Baily had obviously been happy was during the weeks when she and Nick had dated. Heavy sadness pressed in on Delia.

"We've still got a lot of work to do," Matt said. "At the scene and . . . elsewhere."

Delia didn't press for any expansion on "elsewhere." "Where's Billy Meche? In his warm bed, I suppose."

"He isn't in town, and—" Matt said, apparently stopping himself from saying more on the subject of his boss. "You'll have to make do with me."

"Sounds like a fine idea," Delia said. "Now, let's quit the fluff and get down to business. How did Baily . . . do it?"

"Jumped off the roof," Matt said promptly.

Delia's skin contracted. She turned cold, inside and out. "Selfish," she murmured.

"Excuse me?" Nick said.

"You heard me. *Selfish*. Meant to make as much of a mess as possible and upset a whole lot of people."

Silence met her announcement but she wasn't about to retract her comment.

"Baily always works—worked—at night," she said, more for her own benefit than anyone else present. "She liked it that way. Got a lot done while it was quiet. I shouldn't have agreed to it. She was out there alone—except for the occasional nights when Sarah worked, too."

"Nick?" Aurelie said. "Sarah did—"

"Sarah has nothing to do with any of this," Nick said, but Delia thought he spoke uncertainly.

Aurelie didn't take her eyes off him. "Who knew Baily was suicidal?" she said. "She only talked about looking forward to the day when she had her own lab—her own company."

"She talked about that?" Nick asked. "Not to me."

"It was her favorite topic around Sarah. I didn't have much to do with Baily but she told me the same thing."

Delia noted how Matt and Nick stared at each other.

"What is it?" she asked. "What are you two cooking up?"

Matt looked innocent and Nick said, "What d'you mean, cooking up? All I'm doing is trying to think of a reason for this. She must have been working when she decided to go up on the roof. She locked the lab door behind her and used the elevator to the fourth floor, then the stairs to the roof, or that's how it looks."

"Was it quick?" Delia asked. The thought of Baily being dead tormented Delia.

"We'll know that for sure after the autopsy," Matt said.

Aurelie walked to a wall and leaned there with her fists on her hips. "I think she broke her neck."

The intercom buzzed and Matt picked up his phone. Within seconds he excused himself and left the room.

Nick got up quickly and closed the door. "I want to keep this between us," he said, returning to prop himself against Matt's desk. "Baily was working on something that had nothing to do with her job for us. I think that's why she's dead."

"How do you know?" Delia asked.

"From stuff she had on her bench. Or I think that's what I'm going to find when I get a look at it all. Either she got frightened or disgusted with herself, so she ended it all."

Pointing a finger at him, Delia said, "Don't keep things from the police."

"Why throw mud on her name if what she was doing doesn't hurt anyone?" Nick shot back. "It's going away now anyway."

Aurelie crossed her arms tightly. "What are you talking about? Matt's going to be back any second. Quit talking in circles."

"I can't give facts until I've had time with what she was working on," Nick said. "I don't know how long that'll take but I can do it quietly."

"You removed things from the lab?" Aurelie said, her eyebrows rising. "Potential evidence about Baily? Nick—"

"I'm being honest with you," Nick said, his voice barely controlled. He stood up, which meant he looked a long way down into Aurelie's face. "So back off and credit me with enough sense not to step over the line."

"You already have," Aurelie said. Her pointed chin rose. "And you know it. Why would you try to cover up for someone who's already dead?"

"Dammit, you can be cold," Nick told her.

They glared at each other.

"What is it?" Aurelie said. "Guilt. Did you treat her so badly you feel responsible for her jumping off that roof?"

"What a rotten thing to say." He held his ground and Aurelie held hers.

Delia clenched her hands on the arms of her chair. Watching the two of them she felt another, much deeper pang of uncertainty. Without warning, she'd become a surrogate parent and from that day on she considered herself the luckiest woman around. But in the past couple of years she'd had a few premonitions and fears. These moments of passion flared between Nick, Sarah and Aurelie, they flared more often than ever. If deep rifts formed between them, they would all lose too much.

"Let's stay calm," she said. "Just be careful, Nick."

"Aren't I always?"

Aurelie's short laugh joined Delia's.

Matt strode into the room once more, closed the door firmly and went behind his desk. He threw down a folder. "We've got a couple of people in reception asking questions and makin' a nuisance of themselves. They're lookin' for a story."

"Rusty Barnes, you mean?" Delia said. Rusty put out the *Pointe Judah News,* the town's small paper. "How would he know about Baily yet?"

"Not Rusty Barnes," Matt said. "But he won't be far behind once he does know about Baily. This pair must think we're the local information bureau. A man and a woman looking for you." His gesture took them all in. "Before I could stop him, Sampson said something about you being here and the woman tried to cut me off from comin' back here. They've left," he finished flatly.

Delia let her head hang back. "Now what?" she said. "They're here to write a story and they're looking for us? Why—did they say?"

"I didn't let them. You'll probably hear from them, so let me know if they're a problem. First things first. When was the last time you were out at the lab? Nick and Delia—that question's for both of you."

"I don't go there much," Delia said. "About a week ago, I think."

"I was there most of the morning today." This was Nick. "I didn't see Baily, of course."

"We're going to need to question anyone who was there today, including tonight," Matt said. "It's too bad you don't have round-the-clock physical security."

"Oddly enough, Baily helped persuade me we didn't need it," Delia said. "We don't keep money or drugs out there and we're not dealing with formulas that could have any sinister applications. And the building isn't close to anything."

"Spit it out," Nick said, facing Matt. "Say whatever's on your mind."

"I can't get into details," Matt said. His gaze slid away. "The building will be dealt with as a crime scene until you're told it's been released."

"You just got some new information?" Nick asked.

"I'd feel good if I knew all of you were being careful—at least until we have more facts than we do now."

"A crime scene?" Aurelie said. "You think Baily was murdered."

Matt didn't argue.

8

Nick heard the front door close quietly and bolted from his bed. He grabbed a pair of jeans and hopped into them on the way out of his bedroom.

The door to the room he'd given Aurelie stood open and a glance inside proved she wasn't there.

The luminous dial on his watch showed a little before five in the morning.

"Aurelie?" he yelled at the front door, knowing there was no way she'd hear him, particularly if she was well away by now.

She didn't have her car, but knowing her, she wouldn't be above spending what was left of the night in his Audi, just so she could be completely alone with her thoughts.

He wanted to find her in his car.

She hasn't hidden away in a car since we were teenagers. "I hope you've gone into your second childhood," he said aloud, shoving his feet into a pair of downtrodden boat shoes he kept near the front door in case he needed to go outside quickly, like now. Aurelie had been in a quiet mood ever since Matt Boudreaux shuffled them out of the police station through a back door, to avoid the people trying to hunt them down.

The bottoms of his shoes were worn thin and smooth and with his first step he slid on wet mud and only just stopped himself from falling. *"Son of a bitch!"* Rain fell. Not the fine, driving mist of earlier, but a downpour from a black sky quickly assaulted by a hurtling river of forked lightning.

His car was in the carport, right where he'd left it.
Empty.

The Oakdale Mansion Center was large, with satellites of condos, shops, business and professional offices ranged around the old mansion at its center.

Nick made himself stand still. He used both hands to push his dripping hair back and wipe water from his eyes and face. Nothing moved out here. "Aurelie?" he shouted, making a slow circle in place, keeping his fingers where he could repeatedly clear his eyes. Water sluiced from his bare shoulders.

What made her leave?

Could someone have gotten in and taken her?

A glance at Poke Around showed no suggestion of a light inside the shop windows.

Nick ran for the nearest exit to the street. His lungs burned as if they'd explode. Fear and quantities of inhaled rain destroyed his throat. He stared both ways but didn't see as much as a stray animal abroad. Who would be out in this if they didn't have to be?

Thunder rolled. The sound resembled the gathering roar of an avalanche.

When he got his hands on Aurelie he'd shake her till her teeth rattled. She was a runner with several marathons under her belt. Could she be in training? They used to run together before she went away.

Even Aurelie wouldn't run in this.

She wouldn't come out here of her own volition.

He dashed along the verge toward the back of the condos where he lived.

Water squelched beneath his feet and his jeans clung, wet and heavy, to his legs.

Maybe he was already on edge because . . .

He couldn't shake the idea that Baily might have died because she was mistaken for Sarah.

"Aurelie!" His eyes stung and blurred. "Aurelie!"

The killer could have decided to take Aurelie out next.

Shit, he needed help out here.

A deep bark startled him. He skidded to a halt, gasping through his open mouth.

Another bark, this one closer.

Nick bent over with his hands on his knees. He croaked out, "Sucker? She took the goddamn dog for a walk?"

"What are you doing, Nick?"

He didn't look up, didn't need to when he knew he'd found Aurelie. Or she'd found him.

"Nick. Talk to me."

A large tongue traveled from his chin, over his mouth and nose to his forehead. Hoover snuffled at an ear then set about doing water-damage control all over Nick's torso.

Aurelie's laugh didn't amuse Nick. "Don't you ever do what you just did again," he said. "Got that?"

"No."

He straightened up, pausing long enough on the way to rest a hand on the dog's sopping head. Poor Hoover, he just did what came naturally.

The feelings Nick had for Aurelie weren't so gentle. They weren't gentle at all. He reached for her. "Dammit, quit fooling around. We can't afford to be careless. I'm telling you that, and Matt said the same thing. Don't you understand?"

"Calm down," she told him. A hooded, snap-fronted rain slicker covered everything but the lower half of her face. A hand showed only when she pulled the hood back far enough to let her see him. "Would you rather I *didn't* take Hoover out? This is the safest time of the day. No one hangs around looking for victims this late . . . early. It's that sort of no-man's hour. Why don't you have clothes on?"

"I do," he said through his teeth. "But I've always thought it would make sense to go naked in the rain so you wouldn't get any clothes wet."

Aurelie giggled. "I bet your jeans weigh a ton."

Hoover howled, raised his majestic head and bayed at a spot where a moon might have been.

"Shh!" Nick arranged his fingers into two sets of claws and jabbed them at the dog. "You'll wake up the neighbors, dammit. Inside. Now. Both of you."

Inside entailed another slosh through the mud to retrace his steps.

Aurelie made sucking noises when she walked. A look showed the toes of rubber boots shining in a streetlight.

"Sorry I shocked you," she said. "I didn't think, I just left. Hoover always goes between four and five. You could set your clock by it. I never need an alarm."

"Holy . . . Are you saying you get up at this time every day?"

"Yes. I go to bed early. Works for me."

"Wouldn't work for me," he said.

"It doesn't have to."

"It does if you're staying at my place. I don't want

you out here on your own. I already told you that."

"I'm not staying at your place, Nick. As soon as the rental office opens I'll look at the Quarters. If I don't like it there, I'll find something else. I won't disturb you this early in the morning again."

"Sure," he said, and gave Hoover a push. The dog had decided he needed to lean on someone while he walked. "Now I know you take risks like this, how much sleep do you think I'll get after four? No matter where you live."

Hoover kept right on leaning.

They reached the entrance to Oakdale and turned right.

"Nick," Aurelie said, "we're trying to pretend everything isn't falling apart when it is."

"I'm not going to let that happen," he said, and realized she wasn't sucking along at his heels anymore. He turned around. "What are you doing, Rellie?"

"Nothing."

"Then do *something*. Get up."

She sat on the curb with her head down. "Baily was so miserable she jumped off the building."

"Hey, hey, I know." He decided not to remind her that Baily might well have been pushed. "Let's get in and take a hot shower."

She didn't answer.

Hoover waddled over beside her and set his rump down in a good inch of dirty water.

"Don't do that," Aurelie said. "Now I'll have to put you in the bath."

That was a picture Nick didn't want to contemplate. "He'll shake most of it off."

"You talked to Matt on your own," Aurelie said. "What did you tell him?"

"You asked me that on the way back here. I told you not to worry about it."

"Why? Why be secretive? I've got questions I'd be a fool not to have. Did you tell him everything?"

He knew what she was talking about. "I told him very little. All that stuff from years ago doesn't affect him."

"You do know that the truth about us could come out now? The dots could be connected and after that everyone's going to know we took Delia's name but that's all. They'll find out we aren't related to her and she'll be so hurt."

He'd thought of that and just about every other likely eventuality. "What will help her the most is making sure she doesn't doubt our feelings for her. And showing her nothing's going to change. If it happens, which I doubt."

"How do you think Billy Meche and Matt will react if they find out we didn't go to them with information about a big case like this?" She held the hood away from her face and looked at him.

"I can't think about that now."

"We have to," she said. "We need to be ready to deal with it."

Lightning shot a single jagged bolt from heaven to earth. *Whap!* Straight down. Crackling followed, a bit like the invisible rocks-hitting-glass sounds at the end of a firework display. Only this display wasn't over. The thunder came quickly and Nick jumped.

He hauled Aurelie up, ignored a bass growl from Hoover, and moved them along as fast as possible. "You're getting hysterical," he said. "Maybe *I'm* getting hysterical."

"Whatever we are, it's better than crying, and I could do that at any moment. I'm running away—do you understand me? Running away inside my head. I haven't slept at all. Hoover didn't wake me up, I woke him up. I had to get outside and breathe."

"Just you give yourself a chance to get some rest and settle down."

"I'm scared, dammit. I'm so scared. You believe Baily was murdered, don't you? Matt obviously does."

Another light display shot overhead and this time the night split open, or sounded as if it did, almost in the same instant.

"This isn't a good idea," he said, keeping a firm grip on Aurelie's arm. "Come on, cut across the side. It's quicker."

"You do think she was murdered and it could be because she was a bit like Sarah," Aurelie said. "That would mean Sarah was supposed to die."

"I don't know, and I mean that." But only on a technicality. "Grab the dog before we go in. I'll get him into the mudroom."

"Right," Aurelie said meekly. "Sorry for the mess . . . and the nuisance."

"You're not a nuisance," he muttered.

"Yes, I am. Hey—" she poked his arm "—Sabine told me you wouldn't let her in to clean this week. Or last week. What's that about?"

Sabine was Delia's housekeeper, had been for years, and at Delia's insistence Nick had hired her for his place. "I haven't felt like having anyone in. I'll have her back once things settle down."

"Wait."

Nick barely heard her hiss at him through the storm. He drew her beside him and didn't ask questions.

She reached up and when he leaned closer, whispered in his ear. "That truck wasn't at the curb when I left."

He looked and saw a light-colored pickup with a canopy over the bed. "No. Not when I left, either. There's someone sitting in it."

"Let's stay out of sight," Aurelie whispered, tugging on his arm. "They probably haven't seen us."

The driver's door of the truck opened. "Hey, there," a woman called. "Are you Nick Board?"

"Who is it?" Aurelie asked. "D'you know her?"

"I'm Nick Board." He lowered his voice and added to Aurelie, "I doubt it. Who would—could be that woman who was being pushy at the police station. I've heard about writers doing things like this. They get desperate. You hear about things like that."

"She could be dangerous."

The woman pulled an umbrella and a purse of some kind, a very big, sacklike thing, from the space behind her seat. She struggled until the umbrella opened, shut the door and walked across the grass on the turned-inward toes of high-heeled shoes. "How nice of you to be up," she said. "I thought I'd have hours to wait."

"She's nuts," Aurelie murmured.

"Ma'am," Nick said. "It's too early for visitors. What are you here for?"

"Joan Reeves. Of course you're right." She arrived in front of them and looked Aurelie over with a faint smile. "Dreadful weather."

Thick blond hair waved past her shoulders. A short windbreaker over tight, cropped jeans—and worn with pale-colored, very high heels, put her instantly out of place in Pointe Judah. This lady had a land-mark figure; it wouldn't be easy to forget.

"Should we know you?" Nick didn't attempt to introduce Aurelie.

Hoover, who had busied himself draining a puddle and ignoring the arrival of the stranger, chose that instant to deliver a few foghorn blasts.

"Oh, dear." The woman took a backward step. "What is he?"

"A dog," Aurelie said. "Quiet, boy. Good boy."

"Forgive me for my inopportune appearance at your home." The voice had a girlish quality that didn't fit. "I really did intend to sit in my vehicle until I saw signs of you being up and about. Then I was

78

going to ask for an appointment to interview you."

Interview? Geez, she sounded like someone from the press and if she was, it meant he'd already been traced here from California. But Joan Reeves didn't resemble any picture he'd formerly had of reporters. But then, how would he know how a reporter might look? "Calling would have been a better idea."

"Oh, dear, you are angry with me. Come to that, I'm angry with myself. I can be *so* impetuous. I tried to call several times but all I got was a busy signal."

Of course that's all she'd heard. He had made sure of that the moment he and Aurelie got home.

The woman cleared her throat. "I've made a bad first impression. How silly of me. Would you give me another chance and tell me when I could come by and interview you, Mr. Board?"

"You're a reporter."

"No! Why would you think that? I won't bore you with all my credentials except to say that my current job—the one that pays the bills—is with a book factory in New York State." She peered closer, apparently for signs that they understood. "I write books that have other people's names on them—from an outline I'm given. It's really very common, but I'm also working on a project of my own and that's where you come in. Could you give me a little time later?"

Nick began to feel sorry for her. "What kind of project?"

"I already have a contract from a big publisher although I'm not allowed to discuss it yet. I can show you some of the books I've written for the book factory."

He was aware of Aurelie's fingernails in the skin of his arm. Dammit, she was shaking. "Why not call later, Ms. Reeves."

"Oh, I will, thank you very much. And I'll bring a document that says you have to approve anything I write about you."

She wasn't damn well going to write anything about him if he could pull that off. Meanwhile, he'd better not alienate her until he saw where he stood.

Joan Reeves backed away. "I'm at the Roll Inn if you want to get hold of me. I'm not planning to do anything but wait there until I can talk to you." She hesitated.

"Call me later," Nick said. He only wanted to get Aurelie inside the condo.

"I'll call," Joan said, starting to walk backward. "I didn't tell you what I'm working on. It's really exciting. My book is called *Then and Now. Subtitle: Ties That Divide.* Subtitle: *The Lives of Antebellum Houses and the Generations of People They've Owned.*" She paused for breath. "You see how clever that is? The people the houses have owned, not the people who have owned the houses. I have a solid history of Place Lafource and it's early inhabitants but I have to work on the 'now.' I need to know all about you and your sisters."

9

"You're shaking all over," Nick said, helping Aurelie lead Hoover directly into the mudroom. "It's okay. Or are you cold? Of course you are."

"I'm not cold. In this coat, I'm boiling. I'd be boiling without the coat. Nick, it's like, well, is that woman bizarre or am I looking for mutants under every rock? Don't try to soften anything for me. Just give it to me straight. If you think I'm losing my grip, just spit it out."

He laughed but his heart wasn't in it. "You'd have to be strange not to find Joan Reeves unusual. She could be perfectly honorable, but her presentation is something else."

A shower stall stood in one corner. There wasn't a bath, not that getting Hoover into one would be easy. Aurelie pushed the dog inside the glass door and turned on the water. When she was satisfied with the temperature, she closed the door.

Hoover, no fool, blinked at the situation and scooted around to sit in the dry spot immediately behind the stream from the showerhead.

"I need a chair," Aurelie said. She reached in again with a bottle of shampoo and squirted some on the dog.

Nick pulled a wicker-back chair closer and Aurelie stood on it. She hooked an arm over the top of the enclosure, grabbed the showerhead and yanked it back and forth until soapy water and dirt streamed from Hoover's fur.

He caught Aurelie around the waist. "Come on down and let me do that. You'll dislocate your arm." He realized he was grateful she still had on the rain slicker.

"I can manage." And she did. It took fifteen minutes but eventually water ran clear from the animal's coat and Aurelie got down. She cracked the door and squeezed her arm back inside to turn the water off. "That was the easy part. Now—stand still, boy—I've got to dry him. Do you have any old towels you don't care about?"

He figured he would after this and took a pile out of the linen closet.

Aurelie had him put them on the chair then looked at him critically. She waved a finger at his lower regions. "You need to go get those wet jeans off."

"What would be the point? I might as well help with the drying first."

She spread large towels on the floor and unsnapped her slicker. Once she had it off she hung it on the back of the door and turned to him. "D'you have a hair dryer in here?"

"Yes," he said. Just as well his jeans were wet. They had a dampening effect on some things and he needed that. He looked away from her pale pink cotton nightie, low at the neck, sleeveless and reaching just past midthigh, and found the dryer. She had put the darn slicker on over her nightie without bothering to get dressed and now she was behaving as if she were still a skinny little kid.

Hoover didn't need encouragement to move quickly from the shower, but Aurelie had to all but lie on top of him to make him flop in a heap on the towels. She set to work rubbing him down, working from his nose toward his tail. One towel after another piled up in a clean but saturated heap.

Nick plugged in the hair dryer and trained it on the dog. He and Aurelie worked in silence until the animal was damp dry. By that time he lay on his back, feet flopping in ecstasy at having the warm air wiggled back and forth over his tummy.

"Good enough, Hoover," Aurelie said, standing and urging the dog to his feet. "C'mon, boy." She took him from the mudroom and quickly returned to help clean up.

Without warning, she dropped the pile of towels she'd gathered from the floor.

"What?" Nick said. "Why did you do that?"

"All I'm doing is—just racing around, trying not to think." She crossed her arms. Her long black hair stood out from its center part in even tighter curls than usual. "I feel as if we're running down a steep hill and picking up speed. And we don't have any brakes. You know what I mean?"

"Just drive in your heels, Rellie. We know how to do that. We've been doing it for years."

"I don't want anyone's pity."

"I'm not pitying you, dammit."

She poked his ribs. "I didn't mean you, moron!" She dug at him with a sharp finger, advancing while he retreated. "Did you really hear what that woman said. She wants to find out all about you and your *sisters?*"

He made a grab for her hand and caught it. "She's just a woman working on a project and she's real enthusiastic. She doesn't know anything about us. And she won't find out anything we don't want her to know. Rellie, the three of us are fine. Maybe not perfect, but not damaged, either, and she won't be able to make us say things that could make her suspicious." Not a lot, anyway.

"Sometimes I'm not so sure we aren't damaged." She stood close, looking at her feet. "We've had so much good luck. Who would ever expect a busy, important woman like Delia to just about drop out of the life she knew to take care of them? She protected us, made sure we went to the kind of schools we should never have had a chance at. She's always been there for us."

The break in her voice didn't reassure him. "Delia loves the life she has. If she didn't she could have moved on once we had our feet under us. I think she wanted a reason to get off the merry-go-round. She's told us as much, Rellie. Please stop worrying about her."

"That could be because she doesn't want us to feel we've robbed her of something more in her life."

"She was married once, remember? She says he

was a dog and she's better off without him or any other man unless she happens to need or want one for a bit."

"Don't talk like that about her, it doesn't sound nice," Aurelie said, tightening her arms beneath her breasts.

Skinny little kid? Not for a long time. Full and high, he couldn't miss how round her breasts were, or fail to see the pressure of her nipples against the cotton.

Geesh, this was a nightmare.

Uh-uh, a saint he wasn't. Aurelie Board was a dream to look at, a small-scale all-woman with the oval, soft-mouthed face that had become the measure he judged other women against. Her hairline had that heart shape, coming to a sharp point in the center. And she was the least vain female he'd ever met.

He filled his lungs. "Sleep," he said. "Sleep in. You don't have any distance to go to get to work."

"Do you think you can sleep?" she asked. "I don't. Nick, I know I sound childish, but all I want is to go on the way we were. Not having to worry about outsiders, I mean." When she looked at him, her gray eyes shimmered. With both hands flattened on his chest, she rested her cheek on top. "We'll get through it, but what will it cost?"

He held his hands a couple of inches away from her before finally settling them on her back. He held still, afraid to move. "Whatever happens, we haven't done anything wrong. Thanks to my mother, we didn't die in that mine. We'll always stick together and if bits of our stories come out, we'll cope. Maybe some will feel sorry for us. We should try not to fight that, just let it go away."

"You're the sensible one—in theory." Once more she raised her face. This time she put her chin against his chest and he could feel her breath on his skin.

"Would you feel better if you went back to New Orleans for a bit?" He didn't want her to say yes.

"No. My decision on that hasn't changed. I'll go back if and when I can be useful, in whatever capacity I choose to be there."

Her eyes closed, squeezed tightly shut, and tears glittered on her lashes. Nick wrapped his arms tightly around her and pressed his face into her hair. It smelled nice and he rubbed his cheek over it.

Aurelie slid her hands until they rested at the back of his waist.

They swayed a little and he played with the soft ends of her hair. Sometimes people needed the comfort they got from physical contact. He loved the way she felt against him.

The wet jeans weren't inhibiting a thing anymore. He could probably bend iron bars with his dick. Nick settled his teeth together. Even thinking that word with Aurelie in his arms felt crude. But it was true. The reactions he had to her didn't feel wrong. She wasn't untouchable, even if he was having trouble believing that.

He had to hold on a bit longer. She'd get herself together shortly and go to bed. He gritted his teeth again.

"I won't have any peace unless we find out that Baily's death had nothing to do with Colin—with him looking for us, thinking he'd found Sarah and killing her once he'd gotten whatever he wanted out of her. Then we'll feel safer. I never thought I'd pray to find out a woman had killed herself," she said.

"We'd both be fools not to hope for that. It wouldn't bring her back to life if we didn't."

Aurelie sighed. She smoothed her hands up his chest and hooked them over his shoulders. Then he felt her fingers stiffen.

"What is it?" He ducked his head to look into her face and the luminous quality in her eyes let him know she felt a change between them. "It's okay," he said.

"Is it?" For an instant she seemed ready to pull away—or smack him.

He couldn't take his eyes off her mouth, the way her full lips settled together after she spoke. Nick kissed her.

He had kissed her, and she'd kissed him back.

And he had melted her. Nothing had tasted sweeter, until the strangeness of it, the sense of the forbidden, shocked her to her toes. She had felt his reaction to her and folded herself into him as naturally as if they'd been dating all these years instead of living as family.

That brief, sensual warmth had lasted as long as it took her to remember Delia and, most of all, Sarah.

Aurelie wished she could blame her conclusions on her imagination. She couldn't. Her sister was in love with Nick.

Anger, rage at the unfairness of it all, took over Aurelie. What about *her* feelings?

Sarah was older and had been the one to take care of her younger sister when things couldn't get any worse.

What kind of feelings did Nick have for Sarah? For either of them? She only wanted the tension and confusion in her head to go away.

The light in his bedroom had gone out.

That kiss could just as well have happened because the two of them were seeking comfort.

Sure it could.

Aurelie turned toward the window in her room. Early light, heavy with fuzzy gray, pressed into cracks around the blinds. She rolled over and sat up on the edge of the bed, listening to Hoover snore gently.

Nick needed his sleep. His habit of turning off his alarm without realizing what he'd done was legendary. She would give him a little longer to become truly unconscious, then gather her one small bag and leave. Before they saw each other again—alone—she had to have time to let the memory of that kiss fade.

She had a key to Poke Around, so she'd go there and call a cab to get her out to Place Lafource. She needed her own vehicle.

Birds began to sing.

Aurelie got up, waited to be sure Hoover wouldn't stir, and sneaked across Nick's carpets to the kitchen. She wanted coffee, but a Coke would do and she could get that quietly.

"Hey," Nick said and she started wildly. "You thirsty, too?"

He stood on one leg, the opposite foot braced on his knee. When they were all younger, and he'd already had the habit, they'd called him the Stork. She looked at his leg and he promptly put the second foot to the floor.

"Want some juice?" He wasn't smiling and his eyes were watchful.

Aurelie took the glass he offered—his glass—and swallowed some orange juice. "Thanks," she said. Part of her wished she'd stayed in the bedroom, a bigger part wanted to be where she could see him.

He poured a second glass of orange juice and exchanged it for the one he'd been drinking.

"You're making yourself busy because you feel awkward," Aurelie blurted out.

"You think?"

Her body warmed until she knew her face was pink. She blew at stray curls falling in her eyes. "What happened was nothing," she said. "We were both exhausted and we'd had a terrible shock. We were emotional. Forget about it."

Nick's dark blue eyes didn't shift from hers. He drank more juice but never looked away for an instant. Beard shadow darkened his jaw and Aurelie became very aware of how big he was—how big he had always seemed.

Creeping around and trying to leave without his knowing would be silly now. "I'm going to get ready and go over to Poke Around. I can get some boxes unpacked early—before I have to leave to look at apartments."

"Why hurry? You haven't had any sleep."

"I can't sleep in the day."

"I'm exhausted."

She smiled at him. "Get back to bed. You can't go out to the lab until the police release the building."

He put his glass in the sink and took hers, even though she hadn't finished the juice. "Please don't leave without giving us a chance to talk."

"I wish I could talk, but I don't know what to say. It's awful."

"It's not awful, dammit." He grabbed her hand and took it to his mouth. "It's wonderful. I didn't imagine you liked it when I kissed you. You were right there with me. Can't we just go with that? What are you afraid of?" He passed her knuckles back and forth over his mouth.

Aurelie contracted her belly. He might as well have stripped her bare and made love to her right there—her reactions were powerful, exciting, frightening. And he didn't need to ask why she was hesitant. She found her voice. "I'm afraid we've crossed a line that'll push us apart. I'm afraid there's no going back."

"I want to make love to you."

She gasped and tried to free her hand, but he gripped her tightly.

"We've got to stop this," she said. "I'll go right now. Please, Nick, help me to save us."

"From what? From being together? I don't want to and I don't think you do, either. Do you?"

He wore pajama bottoms that rested low on his hips. She tried not to stare at him but failed. Nick wasn't trying to avoid looking at her.

"I've wanted you for a long time," he said. "You're right. There's no going back and I can't pretend anymore. Tell me what my chances are. What do you feel for me?"

"No." She shook her head.

"You don't want me?" Muscles in his jaw sprang hard.

Tears slid, hot, down her face and she let them go. Nick wiped them away.

"Can't you see that this won't work?" she asked him. "We'll hurt other people and we'll hurt ourselves. We would lose something wonderful forever."

"Tell me you don't want me."

Aurelie shook her head again. If she were stronger, she'd lie and say the words. She couldn't do it.

"Hold me," he said.

He threaded his fingers through hers and eased her toward him.

"Stop being afraid," Nick said. "There may not be any going back, but you don't want to. Any more than I do."

She didn't want to. But she pulled her hand from his, whirled around and left the kitchen.

10

No footsteps followed her.

Outside his bedroom door she stopped. Wiping moist palms on her nightie, breathing through her mouth, she went into the room. Dark green walls had begun to glow with the early-morning light. Over the iron bed with its tall, primitive posts, a wooden fan moved slowly.

A breeze reached Aurelie and she saw long, sheer drapes billow from a French door Nick had cracked open.

"I'm afraid to ask what this means," he said from behind her.

"Then don't." She crossed her hands and gripped the hem of her nightie—and drew it slowly over her head.

"My God," Nick said. "Don't you dare do this out of pity."

"Sometimes you should keep your mouth shut." She threw the gown on the bed and stood there shivering, not because she was cool but because she was too hyper to stay still.

Standing close at her back, Nick slid his hands under her arms and supported her breasts. Very slowly, carefully, he stroked them with his thumbs. He kept his left forearm over her aching nipples and flattened his right hand on her belly. Pressed against him, she felt his arousal and arched her back. Cold chased heat deep inside her.

Aurelie settled the back of her head against his chest and let her arms hang at her sides. Slowly but with a fine tremor that showed his struggle to keep control, he stroked her body. His heart beat hard enough for her to feel. She heard her own inside her head.

He touched his mouth to the back of her neck, kissed her there, kissed her spine, moving down, vertebra by vertebra until he knelt and nipped at the very base of her spine. With his mouth pressed to her back, he gripped her thighs and ran his hands up her body to her breasts once more.

Aurelie needed to slip down in front of him. Her legs were weak and a faint humming seethed its way around the places she'd never expected to share with this man.

"Down," she whispered. "I can't stand up."

"C'mon." He eased her to join him on the dark, silky rug. His tongue in her ear sent shivers across her skin. Every touch, carefully, firmly applied, turned up the heat.

Aurelie felt the last vestiges of fight going out of her. She spread her knees and sat astride his thighs, felt him respond beneath her bottom and put a hand beneath herself to hold him against slick, throbbing folds.

"Aurelie," he murmured. "I . . . I don't know how I waited so long."

She didn't have an answer to that but wiggled her bottom until he cried out and spun her to face him.

Nick held her arms, leaned her away so that he could look at her. "Say something," he asked very quietly.

No, she wouldn't put words to this, just as she wouldn't give it up.

Something close to pain passed over his features, but he closed his eyes and kissed her again. He opened their mouths wide, pressed his tongue deep inside hers until she responded with as much force as she could. Aurelie broke contact and he sucked her bottom lip between his teeth. She matched him, move for move, and the morning light turned to darkness again.

Raising her hips, she took him in her fingers and guided herself over him, buried him inside her and swallowed her own cry. Nick shouted aloud and there was no stopping, not for anything, not for either of them.

She felt herself flowering wide, an exquisite pain, and tried to hold back, but the speed of his pelvis, his drive, turned rhythmic and hard and she let go, fell on top of him as he dropped to his back and pulled her over him.

Shock waves fanned from the center of her sensation and she allowed herself to turn heavy and boneless on top of Nick.

He breathed great sighs, kissing her neck again and again. And all the while he stroked her back and buttocks, ran his fingers up into her hair and murmured things she couldn't understand.

"Are you cold?"

She heard that. "Mmm, no. You're obsessed with cold."

"I'm obsessed with you."

He rolled them to their sides, got up, lifting her as he did so, and put her on the bed. He raised her again and threw back the covers. Climbing over her, he lay heavily on his side, still breathing hard, still running his fingers over her.

The sudden sensation of him touching her again, smoothing his way past still-aching skin and flesh, shocked her. Aurelie started to jackknife her knees, but recovered in time to keep them flat on the bed. She crossed her ankles.

"Fly with it," he said against her throat. "It'll be good. You aren't finished yet."

She opened her mouth to protest, but faint stirrings turned into a rush and he proved himself right. Tossing her hips, she grasped him, tried to pull him on top of her, but he placed himself there and made love to her until she threw her arms wide and wailed at the ceiling. The threads to sanity had broken. They clung together, hot, sweating, slipping against each other.

When they rested, limbs entwined, the daylight forced its way into Aurelie's mind. She looked at Nick's face. His eyes were closed, dark lashes moving against his cheeks. His man's mouth, often hard by day, was soft, the lips slightly parted to show a hint of his strong teeth. And a definite paler line outlined those lips.

This was Nick. This was the boy who had looked after her—and Sarah—when they had no one in the world. He had grown to manhood as their rock, the one who would always be there for them. And she'd blown it. They'd blown it.

A little voice told her to snuggle into his arms and enjoy every moment, to take whatever she could get and not look back.

Sometime today she would face Sarah, who had also been ready to slay dragons if that's what it took to keep her little sister safe.

Nick's breathing was deep and even.

Aurelie eased a couple of inches from him and turned onto her back.

Nick didn't stir.

She moved an arm, a leg, pulled the rest of her body closer to the edge of the bed. The feelings she had for this man wouldn't go backward. By tomorrow, or next week, she wouldn't want to go running with him, not as much as she would long to be right where she was now, or where she had been only minutes ago.

Aurelie turned her face toward him, and jumped. Those dark blue eyes stared back. Except for the question she saw there, he seemed expressionless.

"You shocked me," she said, breathless. "I thought you were asleep."

"I know. I'd like to be but I don't dare. You'll leave me."

Covering her face, she struggled to think clearly, to think of something to say that would be right.

The mattress moved and Nick put an arm around her. He began to pull her closer again but she stiffened her body. Nick moved her anyway in the end, she couldn't stop him.

He took her hands from her face and held her wrists on the pillow, rose on his elbows to look down at her. "Stop it," he said.

Her efforts to release her wrists were useless. "Don't hold me down, Nick. You don't want to do something like that."

"Get over the past," he said, his voice rumbly and tough. "We didn't make love because of the past—except for the part that let us get to know each other. I want us to take this wherever it'll go. Maybe it can be something great."

"Let me up," she said. "It's late. I've got to get ready for work."

"Don't be an idiot. It's early."

"No, Nick. It's late. For you and me, it's too late. We've made the one mistake we'll never recover from."

He pushed himself away from her. "Why did you come into my room? You could have walked past the way I thought you would."

"I thought that's what I would do. But I wanted you, too. I'm not going to suggest I'm not as much to blame as you are." She got up and wouldn't let herself search for her nightie.

"Don't go," he said, much quieter now.

Aurelie held her back straight. Her throat hurt so

much with needing to cry yet not wanting to cry in front of Nick. He was right—she could and should have passed his room and gone to her own.

"Dammit, Aurelie!"

She covered her ears and shot around to look at him.

Nick sat on the bed, the white sheet scrambled around his tanned hips. He pointed at her. "Listen to me. You'll get over the guilt. There's no guilt here, no shame, nothing wrong, just two people who could . . . two people who care a lot about each other."

"You're right about me feeling guilty," she told him. "And you know I do, because you feel it yourself."

He leaped to the floor and she thought he would come after her. Instead, he dropped his shoulders, wiped anger from his face, breathed slowly through his nose and said, "Remember one thing. What we just had together isn't nearly enough. It's hardly a start."

She waited, her heart thudding.

Nick pointed a long forefinger at her. "And I am *not* your brother."

11

Eileen Moggeridge managed Poke Around for her sister-in-law, Emma Duhon. Emma's husband, Finn, owned the Oakdale Mansion complex.

Aurelie had dodged Eileen's questions about why

she'd already been at the shop for several hours when Eileen arrived. The Hummer stood in the parking lot and all Aurelie had to do was look past the dusty black vehicle to have a clear view of Nick's condo.

She deliberately turned her back to the outside. As if that would change a thing about the problems she'd been a full party to making.

She polished the espresso machine, a glamorous red affair reminiscent of an old Cadillac. Café tables and chairs stood in front of the counter where pastries, muffins and cookies tantalized from beneath glass domes. Jars of biscotti invited more indiscretion and a range of hand-dipped chocolates beckoned.

Sabine Webb, who "did" for Nick when she wasn't "doing" for Delia out at Place Lafource, pushed the door open with her back and came in with her arms full. "Mornin'," she said, glowing as usual. "Is that your brother's car I see over at his place, Aurelie?"

Aurelie polished with a lot of vigor.

"Hey, girl." Sabine put her face where Aurelie couldn't ignore it. "That Nick, is he home today? Me, I been worryin' about that boy." Since Sabine couldn't be any older than Nick, the term sounded strange, would sound more strange coming from anyone else. "He's not behavin' like himself."

"Nick's home," Aurelie said. She felt herself being watched and caught Eileen staring at her. She smiled and so did Eileen, but not until she'd paused too long.

"What's going on with him, then?" Sabine asked. Her long hair, wound into a zillion tiny braids, shone from the oil she'd added. Tortoiseshell combs at the sides held the braids away from her deep bronze face in heavy loops. She tapped Aurelie's forearm with slender fingers. "Cat got your tongue? You heard me?"

"Well—y'know—yes, of course I heard you." She smiled. There was nothing to be gained by being evasive. "He's been in a bit of a mood."

"A mood?" Sabine shook her head. "Girl, it's time for him to get over his mood. I'm so behind with my work I could just *spit.* I'll do this, then I'll get right over to that Nick and whip him into shape."

"I'd leave him for now," Aurelie said quickly. "He had a late . . . night."

Once more she met Eileen's gaze and her dark eyes held concern.

"We'll see about that," Sabine said. "I've got somethin' you've got to carry, Eileen. You're gonna be right on the cuttin' edge with this. Everyone's gonna want one."

Eileen, tall, voluptuous and exotic, walked over to see Sabine's latest wonder.

"See?" She hauled a pale pink radio from the box she'd brought in and wedged it between two jars of biscotti. A pale blue one followed, a yellow, a green and a white. "Don't go much for the white, myself," she said.

"Radios?" Eileen said.

"Not just any radios, Eileen, so don't you go soundin' all superior like I was missin' a drawer or two in my dresser."

"Never suggested any such thing," Eileen said.

Aurelie leaned on the counter and eyed the green radio. "I like this one."

"Listen to this," Sabine said. She flipped a switch on the green one, pressed a button and stood back with her hands pointed toward it as if she'd just pulled a rabbit out of a hat.

Conversation, talk about politics, droned out.

"I don't get it," Eileen said.

Sabine's hands moved heavenward. "Lordy, do I have to explain every little thing? This is the very latest thing. And what's more, it's been proved, absolutely certain, that it works. Do we or don't we struggle with them rotten armadillos around here? Do we or don't we go to bed at night with gardens full of luscious shrubs, only to get up in the mornin' and find the darn armadillos dug the roots right out from under 'em?"

"It's a problem," Eileen agreed.

"Yes," Sabine said, nodding her head, triumphant. "And what do armadillos hate more'n anythin' else? I'll say it for you so you don't have to stretch your minds too much. Those armadillos can't *stand* talk radio. All you gotta do is put one of these little beauties in a plastic bag—keep out the humidity that way—and leave it snuggled down in them lovely bushes. Turn it on first, of course. But I tell you, there won't be no more armadillos."

Aurelie cleared her throat.

"You want to sell these to me?" Eileen asked.

They usually bought what they carried outright because Emma Duhon believed people mostly needed to be paid right away for what they brought in.

"I'll go you one better," Sabine said, her gorgeous smile casting brilliance in every direction. "I don't want one penny for these until they sellin' out the door so fast you come beggin' to me for more. I can't say fairer than that now, can I?"

"Um—how would we, er—how would we label them?" Aurelie said. "What would we call them?"

"Just you leave that to me. I'll pile 'em up real pretty and if you can't sell 'em, you don't have to keep 'em. How's that?"

"Wonderful," Eileen said. "Yes, that'll do just fine."

"I'll do it then," Sabine said and set about making a radio pyramid on a direct line with the door. "What put that Nick in a snit, then?"

"I'm not sure," Aurelie said promptly. "Where did you get those pretty radios?"

"Armadilla-killas," Sabine corrected. "My Ed got 'em. A fellow was sellin' 'em at a market over in Lafayette. Ed got 'em cheap on account of he took 'em all. Smart man, my Ed."

Ed Webb, a pale, sinewy man who never tanned, even though he spent most of his days taking care of the grounds at Place Lafource, was renowned for his many "good deals." He didn't shine as a conversationalist but his love for his Sabine showed and Aurelie really liked him for that.

"Whooee," Sabine said in her rich voice. "I do believe you've got trouble on the way."

"Who?" Eileen said, immediately craning to see around hanging flights of battery-driven bumblebees. "Oh, lordy, not at this hour of the day. Lobelia Forestier of all people. What's she doing here?"

"Ooh, gatherin' gossip, I'd say," Sabine said. "And if we're lucky, maybe sharin' a little. I'll have me a café au lait, please, Aurelie. I know how to use the machine if you're too busy."

"Sit down and be waited on," Aurelie said. She didn't look forward to hearing whatever Lobelia Forestier might have on her mind. President of the Chamber of Commerce, Lobelia's primary function was spreading gossip and interfering with town business.

"Don't stare, either of you," Eileen said. "She'll take it as a compliment."

Aurelie chuckled while Sabine snapped her fingers to music in her mind.

"She's surely takin' her time," Sabine said when the shop bell didn't immediately ring. "If she's pullin' weeds and lookin' smug, don't go gettin' mad. Let her do it. I could give a rat's hiney if someone gets pleasure out of pickin' on me, so long as they're helping me at the same time."

Eileen and Aurelie sniggered explosively. "Hold it," Eileen said. "Keep your heads down but she's talkin' to someone I don't know. Not that I know so many people."

"Who is it?" Sabine whispered.

"She can't hear us," Eileen said. "No need to whisper. It's a woman. That Lobelia is gabbin' away like she's met Santa Claus and he's taking down her list."

Aurelie put the café au lait in front of Sabine, together with one of the lemon cheesecake and shortbread bars she loved and started checking a rack of clothing. "We need to rotate some of these into the back room," she said. "There's so much out there and I've heard merchandise should be moved around."

"You would have learned that in law school," Eileen said.

Aurelie looked at her sharply, but decided the remark was supposed to be a joke. "You'd be surprised what you learn in law school."

Allowing her eyes to wander, just enough to see Lobelia in an animated chat with Joan Reeves . . . Well, hell, that tore it. Or it could. Given the hooded rain slicker and less-than-perfect light conditions, Joan wouldn't necessarily remember Aurelie. Her attention had all been on Nick.

"Now we've got a photographer," Eileen said. "He's taking shots all around the place. Mmm-mmm, nice lookin', too. Could be I should offer to take some photos of him."

Eileen was pretty tight with Matt Boudreaux but she made certain to let people know there was no exclusive arrangement. Aurelie—together with most of the town—wondered if there was more to it than Eileen wanted them to know.

The photographer worked like the pro he obviously was. His equipment was strictly professional.

"Damn," Aurelie said under her breath. The man had joined Joan Reeves and Lobelia.

"If someone doesn't tell me *exactly* what's goin' on out there I'll have to go stand in the window and look for myself," Sabine said.

"Lobelia's talking to a woman and a photographer," Eileen said. "How can we know anything else? We can't hear, can we?"

"Guess not," Sabine said.

"Lobelia looks too happy." Aurelie turned away again.

"They're comin' this way," Eileen said. "Be busy, both of you."

"I'm busy with my cheesecake," Sabine said, chewing. "Why don't you two join me."

The shop bell rang and Aurelie talked herself out of hiding in a pile of silk jackets and heading for the stockroom. She did go to the opposite side of the shop and check out the water situation in a row of small pigs made of live ivy growing on wire forms.

"Mornin'," Lobelia said loudly enough to greet folks for a mile around. "Looks like I've come at the right time. Aurelie, I heard you were back. You didn't come to the chamber to see me. What have I done to you? I thought we were friends."

Aurelie groaned. "Hello, Lobelia." She had to face

105

the woman. "I have been so busy, you wouldn't believe it. Between moving back to Pointe Judah and finding a job it's been hectic." She straightened several candles in their holders.

"Hello there," Joan Reeves said, a big smile on her striking face. She came toward Aurelie with a hand extended. "How great to meet you again so soon. I am so sorry about early this morning. What a dolt I can be. Oh, this is Vic Gross. He's an old friend and he's helping me with the book. Vic's a photographer and his photographs could make anything look good."

Blond, green-eyed Vic had a charming smile and he looked amused at the buildup. "Nice to meet you." He shook Aurelie's hand and looked around. "Nice to meet all of you."

Vic got a warm welcome of his own and his comfort with female approval showed.

"You mean you're workin' here at the shop, Aurelie?" Lobelia asked. "What happened to the fancy lawyer job?"

"I'm taking a break," Aurelie said, hoping the least she could expect from this encounter was that she wouldn't have to repeat the story too often. Lobelia was likely to do it for her. "It was time to come home and be with my own people."

"Well, I can surely understand that," Lobelia said. "Never did like big cities myself. Now, you know it's not my way to talk about unpleasant things, but this town deserves to know what happened last night." She had taken to having her gray hair dyed a shade of light brown and replaced tight curls with a softer look. Nothing would soften the sharp pleasure in her eyes.

Sabine dropped the end of her cheescake pastry; she'd apparently forgotten it was still between her fingers. "What are you talkin' about, Lobelia? You look like somebody died."

If she could do it without drawing attention, Aurelie would sit down. She wanted to be somewhere else. Joan Reeves's attention centered on Lobelia, which was a good thing. The longer she was diverted from Aurelie, the better, but Matt had said there should be no discussion about Baily's death.

"You have a truly unfortunate turn of phrase, Sabine Webb," Lobelia said. "One day you'll learn to think before sayin' something like that. Aurelie, you were out there, weren't you?"

"I can't talk about it," Aurelie said. "Any questions should go to Matt Boudreaux." Even that would earn her black marks from Matt.

Lobelia drew herself up and her cheeks turned bright pink under a liberal coating of face powder. "If there's something going on that could put other people in danger, we have a right to know. Who was it they found dead in the rose beds?"

"Really," Aurelie said, annoyed by the way information spread in Pointe Judah, "I've been told this is a police matter. But I don't think there's anything to worry about," Aurelie said, praying she was right.

"Then why not tell us about it instead of being secretive. There's something nasty about that secretive nature of yours. I'm going to have to speak to Delia about it. She wouldn't like it one bit, not one bit, if she thought you were deliberately frightening folks."

"Lobelia," Eileen cut in. "Have a word with Matt. He'll put your mind at rest. Anyone else for coffee?"

"No, thanks," Lobelia said and the others shook their heads, no.

"I spoke with your husband on the phone," Joan Reeves said, smiling at Aurelie. "He is such a nice man, but you know that. We're getting together this afternoon."

Aurelie didn't dare meet any of her friends' eyes. How could this be happening to her?

"I can't think of another couple who would put up with an interruption before five in the morning and still treat me with the sort of kindness you and Nick did."

12

"If it was you, you'd want to know all about it," Sarah said. She giggled—again—and instantly knew her mistake. "Sorry. That just slipped out. Tell me what everyone said, though, Rellie. I tell you *everything*."

They rode in the Hummer with Hoover stationed just behind them where he could poke his head forward and keep his eyes on the road, or what he could see of it in rapidly falling darkness.

"Stop laughing," Aurelie said. "Stop it right now, Sarah, or I'll . . . Well, I will, so don't push it."

"I'll try," Sarah said, pressing her lips together. No good. She choked and snuffled.

"You are such a baby," Aurelie said. "Worse than . . . than that. You're like a junior-high schoolgirl. A mean one. Don't ask me again. Now let me drive. I don't want to be late for dinner. Delia sounded serious about something."

A couple of hours earlier Sarah had hitched a ride to Oakdale with Ed Webb, Sabine's husband. She'd been working at home on the computer all day then decided to drop some materials with the printer they used locally. Delia believed in supporting businesses in town.

Around closing time, Sarah had turned up at Poke Around to rendezvous with her sister, and Delia had called to ask them to come to dinner that evening. Aurelie was right, Delia hadn't been in the mood for small talk, but she'd made it clear the invitation was more of a summons.

Rather than leave the shop on time, Aurelie had hung around, feeding Sarah coffee and deliberately finding more things to do until it started getting dark and Sarah insisted on leaving.

"Why didn't you want to leave when the shop closed?" Sarah asked.

"Sit, Hoover," Aurelie said. "That's a good boy." She didn't answer Sarah.

"Don't stay mad at me, sis. You can't blame me for

being curious. Eileen said just enough about that Joan Reeves coming in to make me *die* for more. I can't believe Sabine and Lobelia were there, too. Hey, you wouldn't want Lobelia Forestier spreading our business around town when I don't even know what our business is, would you?"

Not a word, not a flicker.

"C'mon. What did you say when that woman called Nick your husband?" Apart from Eileen's sketchy description of Joan Reeves's visit to Poke Around, the dreamy photographer she'd brought with her, and what she'd said in front of everyone, Sarah hadn't heard the juicy details.

Aurelie blinked rapidly. "You don't give up, do you? All right. But then, drop it. I said he isn't my husband. I told her I was spending the night at his place and we'd gone out to walk my dog."

Sarah snorted. "You *didn't.*"

"I did." Aurelie glared at her. "What's wrong with that?"

"It doesn't sound better than the other to me."

Aurelie actually looked stricken. "Don't say things like that." She swallowed audibly and moisture sprang along her lower lashes.

"Oh, don't be silly," Sarah said. She kept smiling and joking, but having Aurelie spend the night at Nick's place had upset her. "You know I'm just fooling around. It sounded funny when you said it, is all. Let's change the subject. So now Lobelia knows you're looking for somewhere to live, she wants you to look at the apartment over Lynette and Frances's salon?"

"Yes. I think it's a great idea. Everyone knows those two. They're good friends of Emma Duhon, and Frances does Sabine's hair."

"I thought you were set on the Quarters at Oakdale," Sarah said.

"I changed my mind. I don't need to be that close to work."

Aurelie's brusque replies were starting to irritate Sarah.

Aurelie edged to a stop at the junction with Rice Street. The next turn, small enough to miss real easily, was the entrance to a little strip of shops tucked in behind Main Street. That's where Lynette Cayler and Frances Broussard ran their salon. Aurelie slowed to a crawl again.

The sisters peered down the gloomy alley. "Does anyone else live back there?" Sarah asked.

"I have no idea," Aurelie told her. "A spotlight or two on the outside of the building and it'll be daylight at midnight. Don't worry."

"Let's drive down there and take a look."

Without a word, Aurelie turned the wheel hard and shot down the alley to where it opened into a parking area for six or seven shops, including the salon. The brakes squealed and she pulled the Hummer to a stop.

"What was that for?" Sarah asked. "What's the matter with you?"

Aurelie stared ahead at darkened shop windows. "Did you see Nick at all today?" she asked.

"No." Sarah's tummy did a flip. "I thought he might come over but I haven't seen him at all. He's not at his place and he didn't answer his phone—again. He's making a habit of that." She felt uneasy.

"So he's turned into the Invisible Man." Aurelie knew she couldn't play completely dumb with Sarah any longer. "He was meeting with that Joan Reeves this afternoon, she didn't say where. Like I said, she's writing a book on the generations of people who have lived in antebellum houses. She wants to know all about the current family attached to Place Lafource." Sarah hadn't mentioned Baily, which meant she didn't know about the death.

Sarah rolled down her window. After another scorching day, the wind still held its heat. "I don't like the sound of her book. I hope we can stop her from giving our real names or where we live."

"Nick won't tell Joan Reeves anything that could be difficult for us," Aurelie said. "Although I don't think there's much hope that she won't publish something anyway. Having the photographer with her means she intends to have photographs of Place Lafource and of us. Why would she do that if she didn't intend to mention us directly?"

Sarah jerked her head away from Hoover's tongue. "We'll have to find out if we can insist on privacy. I think we can, I just don't know the rules."

"Can you complain when someone writes the truth

about you?" Aurelie asked. Her palms sweated on the wheel. "I'd have to check. Have you talked to Delia today? About anything else but dinner?"

"Nope. Nothing except for the grand summons. You know how she loves a buildup. She didn't have any intention of tipping her hand before she could get us lined up in front of her."

"I know. She may just want to get us all together," Aurelie said. It made sense that Delia would expect Sarah to have found out about Baily's death by now. This dinner was for some other reason, but someone had to break the news to Sarah.

"I wonder if Nick's coming."

Aurelie shook her head silently. From the way he'd kept to himself today he couldn't want to be with her any more than she wanted to be with him.

She would just like to know he was okay.

Screaming wouldn't help but it might feel good.

"What do you really think's on Delia's mind?" Sarah asked.

"No idea," Aurelie said. "Um, Matt didn't call you, did he?" If she could save Sarah the unpleasantness of hearing that Matt, Nick and Aurelie wondered if Sarah had been the one intended to end up in the rose-bushes, she would.

Sarah drummed her fingertips on her thigh. "You are being secretive. I thought you were. You wouldn't ask about Matt talking to me if you didn't have something on your mind."

"Sure I would. He's a good friend. He could have

113

called you. Do you think he's really interested in Eileen?"

"Yes." Sarah sounded short-tempered. "Are you going to tell me what all the secrecy is about?"

"Secrecy!" Aurelie hammered the wheel. "There's that word again. D'you know that Lobelia Forestier said I was secretive? She had the nerve to tell everyone I had a *nasty* habit of being secretive and she was thinking of going to Delia about it."

Sarah snickered. "Sounds about right to me." She pulled herself together. "Let's get serious. Delia used that voice she has when she's about to hand down final judgment on something."

"Okay," Aurelie said, and put on the handbrake. "I might have known I'd end up being the one who told you this." Now she sounded petulant and didn't like it. "I mean, I hoped you knew about it by now. You ought to. Delia should have made sure she came and told you."

"Stop it!" Sarah turned sideways in her seat. "Rellie, please, what are you talking about? Don't do this to me."

"Baily . . . Baily Morris died last night. Out at the lab."

"No." Sarah shuddered and shook her head. "*No.* Baily? No, that can't be."

"She, er, she fell off the roof."

Sarah put fists to her cheeks. "What?" She frowned at Aurelie. "She fell off the roof? Why didn't anyone let me know? We couldn't stand each other but that

114

wasn't her fault. Not really. It was because of Nick. Damn, I'm babbling."

Aurelie decided to keep quiet.

"She always seemed to want to outdo me," Sarah said. "Nick and I get along so well, and she had to work hard just to get him to ask her out. Not that it lasted. She was a mental case. No, no, forget I said that. Baily was highly strung. My God, Rellie, how did she fall?"

"I don't know." That much was the truth.

Sarah started to cry quietly.

Aurelie put her arms around her. "You're shocked," she said. "It was unbelievable. They found her in the rose gardens in front of the lab."

"No. Don't say it. *No.*" Sniffing, she wiped the back of a wrist across her eyes. "Listen to what you're saying. Baily wasn't . . . I mean, she didn't want to break up with Nick, but she wanted to live. If anything, when she couldn't make it stick with Nick, she blamed the family. I think she wanted to show us all what a success she was going to make of her life. Rellie? Did she trip?"

"They mentioned suicide."

Sarah let out a long, long breath, faced front again and rested her head back. She closed her eyes and didn't try to stop Hoover from licking her gently. "I can't stand it," she said. "I feel so guilty."

Aurelie knew what she meant. "Because you didn't like her? I didn't like her, but what happened wasn't my fault." Even as she spoke, her own throat grew tight. She detested the pictures that formed in her mind, pictures of Baily twisted up the way she had been.

"Delia knows about this?" Sarah asked.

"Yes."

"I can't believe she didn't say anything on the phone." Sarah said. "Sometimes she behaves as if bad things will go away if she doesn't acknowledge them."

"I know," Aurelie said. "It could be an irritation but it may be what helped her to deal with getting three teenagers dumped in her lap, and all the stuff she went through to keep us together."

Sarah gave a short laugh. "Remember how she just sailed through the whole thing? You talked about Matt. Were—dumb question—of course the police were called."

"Nick and I went out there," Aurelie said, turning her face away. "I was so sure you'd know right away, this morning, when you couldn't get into the lab."

"What do you mean? I haven't been out there today. I didn't feel like it after getting so shaken up yesterday."

"Matt called Nick on his cell last night, when we were driving to Oakdale from your place." Driving to Oakdale and about to break an unwritten rule between them.

It wasn't a rule at all, dammit.

"You didn't see her?" Sarah almost whispered.

"I did. But I wish I hadn't." And all day she had

driven thoughts of what happened from her mind. "The lab is closed off as a crime scene, or potential crime scene."

"Crime?" Sarah shot upright. "Suicide isn't a crime—not that way."

"If it was suicide."

"Oh." Sarah found Aurelie's hand and held it. "Do they think she was murdered?"

"Sarah, I haven't heard another thing about it all day. I kept expecting Matt to contact me."

"I bet he spoke to Nick," Sarah said, sounding upset again. "Isn't that the way it always is. The guys stick together as if we don't exist."

"Could be. Could be Matt's had his hands too full to be chatting to anyone. This is a big thing in a little town."

Sarah put her elbows on her knees and cradled her chin in her hands. "We're not talking about what's really on our minds," she said. "Colin Fox. It's not knowing if he's dead or alive, or if he would actually come after us that's driving us mad."

"I keep trying to push him out of my mind. But I can't believe someone won't find out about all of us and come after us. The press, I mean—or the police out there."

Sarah rocked her head from side to side. "The only thing we ought to care about is staying safe. Staying *alive*. We're handicapped because we don't think we should go to the police." She put her forehead on her fists. "We can't be blamed for being afraid. Rellie, you don't think Baily's death has anything to do with Colin, do you?"

"I've thought about it and I can't see how." Until more information came from Matt there was no point terrifying Sarah. Aurelie squeezed her sister's fingers. "We should get to Delia's. Can you face that yet?"

"I guess so."

Aurelie wasn't sure she could, but she turned the Hummer around heading towards Main Street.

"What about Baily's family?" Sarah asked. "They must have contacted them."

"I don't know anything about that." Aurelie looked both ways and waited for a truck to pass before turning right. Once on the street again, the town seemed too bright. Music blared from the tavern and a band of people loitered outside, some of them dancing. "I thought Lobelia was going to start blabbing all the details when she came in. But she hadn't heard much, so she was just fishing for answers."

"Give her time. If she's not up to speed now, she will be by morning."

"Matt wants us to be careful." She didn't want to frighten Sarah, but these things had to be said.

"I don't see what it's got to do with us."

One thing Aurelie wasn't going to mention was how much Baily had resembled Sarah lying there dead. "We had to go to the police station really late," Aurelie said. "Joan Reeves and her sidekick showed up."

"How could they have found out about Baily?"

It wasn't fair that she'd got stuck explaining all this to Sarah. "They weren't there because of Baily. They were looking for us—or Nick, from the way Joan sounded."

"Now I'm mad," Sarah muttered. "All this going on and not one word said to me. Those people could have come banging on my door and Nick hasn't even explained exactly how he wants it handled."

"No, he hasn't." Aurelie hadn't thought of that before. "They don't know anything about our pasts yet."

"If they do enough poking they could find stuff out. But don't worry. They obviously know nothing about The Refuge."

That was true. "If Joan Reeves gets any inkling the three of us were at The Refuge, she'll be changing the subject of her book in a hurry. She wants to make her mark. She was just sitting outside Nick's waiting for it to get light."

"I bet Nick got rid of her quickly."

"He did." Now Aurelie wanted to change the subject. "It was raining so hard, Hoover got all muddy. I had to put him in the shower when we got inside."

"Did you manage to get Nick to help you? I can't see him doing anything like that."

"Why not? He's a very physical man." Her teeth closed together hard. Nick was physical, yes. Her belly tightened until it ached.

"I didn't say he wasn't. I didn't think dogs were his thing, though."

Aurelie let it go.

A scatter of lights spread out where the trailer park was located. Set back from the road, in daylight parts of it were seedy.

"It won't be long now," Sarah said. "Am I crazy to be nervous about this get-together?"

"I'm nervous about it." Aurelie concentrated on her driving.

The Hummer, which Sarah coveted, was too big for Pointe Judah and absolutely too big for Aurelie, who had bought it from one of the partners in her old law firm.

"Why *did* you buy the Hummer?" Sarah asked. She had wanted to ask for months.

"For Hoover."

"For a *dog?*" Laughter bubbled up again and it felt good—but maybe she was out of control.

"Yes, my dog who is a big boy, in case you haven't noticed. And the partner sold this thing so cheap I couldn't afford not to buy it."

"I'm glad you watch your pennies."

Aurelie sighed. "I didn't like the way Delia sounded when she spoke to me, either." She drove fairly slowly, not anxious to get to their destination. "I think it's something big."

"What are you talking about?" Sarah asked. "We know what it's about now. You already did. Baily. I don't know what Delia's likely to say about it, though."

Aurelie considered before saying, "Mmm—no. I

think she's got something else on her mind." She took off along the winding road that led to Place Lafource.

"The Hummer handles so well," she said. "I admit I used to feel safe going anywhere in it back in New Orleans. Have Hummer and Hoover, will travel." She smiled at Sarah, who frowned at nothing in particular.

"I am so nervous," Sarah said. "Rellie, I kind of got used to the idea that we're all right. I have ever since . . . you know. When we got away and ended up with Mary and Nick. You know what I mean?"

"Oh, yes. Count me in as one more ostrich."

"It's been so good all these years since we went to Delia. We've got new lives and I like them."

Aurelie said yes carefully. There were things they never discussed and she didn't want to go there now.

"No one will ever find out, will they?"

"Don't," Aurelie said. "We promised each other we would never talk about it and we haven't."

"But with everything else happening, it might be that it'll come—"

"No, it won't. There wasn't anyone to know. Who cared? No one. We were alone there. Almost alone."

"Someone must have wondered once they found her. We did go to school before, so they had to notice when we quit."

"They would think relatives took us afterward," Aurelie said. "That's what happens. An aunt or an uncle takes you in."

"Not us," Sarah said. "No one came for us, Rellie. And there was her."

"Please," Aurelie said, desperate. "If we have to talk about this, let it be another time. But I don't want to. Not ever. I don't want to think of it. Sarah, please—"

"Okay." Sarah's voice shrank away. "I'm sorry. I won't say anything else. You're right. Nobody knows anyway—how would they?"

"Leave it!"

"Yes," Sarah said quietly. "It's just all the shock."

Aurelie nodded. She could hardly breathe or swallow. "If you have to think of it at all, remember how many times Mrs. Harris told us she wanted to die."

13

Aurelie caught a glimpse of the lights at Place Lafource. "Let's get this thing with Delia over."

"Yes. I hope Nick is there."

Sarah's guesthouse stood to the left, inside the entrance to the estate. Aurelie drove past without a glance and took the sweeping right fork in the bifurcated driveway through lush grounds. Lamps with three globes apiece stood no more than fifty yards apart and showed off the heavily laden crowns of mature oleander bushes. Through the open window of the vehicle, Aurelie smelled the rich scents of gardenias and roses.

The driveway widened in front of the antebellum house. Uplighting cast the shadows of giant columns in dark gray bands on the stark white facade.

"Oh, my," Aurelie said. "Look at that."

Sarah looked. Up on the wide gallery, seated on a bench outside the open front door, sat Delia. Delia staring straight ahead with her hands pressed between her knees.

"Let it go that she didn't tell you about Baily Morris sooner," Aurelie said. "Okay? I'm sure Delia thought someone else had. And we all thought Delia had."

"I don't intend to make a fuss about anything," Sarah said. "Better leave Hoover here."

Aurelie unlocked the doors and slid out. "Here boy," she said, looking at Sarah across the front seats. "Delia likes animals."

"*I* like animals, dammit," Sarah snapped back. "Sometimes they have a way of complicating difficult moments, that's all. I think you're missing some of the normal instincts most of us have."

Aurelie couldn't keep up the sniping. Her heart felt lodged in her throat and she couldn't stop checking around in case Nick popped up from somewhere. She was sure she couldn't face him.

"You took your sweet time," Delia said, her voice ringing out on the quiet evening air. She stood up and took long, slow steps across the gallery in a pair of high wedge shoes that shimmered. Delia liked to dress in the evenings and tonight was no exception. The halter bodice of her long white dress glittered.

"Look at us," Sarah muttered. "We should have changed."

"I can't worry about all that tonight," Aurelie said.

"Don't whisper." Delia waited at the top of the steps. When the dog galloped to greet her she did the unexpected—which was what they expected of her—and sat down on the top step to take the animal's big head in her arms. "Sweet fella," she said. "Lovely boy."

"He'll slobber on your dress," Sarah told her.

Delia planted a kiss on the sprouting fur between Hoover's eyes. "You can slobber on me any old time," she said, and got up again. "Inside, both of you."

Sarah and Aurelie climbed the steps to the gallery, but Delia continued to stare toward the driveway.

"Are you waiting for Nick?" Aurelie asked, although she knew what the answer would be.

"He's in one of those unpleasant new moods of his," Delia said. "I haven't spoken with him all day but I've left messages. He knows he's expected." She frowned. "I shouldn't be blaming him for feeling the way he does," she added quickly.

Knowing he was expected didn't mean Nick would come, Aurelie thought, not tonight. If she were smart, she'd hope he wouldn't. But there were reactions she couldn't control.

"Let's go in," Delia said. "Sabine has cooked us a feast. She won't be amused if it gets spoiled."

Now Aurelie was sure she should have changed. They wandered through the big hall with its cavernous ceiling painted with great red and pink poppy blooms that spilled and dripped over the tops of walls the color of pale raspberries. Stairs rose from the center to a straight balcony that led to rooms on both sides of the second floor.

The floors themselves were of the original wide wooden planks polished to a deep glow by generations of wear and careful polishing.

"Little dining room," Delia said, lengthening her stride. Her perfect, long legs made appearances through a slit in one side of her skirt. Diamonds flashed at her ears with each turn of her head.

Sarah pretended to scuff her sandal-clad feet across the floor and Delia laughed. "Stop that right now," she said. "You both look dreadful. Don't make it any worse."

The little dining room, as Delia called it, was decorated in shades of green with a circular, koa-wood table laden tonight with china and silver and enough flowers to soak the air with perfume.

In the mornings the room was used for breakfast. Covered dishes loaded the sideboard, newspapers littered every available surface, and the atmosphere was casual. Growing up with Delia had been a crash course in living the way Nick, Sarah and Aurelie could not have imagined living before they met her.

In a single flash, as if through a sharp lens, Aurelie pictured a house set back on a windy hill not far from the ocean in Oregon. Weathered gray siding groaned and squealed with each fresh gust, and she reached for the handle on the peeling front door, anxious to get inside. Always small for her age, her too-long woolen coat flapped around her ankles. There were holes in the heels of her cotton socks, and a nail coming through the sole of one shoe poked her foot.

Aurelie drew in a quick gasp. She glanced around Delia's little dining room, shaken by the vivid image she had seen. This was happening because she and Sarah had done what they were never to do, what they'd avoided by silent agreement since they left that place—they had spoken of it.

A light touch on her arm startled her. She looked into Sarah's eyes. Neither of them smiled but understanding passed between them.

Carrying a silver tray and wearing a slinky black dress, Sabine sashayed into the room, a gardenia tucked behind one ear. "Mint juleps," she said. "It's a good thing my Ed knows how to make 'em because we surely didn't have 'em at my house." Her laughter surged. "Where's that Nick? He could get to be a pain in my rear if he keeps up this sulkin'."

"Nick never sulks," Delia said mildly and armed herself with a mint julep.

Sabine smacked a fist on one hip. "That so? Well, he wouldn't let me inside his place today. Did I tell you all that? Two weeks, he's made me miss, coming up on three. I used my key and yelled out like one of those chickens Lobelia Forestier's got. Cocks, I guess, and he still looked at me like he was seein' a one-legged elephant. Shut in there with that Joan Reeves and her pretty photographer, he was, and he told me there was nothin' for me to do. Ha! I got out

126

of there quick, I can tell you. Now he's late for dinner."

On evenings when Delia wanted something really special, she got Sabine to cook, mostly because Sabine's feelings got hurt if she wasn't asked. The rest of the time another woman, Betty Valenti, dealt with meals.

"Thanks for the drinks," Delia said. She set her own drink down and handed glasses to Aurelie and Sarah. "These should be good for anything that's bothering us. Sabine, be a love and serve on the sideboard. Something tells me we aren't going to make this into a graceful evening." Delia drained her glass and took another.

Sabine narrowed her gaze at Delia and the second glass. "On the sideboard?" she said, her voice reaching its rich upper register once more. "My baked freshwater bass on the sideboard? My oysters in champagne. My—"

"You are a wizard," Delia said. "But I feel a messy evening coming on, don't you?"

Sabine studied Aurelie and Sarah, cast a narrow eye over Hoover, stretched on the cool marble before the fireplace, and looked at her watch. "Yes, ma'am, I surely do. The sideboard it is." Sabine ran the domestic affairs at Lafource and Delia admitted she would have been a disaster without her.

As soon as Sabine left the room, Sarah said, "You didn't tell us this really was a formal affair. Now I feel terrible."

"Don't," Delia said. "You know I have more fun getting ready for things than doing them. I don't really like a lot of fuss, but if you never practice, you fall apart when you do have to pull off a social masterpiece."

"You gave it all up for us," Sarah said.

"No, I didn't," Delia said, sweeping Sarah into a hug. "You silly girl. You saved me, you three. Thank goodness."

Aurelie wanted desperately to enter into the conversation and help lighten the mood. She couldn't, not when she didn't see how Nick could make an excuse for not showing up at dinner sooner or later.

She took a long swallow of the sweetened bourbon and mint. This was a drink she liked, but since one of them could loosen her tongue enough to embarrass her, she had to be careful.

"What's the matter with you, Aurelie?"

Delia's question, sharp and sounding as if asked by a stranger, startled her. "Nothing," she said, forcing a smile. "What are we celebrating?"

High color spread over Delia's cheekbones. "Yes, there certainly is something wrong with you. You've hardly said a word since you arrived."

Aurelie looked into her drink. "These past couple of days haven't been easy. I wish I were doing better with everything."

"They haven't been easy for any of us," Delia said.

Aurelie turned up the corners of her mouth. "I know. Forgive me for being self-involved." And muddled, and guilty, and for feeling . . . *dirty*.

Delia finished the second drink but carried the empty glass with her. "They've got to know whether or not Baily killed herself by now," she said. "Don't they?"

"I don't know." Panic began to uncurl.

Sarah glanced at Aurelie. Now they could be sure Delia had simply forgotten to say anything to Sarah.

Delia put down her glass. "I'm sorry. I'm supposed to be the one who holds it all together. Forget this little hiccup." She sniffed and ran her fingers through her hair. "You'll understand why I'm so not myself— if Nick ever bothers to get here."

"Hello."

He came into the room. Unshaven, wearing a shapeless cotton sweater with a baggy neck and ragged jeans, Nick passed up the juleps and poured himself a Scotch. He turned to face them, raised his glass and said, "Here's to whatever." And his gaze settled on Aurelie.

Sarah hurried into the path of that gaze and rubbed Nick's chest. She kissed his cheek and stood with her back to the room. "Let yourself grieve," she said. "But don't suffer more than you have to. Mary's been at peace for a long time."

Very encouraging and so darn pat. Sarah, Aurelie couldn't help but notice, dripped over Nick, her voice loaded with sympathy. Only a fool wouldn't see what she really felt for him. Sarah was in love with Nick. And short of a miracle, all three of them were going to lose what they had treasured most: their family.

They could become three islands.

Nick looked past Sarah, reconnected with Aurelie. His mouth jerked down at the corners.

So he was hurt. Big deal. So was she. One of them should have had the strength to be the anchor for both of them and it hadn't been her. She looked back at him, at his blue-turned-black eyes. Telling herself Nick should have been the one to keep their friendship safe was childish. She owed him more than that.

He raised his glass to her alone and took another swallow of his Scotch.

"Well, now." Delia gave her hair a theatrical shake. "I expect you all wonder why I've called you here tonight."

Nick heard Delia, registered that she didn't sound like herself, but couldn't look away from Aurelie. She obviously wasn't any more at peace than he was. And Sarah wasn't helping him. Her almost cloying attention made him squirm. It wasn't like her to fawn on anyone.

Sabine came in with a covered dish in her hands and put it on the sideboard. One of the girls who helped in the house followed up with a basket of bread draped with white linen and smelling fragrant the way only Sabine's fresh-baked bread smelled.

"Come into my study," Delia said abruptly. She turned around, her skirt whipping about her legs, and led the way from the little dining room and through double doors into the one place in the house she kept mostly to herself. "I was going to wait until after dinner for this but the strain is too much. We'll do it now."

Nick caught the frown on Sabine's face and settled a hand on her shoulder. "Try not to worry about the food," he said in a low voice. "This is one of those evenings. Every family has them." They rarely had, but Sabine nodded as if she understood.

"Close the doors," Delia said.

Nick did as she asked. He couldn't keep his eyes away from Aurelie. She carried a glass and seemed more interested in its contents than was usual for her. That, or she'd do anything rather than look at him.

Sarah was still with him, her hand hooked under his arm.

Delia's study resembled an eighteenth-century flight of fancy in some French nobleman's home. Since the house had originally belonged to a French family, the motif seemed appropriate. From plaster cherubs, fruit, flowers and musical instruments on the ceiling, to ornate oval medallions surrounding paintings of rosy-faced children, rococo dominated. Nick supposed the room and its furnishings were beautiful if you liked that kind of thing.

"Sit down," Delia said. She faced them, and Nick held his breath. The big smile was gone and for the first time he realized she had left her forties behind some years earlier. "Sit down," she repeated. Behind her, one of the oval wall medallions stood open to display a hidden safe. He'd never known it was there and was sure Sarah and Aurelie were also seeing it for the first time.

Nick cast around, grabbed delicate gilt and upholstery chairs for Sarah and Aurelie and went toward Delia.

She held up a hand. "No," she said. "I'm fine. You sit down, too. I'd rather stand."

So would he, but he perched on the arm of a divan.

"I'm sure you remember the day you came to me in Savannah." Delia's smile trembled and he feared she might cry—or shriek. "Do you remember?"

They all murmured that they did.

"Your mother gave you something to bring to me, Nick. You used to ask about it but then you stopped. I really did expect you to push for answers again long before now."

Sarah and Aurelie didn't move a muscle. They kept their eyes on Delia.

"Nick?" Delia said.

He wasn't sure what she wanted him to say. "I assumed she sent some sort of instructions to you. A request, too, I guess. But I could tell it upset you when I mentioned it so I gave it up."

"She did send me a letter. She also sent one to you. Her instructions to me were that I should give you the letter if I heard something had happened to her. If I found out she had died."

Nick couldn't look at Delia anymore.

"She thought I'd be doing this a long time ago. You see, she didn't expect to live long. She wrote that she could be dead by the time you got to me."

"So she knew what might happen even when she

was sending us away?" Aurelie asked. "I wish she'd come with us."

Nick didn't trust himself to speak. He should have insisted his mother leave with him. If he had absolutely refused to go without her, she would have gone. Or he thought she would have.

"Sometimes I've managed to forget this was here," Delia said, turning to the safe. "For a long time."

"I can't stand this," Sarah said. "What did Mary write?"

"To Nick?" Delia looked at her. "I don't know. I never read his letter. Now he can find out for himself."

From the back of the lowest shelf in the safe, Delia removed a padded envelope she'd rolled down at the top. She opened it and took out a letter-size envelope.

Nick remembered, all too well, the night when Mary Chance had taken that same envelope and dropped it into the bigger one to make it easier for him to carry what was inside while they traveled. The packet had been heavier than he'd expected, and lumpy. He had guarded it like a last connection to his mother—which it had become.

"There's something else here, too," Delia said, pulling out a manila envelope and prying open the metal fastener on the back. "Mary wrote to me that you'd know what to do with this once you read your letter, Nick." Her voice jerked, and moisture glistening on her face blew him away. Delia didn't sweat.

"Why did you wait so long?" Nick said, his pulse

pounding. "After a couple of years went by with no word, you must have known she probably wasn't coming back. It could have made things easier if I'd stopped hoping she would turn up."

Delia looked directly at him. "I waited because I was afraid. I didn't want things to change between the four of us. I still don't want them to. How could I know there wasn't something in here that would take you away from me? I don't know now."

Aurelie did raise her eyes to his then. She shook her head slightly and he understood, even if he did resent the suggestion that he didn't know how and when to do the right thing. "Nothing will change between us," he said. Aurelie studied her glass again.

"I hope not." Delia slid the contents onto her desk. And it looked as if the so-called private mail had already been opened.

Delia frowned, checked what had fallen out and pulled open the top, right desk drawer. She looked at several pieces of correspondence from inside, checked mailing dates against the one on the letter she'd dropped on her desk pad and looked inside the package, a medium-size bag folded and taped. Then she turned back to the mostly empty safe and searched each shelf.

"Gone," she said, facing them again. "They were here when I opened the safe earlier. Someone's taken them and left one of my invoices instead. And the bag's different. It's got sand in it—probably from my Zen garden."

14

"What are you doing here?" Aurelie asked.

"Nice welcome," Nick said. He folded the paper he'd been reading. "I'm doing what you're doing, trying to make sure we all do the right thing."

Seven in the morning, and he was back in the little green dining room—the breakfast room at this time of day—that opened into Delia's study. He'd been there an hour already and all he could get from the one woman who came in early each day was that Delia wasn't up yet. Betty Valenti had brought him coffee and croissants then disappeared hurriedly.

Aurelie wore her hair strained back and wound into a knot that was already unraveling. A white blouse and beige linen suit reminded Nick that she was a lawyer. This morning she looked the part.

"Where's Delia?" she asked. Pink color had already risen along her cheekbones. "In her office?"

He shook his head, no. "Betty says she isn't up yet."

"She's always up by five-thirty. I'll go and find her."

"Betty told me Delia left instructions she's not to be disturbed."

"When? When did she leave instructions with Betty who doesn't get in here until just before Delia gets up? Did Betty take her coffee up yet?"

"You sound like a lawyer."

"I *am* a lawyer," she said with not a glimmer of a smile.

"Sure you are. But I'm not your witness, Counselor."

"Give me a break," she said and pressed her lips together.

This shouldn't be happening, not after what they'd shared. Not *because* of what they'd shared. "What am I supposed to do, Aurelie? What can I say? Or dare to say without you getting even madder at me?"

"Nothing."

"So you admit you're mad at me," he said. She didn't have the right to be but he couldn't resent the way she felt. "That's how you handle things you can't deal with. The personal stuff. You get angry. The last thing I want is for you to be angry because of me."

"I'm not." She raised her chin and he saw her swallow. "Is Betty in the kitchen?"

"You wanted us to make love."

"Don't." She glanced behind her as if expecting to see someone there. "Leave it, please, leave it."

He spoke softly. "Did you make love with me because you were horny?"

Her eyes glittered and she put a fist to her mouth.

"I'm sorry. That was too blunt. Goddammit, woman, I don't have any more experience with this situation than you do but we've got to get through it. Sure, there's big stuff going on that'll keep everyone busy until it's over. But it will be over and you and I will still be here. Then what?"

Aurelie pulled out a chair across the table from his and sat down hard. She looked at him. He didn't want to see the turmoil she felt but it was right there in her eyes. And she was afraid to speak in case she broke down.

Betty had only brought one cup but the pot of coffee was hot. He poured a refill and pushed it across the table. "Take a deep breath. And please try to listen to me. I'll try not to be offensive again."

She picked up the cup and swallowed several sips of coffee.

"If I thought it would help, I'd suggest we forget what happened." He was glad it wouldn't help because he didn't intend to forget a moment of it. "There was a lot of feeling between us. I actually thought it was going to be all right."

"It shouldn't have happened."

He stopped himself from snapping back at her. Instead he took his time to say, "For me, it was so all right, Aurelie. I'm not going to apologize for that. But it wasn't for you. Do you want me to go away somewhere? Would it help if I got lost? I'll do it."

"No, you won't. Threats aren't going to make this any easier."

She didn't want him to leave. He almost grinned.

"If anyone goes it'll be me," Aurelie said.

"Now who's threatening?" If she went, he'd follow, which might be a great idea. "Why are you so upset? What we did was normal. It was healthy. It was damn healthy for me. I don't know how much longer I could have controlled—"

She set the cup down carefully. "Good idea to stop

right there," she said. "Your mouth does have a way of digging deeper holes. Don't mention it again. If we try hard enough, we can hope to put the mistake behind us. We were both overemotional. That's what happened. Emotion got away from us and we just . . . we just . . . it did."

This was the most he could hope for now. Not that it would change a thing for him—except for making him work on better timing. He hadn't had nearly enough of her.

"We should never mention what happened again," Aurelie said.

When her very blue eyes filled with conviction, understanding why she made a good lawyer was easy. "You're right," he said.

"Right."

Move on. "You feel the way I do, don't you?"

"Nick!"

Before she had time to get really ruffled again, he added, "About last night. The letters. Delia's wrong on this one."

"Oh." The pink returned to her face. "Yes, I do."

"I don't know why I didn't argue last night—"

"I do," Aurelie cut in. "You didn't want to make her any more upset than she already was. I felt the same way and I bet Sarah did, too. We've got to report the theft."

Amazingly, he felt some of the tension between them lessen. "Even if it can bring a heap more trouble on our heads," he said. "Yeah. We don't have a choice. We're going to have to dig Delia out of her hiding place."

"She feels threatened. For us, all of us. She can't accept that it isn't possible to keep some things private indefinitely."

Betty opened the door and poked her head into the room. When she saw Aurelie, she said, "You need a cup. You should have called for me. I'll get it right away." Then her eyes moved left and she whistled. Betty often punctuated her train of thought with a single whistle. "Matt Boudreaux is here. He's got another policeman with him. I've already told them Miss Delia isn't entertaining guests this morning. Did that bother Matt Boudreaux? Uh-uh. The two of them are out there, standing by the door. You got a message for them, Nick?"

"You're a gem, Betty," Nick said. "You were right to fend them off and come to me. I think the best way to deal with them now is to let them come in. Yes, do that. Delia will appreciate it if we take care of them. You know how she approves of hospitality. Yes, and if you can spare the time, would you bring more coffee and cups for them—just in case they'd like that."

Aurelie watched the exchange, fascinated by the adoring expression on Betty's face. How come a good-looking man with a sweet tongue could manipulate most women?

"I tell you," Betty said, "I almost thought the same thing myself. It's lucky you were here to put it into words, Nick." Off she went, humming.

Aurelie waited until Nick looked at her and pretended to gag herself with a forefinger.

He laughed.

She laughed, too, before they both fell silent.

"Do we mention last night to Matt?" Nick asked.

"I'm not sure. You don't think Delia called him here because of the letter, do you?"

"We'll know as soon as he comes in here. Let him suggest the topic."

"Suggest the topic," she repeated. "Cute. I must remember to use that."

"Why would he bring another cop with him just to ask questions?" Nick asked.

She had no idea, but the door opened again to admit Matt and a policeman of similar age, so she didn't have to come up with an answer.

"Come on in," Nick said.

"'Mornin'," Matt said. "'Mornin', Aurelie. How are you doin'?"

"Very well," she said, but her spine felt prickly. Instinct put her on alert and she suddenly dreaded whatever Matt had come to say.

"Thought I'd bring Buck Dupiere out to meet y'all. He's going to be taking my job."

Aurelie's mind went blank. Matt was trusted locally and expected to follow Billy Meche in the chief's chair eventually. "I'm sorry to hear that," she said.

Buck Dupiere laughed, low and memorably. "A sad time, hmm? You'll have to let me help you get over it." He had the build of a middleweight boxer, but not

140

the nose. Buck's nose, narrow and straight, didn't look as if it had ever been punched. His short, dark hair had a good acquaintance with expert styling, though, and a killer smile drove just the right number of lines from the corners of greenish eyes. Naturally, the smile also produced winsome dimples.

Men. They were so obvious and this one had *womanizer* etched into his attitude.

"Dupiere?" Nick asked. "Is that your name?" He managed to make a simple enough question sound insulting.

"Surely is," Dupiere said. "And you must be Nick Board. Pleased to meet you."

Nick looked at the man with the kind of expressionless face that Aurelie decided was threatening. He was reacting to Buck Dupiere sounding a little flirtatious toward her. Ridiculous.

"I'm going to be taking over as chief," Matt said.

Aurelie frowned at Nick and they both gave Matt their full attention.

"Billy's decided not to come back to the department," Matt said. "With all the vacation he's got stacked up, he's close enough to be able to retire with his full pension and he thinks that's the best thing. So does his wife. I knew this was happening but I wanted to wait until Buck got here to say anything. He comes highly recommended and he wants to move out of the big city. So everything's coming together. Not that we won't miss Billy," he added quickly.

"Congratulations," Nick said. He turned to Buck

and said, "Good luck with the new job," but not with any enthusiasm.

Betty came in with a tray and set it on the sideboard. Another pot of coffee, cups and more fresh croissants. She actually winked at Nick before backing out of the room.

"Have a seat, both of you," Aurelie said and got up to pour coffee for everyone. "I'd better go and tell Delia you're here."

"Or not," Nick said quickly, and without looking at her. "She's pretty tired. We had a late night."

"Talking about Baily's death?" Matt asked.

"Not entirely."

Aurelie carried cups to the table and returned with the croissants, butter, honey and homemade peach preserves. Betty took instructions seriously.

"Thanks," both cops said. Matt leaned toward Nick. "What does 'not entirely' mean?"

So much for letting the police suggest the topic. "Mostly we talked about Baily," Aurelie said before Nick could reveal more than ought to be revealed. It was likely that Delia would feel betrayed if they didn't let her be the one to talk about yesterday's theft. "We wondered if you'd contacted the Morris family."

"Her father," Matt said promptly. "They haven't had a lot to do with each other for a few years. He said her mother is an archaeologist and on a dig somewhere. I got the impression Baily's folks figured they'd done their job when she left home."

"You wonder why some people have children," Aurelie said and felt stupid. "I know everyone says that. I feel badly for Baily, that's all."

Delia walked in silently, her feet bare. "Don't stop for me," she said, her voice tight. Most redheads would avoid the red brocade kaftan she wore, but on her it was spectacular. "Why do you feel badly for Baily, Aurelie? Other than the obvious reason."

Both policemen were on their feet, Dupiere holding a chair for Delia. She smiled, assessing him, and sat down.

"Baily Morris didn't have real close family ties, Miz . . . Delia," Matt said. "Aurelie was sympathizing over that."

"Thank you for speaking on her behalf," Delia said. "What are you two here for?"

"Yes, ma'am," Matt said. "First, this is Deputy Chief Buck Dupiere. He's taking my place. Billy's retiring and I'm filling his spot."

"Congratulations," Delia said.

"We won't take up much of your time," Matt said. "Just to bring you up-to-date, I've decided to put extra surveillance out in this area. We'll have a car drive through regularly. You have an alarm system. Please use it."

Delia stayed in her chair but turned to look at Matt. "I beg your pardon?"

"This is for your security. Routine precautions."

"Routine?" Aurelie crossed her arms.

"I thought we agreed to keep this among ourselves,"

Delia said. She stood up and pointed at Nick. "You should have talked to me first, not called these people in so I didn't have a chance to help make the decision."

"Delia—"

"No, Nick. There's nothing you can say."

Matt cleared his throat. His and Dupiere's silence should have warned Delia to be cautious. It didn't.

"There wasn't a theft, Matt," she said. "I played a silly joke and made too good a job of it. I shouldn't have done it and I was wrong. Thanks for coming but we don't have anything to report."

"Sounds like you folks had too much fun last night," Matt said, but Aurelie didn't fool herself they wouldn't hear about Delia's announcement again. "We came over to talk about security because the pathologist is certain Baily was murdered."

Nick propped his elbows on the table and tapped his fingers together. Aurelie expected him to speak but his gaze lost its focus.

"You said it was suicide," Delia said.

"I said it could be suicide," Matt told her. "And we all hoped it was because that would be better than murder. But murder is what we've got."

"What makes you so sure?" Aurelie said.

"I'm not the pathologist, but marks on the body tell the guy who is that Baily was helped off that roof."

"What kind of marks?" Aurelie said.

"Those details haven't been released yet."

"You mean you know all the details but you're not telling us." She stared Matt in the eye.

"You might be right about that," he said. "Your lab is now a definite crime scene. We can't be certain when we'll be able to release it. The crime folks have already done a lot of work but they'll be going over everything again."

Delia massaged her temples. "We'll make sure none of the staff go in until you're finished. They're already on alert."

"Where's Sarah?" Matt asked. "Sorry to put you out even more, but if you could ask her to come and see us, I'd appreciate it."

"Why?" Delia asked, springing to her feet. "Sarah doesn't know anything about what happened to Baily. None of us do."

"I'm sure you're right," Matt said. "But I need to talk to each of you, alone. The best time for that is now. I asked you where Sarah is."

Aurelie had never seen this harsh side of Matt Boudreaux. "She's at home," she said. "In her house, in the grounds here."

"Fair enough," Matt said. "Buck, I'd appreciate it if you'd pick up Sarah Board and bring her here. The house Aurelie's talking about is the one you see as you come through the front gates."

15

Matt and Buck carried a bucket of fish fry from a mobile canteen set up for business at a picnic area close to the bayou. The picnic area was also an easy walk from the trailer park. Thinking about the shrimp fried in spiced-up cornmeal tickled Matt's appetite. Even more than that, the aroma wafting from the paper bucket made his mouth water.

"There's a table over there," Buck said. "No shade, though."

"Sun's movin'," Matt said. "We'll manage."

Laughing kids raced around while their mothers talked, and clusters of workers from a nearby construction site plowed through heaps of food. A band of teens gyrated around a boom box, eating burgers and fries and tossing the empty wrappers on the grass.

"I see the local youth take littering laws real seriously," Buck said. "About as seriously as they take the law in general."

Matt slid the fish fry onto a wooden table and sat sideways on one of the attached benches where he could keep an eye on the area—and move fast if he had to. Buck assumed a similar position on the opposite bench and passed Matt his coffee, set down his own and a bag containing two huge squares of cold bread pudding.

Buck dived into the shrimp. He watched traffic on

the bayou and Matt felt him waiting for an opportunity to discuss their long visit with the Boards.

The shrimp still sizzled a little and they crunched between the teeth. They were small enough that the tails had been left on—Matt's favorite kind. He took a gulp of coffee.

Buck swung the open side of the bread-pudding bag toward him and broke off a piece. He ate, a faint smile of pleasure on his face.

"So what d'you think?" Matt asked.

Wiggling a slightly greasy forefinger, Buck said, "I'm the new kid on the block. You're the one with all the background on these people. You tell me what you got out of all that."

"Damn." Matt put in several more shrimp and chewed. "I didn't think you'd fall for that. When it gets out the death *was* murder, we're going to get some press interest. But a probable random hit won't be interesting for long. Especially if we get the perp."

"You don't think any of the Boards were involved, do you?" Buck asked.

Matt shook his head, no. The boom box had edged up even higher and the heat of midday started to wear on him. He slapped a mosquito on his forearm. "My knee-jerk is to say no, but that could be because I know them. And I like them. But they've never seemed to fit in. I don't mean they're difficult, just different. They're telling us as little as they can."

"If that doesn't have anything to do with the Baily Morris case we don't need to worry about it."

"Right," Matt said.

"They didn't like Baily," Buck said.

"I picked up on that," Matt said. "We're going to have to find out why."

"Plenty of nice people have turned killer if they were provoked enough."

Matt enjoyed Buck. The man had a quick mind and a straightforward delivery. "If Baily had provoked the Boards, why wasn't she just fired?"

"Delia kept saying she was a good chemist," Buck said.

"Sarah didn't," Matt said, offhand. He broke up some shrimp and tossed the pieces to a skinny tabby cat with hopeful yellow eyes. "Did you notice how quiet she was?"

"I didn't think it was important," Buck said. "She seemed real on edge about the whole thing. Maybe she's more shaken up about the killing than the others."

"You wouldn't blame her if you'd seen Baily Morris."

Buck drained his coffee and looked into the dregs. "Of course you're going to explain that."

"Baily looked a lot like Sarah, that's who I thought it was when I arrived at the scene. Nick and Aurelie came out to the crime scene and I know they thought the same thing at first."

"Sarah's unusual," Buck said. "A looker, too. I've never seen a woman like her before. Are you sure there isn't some other connection between Baily and the Boards, other than her being a chemist—the same as Sarah—and the two of them being alike enough to be mistaken for one another?"

"In death," Matt pointed out. "With Baily lying mostly on her face and in the same kind of white coat Sarah wears for work." Nevertheless, Buck's thoughts appeared to be going in the same direction as Matt's.

A small girl, her tightly curled black hair decorated all over with minute, brightly colored plastic butterflies, stationed herself at the end of the table. Her huge eyes alternated attention between the two cops and the rivulets of melting ice cream she chased down a cone with her tongue.

Buck and Matt waved at her and smiled. She had her priorities straight and kept after the marauding ice cream.

Buck went after more bread pudding. "Delia put the lid on any talk of theft," he said. "I'd say she was desperate to shut it off."

"We can't investigate an unreported theft. And she said there wasn't one anyway." Matt studied the girl who knelt on the ground and rested the tip of her cone on the end of the bench while she ate steadily. "That's a good idea," he told her. "That way the ice cream comin' through the bottom will only mess up the bench."

She raised her face momentarily. "Won't come out with the hole on here."

Matt met Buck's eyes and they grinned.

"Nick and Baily dated for a while," Matt said. "Then they stopped and Baily didn't look happy."

"Did Nick?"

"Not particularly. But that could have been for any number of reasons on either side. I didn't get a straight answer on when she started working nights at the lab."

"Noticed that," Buck said.

"It could be important, particularly if it had anything to do with a setup for her murder." Matt noticed the child had rivulets of ice cream drying on her face, neck and T-shirt. More of the stuff mixed with dusty mud on her hands. "Where's your momma?" he asked her.

The girl turned a little and pointed to one of the groups of moms.

"Maybe you should check in with her."

That got him a shake of the head. "My name's Crystal-Mae," she said. "Yesterday was my birthday."

Matt hummed. "I bet you were four," he said.

She gave him a "you're stuck on stupid" look.

Buck laughed. "I bet she turned six."

"How would you know that?"

"Are you six now, Crystal-Mae?" Buck said, and when she nodded seriously he added, "I figured you were because you're so grown up. Now, I want you to go back and be with your momma before she gets worried about you."

Crystal-Mae frowned but followed instructions.

"How did you do that?" Matt asked. "And how did you know she was six? She's no bigger than a bean."

"A good guess."

"The Boards didn't like it when you told them they have to be fingerprinted," Matt said. "But I didn't think they would. I wish folks would understand that a lot of things are routine."

"Yeah. What did Aurelie say when you mentioned the missing briefcase?" Buck asked.

"She asked how I knew Baily had a briefcase. She wanted me to explain how we knew about it if it wasn't at the lab and said we should look around Baily's home." Matt replied.

"So you said another member of the staff mentioned the bag and we already looked at Baily's place?"

Matt started on his own bread pudding. "No. I don't see where I have to answer suspects' questions."

Buck didn't comment on Matt calling the Board family suspects. "Sarah's reaction was similar," he said. "And Delia's. How about Nick's?"

"Acted like he didn't know what I was talking about. Which could mean he does know."

"Might not, too."

"This stuff is good," Matt said of the pudding. "Loaded with fruit. Truth is, we don't know much of anything for certain. Except Baily didn't die of natural causes. And a fair number of people knew she spent time on her own out there—at night."

"How many people work there?" Buck asked.

151

"Not a lot. Seventeen without the service folks. That includes a manager and his staff. Sampson and Fildew are working on getting statements from each of them. Carly Gibson's dealing with the security company. That's a long shot and so is the cleaning service. They were the ones who found the body."

"We need those fingerprints today," Buck said, raising an eyebrow at Matt. "It won't be so pretty if we have to follow up on the Boards."

"We won't," Matt said. "They'll end up cooperating." He thought he was right but if not, they'd be brought in just like anyone else.

A clear bass voice, strongly Cajun in lilt, reached them from a fishing boat puttering along the middle of the bayou. The man traveled in his own pleasant bubble, and the rhythm of "Viva La Money" set Matt's toes tapping.

"It's good to be here," Buck said. "I should have gotten out of N'awlins sooner. It hasn't been good to me for a long time."

Matt already knew why Buck, a New Orleans homicide detective until a couple of months ago, had left his job. Despite Buck's insistence that the decision had been a no-brainer, Matt had enough details to figure out the break had come with a lot of bad feelings. Someone over there didn't like Buck much but that hadn't messed with his record.

"I want to get back and see how we're doing with prints and interviews," Matt said. "I told Sampson and Fildew not to release anyone who doesn't answer questions satisfactorily. Carly Gibson doesn't need to be reminded about those things."

"It's too damn hot here," Buck said. He dropped the empty coffee cups into the fish bucket and carried them to a garbage can. When he got back to the table, he stared past Matt and frowned. "Company heading this way."

Matt promptly looked over his shoulder and located Rusty Barnes, who came across the bleached grass with that woman, Joan Reeves, in tow. "Shee-it," he muttered. "How would they know where to find us?"

"I did call in to the station from Place Lafource," Buck said. "I told the desk we were stopping here on the way back."

"Why?" Matt said while the unwelcome guests got closer.

"I'm expectin' a piece of mail there. I was checkin' on it."

"Hey," Rusty shouted. "Nice life you cops have."

"Just one big round of fun," Matt said. He liked Rusty Barnes when he wasn't being a reporter.

"Good to see you, Matt," Rusty said, dropping a shoulder bag to the ground so he could shake hands. "This is Joan Reeves. She's writing—"

"We've met," Matt said.

"We haven't. I'm Buck Dupiere." Buck smiled at the tall, stacked Joan Reeves, who responded with a demure lowering of the eyelashes that didn't match the impression she gave.

"How are you?" she asked and put her hand in Buck's.

He held it too long, but Matt already had his new deputy chief pegged as a ladies' man.

"What are you writing?" Buck asked.

"A book on people who live in antebellum houses. A history of the houses and whose lives they've impacted. Past and present," Joan said in her light voice. "We shouldn't be interrupting you while you're having lunch." She cocked her head to look into Buck's face.

"Glad to help in any way I can," Buck said.

"Thank you," Joan said, dipping a little. Her blond hair shone in the sunlight, so did her light brown eyes. "I'm hoping I can get some input from folks who've lived around here—especially if their families have been here for generations. I'm working on Place Lafource now."

Matt expected Buck to say he'd been a homicide detective in New Orleans and didn't know anything about Place Lafource.

"Matt's folks settled here several generations ago," Buck said. "But there's no time to talk about it now."

Rusty picked up his bag. A slim, fit man with dark red hair, he had a reputation for being a straight shooter, and for never staying in one place long. "Could you give Joan some time when you're off the clock?" he said to Matt, already backing away.

Joan shook her head. "I couldn't ask you to do that," she said. "I know how hard you work. I'll drop by the station and make an appointment—if that's okay?"

"Maybe we can do better than that," Buck said. "I'm a longtime Louisianan and there may be some useful points I can pass on to you. Will you be in town for a while?"

"I'm sure I will be," Joan said.

"Interested in dinner?"

Matt caught Rusty's glance and they both made sure they didn't show whatever they were thinking.

"If that's an invitation," Joan said, "Then the answer is, yes."

16

"I've got to go," Aurelie said. She hadn't wanted to come back to Delia's after work in the first place.

"Go then," Sarah said. "Run away. That's what you do best. Instead of sticking around and figuring things out, you run."

"How can you say that to me? If I've done some running away it's been because I didn't have a choice. And you ran with me, Sarah, so let's not go there."

"I wasn't in New Orleans when you couldn't take the heat. You scuttled back here all on your own."

"That's not playing fair," Aurelie said. "I can't believe you'd get so low. I'm not going to repeat my reasons for leaving the practice. My only mistake then was to come home."

Nick looked at them over his shoulder. They were in the place that had been their favorite retreat since they came to Place Lafource. The conservatory. Palm crowns touched the glass in a two-story-high roof. Orchids bloomed everywhere, even trailed flowers and leaves onto the old green-and-white stone floor tiles.

"Why don't you say what you're thinking?" Aurelie said to Nick. "You've hardly said a word since you got here. Did you get in to have your fingerprints taken today?"

"Of course I did," he said. "Bickering isn't going to help us. Why don't you two calm down. I'm the one with the decisions to make."

"I'm sick of this," Aurelie said. "What's the point of staying here, staring at one another and panicking?"

"Are you panicking?" Nick asked.

"I don't panic," she told him. "I was talking about you two. Holed up here trying to figure out the impossible. We don't have a choice. Before we get hauled in for obstruction of justice, we have to tell the whole truth about everything. We know Colin has to be behind this."

"We're trapped." Sarah reached the end of a walkway between beds and spun back. "Do you realize that? After all we got through together—and before we were together—we're finally stuck. I don't see a way out."

"Garbage," Nick said. Like Sarah, he wore shorts, sandals and a polo shirt and looked fresh as long as you didn't see his face too close up. "We never have to stay in a box unless we give up. I don't give up. But you two worry me. We can't afford to have you crack up or it will be all over. I want to find out if we can finger Colin."

"Yes," Aurelie said. "Present the cops with as close to a wrapped-up case as we can."

"If Matt gets wind of what's really going on here—he'll insist on going to the cops in California. He'll have to. Details will get out and any one of us could be Colin's next victim."

"Darn, don't state the obvious again," Aurelie said.

"Why is Delia outside with Hoover?" Arms akimbo, Sarah stared out into rapidly fading dark pink light. Since that morning's unpleasant interludes with Matt and Buck, the four of them had gone in different directions, keeping busy, going through the motions of being in control. No matter what Nick said, they were no longer in any driver's seat.

"As long as Delia's out there, she's not in here stirring things up." Nick sounded nothing like himself. "She's always enjoyed a good purple evening."

"Hoover's having a good time, too." Aurelie smiled at her pooch, whose snout never left the ground. She hoped he didn't manage to contract a stomach ulcer with all the crap he ingested.

"I want everyone here in the house tonight," Nick said. "The alarm system's been thoroughly checked and as long as you all use your heads, you should be okay."

Aurelie got out of her basket chair and stood parallel with Nick, facing out, but with several feet between them. "You can be an ass," she said. "Have I told you that lately?"

"I wouldn't be surprised," Nick said. He glanced sideways at Aurelie. Looking at her brought him hope. As long as she was within reaching distance he felt powerful, and he had purpose. "Are you calling me an ass now?"

She looked back at him. Tired, her once crisp beige suit rumpled, it seemed as if she needed the hug he was all too ready to give her. He wanted her so badly she turned his heart. The stare she gave, that bright and intense blue, looked inscrutable in a pale face. He sensed her considering the next words out of her mouth and tried giving her a grin.

"That's what I'm calling you," she said, but smiling just a little herself. "You're an ass, Nick Board. We've been here forty-five minutes and accomplished nothing. But you've managed to put Sarah, Delia and me down just the same. You're the only one with decisions to make. If *we* keep our heads the bogeymen will be kept at bay. We women, that is, according to you."

"I didn't say anything like that." Women had a way of twisting a man's words. "You're looking for things to get upset about."

"You did say them," Sarah said from the far end of the conservatory. "You don't even know you're putting us down."

"Thank you, Sarah," Aurelie said with a smug downturn of the mouth.

"Why would someone break in?" Sarah said. "For them to take Nick's letter and whatever was in the

158

package when it was put in the safe means they knew exactly what they wanted. Now they've got it and they don't need to come back."

"Use your head," Aurelie said. "They may have what they want, but they could just as well want us all dead. That would make things tidy for them. I wish Delia had read the letter so we'd have some idea what we might be up against."

Nick grunted assent. "I'm bummed she won't hire a regular security company to patrol the outside. There are too many windows in this place. She admits the doors to that little terrace outside her study were open throughout the afternoon yesterday. Whoever took that stuff didn't even have to break in."

Aurelie sat on a wicker couch with loose, faded floral cushions and Nick joined her there with his jaw set as if daring her to say she didn't want him near her. She did want him near her, but she didn't trust her own reactions.

"I got the keys to my new apartment this afternoon," she said. "It's furnished, Sarah, so I may leave my stuff in storage when it finally gets here."

"This is the place in that strip mall?" Nick asked. "What made you go there when you could have been at Oakdale?"

Near you? "I don't want to live where I can almost see the place where I work," she said. The excuse had begun to feel real. "Frances Broussard showed me around. It's nice. Small but cozy. I don't need anything big."

"It's dark back by those shops," Sarah said. "Aurelie and I drove in there last night to take a look. I didn't think you'd go ahead with it, Rellie."

"Because you said it was too dark?" She took a breath. "Sorry. You care about me, thank God, but I make up my own mind. They are going to get spotlights put up. They'll be on motion sensors. Frances said they've been thinking of doing it anyway."

"You'll stay here for now, though," Nick said. "With Matt sending a car around regularly and all of you together you'll be safer."

"Safer from what?" Aurelie said. Her temper rose again. "Sure I'm scared, but all we've got is speculation. I'll be staying in my apartment tonight. I'm looking forward to it. I was going to ask you to take Hoover to your place, Nick. He gets anxious when there's a lot of running in and out. I'll get him in the morning."

"I'm not comfortable with you moving into that place," Nick said.

"Lighten up a bit," Aurelie said. "We don't even know if we're at risk other than from you getting arrested for interfering with evidence in a murder investigation."

"Don't," Sarah said.

"You of all people should be scared, Sarah," Aurelie said.

"Why? What does that mean?"

She was stupid, Aurelie thought, stupid and out of control. "Nothing."

"I haven't had a chance to take a good look at what Baily was working on before she went up to the roof," Nick said. "I need to get that done."

He was trying to change the subject, Aurelie thought. Sarah stared at her as if she hadn't heard a word Nick had said.

"You did mean something. I, of all people, should be scared. That's what you said." Sarah approached, a yellow orchid whirling between finger and thumb. "I am scared now, so don't try and put me off again."

"Aurelie meant she thinks we all need to be cautious until we know this thing's over."

"No, she didn't."

Hoover shot into the conservatory, his beard dripping red spots on the tiles.

"Oh, Hoover, what did you do to yourself?" Aurelie dropped to her knees and took her big pet's head in her hands. "You've cut your mouth."

"He was eating berries," Delia said. She closed the door behind her with something close to regret in her expression. "There's paper towel in the little painted cupboard."

Aurelie found the towels, wiped off Hoover's mouth and cleaned up the floor. The dog went immediately to Nick and rested his jaw on the man's knees. Aurelie had noticed her pet showed traitorous tendencies to adore him.

Goose bumps rose on her arms and legs.

Each time he looked at her she had no doubt he was thinking about them making love. She contracted everything in her body that would contract and held herself stiff. Whenever she was alone and let her mind wander, she imagined Nick naked and enjoyed the experience too much.

"We've been talking," Nick said to Delia. "I called the security people and the alarms checked out fine. With a cop car coming around regularly and all of you staying here together, I think you should all be okay."

Delia wore a large hat with a floppy brim, and an orange cotton shirt and pants. Her toenails were painted the same shade of orange, and when she flung her gardening gloves aside, her fingernails matched.

"Aurelie's got some idea of moving into a little hole of an apartment over that salon Lynette Cayler and Frances Broussard run. Talk her out of it, will you, Delia? She won't listen to us."

Aurelie and Sarah squinted at each other and shook their heads, waiting for Delia's reaction.

Nick carried right on. "We should get our stories straight about Baily's briefcase. I would have told Matt about it right out but I don't want him looking any closer at us."

"At you, you mean," Aurelie said. "You're the one who took the thing. I still can't imagine why."

"Because," Nick said, patiently enough to make her teeth itch, "at that point we thought Baily had killed herself and it looked as if she could have been suffering from a major dose of guilt."

"But she was already dead," Sarah said. "It didn't matter anymore."

"It mattered to me to save her reputation if I could." He turned his eyes away. "She hadn't been happy and if she was trying to get back by developing a knockoff product at the lab, I wanted to take it out of the picture."

"Get back at you, you mean," Aurelie said.

He faced her and she saw she'd hurt him. "I'm not proud of the way things turned out between us. I didn't give her enough of a chance."

Aurelie reminded herself that one of the nicest things about Nick was his sense of fair play. "I think you did," she told him. "She needed time to heal. And she would have if someone hadn't taken the chance away from her."

"Did you decide what you intend to tell the police about that briefcase?" Delia asked. "And about what went missing yesterday?"

"Not exactly," Sarah said. "I'm not sure we can reach a consensus."

"We have to." Delia took off her hat. Her thick hair shone. There was a harsh set to her mouth. "First we deal with our behavior from now on. We don't huddle together here and change the way we live. I won't do that."

Aurelie barely stopped herself from kissing the woman.

"If there's a way to make sure we look guilty of something, that's it," Delia said. "I want you to tell the truth about Baily's briefcase, Nick. Your reasons for what you did were honorable. Baily was already dead when you took it, too, so it can't tie you to anything."

"I'm sure someone could find a way to incriminate me anyway," Nick said. "Only, I'm not guilty. I'm also not worried about it. Leave it to me."

After a tap at the door from the house, Sabine came down the steps into the conservatory with her husband behind her. She looked around at the Boards and slapped her hands into the folds of a long green skirt. "Will you look at the four of you? You'd think you was goin' to a funeral, you look so miserable."

Nick felt like saying they probably would be going to a funeral—Baily's—but didn't.

"We wanted a word with you," Sabine said, urging Ed forward. He wore one of the khaki jumpsuits he used for work. "Come on now, Ed. You back me up with this."

He smiled at her and there was no doubt who was the center of his life. Very thin, he was a freckled man with white skin and curly brown hair.

"There's all kinds of talk going on now. Information always leaks out and they know Baily was murdered," Sabine said. "Isn't that right, Ed?"

He nodded.

"Ed and me are telling folks to mind their business. They don't know what they're talking about, but you know how it is. A chance for some gossip and the tongue waggers crawl out of their holes. Isn't that right, Ed?"

Ed nodded. Then he nodded seriously at Delia, who nodded back. She relied on Ed and Sabine to keep the estate up and running. She had complete faith in them and Nick felt the same way.

"We know Baily was murdered and you must be real worried about this," Sabine said. "This is none of our business, but you know we're just the two of us and we think we could help out till this nonsense goes away. Unless you got other plans." She turned to Nick. "Have you already arranged for someone to live in here, just so there's a warm body to wake up if Miss Delia needs anything?"

Amazingly, Delia didn't say a word.

"No," Nick said. "We haven't done that."

Sabine elbowed Ed. He cleared his throat, shifted his feet. "We could stay in the old servants' quarters," he said. "Sabine, she says there's still a bell in Miss Delia's room and it rings over there. We don't think there's anything to worry about, but a person can get uptight after a murder. It's natural."

Tears actually stood in Delia's eyes. She sniffed and straightened her back. "What a sensible idea," she said. "Thank you. It'll be convenient for you and very convenient for me. And no one can make something out of live-in staff. It's common."

Delia had just accepted help. Nick didn't remember an occasion when she'd done so without an unpleasant struggle. And she wasn't a woman who knew fear, so why the change?

Would she do anything rather than have the roles

reversed? That could be it, Delia wasn't ready to have the adults she considered her children try to take care of her.

"Well, then," Sabine said. She was pleased and it showed. "We'll go put our things in there. And Ed's goin' to test that bell. I got my cell phone, too, Miss Delia. So you can get us that way, too. Not that you'll need to reach us. It's just knowing you could."

Delia waited barely long enough for Ed and Sabine to be out of earshot before grinning around and saying, "There, now, you three can stop worrying about me."

Aurelie said, "How convenient. Did you call the Webbs and arrange that little scene?"

"That's a silly suggestion," Delia said, but she didn't meet any eyes. "They're thoughtful people. And as Sabine said, I won't need them, but they'll be there."

But no one would be with either Aurelie or Sarah. Nick crossed his arms. "Good. We'll all feel better. One more thing and we'll get lost. Have you thought about that letter? We need to report the theft."

"I've thought about it," Delia said promptly. "I want to wait until this dreadful thing with Baily's been cleared up. If we mention the letters now, Matt Boudreaux and his new friend will be all over us trying to make a connection that isn't there."

"It might be there," Aurelie said.

"No." Delia shook her head. "It isn't. Later our problem can be dealt with on its own and there'll be no need for anyone to stir up a big fuss about the past."

Nick couldn't look away from Aurelie. When she made a decision she stuck with it and she'd made one now.

"I know I shouldn't make a big deal about it," Sarah said, "but I'm so sad Mary's letter is gone. It was all Nick had of her."

"Whoever took it must have thought it was something important," Nick said. "I mean, in some way other than the sentimental value."

"You never looked inside the package?" Sarah asked Delia.

"No." Delia shook her head. "I felt that if I did, it would be like saying Mary wouldn't be coming back. I couldn't do it."

"Tell the police tonight," Aurelie said. "Nick, just do it. Tell the whole thing from the beginning at The Refuge. It's the right thing and we'll all cope with the fallout. If Colin's in Pointe Judah, if he murdered Baily, possibly by mistake, and he intends to deal with all of us, we need official help."

"What's that dog got?" Delia asked, making a grab for Hoover, who clumsily evaded her and loped away between the tropical beds. "He's chewing something."

Nick went after the dog, his sandals crunching on what looked like little white pills the animal had dropped from a mouthful.

"Drugs," Aurelie said. "Get him, Nick."

He caught Hoover and pried open his mouth to find a heap of lumpy white mush inside. Hoover coughed and spat. He dropped to the floor, whining and covering his nose with his paws.

Kneeling, Nick sat back on his heels and laughed.

"What?" Aurelie asked, throwing herself down beside her animal. "What are you laughing at, you idiot?"

"Isn't it Ed who eats those really strong mints in a tin?"

Aurelie went limp and rolled her eyes. "Yes. Is that—"

"Yep, Hoover got the mints and he doesn't like 'em. He'll probably throw up."

Aurelie punched his arm. "That's not funny."

"Sure it is. He's not my dog."

She bumped shoulders with him and he thought he might be having the second-best moment of his life. "I'll take him home with me till you get settled. And he'd better not upchuck in *my* car."

"Have you two stopped being good buddies?" Sarah asked. When Nick looked up at her he saw she was close to tears. "If you have, would you answer a question for me? Or don't I matter at all?"

"Of course you do," Nick said, getting up and pulling Aurelie with him. He looked closely at Sarah. "What is it, Sarah? Tell us."

"Did you think Aurelie could tell me I ought to be really scared and I wouldn't notice?" She turned to Aurelie. "I am scared. I'm so scared *I* could pass out."

"Come here, Sarah," Delia said, hurrying toward them with her arms held out. "We're all upset and not thinking straight. Matt Boudreaux told me it was only for a moment that he thought Baily was you. And Nick and Aurelie knew it wasn't you as soon as they got a really good look at the body. Isn't that right, Nick?"

17

She had a big, careless mouth and she had hurt her sister. Aurelie left the house by the front door and cut right toward one of two groves of giant oaks that flanked the building.

All that talk about making sure Delia was safe, but there hadn't been a way to console Sarah after she learned that people who knew them both well had at first mistaken Baily's body for hers.

Sarah had kept saying, "You thought it was me. You thought I was dead. Now you think it was supposed to be me." And she wouldn't be comforted.

Nick had suggested Aurelie should leave because she intended to empty her things out of the Hummer and into her new apartment before she went to bed. She had left the vehicle at Sarah's and the two of them had walked to the house together.

When Sarah settled down enough to go back to the guesthouse, Nick intended to check it out before leaving her there. Aurelie had offered to stay with her sister but, like all of them, Sarah insisted on exerting her own independence.

It stunk that Delia had walked right into a bad situation and made it worse, but there was never malice in her heart.

Aurelie felt a little guilty. With emotion running so high, Nick and the others had forgotten the Hummer wasn't parked outside Place Lafource, or they wouldn't have let her go out alone to the guesthouse. Which was silly when it was only a short walk away.

The sun was an old memory now. Clumps of inky foliage crowded a smoke-gray sky. Despite the problems they faced, Aurelie relaxed as she walked. Her one regret about Lafource was that they hadn't lived there as children. These grounds would make a dream playground.

Perhaps their children, Nick's, Sarah's and her own would be there one day.

A sudden sharp beat of her heart came with making a connection between herself, Nick and children. The two of them had played a very adult game together, and the wonder of it still messed with her mind.

The path wound back and forth between the trees so that by daylight it made a pleasant stroll between all the woodland shrubs that grew on either side. Where it came close to the driveway, the lights penetrated in places, but the deeper bends took her into almost absolute darkness. Aurelie looked upward again. Trees almost touched overhead in this spot. She became aware of how the low thicket came alive at night. Sounds swelled, a sibilant background, the katydid and didn't cries, and the boisterous ruckus from cicadas.

The noise grew until it grated on Aurelie.

She walked faster.

There was a lot to do before she could sleep. Humidity drained her and tonight wet heat wrapped her as if she wore plastic film.

"You shouldn't have left the mutt behind," a muffled voice said.

Aurelie jumped madly and checked her stride. She looked over her shoulder, one way and then the other, didn't see anyone and broke into a run, her arms pumping.

Crashing came from the undergrowth, to her right. Or was it to her left?

She tried to scream but couldn't make a sound.

"Where's the stone?"

She tried again but still couldn't scream and if she did, who would hear? She had gone so deeply into the oaks, so far from the driveway. *Keep moving.*

"Tell me where it is and I'll go," he said. And it was a man. "You'll never hear from me again."

Aurelie ran on, every breath loud and painful. When she dared, she peered behind her, and into the dark trunks that hemmed her in, but couldn't see anyone.

"You're making this difficult. Your choice."

Arriving at her back as if from the clamoring air, he shot an arm around her neck and held it in the iron crook of his elbow. She couldn't take another step.

"I don't like killing people," he said.

Panting, she plucked at his arm but only succeeded in causing him to grip even tighter. Her head felt as if it would explode and every one of her muscles shook. She fought for each breath now.

Think. She couldn't. Her mind spun, wouldn't settle. "I don't know what you're talking about." Her voice sounded distant and husky. "Let me go. We'll forget this happened."

"You sound like a cliché," he said and chuckled. "This isn't hard. You people have got something that doesn't belong to you and I want it. Because it does belong to me. I'm not trying to steal anything, just get back my property."

Aurelie twisted, slammed her heels down on his toes—and knew the huge mistake she'd made.

"Bitch," he hissed, spewing rage in that single word. With one hand he wrestled a bag that smelled of old potatoes over her head. His hands around her neck, he gathered the bottom of the bag tight and she heard tape rip from a roll, tape he used to secure the bag.

His hands moved swiftly from her neck to force her arms behind her back. More tape bound her wrists together. Her bones pressed into one another and with each attempt to move them, they chafed on the edges of the tape.

"You're making too much noise," he said. "Pity, that. Makes it harder to get my answers, but I'll have to shut you up."

"I'll be quiet," she said, blinded by brilliant spots of light sparking in eyes that saw nothing else. Sweat soaked her clothes.

He was much bigger than her but that's all she could tell.

With no warning, he spread fingers over her collarbones and pushed so hard she moaned.

Down among stickery twigs, thorns and the blunt ends of branches she went. This time the sound she made was the *whump* of her emptying lungs. Under her diaphragm, a burning ache penetrated upward. And she kept falling until she settled where she felt the brush rise all around her and a bed of stones at her back. Dozens of sharp objects stuck into her through her blouse and against her bare arms where she'd rolled up her sleeves. Her neck and legs stung. Too hot, she'd taken off her jacket and couldn't remember where she'd left it.

She screamed, opened her mouth wide and let loose a full-throated shriek. And he slammed a hand over her face so hard she heard a cracking sound from her nose and pain blasted into her eyes and cheeks.

"The Vulture," the man said, the sound hateful. Grinding, hissing, threatening the worst. He spread his whole weight on top of her. "You know the story of the Vulture. How that stone you all took was nicknamed after the kind of bird that killed anyone who tried to get the ruby. Where is it?"

"I don't understand," she said. "If I did, I'd tell you, wouldn't I?"

He gave his raspy chuckle again. "Would you? By the time I got into that study, the ruby was gone. Has Nick still got it, or has it passed to someone else? I don't think so. I don't think he knows how to get rid of it and he hasn't had enough time. He's got three days to give it to me, or I'll be back to finish what I'm going to start."

He sat astride her hips and opened her blouse, tore the buttons away.

With her arms behind her, Aurelie was helpless. She swallowed bile and her face burned with shame and fear.

He pulled her bra above her breasts and twisted them in his hands.

Aurelie squirmed. Her cries gurgled in her throat.

"That hurts, hmm?" he asked. "I could make it hurt a lot more. I expect you already heard all about the Vulture Ruby from someone else."

She didn't dare speak.

His weight shifted and he moved higher over her body. The zipper opening on his pants sounded like a rifle report in her ears. *Please don't let him rape me.*

She heard him rip open a condom and struggled ineffectually. He brought the side of a hand down again, hard, on her breastbone. Again her lungs wouldn't fill.

He moved his penis over her breasts, spent time flipping the tips of her nipples back and forth. She could feel the rubber sheath. He didn't intend to leave any DNA behind.

"Are you remembering anything about the ruby now?" He filled a hand with one of her breasts and squeezed.

Aurelie tried to push herself into the ground. Blackness edged her mind.

"I'm having a good time but I've got to get my answer and move on," he said. "Vultures start with the soft parts of a body, don't they? But you know all about that story. First the eyes." A pointed object struck through the bag and into the skin just shy of her right eye. "They have such sharp beaks and they're so hungry." The same needlelike attack hit her nipples.

She began to scream but he crammed a hand over her mouth again. "Don't pretend that hurts. It feels good. It's only when the vulture pulls these things off that you pass out." He pinched a nipple and pulled hard, pulled until her body arched up from the sticks and stones. "Fuck, I mustn't kill you tonight, even if we do have fun first. But I want to kill you. And I want to see their faces when they find you. They have no stomach for mutilation."

He was cold, completely, icily cold, and every word he spoke was meant to terrify her. She boiled and sweated and her brain felt on fire, but this man considered each move he made and took his time about it. She strained to listen, hoping she'd hear the Audi. There was nothing.

Swiftly, he undid her slacks and yanked them, with her panties, down around her hips.

Aurelie cried silently, the tears squeezing from the corners of her eyes. His fingers on her skin turned her belly liquid and crawling. She sucked fine, gritty dirt from the bag into her nose and mouth.

Where was Nick? He should have left the house with Sarah by now. The moment he saw the Hummer still parked outside the guesthouse he'd know something was wrong.

"A big black bird could feel like this." He used his fingertips to stroke her belly. "Feel how soft it is."

Horrified almost to madness, Aurelie cried, "Leave me alone. Please, leave me alone."

"A vulture wouldn't feel so soft if it attacked you." He jabbed her belly with his penis, jabbed it again. "And men can be just as dangerous."

Aurelie screamed and once more he silenced her. He fluttered his fingers over her belly again. She thrashed, whipped her hips from side to side.

"What was stolen from me is soft. Big and smooth and worth a king's life."

"I can't understand you." Aurelie cried and couldn't stop. And she hated herself for being weak. People like him liked to know their victims were scared sick.

"Smooth, dark—the darkest fire ever seen in a ruby, the price of a king's life," he said. "You know what I'm saying? The sooner you tell me what I need to know, the sooner you'll be free."

Aurelie clamped her teeth together and stiffened her body.

"They say rubbing a stone like that causes warmth that reaches inside you."

"Stop it." Her gut burned. "Get away."

Close beside her, the man groped her breasts again, and he took what felt like a bird's claw and scratched it across her belly. "They grip with their claws and they—" he spread spiked talons and drove them into her assaulted flesh "—and tear with their beaks.

"Now, you're overheated. I'll help you cool off." With that he swept her slacks and underpants to her knees and caressed her body with humiliating intimacy.

In seconds, he wound more tape around the bag that covered her head, placed it to keep her mouth shut.

"Now listen. Tell Nick he has three days to give me what's mine. I'll let him know how to get it to me. Understand?"

She nodded her head.

"If he doesn't do as he's told, there's a price to be paid. It's been paid before. Someone he cares about will suffer and die. In case he doesn't know the story, tell him my stone, Vulture, got its name for the price paid by the ones who stole it down through the centuries. Each of them was staked out to die in the sun, but the vultures got them first. The strongest were still alive when they were already blind and still alive while their organs and guts were torn from their bellies.

"A man can inflict the same deadly wounds."

18

He ripped the tape from her wrists and threw her, facedown, into the taller bushes. Aurelie closed numb hands around clumps of plants and held on. Her mind raced and her eyes stung.

"Don't turn around," he said, and, shoving at her neck, he tore the sack from her head. Then he was gone, as silently as he'd come, and she lay, swallowing air.

Crashing in the trees. He would come back and kill her after all.

No.

She covered her head.

Aurelie gradually pulled the heels of her hands from her ears.

Not another sound but for the critters.

Her bruised body throbbed.

Pulling her clothes together as best she could, Aurelie struggled to her feet. It was too dark to see what injuries he'd inflicted; she touched her nose and just as quickly pulled her hand away. She tasted blood.

This time she would do things her way. There would be no asking advice or permission from the family. They would only slow her down and try to change her mind. Aurelie knew what must be done.

Stumbling, moving as fast as she could, she reached the Hummer.

Her keys? They were in her jacket pocket, she was sure of it, but she didn't know where the jacket was.

She couldn't go back.

Aurelie looked over her shoulder and the trees felt as if they had closed the pathway behind her.

Desperate, she tried Nick's Audi. Even if she could take it, she wouldn't. She shoved her hands in her pants pockets—and found her own keys.

"Hurry up," she told herself, trembling with relief. "Hurry." She threw open the driver's door on her vehicle, clambered inside and turned it on. In seconds she drove from the grounds at Place Lafource, her tires screeching.

All the way to town she repeatedly checked the rearview mirror but didn't see any following lights. And she opened her window, took her foot off the gas and didn't hear another engine.

Driving faster than she ever drove, she made it to the strip mall, parked as close as she could to the door beside the salon, the door leading up to her new apartment. She shot from the vehicle, locked it, and then used the key Frances Brossard had given her for the apartment door.

Inside, she put on the dead bolt and chain, and took the stairs so fast she tripped repeatedly all the way to a tiny, square landing at the top.

The apartment consisted of two fairly small rooms. And a tight bathroom off the bedroom. The kitchen and dining nook were part of the living room. In the bedroom, she locked the door from the inside. She already had two bags of personal things there and within minutes she stood under hot, if slightly rusty, water in the shower, washing herself with an existing bar of plain soap. The stream stung her bruised body. Scratches and small puncture wounds traversed her belly and ribs. More wounds the size of large pinpricks surrounded her nipples and she still couldn't touch her face—which she had yet to look at in the mirror.

A new bottle of glow-in-the-dark orange-colored shampoo stood in the shower pan and she drenched her hair with it, wrinkling her nose at the strong tangerine scent.

Rinsing with a blast of water, she tried to control her racing heart and the thundering at her temples.

She would not waver in what she had decided to do.

Gingerly, she patted dry and smoothed antibacterial cream over a good deal of her body. She pulled on clothes, a blue T-shirt that looked as if it had been cut on the bias and bleach-spotted jeans.

In front of the mirror, she leaned forward to survey her face. What a mess. The jab beside her right eye had made a quarter-inch wound that probably needed a butterfly dressing. Her nose had swollen. Carefully, she touched the bone, but although it felt bruised it didn't seem displaced. She wiped off a few specks of blood but felt sorry for herself when a thin, pink stream started to flow from her left nostril.

Moving as quickly as pain allowed, she raked at her hair with a wide-toothed comb, grimacing each time it tore at tangles. Eventually her thick black curls made a triangular shape from her crown to the ends. She tossed down the comb and returned to the bedroom.

This was it. All the subterfuge was over. It was up to her to save the people she loved from their own folly.

Holding a wad of tissues to her nose, she left the apartment again, this time with the gun she hadn't told anyone she owned. Stuffing it into the waistband of her jeans, she pulled the T-shirt over the top. She had a license to carry and it was her business.

She didn't make a phone call until she was behind the wheel of the Hummer and driving. A woman on the desk at the police station answered. "How can I help you?"

"This is Aurelie Board. I'm coming there now. I need to speak with Matt Boudreaux and I think he'd want to talk to me."

"Yes, Aurelie. This is Officer Carly Gibson. Matt's here, would you like to speak with him?"

No, she didn't want any opportunity to change her mind about what she'd decided to do. "I'll be there in a few minutes. I'll talk to him then. Thanks."

She made it to the station in record time and, still driving too fast, bumped over exposed tree roots in the parking lot. The Hummer had great suspension, but the bouncing pulled at her injured skin. The engine scarcely died before she was out and running for the building.

"Aurelie!" Carly Gibson looked up and hurried from behind a desk. "What's happened? Has there been an accident?"

"You could say that," Aurelie said. At last the adrenaline ebbed and she felt weak. She trembled inside and put a hand on Carly's solid shoulder.

"Sit down," Carly said. Worn in a single braid, her blond hair hung down her back and swung when she walked. She reminded Aurelie of a pretty, well-padded Dutch girl.

"I need Matt," she said in a wobbly voice. "I'm sorry for roaring in like this."

He must have heard the commotion because Matt appeared with Buck Dupiere behind him. The two of them approached her swiftly. Matt took her by the shoulders and looked closely at her face. "Someone punched you, didn't they?"

She nodded.

"Any idea where he is now?"

"No."

Buck put a hand to her chin and turned it. "This is a puncture wound," he said of the cut by her eye. "Did he stab you with something?"

Aurelie nodded again.

"Rat," Carly said. "Wish I'd been there, but he probably wouldn't have picked on someone his own size."

Aurelie giggled, then felt stricken at the idea of losing control. "He was a lot bigger than you, Carly."

A stream of harsh language blasted the air and none

of it sounded like Matt Boudreaux's usual vocabulary. His face was set and his usually slow Cajun temper looked to be on the boil. He put an arm around her shoulders and hustled her toward his office—the office that used to belong to Billy Meche.

Quietly he said, "Do we need to think about a rape kit?"

She shook her head, no, and felt sickened.

"Get me a first-aid kit," Buck said to Carly. "And some coffee and something for the headache she's got. You do have a headache, Aurelie?"

"I hurt all over," she said, in no mood to be courageous.

"Aurelie?" She heard Nick's voice a moment before she saw him in the office doorway, struggling with Hoover to be first through. "What are you doing . . . Fuck!"

"Watch your mouth," Matt said, evidently forgetting the blue barrage he'd just let loose.

Hoover loped rapidly toward her, whimpering all the way. He brushed around her legs, all but knocking her over.

"Look at that," Buck said. "He knows something's wrong with the boss."

Stiffness had settled in and Aurelie carefully bent her knees to stroke Hoover—and to take a chewed ballpoint pen from his mouth.

Nick pried her out of Matt's arm and half carried her into the office. He looked from one uncomfortable chair to another and Buck held up a hand. "Just a minute." He hurried next door, to what had been Matt's office but was now his, and manhandled in an ugly, sagging, red leather recliner. "You don't have to look at it," he told Aurelie. "Just sit in it and try not to fall asleep yet."

She sat down. Buck pushed the back so that the footrest came up and she sank into the age-softened leather. He was right, she could have slept there—if she didn't hurt in so many places and if she wasn't horribly scared.

"What's happened to you?" Nick said. He knelt down and looked closely at her face. "Who did it?"

"I don't know, but I've got to be ready the next time."

"Next time?" he said explosively. He held her hand tightly. "No next time. Tell me what he did to you." His voice dropped and she read fear in his face.

"He beat me up. Scratched me up. Scared the devil out of me. Threatened me. Pushed me around. And did I say he threatened me? Big-time. Do as he wants or he'll pull my insides out a bit at a time."

"Are you serious?" Matt said.

"No, I'm making it all up for fun. And I inflicted the wounds myself."

"What did he make the one by your eye with?" Matt asked. He waved Carly in and she put a large first-aid kit on a chair, then pulled the chair close to Aurelie.

She started to answer Matt but stopped. She didn't know the truth for sure.

"Did he have a knife?" Nick said. "It was a man?"

184

"A man," she said.

"Aurelie, did he . . . did he assault you sexually?" Nick said.

"That depends on what you mean by sexually."

His face lost all color.

The way he cared for her showed. She hoped she was the only one who saw how personal his anger was.

"Spell it out, Rellie," he said.

"He didn't in the normal sense," she said. She touched her face. "But he's a sick puppy. I think he did this with a claw from a dead bird."

Aurelie saw Nick's eyes fix. She looked at the others and they'd stopped moving around. Four disbelieving faces confronted her.

"A bird's claw?" Matt said finally. "Like—" He raised and lowered his arms a couple of times, then quickly crossed them. "You saw this?"

"Yes. No." She sat up straighter. "He kept talking about a vulture."

"You're kidding," Buck said.

"Carly," Matt said. "Get on to the clinic and see if they can send someone over. Mention dead bird claws and rabies."

Aurelie's face felt stiff and cold. "I wasn't bitten by a bird. There was no bird. But it felt like he stuck a claw into my face and I think that's what he used to scratch up . . . other parts of me. He's very sick. His thing is to creep you out and he did a fine job with me."

"I'm taking you to a hospital," Nick said.

"No," Aurelie said patiently. "I'll go to a hospital when I've said what I came here to say. Anyway, a scratch from a dead claw's no big deal."

Nick's pupils dilated. "You aren't thinking. We're going now." He stood up and Hoover bayed.

"Shit," Buck said. "That's a helluva bark."

"If you touch me, Nick, I'll scream," Aurelie said. If she'd ever had any control in this situation, she'd lost it. Now she'd get it back again. "I'd like some water, please. And whatever you were going to give me for a headache, Buck."

"Gotcha," he said and hurried from the office.

Nick started to speak but Aurelie shushed him. "If the claw—if it was a claw—gave me rabies, I've got plenty of time to start the shots. Even I know that much."

"I don't want to wait," he said. "Matt, talk to her."

"She's right, there's time. Can you give me a description of the guy?"

"No. He put a bag over my head and taped it around my neck. Would you two mind sitting down? It hurts to look so far up."

Nick and Matt hurriedly pulled up chairs. "Where did this happen?" Nick asked, apparently oblivious to Matt's irritated glances. The cop didn't like the civilian walking on official territory.

"On the path between the house and the guest-house," Aurelie said. "You know how it snakes in and out of the trees. He got me way back in. From behind.

There wasn't any light. He put me in a hammerlock and bagged my head. He was fast. He taped my wrists together behind my back."

"What were you doing there?" Nick asked. "You were going to drive right to your apartment."

"My car was at the guesthouse."

Nick scrubbed at his face and slowly pulled them down far enough for his eyes to be visible over his fingertips. "Dammit. You shouldn't have walked on that path alone."

"Did this man speak?" Matt asked.

"Oh, yes. I don't know who he was. I do think he was quite big. And he was strong. He didn't have any trouble picking me up and throwing me."

"My God," Nick said.

"Tell me what he said and did," Matt said. "Don't leave anything out."

Aurelie gave it to him move for move, word for word, leaving out only the embarrassing bits. If she had to talk about the rest of it later, it wasn't going to be in front of Nick.

"We need to find out if your nose is broken," Buck said when he had returned to stand over her while she took the pills and emptied a big glass of water in a few gulps. "It doesn't look crooked."

"Right now I don't care if it is," Aurelie said, absolutely honest.

"Could just as well have been a knifepoint," she said.

"I wish I'd had some idea of what was going on," Nick said.

If Aurelie didn't know better, she'd think she was a bit drunk. "I drove back to the apartment to get cleaned up and put cream on the scratches before I came here. Why are you here, Nick?" She hadn't questioned his presence until this moment.

"I've got business with Matt. So you were attacked at home but instead of coming to me when that freak let you go, you went to take a shower and drive here?"

"Yes."

"Aurelie—"

"You said you have business with Matt. I've got business with him, too. There's a sick killer on the loose and I can't hold back any information that could help track him down."

"He didn't kill you," Nick said. "He just played a dumb trick."

"If someone did to you what he did to me, you might not brush it off as a dumb trick. From what he said, we've got three days to do what he wants or he'll be back. He described how he'd kill me if that has to happen. I think I'd like to pass."

"Damn." Nick slid forward on the chair and stretched out his legs. He ran his fingers into his hair. "He wanted to scare you and he made a good job of it."

"He'd have scared you, too," Aurelie said. "I think he killed Baily for exactly the reason we thought— because he thought she was Sarah."

"The same guy?" Nick said.

"Yes, the same guy. How many homicidal lunatics do you think we've got in this town? He may not have intended Baily to fall off the roof, though. Have you thought of that? He could have done to her what he did to me—try to terrify her into giving him the information he wants."

After packing up the first-aid kit, Carly brought in a tray filled with coffee mugs and offered them around. "Dr. Halpern's on his way over," she said.

Aurelie puffed at a curl that had dried and strayed over her face. "I'm not going to consult a doctor here."

"Be reasonable," Nick said. "At least he can decide what treatment you need."

"I'd like to go to the clinic myself. After I finish here."

"The doctor's already coming," Carly said, but she looked sympathetic. "It'll be okay. You can be in a room with him on your own."

Nick looked about to argue but closed his mouth.

"Matt," Aurelie said. "I need to tell you some things that we've been keeping quiet about. We didn't do it to make life hard for you. We've learned to keep our business to ourselves, is all."

Nick jumped to his feet and paced. "You didn't need to come and get yourself mixed up in all this," he said. "I was about to fill Matt and Buck in when you got here. That's why I came."

"Did you tell them about Baily's briefcase?"

Something close to hurt entered Nick's expression.

"I intended to. I also intend to discuss our background. Yours, mine and Sarah's."

"And the theft, Nick. That's probably the most important for the moment."

"That, too." He looked unhappy enough to make her doubt just how clean he had planned to come. "We can't leave anything out anymore."

"Including Colin?"

He stared at her. "Yes, including Colin."

"Good. You think he's here, don't you?" She touched her tummy and winced. "It's the creepiest thing I can think of."

"Can we settle down a bit before we spill everything?" Nick said. "There's a lot to say."

"Who is Colin?" Buck asked.

Aurelie looked at Nick. He shook his head. "He led the commune my mother went into when she was expecting me. He became her partner. Then he killed her."

"You can't prove that, can you?" Matt said.

"No, but all I need is time."

"Yes," Aurelie said. "That's another reason Colin wants to get rid of us all. We're untidy and we may be able to cause him big trouble. But he wants his priceless ruby back first. He said it was called the Vulture Ruby."

Silence met her statement.

"He said the stone was smooth and dark and talked about a king's life and people dying for it—being torn apart by vultures. The stone gets warm when you rub it. He said that, too."

"That's all real clear," Matt said.

Nick had been carrying his coffee mug around. He took a mouthful and grimaced. "Cold. Look, there's about sixteen or so years of history to go over. I know we can't afford to put it off, but let's see to Aurelie and get her back to Delia. She'll be looked after there."

"I'm not going anywhere to be looked after," Aurelie said. "Thanks for the offer anyway. I've got my own past to deal with. Sarah and I both do." She realized she should have Sarah's agreement before going on.

"Good evening all." A man wearing a navy blue tracksuit stood in the open doorway. He carried a bag that suggested to Aurelie he was the doctor. "Mitch Halpern. Who's the patient?"

"She is," Nick said promptly, pointing at Aurelie. "Someone attacked her. She isn't sure but she thinks he used a claw from a dead bird to scratch her."

Halpern, around six feet, muscular, hard-jawed and with dark blond hair, raised his eyebrows. "Is that some kind of voodoo ritual around here?" he asked. "Or maybe a fertility rite?"

Carly laughed but collected herself quickly.

"I don't know anything about voodoo," Aurelie said. "But what he did hurt."

"D'you know who he is?" Halpern asked.

Aurelie sighed. "Here we go again. No, I don't know him. He grabbed me from behind and put a bag over my head. I could need a shot of antibiotics

191

because I can't be sure I got all the cuts clean enough. But I tried. I really scrubbed them." She winced.

"We'll decide what we need to do," Dr. Halpern said. He had the kind of eyes that seemed permanently narrowed. They were hazel and filled with humor. "We'll find out when you had your last tetanus shot. You're holding your abdomen. Scratch you there, did he?"

"Yes," she said and barely stopped herself from slapping him away when he lifted the front of her T-shirt a couple of inches.

"Somebody got busy here," he said. "Whoever did this meant business. Could have been from claws. Chicken, maybe. Having this jammed in your waistband isn't helping, either. Do you always carry?"

The other three men crowded around. She knocked Nick's hand away when he attempted to take the gun, then slid it out and gave it to Matt. "Take a look," she told him. "It's pretty in its own way."

"I didn't know you had a gun," Nick said.

Aurelie gave him a small smile. "Seems like a good idea," she told him. "Don't you approve?"

He shrugged. "I'm probably overreacting to everything at the moment. I can't stand it that you need to tote a firearm around."

"Businesslike piece," Buck said of the 9 mm Glock. "Isn't it heavy for you?"

"It's perfect for me," Aurelie said. "I'm a woman who lives alone, and I've got a license."

"Do you know how to use it?" Buck asked.

"Yes." The question annoyed her.

"I take it you didn't have it with you when you met bird man," Dr. Halpern said, more interested in examining her than the gun.

"I don't believe him, but he suggested it could be a vulture's claw. No, I didn't have my gun. But the next time he shows up, I will."

"I don't think that's a good idea," Matt said. "Using a gun for show can get a woman into big trouble."

"It could get a woman or a man into trouble," she said. "But I have no intention of using it for show."

19

"I don't know what to say," Aurelie told Nick.

"Thanks would do it," he said. He had followed her back to her new apartment and carried in all the boxes and bags packed in the Hummer. He put down Hoover's oversize fuzzy bed and smiled at Aurelie. "I'm glad to do it. Everything's upstairs now."

Hoover climbed into his bed and turned around and around before flopping down. He sighed and closed his eyes.

"Is he actually a guard dog?" Nick asked.

"Of course. He looks scary."

"Would he bite an intruder?"

"Intrude and find out."

"Ouch." Nick grinned. They were actually relaxed together. Too bad he couldn't trust the resumption of diplomatic relations to continue.

Draped on a cushy lilac-colored velvet sofa, Aurelie rested her head on one overstuffed arm. "I don't like getting those shots," she said. "Why couldn't I wait to see if there could be a problem before that sexy doctor started shooting me up?"

If she'd hoped to annoy him, she'd failed. He cocked his head to one side. "The sexy doctor knows his stuff. The shots are precautionary and they can't wait. Anyway, they used to be a big deal but they're nothing now."

"Says you." She frowned at him. "Thanks a lot for helping me out. You'd better get home and sleep. Matt made it sound as if we could expect business tomorrow."

"Security became an even bigger issue tonight," he said, her scratched face annoying him all over again. "You bet we'll have business to do."

He found Hoover's bowls, filled one with water and rooted around until he found a bag of food so he could pour some in the second bowl. These he put down in the kitchen.

The dog swayed slowly up behind him, nosed him aside and somehow sucked about half the bowl of food into his mouth at one time. He retraced his steps, climbed back into his bed and spat out a heap of kibble. These he ate a few at a time.

Nick shook his head.

Next he turned to the bedroom, and stood in the doorway with his arms crossed. "Do you have to climb over the bed to get to the bathroom in here?"

"Not quite," Aurelie told him. "Now you've seen everything there is to see in this place. And I like it, which is what counts."

"You sound defensive, Rellie."

"I can see what you're thinking," she said. "You think it's too small."

Anything he said could be wrong. "Where's your bedding?"

"In the green box . . . No, Nick, you don't have to do any of that. I'll be fine now, thanks."

"It's no trouble."

"You're a good guy, Nick Board. You always have been." Aurelie swung her feet to the floor but stayed on the couch. "Since Sarah and I were kids you've been looking out for us. Do you know how special that is?"

"It's been special for me, too."

He located the green box. His personal battle raged. If he played it safe, behaved like a choirboy, there was a chance they could return to a semblance of the way their lives had been. Without using the words, Aurelie had just offered him a rope to hold while he crossed back to the safe side of the river.

The safe side of the river wouldn't be enough. He'd slip and make another intimate move. Or, glory hallelujah, she could make the slip. He almost laughed at himself.

The only sheets he found in the box were flannel. The ones on the top had holly sprigs all over them. "Why are these sheets here?" he asked. "Flannel. There must be another box."

"The holly ones are on top. Those are my favorites, but leave them, please. I'm not an invalid."

Nick pulled out the holly sheets. "You're kidding," he said. "You don't sleep in these things? They've got to be so hot."

"I like them."

He didn't miss a subtle change in her tone, a moving away. "Aurelie? You okay?"

"Great."

"Why do you do that?" He went back to sit on the couch with her. "You're not feeling great so why do you say you are?"

She drew up her shoulders. "It must be a habit. I didn't know I was doing it. I think Matt got more than he planned on tonight, don't you?"

Which meant he was supposed to change the subject. "Yes. Now it's all out, or most of it, I don't know how we ever thought we'd keep our past quiet forever."

"We thought we could because that's the way we wanted it to be. Matt may have seemed low-key about the information, but he was really mad we didn't tell him about the theft as soon as we knew about it."

Matt hadn't tried very hard to cover his feelings. "I don't blame him," Nick said. "Delia messed with everything. She didn't realize what she was doing, but you know how cops are. Don't touch their crime scenes."

"They're right," Aurelie said. "It's as much our

fault as Delia's. We should have insisted on calling Matt immediately."

"We did what we've always done," Nick said. "We closed ranks. It's worked for years so it's a habit."

"It's not going to work anymore," Aurelie said.

"No. But I did feel the ice melt between Matt and me this evening. He'd started treating me like a suspect—or a stranger. We've always been close."

"You can thank me for that," Aurelie said. "You couldn't be roughing me up and be at the police station at the same time. Glad I could give you an alibi."

Her crooked smile made him sigh.

"I'd rather I'd been the one he went after," he said.

"I know that."

He got up again and returned to the bedroom. Climbing around the bed to get the sheets on wasn't easy for a big man. The thought of flannel sheets with holly on them, in Louisiana at this time of year, puzzled him. And amused him. Who knew why people did what they did?

"Nick."

He threw the pillows on the bed and went back to the living room.

"What does this place remind you of?" Aurelie asked.

"Well . . ." Besides the lavender couch there was a matching chair, all curves and softness, and a purple carpet. Two small tables in front of the couch had circular glass tops balanced on painted wooden bases resembling the balls sometimes pictured on the noses of cartoon sea lions. "I don't know." Any opinion he gave could be a disaster.

Aurelie laughed and the sound made him grin. She hadn't laughed much in the past few days.

"What's funny?"

"Look at the chandelier."

The chandelier, suspended low over a kitchen table covered with a star-splotched cloth, sported dangling wooden hearts, flowers, caterpillars . . . and kites, all painted in bright shades. "Interesting," he said.

"That's a loaded word," Aurelie said. "But you still don't know what this place reminds you of?"

He started to shake his head but frowned instead. "A child's place?"

Aurelie pointed a long forefinger at him. "You got it!"

Nick perched on the chair. He wasn't sure what he was supposed to say or how he should react.

"It's like every little girl's dream," she said. "It's adult whimsy, really, but I just got the impression that some children—the ones with parents who live to make them happy—could come up with a miniature version of this."

He might not be Mr. Sensitive, but he knew longing when he heard it. "This is pretty miniature, Rellie."

"Both Lynette and Frances are whimsy types," Aurelie said. "I can imagine them thinking this would make someone happy . . . Maybe make them feel safe."

He breathed deeply. An edginess attacked him. This

was going to be one of those make-or-break moments when a man had better not put his foot in his mouth. "Does it make you feel safe? Is that why you wanted it?"

The smile she gave him lit up her face.

Score one for Nick, and her happiness made him feel triumphant.

"Exactly," she said. "If I spread my arms and ran around I could touch all the walls in no time. With the bedroom door open, I can see the whole place. It would be hard for anyone to hide in here. And it's cozy. And there's no upstairs. I hate upper floors. They were the only thing that freaked me out at Lafource." She shut her mouth as abruptly as she'd taken off with her rush of enthusiasm.

"Upstairs?" Nick moved beside her again and studied her face, her eyes. "Why would you dislike a place with an upstairs?"

Stricken. Deep in Aurelie's eyes lay revived pain. "No reason," she said. "I don't even know why I said that. Thank you for helping me out and looking after Hoover and everything. Lock your doors tonight, hmm?"

This time he didn't feel like backing off. "You're scared. Big surprise. We're in the middle of some-thing damn scary. I'm not going to tiptoe away just because you tell me to and leave you here to work yourself into a basket case."

"I'm not going to do that." She turned her face away. "I tend to tell you whatever comes into my head. I guess I should be more careful with that."

"That's a threat. Or at least a warning not to try to get too close. Why? If any two people should be close it's you and I. I won't be going anywhere, so get used to it." *Here it comes.* He braced himself to be told off.

"Sarah and I don't talk about it—about being children," Aurelie said. "Once or twice we've mentioned it and it's made us upset. It doesn't seem to matter how far away we get from all that, it's still painful. It all comes back."

Nick sat quietly. He couldn't know the right thing to say so he didn't say anything.

"Mrs. Harris lived upstairs. At the house where Sarah and I were from when we were really little until we left. She'd call us by banging on the floor with a stick."

"Mrs. Harris?"

"We think she was our grandmother, our dad's mother, only she said we had to call her Mrs. Harris. She wasn't always upstairs, just for the last five years after she got sick."

"I'm sorry," he said. "There must have been other people around."

Aurelie shook her head. "No. Mrs. Harris got our clothes out of a catalog. The groceries were delivered from the town. We went to school but we weren't allowed to say anything about Mrs. Harris or why we lived with her. We were only supposed to say she was our guardian if someone asked."

"Rellie—"

"I've got to get it out now. I always thought that if I ever did, it should be with Sarah, but I'm only telling you, and she has to make up her own mind if she ever wants to talk about it. It was in Oregon. On a cliff. We could look at the sea. The house used to be white but the paint mostly came off and Mrs. Harris didn't want anyone coming around any more than they had to, so it stayed that way. We looked after ourselves, and when she got really ill, we looked after her, too."

Nick glanced around the room. "No wonder this seems so special to you."

She hunched her shoulders. "I've been over it a long time now."

He barely stopped himself from arguing.

"We walked into town to school. Other kids made fun because our clothes were funny. Sort of old-fashioned. But they were good quality—at least to begin with. It got cold in winter because we didn't have proper things for the seasons. I think that's because Mrs. Harris didn't go anywhere, so she didn't think about it."

"Poor kids," Nick muttered.

"No, we were fine. We didn't go hungry."

Just short of about everything else a child needs. "That's good."

"When Mrs. Harris couldn't move much anymore, she stayed in her bed and we went up when she banged the floor. It was dark up there and we were afraid she'd be waiting somewhere and jump out at

201

us. Which was stupid because she could hardly move. She didn't complain, just said even less and asked for what she wanted. Soup. Tea."

"This is making me furious," he said, probably unwisely. "Someone should have been checking in on you. Where were your parents?"

"She said our mother led our father into bad ways—her term—and they did drugs and loved San Francisco and what she called the wild life. She said our mother died and our dad left us with her. He never came back. I think she was ashamed because our dad was her only child and she couldn't feel proud of him."

"So you girls had to suffer."

She wrinkled up her nose. "We did the wrong thing in the end. I can't make excuses, but we panicked. She didn't bang on the floor one night and eventually we crept up there. Mrs. Harris was asleep so we just went down again. We slept down there and everything."

Nick decided he had to let her find her own way from here on.

Aurelie looked at him, and away again. "We had a phone but it never rang. Mrs. Harris used it to call the grocery order in, is all. We kept picking it up in case she was talking, but she wasn't, not for two days. And she didn't bang on the floor. So we went up again. She was still asleep." She rubbed her face. "She hadn't moved since the last time."

"Did you touch her?" Nick asked quietly.

Aurelie shook her head. "We were too afraid. But we said her name and she didn't answer."

"She was dead."

"I suppose. But we didn't get help. We didn't get a doctor or anything. We could have gone to town and found someone. They would have helped her."

He wouldn't let himself ask the "why" question.

"Mrs. Harris said she was all we had and when something happened to her they'd put us in a home—probably separate homes. She wasn't mean about it, just making sure we were prepared."

Not mean?

"We knew about that from when we were real small." She found his hand and held it tightly. "Of course, I know what happened. Sarah and I both do. But we also know we were selfish in the end. We just wanted to get away and stay together. So we left. We left her there and made our way to San Francisco. There was money in the house and we took it and caught buses. We went to San Francisco because we thought we might be able to find our mom or dad."

He tried to hold her but she wouldn't let him. "You led a sheltered life. You were scared and you did the best you could. No one could have brought that woman back to life."

"No, but we could have shown some respect. Even if we called the operator and had them send someone. We could still have got away. But we wanted as much time as we could get before someone looked for us, so we just left, left her there like that."

"It was a long time ago."

Her grip on his hand got tighter. "But you don't get over wondering if you're flawed, Nick. If it came down to a choice, would you always save your own skin?"

"I know you well enough to remind you how much you care about other people. You couldn't help Mrs. Harris but you could try to help yourselves."

She nodded slowly. "I don't ever want to have to make that kind of decision again."

"You won't have to."

"How can you know that?"

"I do, that's all," he said. "I'm glad you told me. It explains some things."

She drew her bare feet onto the couch, sat cross-legged and gave him a record-breaking frown.

"What?" he asked.

"Just take care of yourself, Nick. And remember what I said about locking your doors properly."

He stared at her. "You know, you're manipulative. You're trying to manipulate me now. Why don't you tell me what you really want? You don't look ready to be here on your own to me."

"I got shaken up," she said. "But I'll be okay."

"We have to hang together or it'll be a whole lot tougher to make it through," Nick said.

"I know."

"Isn't that better than not having anyone to keep you company when you need it?"

"Of course it is. But I'm scared. There, I've said it, I'm absolutely freakin' terrified."

"Really?" He sat on his hands to stop himself from reaching for her again. "You sissy. Stiffen that back. Lift that chin—"

"Shut up before I jump you," she said.

"Promise?"

She let her head flop against the back of the couch and closed her eyes. Her throat jerked and, as he'd feared, tears coursed from beneath her lids.

"Don't, Rellie," he said quietly. "I'm only trying to lighten things up." Even if he did manage to pepper his comments with innuendo, dammit.

"That man thinks we've got something of his," she said. "It doesn't matter if we do or not, he's not sane. Sane people don't do what he did to me tonight. What am I saying? Of course he's not sane. Baily's dead and you know he did that, too. We're supposed to sit here and wait for him to figure out his next move."

"We're not doing that."

She looked at him. "We're not? How can you say that? Where is he? Does one person in this town have any idea where Colin is? Where he's hiding and watching us from? If we don't find his ruby, he's going to pick us off one by one. He's probably going to do it anyway because he can't afford to leave any witnesses behind."

"From what Matt said before he left, he's going to come up with a workable safety plan. More important, they're going to cast a net and catch Colin."

"I'm glad they're so sure of themselves."

Nick wanted her to feel just as sure.

"While you were with the doc, Matt, Buck and I made a few decisions. One of them was to involve the community. We've got able-bodied people who will gladly step forward on an invitation basis. We can't risk panic or we won't get anywhere."

"Sounds like you really are back on the friendly side with Matt," Aurelie said. "Or Matt and Buck want to keep you close."

He leaned closer. "Aren't you the cynic? You think my old friend has me pegged as a homicidal maniac and he's trying to get me to give myself away?"

"Guilty people often join in with searches for their own victims, or the killers of their own victims," Aurelie said.

"If I were a paranoid type I'd be getting jumpy."

"Thinking aloud, that's all I was doing," Aurelie said. "And I'm probably wrong."

"You could be right," Nick said. "But it would have been some feat for me to be attacking . . . I don't even want to talk about this anymore. You've made a good point."

"Forget I said it. Put it down to early legal training."

He inclined his head. "We'll beat this thing. As long as we're smart, we will."

"When you talk like that it seems possible," Aurelie said.

"It is. Believe it."

Nick reached for her hand again and she let him hold it. He hardly dared to hope she wouldn't pull it away again. "Listen. I'm not going to let anything happen to you, or to Delia or Sarah." He must give her confidence. As long as no mistakes were made, Colin wouldn't get to them except through him and a police department he trusted. "We've got Matt, Buck and as many other pros as we need on our side. We can call in extra help if we need it. This town isn't going to sit back and let this man scare people into hiding in their homes."

She squeezed his hand. "Matt will get in touch with the police on the West Coast," she said. "That's protocol."

"I don't think he'll follow protocol just yet. You know all too well how these cops are, they want to keep other agencies out of their jurisdiction for as long as possible."

"Maybe I'll stay in here and not go out until it's all over," Aurelie said.

Not such a bad idea. "I'm not Superman, but I'm close." He laughed, and so did she. "I can look after you."

"I've done a good job of looking after myself," she said. "I like it when a man opens a door for me, but if one doesn't show up I can do the job myself. Do you understand, Nick?"

He raised her hand to his mouth, keeping his eyes on hers, and rested her knuckles against his lips. "I understand you very well."

She didn't look away. "How are we going to cope? You and me? With each other?"

Nick turned her hand over and traced the lines on her palm. "There's always that, isn't there?"

"When we crossed the line, we made sure there always would be, yes." Her hair, completely dry, shone blue-black. "We could make a promise to put our personal issues aside until the crisis is over."

"Yes. And that's what you want to do?"

"I said we could do that," Aurelie said. "Or we could try."

"I don't want to." He couldn't help himself, he had to say it.

Aurelie stood, her hand still in his. "Then I'm scared for us."

Nick pulled her until she bent over him. He kept on pulling, raised his chin, watched her mouth come closer. She could choose to stop this anytime she felt like it.

Aurelie didn't feel like it. Their lips met, softly, then urgently, and she overbalanced onto his lap.

Nick's lap didn't offer a soft landing.

Stretching around to hold him irritated her wounds, but it didn't matter. Not now.

They kissed every way a man and woman could kiss, or so Aurelie thought until he showed her a few more variations.

Breathless, they fell, face-to-face, on the couch, their arms and bodies entwined and Nick stopping Aurelie from falling off. And he kissed her some more.

"We'd better stop," he said at last. "You're injured."

She pushed her face beneath his chin and nipped at the skin over his collarbone.

"Seriously, sweets, you're damaged."

Rising over him, she took his face in her hands. "Watch who you call damaged. Thanks to the good doctor, I'm not feeling much pain but I am feeling . . . strong. Do you feel strong?"

"Very strong."

"Think about this, Nick. If we mess up, really mess up, there won't be any picking up the pieces."

He pushed his fingers into her hair and held it back. "I think you're a dramatist."

That wasn't the answer she wanted. "So you believe we can fool around until you get bored, then go back to being pretend brother and sister?"

"Oh, no, I surely don't," he said. "I don't think that at all. I do think that if you don't go to bed now, on your own, and I don't get out of here, your new home is going to be the site of some serious sex."

As he suggested, keeping up the kidding around would only lead to one thing. She sat up beside him, turned away. It was up to her.

"Damn you," she said.

He ran a finger down her back. "What did I do to deserve that?"

Aurelie looked over her shoulder at him. The corners of his mouth turned up but his eyes were very serious. "Tread lightly," she told him.

"And carry a big stick?" he asked softly, his brows flickering upward in the middle. "I want to kiss you again."

No, he didn't, she thought, but he'd take whatever

he could get. She sighed and swiveled toward him again. He leaned to kiss her and put a hand on her breast.

Aurelie winced.

"Hey." Nick sat straight. He removed his hand from her breast. "That hurts?"

"I hit most things when I fell," she said.

He stopped her from getting up. "Show me."

"No!" She forced a laugh. "What a line."

Gently, he pulled up her T-shirt. The expression on his face changed from concern to anger. "I'll kill him," he said. "Anyone who would do that shouldn't be walking around."

Aurelie tugged the T-shirt from his fingers and he grimaced at her. "Sorry. I've got a temper, too. He's got to be stopped."

She settled her forehead on Nick's shoulder and he put his arms around her. "Do you want to stay tonight?" His stillness didn't surprise her. He hadn't expected her to make the moves.

"You know I do."

A jarring buzz sent them jumping away from each other. "It's the intercom," Aurelie said.

Nick blinked and cleared his throat. "I wouldn't have expected one here. I'm glad there is."

Aurelie went to the wall box and pressed a button. "Yes?"

"Rellie? For God's sake, open up. I can't find Nick anywhere."

Nick mouthed, "Sarah?"

She nodded and said, "Come up." She buzzed the door open and glanced around the room. It looked as if someone was moving in, nothing more.

Nick watched her, she felt it and looked at him. "This is not wrong," he said quietly.

Hoover roused himself and gave a halfhearted bark.

"It feels wrong," Aurelie said, listening for Sarah's footsteps on the stairs. "But you're right. What's taking her so long?"

Suddenly intensely anxious, Aurelie left the room and ran down to the open front door. The light at the bottom of the stairs cast a dull glow.

Aurelie put a hand to her stomach. "Sarah?" The door had clicked open and stood cracked, but that was all. "Sarah?" She threw open the door and hurried outside.

Sarah stood a few yards away looking at Nick's Audi. Aurelie couldn't see her face. "Nick's here," she said, her mouth dry. "He came to help me get my stuff upstairs."

"I didn't see his car when I drove in," Sarah said in a tight little voice. "Your Hummer hid it."

"Hey, Sarah," Nick said, jogging to join them.

"You said you were going home," Sarah said.

"I intended to," he said. "I ended up at the cop shop instead. It's been quite a night. You'd better come inside and hear all the news."

"Oh, Nick." Surging toward him, Sarah hugged Nick. "Thank God you're okay. I went to Oakdale and I was so scared when you weren't there." She pressed her lips to his cheek and closed her eyes.

20

"She's avoiding us," Aurelie said of Delia. "I'm not imagining that, am I?"

"No," Nick said. "And her timing couldn't be worse."

"You mean time's running out, don't you?" Aurelie said, walking beside him through Place Lafource, heading for the conservatory and the pool area beyond.

Nick had to be tired. Aurelie's eyes felt gritty and she couldn't get Sarah, or the hours of talk the three of them had shared, out of her head. After that, the night had been short before Nick returned to pick her up again. She was grateful Sarah had opted to sleep in rather than face another potential confrontation with Delia first thing this morning.

"Keep your voice down," Nick said. They stepped into the misty, palm-filled conservatory.

Aurelie's irritation got away from her. "It is down. He didn't give me the hour, but by my figuring, we've got three days and two nights before that rotten man figures out another way to get at one of us."

"Where the hell is she?" Nick asked. In daylight, the pool was clearly visible from the windows. "Sabine said she'd gone out there. I don't see any chairs. I don't see Delia."

"Did you hear what I said?" Aurelie asked.

Nick leaned on a copper window frame. "Yes, I

heard. And I shouldn't feel mad at you, but I feel mad at everyone, including you. Nothing's moving fast enough, and it's got to. I'm not waiting around for other people to act anymore."

His phone rang and he looked at the readout before excusing himself and walking away through the palms.

Aurelie listened. Why should he think she'd shut her ears just because he signaled the call was private?

The "Yes, yes, thanks. I got your message. Thanks for getting back to me again. Okay, see you then," didn't give any clues about either the caller or the reason for the call. Funny how she'd almost stopped factoring in the ordinary matters of life. She expected any conversation to be significant.

Nick came back. He looked at her intently, so much so that she almost turned away. "Quit worrying," he told her. "And I don't mean I think you can shut everything off, but victims are just that. You're no victim. Not one of us is a victim."

"I know," she said. "But wouldn't it be great if all of this would just go away?"

"No," he said. "My mother was murdered. That doesn't get to go away. Plus, it can't suddenly be a coincidence that unwanted company arrived in Pointe Judah not even three weeks after the grave was found."

"I'm sorry, Nick."

"No, I am." He looked at her face, then did a quick study of her feet and back. "Even when you're tired you look great. I resent not being able to concentrate on you."

Aurelie took in a shaky breath. "Don't say that."

"Why not? It's true." The corners of his mouth turned up and she got a shadowed blue stare. "I knew a long time ago that I wouldn't be able to keep on pretending with you. Thank God I don't have to anymore. You know how I feel, and you know what I'm thinking right now, just looking at you."

She ought to be slicker than she was, more ready with a comeback, but anything she said would probably give her away. Wanting him consumed her.

"Don't you have anything to say?" he asked softly. "How long are you going to make me wait?"

"Wait?"

"Before we can stop playing brother and sister."

If she could look at him without wanting to kiss him, it would help. Learning to dislike him would be even better. But everything about Nick made her ache with longing.

"Aurelie?"

"You're going too fast for me," she said.

"Sixteen, almost seventeen years is fast?"

She wouldn't tell him, but it felt as if they'd always been together. This was a scary time, being afraid to let things happen with them when they'd already gone too far to turn back.

Seeing Sarah look at Nick as she had in the night had buckled Aurelie's confidence in being able to cope with the situation. She and Nick hadn't discussed it, but he must know, he must have felt Sarah's reactions to him. And if she had seen the moment when Sarah wondered what he was doing at Aurelie's apartment when he had supposedly gone home, then so had he. Any suspicion had been neatly snuffed out when Nick explained the events of the night, but Aurelie didn't want to repeat the experience.

"Are you working today?" he asked.

"Yes. I'm looking forward to it. It gets too busy for me to think about anything but making sure merchandise that still belongs to us stays in the store."

"Shoplifting?"

"Not a lot, but enough."

"What time do you get off?"

Nick's unflinching look made it impossible for her to concentrate on avoiding the question.

"Around six," she said.

"I'll pick you up."

"Nick—"

"How many times have you been running since you got back?"

She frowned. "I . . . haven't. It's been busy, Nick."

"We'll run late this afternoon. It'll be good for both of us. We'll have to take it easy because of—" He waved a hand toward her. "I don't want you to do more than you should."

She could fight him now or fight him later. Later sounded better.

Early sun through a window caught the face on his

black watch. His forearms were strongly muscled, his hands broad and capable in appearance. Nick's skin had a permanent tan, and his presence felt solid, rugged. He was a physically big man but his very presence took up a lot of space. Aurelie smiled at him and he raised an eyebrow in question.

"I was thinking you don't change a lot," she said, caught off guard. "You're bigger, stronger, more mature . . . maybe even smarter, although you must have been brilliant all along. You used to tell us you were." She had to grin. "But you're comfortable with yourself. You were confident even when I first knew you and I like that."

"Thanks. I think," he said. But he returned her smile. "Hmm. You don't change, either. And you're more mature, I guess. I'm not ready to commit myself on the other stuff."

She'd have to think about that—later. "So, what do we do about Delia? She isn't out there but she must have told Sabine to say she was."

"Which means she's definitely avoiding us," Nick said. "Which means we're definitely going to track her down."

He opened a door and stepped outside. Aurelie followed. A walk past rose beds and well-tended shrubs led straight to the pool where a white marble wall surrounded turquoise water. A disturbing fountain, a Minotaur wound about with sinuous snakes, gushed water in the center, and urns built into the wall spilled flowers in full bloom.

The only human in sight was Ed Webb, who waved and went back to cleaning the pool.

"This is a waste of time," Nick said. "The cabana's all closed up, too."

Delia liked the doors in the low stone pool building to stand open so diaphanous curtains the color of the water could billow. Shocking-purple bougainvillea loaded the tile roof and made an unreal contrast to the white walls.

"Just a minute," Aurelie said. She sprinted away from Nick and around the pool to the nearest cabana door, which she opened. A look inside proved her hunch. Delia's auburn hair showed above the back of a white wicker chaise.

Chairs, sofas and chaises stood in groups. Showers and changing rooms occupied a twin wing of the cabana.

Aurelie stuck her head back through the door and waved at Nick. She beckoned for him to come.

"You found me," Delia said, not turning around. "I knew it was too much to hope you wouldn't."

"Hi, Delia," Aurelie said. Nick arrived and she rolled her eyes at him. "Nick and I make a special trip to spend time with you and look what we get. You try not to see us."

Nick closed the door behind them and put a hand on Aurelie's shoulder to steer her across the long room. "Hey, Delia. Did you have breakfast yet?"

"Hours ago," she said, raising an arm straight up and wiggling her fingers at them. "I'm not trying to avoid you. Even iron ladies need refuge from time to time."

Sticking close together, Nick and Aurelie skirted the chaise and pulled up chairs. "We've got some questions for you," Nick said and Aurelie heard how he hurried the words out.

A simple pink blouse and jeans were unusual garb for Delia. Her makeup was as ever—perfect—and her hair glorious. "I didn't think you were coming to tell me how much you love me," she said. "I've got a question or two of my own."

Delia chuckled, and her serious expression was transformed—only to dissolve into horror. "My God, Aurelie. Your face. Your face! What's happened?"

"I was attacked by a man. Last night outside this house."

Delia's hands fluttered. "Why didn't I know this before now? Oh, my poor girl."

"I'm going to be all right," Aurelie said. "It's superficial, but—"

"But we need to fill you in," Nick said and told her the entire story, including everything that had been said to Matt. "I think we'll all feel better now," he finished.

"Yes," Delia said, subdued. "I'm glad they insisted on the doctor, Aurelie. I suppose you've already had to give up the briefcase, Nick. Did you get a chance to look at whatever Baily was experimenting with?"

Nick gave her a half smile. Growing up with the highly competitive Boards would have taught Delia the art of quick recovery and early attack. "I looked," he said. "Simple stuff really and she wasn't very far along with it. Remember the formula we decided we'd call WB Forever Forty?"

Aurelie looked blank.

"An old idea," Nick said to her. "A bit like the stuff you can use on cracked china to fill in the crazes, only this fills in skin lines. We think our product is going to be very successful. Apparently, Baily was taking it apart so she could put it back together. I assume under another label and with a few tweaks."

"Like filling in china cracks?" Aurelie said, wrinkling her nose. "You're kidding? What happens when the person moves her face?"

Nick rested a hand on top of his head and grinned at her. "The skin doesn't fall apart again, if that's what you're thinking. The formula works well."

"It's Nick's baby," Delia said speculatively. "I wonder if that made it even more appealing for Baily to rip off."

Aurelie felt sorry for Nick. "Sounds to me as if she knew a good thing when she saw it and it wouldn't have mattered who invented it."

"Thank you for that," Nick said. She touched him in so many ways, big and little. And even if she thought she didn't, she showed she cared about him.

Delia didn't seem convinced. "If she was stealing for someone else, it could have had something to do with her death."

"You're looking for escape hatches," Nick said,

knowing just how she felt. "I've told Matt Boudreaux about it and it's duly noted."

"WB Forever Forty?" Aurelie gave him one of her puzzled squints. "That's what you're going to call it? It's awful."

"The idea—" he told her patiently "—and we weren't serious about the name—was that for the older women the thought of never looking a day over forty would be appealing.

"Delia, let's get back to the main topic. I know I haven't pushed you on this, but I've got to now. With the letter my mother sent for me, there was one for you, as well. That wasn't with mine in the safe, was it?"

Delia's high cheekbones flamed. She shook her head, no, lowered her eyelashes and gave a shuddering sigh. "I should have taken the three of you out of the country back then. I could have married that man with a villa outside Rome—he just about had his own army, you know—and you'd have had private tutors. I could have run the business from there and none of this would ever have become an issue."

Nick looked at Aurelie. She leaned forward in her chair and said, "You hated the Roman and so did we. You said he wanted your money, I remember that clearly."

"Rubbish," Delia said. "He had plenty of money."

"Could we get our feet back on earth?" Nick said. "You can't hide three people forever. Concentrate on the letter. You didn't say what was in it but you must have read it. Mom asked you some things, didn't she? Like whether or not you could take in three kids you'd never seen before?"

"I would have done anything she asked of me," Delia said. "She had a horrible time of it but she never felt sorry for herself."

Nick's gut contracted. "You said you'd tell me about her life when the time was right. You still haven't done that. But . . . " He couldn't allow himself to be diverted again. "We need that letter to you from my mother. With the other one missing, it's all we've got and there could be a clue in it." And he wanted to read it anyway, to see his mother's writing and imagine what she'd been thinking when she sent them off that evening.

"I don't see how it could help," Delia said. "There aren't any clues. Let's not go there now."

She was threatened, and frightened.

"Hey," Nick said, furious with himself for being so damn clumsy. "This is important for all of us. I'm looking for a way to protect the family."

"I've always protected us," Delia said. "It's my job."

"For God's sake," Nick said. "The three of us have been adults for a long time. It's our turn to look after you."

"Don't you raise your voice to me," Delia said. "I'm not a doddering old fool and I don't need to be looked after. People who have worked with me for years would be amazed by that suggestion."

Aurelie couldn't stand watching this. "Delia, we love you. You gave up so much for us."

"No, I didn't," Delia snapped. "Everything I did was selfish. I did it for myself because I wanted you and I'm going to keep on doing it, so you can all settle down. I've already taken the necessary steps to ensure that creature doesn't get near any of you again. I was going to speak with you about it today and I will. I still have a few details to clear up. It's going to be necessary for all of you to move into this house for the present."

Nick slumped in his chair, rested his head against the back and closed his eyes.

"Before everything explodes," Aurelie said. "And that's going to happen real soon. But before it does, I've got to tell you something. Delia, you're the only mother Sarah and I have ever known. We wouldn't choose another one, either, so we think we're blessed that you took us in."

Delia turned to her. "You never told me that before." Moisture welled along her lashes.

"Sarah and I try not to think about the past." She glanced at Nick. "Before we were with Mary, I mean. I doubt if we ever will—that's probably why we've never mentioned not having a mother."

Nick had raised his head. "Everyone has a mother, Rellie."

"Everyone is born," she said with a faint smile. "Let's leave it at that. I just want you to know how much you mean to me, Delia."

Delia patted her mouth with trembling fingertips and Aurelie popped up to plant a quick kiss on her forehead.

"I'd like to read the letter Mom sent to you," Nick said.

His attitude annoyed Aurelie. Just because he was uncomfortable witnessing emotion shouldn't mean he had to sound angry.

"As you've said, the letter was to me." Delia pulled a silk cushion from behind her back and put it on her lap. She pulled at crushed tassels.

"If you don't want to actually let me see it, tell me what's in it."

"I got it a long time ago," Delia said. "I don't remember."

Now Nick was convinced he had to pursue this with her. He couldn't imagine what, but she was hiding something. "You're a busy woman," he said. "I don't expect you to remember every word of a letter from sixteen years ago, but apart from asking if you could look after us, was there anything that could be helpful to us now? Did she talk about Colin? Maybe he'd discussed some plans for the future as if she'd be sharing them with him, or . . . What about the bag that's got sand in it now? What was in it before? Did she say?"

Delia got up, sending the pillow sliding over the marble floor. "I don't remember, I tell you. Please don't talk about it anymore. If I decide I want to, I'll let you know."

Nick stood, as well. He hadn't known what to

expect but this exact scenario hadn't even entered his mind. "You're hiding something. What? Please, don't do this if there's something that could make a difference, a good difference."

"It couldn't," she said, backing away, bumping into a chair.

"Stop it, Nick," Aurelie said, on her feet and going to Delia. "If Delia had information that would help us, we'd already have it."

He'd like to believe that, Nick thought. Delia's behavior in the past few minutes made it unlikely in his mind, but some of Aurelie's instincts were right. He had been forceful enough, for now, and needed to ease off. "I'm sorry," he said. "Forgive me. I'm frustrated."

She didn't answer.

"Forget what I said about the letter. If you ever feel like sharing it, you will."

"I want the three of you back in this house by tonight," Delia said, her voice small.

"Did you come up with that idea all on your own?" Nick asked.

The cautious look Delia gave him answered his question.

"You didn't, did you?"

"I can't take any risks with your safety, don't you understand that?" Delia asked. She had stopped moving away. "Whatever I'm doing, I've thought through."

"Including going to Finn Duhon and asking him to help you find professional protection?"

Aurelie caught at Nick's arm. "What are you

talking about? You sound wild. What about Finn Duhon?"

"I like Finn," Delia said. "I knew him when his father Tom was still chief of police here. And I was glad when he came back to Pointe Judah to live again. He and Emma are a real asset to the town."

Nick could see that Aurelie wanted more explanations. "Finn is a former Ranger with a reputation as a tough man," he said. "A hero."

"He owns Oakdale," Aurelie said. "I know who he is. He's great. Did you forget Emma owns Poke Around? I see her when she comes in to the store, and Finn shows up occasionally. What do they have to do with anything?"

"Delia decided Finn's the one to make sure we keep on breathing. And bring Colin to justice, I guess—or kill him and put us all out of our misery."

"Did Finn contact you?" Delia asked Nick. "Did he call and tell you that I'm asking him to help? Why would he do that?"

"Yes, he did. For two reasons," Nick said. "The request sounds damned odd and he wanted to be sure you were okay, not under excessive strain or anything. After that he didn't have any choice but to explain—at least as much as he's got anyway. Why didn't you come to me first? How do you think I feel that you consider another man more capable of looking after you than I am?"

"For the second time," Delia said, "I don't need anyone to look after me."

"Stop it," Aurelie said, planting her hands on her

hips. "What we need is to take care of ourselves, all of us. I don't blame you for hating the idea of someone you know, a peer, being asked to babysit you," she told Nick. "But can we calm down? We won't get anything done this way."

Nick smiled. Aurelie had that effect on him, especially when she showed her take-charge side. "Yes," he said. "You're right. Sorry, Delia."

"I've made a lot of mistakes," she said quietly. "Lots of them. But mostly because I wanted the best for everyone."

Aurelie created her own diversion by going after the cushion that fell when Delia had stood up. Right here, between the three of them, something was cracking apart. Aurelie wanted to head the whole thing off if it couldn't be fixed afterward.

"You deserve an apology from me," Delia said. "More than one, but one will do. Where's Sarah?"

"At her place," Aurelie said.

Delia picked up a phone from a nearby table and dialed. She didn't wait long before she said, "Good morning, Sarah. Please meet me in my rooms . . . Now. Nick and Aurelie are already here." She gazed into the distance, flinching once before she said, "You can't hide from what's going on. You can't stay in bed and hope a killer dies of a hangnail by the time you get up. We'll see you in a few minutes."

This was no hot-chocolate-and-cookies invitation to Delia's pink, green and lavender boudoir, the room

226

which, like her bedroom, she had kept as it was in the late 1800s when a Mrs. Lafource, wife of Colonel Lafource, actually lived in the house and these had been her rooms. Today's visit to Delia's faithfully refurbished lair felt like a court appearance with a lot of doubt about who the accused might be.

Delia stood beside an empty, white bamboo bird-cage where her beloved parakeet, Yuri, lived when he wasn't taking long baths in his mistress's claw-foot tub. Aurelie could hear voices coming from the bathroom, one was Yuri's delivered with a heavy Russian accent (the bird had been a gift to Delia from an admiring Russian playboy who'd trained him to talk), and the second voice, Sabine's, her rich tones punctuated with laughter.

"Yuri is taking a bath," Delia said as if this was news. She waved a hand toward the bathroom. "He needs lots of attention, lots of games. Sit down. Sarah shouldn't be long." She turned away and raised a lace drape from a window set into an alcove.

White silk draperies tinted a shell-pink looped above the curved top of the window and fell on either side to settle in soft heaps on pale green carpet. The same fabric, supported by gilded cherubs, formed soft puffs over a mahogany daybed.

Aurelie never quite got used to the opulence in these rooms but she did understand why Delia had wanted to preserve a little piece of history. "Did Sarah say she was coming right over?" If she had, she should have arrived.

"More or less."

Aurelie looked at Nick, who had also remained standing. "I hope she gets here soon," he said. "I've got meetings all day. So do both of you—or at least you've got things to do other than wait around for Sarah."

"I hear my name," Sarah said, walking in and going directly to the daybed, where she flopped down on lavender velvet pillows and hauled up her feet, without removing her sandals. "Okay, Delia, here I am. What's so important?"

Nick strolled to the daybed, pulled off Sarah's sandals and deposited them on the floor.

"Thanks," she said with a sweet smile.

He nodded and his attention wandered back to Aurelie—again. She wore a deep green sundress that fitted snugly over her breasts and showed off a small waist. The full skirt swirled around her knees when she walked. Her black hair was pulled back again, which he didn't like, but plenty of curls had already wiggled free.

"Why are you staring at Aurelie, Nick?" Sarah said, jarring him. She rushed on and when she bent her head back, Aurelie knew she was watching their old trick to hide tears. Sarah looked at them again. "You two have turned into the Bobbsey Twins. 'Wherever you go, I go.' Isn't that the way the song goes?"

No one answered.

Sarah pointed. "You look guilty, Rellie. Is this meeting about you? What have you done—apart from getting your face messed up?"

Aurelie said, "No, it's not about me," and picked up a book on New Orleans's monuments. She didn't want Sarah to see her blush. Sarah wasn't mean, she didn't say cruel things the way she just had.

"The only one who *did* anything is me," Delia said. She opened a door on a tall cabinet, revealing small drawers inside. "I made a mistake because I didn't think before I acted on something I'll regret forever."

Sarah frowned. She folded her arms across her middle, bare between a black cotton blouse with the tails tied up and a pair of low-slung denim cutoffs.

"Yesterday I wrote down everything I could remember. I shouldn't have had to." Delia pulled out a drawer and took out an unfolded sheet of paper. This she carried with her to a spot by the window.

"Colin Fox started The Refuge and seemed to care about people in need. Mary already had you, Nick, when she met Colin. On Haight Street. You were three and she was making her way as best she could. In San Francisco, as you know. Colin must have fallen for Mary—no surprise there—and the three of you went on together."

He hadn't known he was three before his mother got involved with Colin.

Yuri shouted something Aurelie didn't understand and she heard the bathroom door open. Sabine, smiling and holding the purple-headed bird in both hands, came into the boudoir. She stopped when she saw all of them.

"I'll pop this boy in his house and go make coffee," she said.

"No coffee for me, thanks," Aurelie said.

"Not for any of us now, thank you, Sabine," Delia said.

Sabine looked briefly at each of their faces and her smile faded. "Okay, Mr. Yuri, playtime is over for you." She approached the cage and Nick opened it for her. In went Yuri and Nick closed the cage.

"It's none of my business," Sabine started, "but—"

"Don't worry about us," Delia said. "This is just a family summit. Everything's fine."

"Summit, hmm?" Sabine said. "From what I know, those are when a whole lot of talkin' goes on and nothin' gets done."

Sarah laughed, too loudly and too long. They were all nervous, Aurelie realized and wished she could comfort her sister. She was hurting. She had begun to piece together, or at least to suspect, that there was more than simple friendship between Aurelie and Nick.

Yuri squawked and opened his beak to make a clicking sound. Then he said, clearly, and with strongly Russian overtones, "Come to your sexy *Psittacula cyanocephala*" over and over until Delia threw a velvet cloth over his cage.

"I wish he'd forget the name of his species. What a silly thing to teach a bird." Slightly pink in the face, she added, "It doesn't take him long to move on from purple-headed parakeet to . . . well, you can guess. He does get rude."

Sabine grinned and left the room.

Nobody laughed at the bird.

"I can't deal with this," Delia said abruptly. She crumpled the piece of paper. "I didn't show you the letter because I didn't want you to read it. I was afraid it could make you feel too independent. We became a family and I wanted us to stay that way." She fumbled with a box of tissues.

Nick couldn't look at anyone. He bowed his head.

"Mary provided for you. She sent that . . . that *thing* for me to sell. She said it was worth a fortune and I should sell it and use the money to bring you up. Mary said if you were old enough, Nick, you'd find out how and make sure it got done. She believed in you absolutely. But we didn't need it. I had plenty and anyway, it's been stolen now. There, now I've told you and you'll be furious with me."

Thing? "You mean what Mom sent in that bag, don't you? And now it's been stolen. I'm not furious. It wasn't your fault it was stolen."

"Yes, it was. That ruby was in the bag—or that's what Mary said. I never looked at it. If I'd sold the stone like Mary asked me to, it wouldn't have been there to steal. But that's not what I meant."

Sarah propelled herself from the daybed. She went to Delia and pulled her into a hug. "It doesn't matter," she said. "You couldn't do anything to make us mad at you."

Despite the way his spine prickled, Nick smiled. Among the three of them, Sarah was the spontaneous one and this was a moment when he was glad for it.

Delia hugged Sarah back. "Mary wrote that It was a Burmese pigeon's blood ruby called— Oh, I knew I wouldn't forget the name, but I think I have."

"It's in the letter, isn't it?" Nick asked. He wouldn't give a shit about any ruby, only this one could have brought major trouble to town.

"I think it was Yama Dharma. Nicknamed the Vulture Ruby. A king once bought his life with it. Some horrible people were going to kill him."

Aurelie realized her mouth was open and shut it. She turned to Nick. "Do you understand any of this?"

"Only that my mother sent that envelope with us, and the letters and the small package were inside. I guess there was a ruby in it and now it's been stolen. With any luck it was stolen by Colin and now he'll get lost and leave us alone."

She nodded, then shook her head, no. "Nick, think, if—"

"I already am thinking. You were attacked after the robbery, which means someone who was after the ruby didn't get it. If that's what the guy wanted. That letter is really important, Delia."

Delia broke free of Sarah's embrace and sat down hard on an upholstered bench. "Let me finish, please. I didn't have the right to sell that ruby because it wasn't Mary's. Any more than it was that Colin's. Who knows where it came from, but someone stole it. They must have. Of course I didn't want any money to care for you, but I wasn't going to sell a stolen ruby worth millions anyway."

"Millions?" Nick and Aurelie said together.

"That's what Mary wrote. I can't remember how many carats she said it was, but it was hundreds. And there's a story about a thief and a vulture—what that man told you about, I think, Aurelie, but I didn't read it closely. It frightened me."

Nick held out his hand. "Let me read it, please, Delia."

She threw the ball of paper on the floor. "That's just where I tried to make a list of what I remembered from Mary's letter. I burned that years ago."

21

The first scream broke the silence in Delia's rooms.

Someone screamed again, a woman, the sound soaring upward from somewhere in the grounds behind the house.

Delia turned to look outside, but Nick moved her aside and threw the window all the way open. He couldn't see anything unusual, but another scream sounded and this time complete panic raised it higher.

Running, he left the suite and took the stairs down to the first floor several at a time—and cannonballed into Betty Valenti on her way in from scrubbing the front steps. Her bucket of water upended on the wooden hall floor, but she left it and pushed him toward the passageway leading to the rooms at the back of the house.

"You heard it," she said, even as the noise came once more. "Go, go, Mr. Nick."

He went, aware in some small area of his brain that at least he wouldn't find Aurelie, Sarah or Delia when he reached the terrified-sounding woman.

Betty wasn't far behind him when he took a side door out of the house and skidded to a halt on a path. The screams had stopped, replaced by desperate cries for help.

"At the back," he said and ran on, hearing more sets of footfalls behind him. He knew at least Aurelie and Sarah must be following.

Aurelie shouted, "The pool, Nick," and he went in that direction, leaping over flower beds and scrunching across expanses of crushed rock until he saw first the white marble wall, then the turquoise waters of the pool.

"I don't see anything," he called, hurdling a low hedge and throwing out his arms to steady his balance.

But then he did.

In the pool, water up to her raised chin, stood Sabine. Even at a distance he could see wildness in her eyes.

"Hold on, Sabine," he shouted. "I'll be right there."

"She can't swim!" Aurelie's voice was breathless. "Hurry."

He kicked off his shoes as he went and put one hand on the wall to vault into the water.

"There's blood, Nick," Aurelie shouted. "There's blood on the wall here."

"It's okay," he said to Sabine, keeping his attention on her face, willing her to look at him while he waded toward her where she stood as far out as she could get without swimming. "You're all right. You're safe now."

She looked back at him, then away, toward the fountain.

Nick reached her and put an arm around her waist. He pulled her backward until her shoulders were clear of the water.

Tears ran down her already wet face. She grabbed him and he felt her shake. "Ed," she said, her voice scratchy and breaking. "Get Ed." And she pointed.

Nick looked over his shoulder, then turned around, taking his arm from Sabine as he did so. He kicked off from the bottom and swam, cursing the clothes that weighed him down.

On the fountain, suspended by the head of a stone snake snagged through a hole in the back of his work shirt, hung Ed Webb.

22

Police and quickly assembled volunteers had started searching the grounds. Matt Boudreaux, his hands clasped behind his back, stood in the middle of the kitchen, waiting to get into the quarters where a doctor and a team of medics were attending to Ed.

Ed had insisted that although he was woozy, he didn't need to be hospitalized and Sabine backed him up.

"Broad daylight," Nick said, and started to pace. "How does a man get attacked in broad daylight and hung on a goddamn fountain in the middle of a pool?"

"Once they let us talk to him we intend to find out," Matt said.

"He's not in such bad shape," Nick said. "When I first saw him, I thought he was dead, but we should be able to talk to him shortly."

"*I'll* be able to question him," Matt said abruptly.

After an uncomfortable silence, Nick said, "Back off, Matt. Don't take it out on me because you haven't gotten anywhere with this case." His own talk of thawing relations with Matt had been premature.

Matt's face set. He looked toward the door leading to the area where Ed and Sabine were staying. "They never used to live here," he said. "Why are they here now?"

"My domestic arrangements are none of your business," Delia said. To this point she had sat quietly at the kitchen table with Aurelie and Sarah.

Matt's chest expanded. "Everything to do with the ongoing investigation is my business, ma'am. The question was simple enough. And I think you've been cagey enough up to now, don't you? Without Aurelie's nasty experience you'd still be keepin' the truth from me. You all would."

"Well, we're not, and I can't imagine what's wrong with you," Delia said. "I don't like your attitude."

Aurelie almost groaned aloud.

"I regret that," Matt said. "I have a job to do and decisions to make. I intend to do both in whatever way I think will be best."

"Are you still expecting a meeting with us later?" Nick asked. He couldn't guess why, but Matt seemed to be erecting another frosty screen.

"I don't see any point," he said. "I'm going to hope you quit holdin' back information and let me know if there's somethin' you figure I should know. So far you've shown that you'll open up when you feel like it. You've been hindering this investigation." He looked from one to the other of them. "I believe you're good people but you've been misguided over this."

"You talked about getting some trusted local people together to discuss a plan," Nick said.

"The plan's been made. The fewer involved, the better—the easier to be sure who knows what."

"That's just plain nasty," Sarah said, surprising the rest of them. "I don't know what put a bug up your ass, Matt Boudreaux, but you're going to regret it."

Nick hid a grin. The un-Sarahlike comment was more effective for its shock value.

Matt ignored her. "We'll be finished with the lab by later today," he said. "Feel free to go back in there, then."

Buck Dupiere knocked on the door from outside into the kitchen and came in.

"Glad you could finally join us," Matt said. Apparently there was enough nastiness to spread around.

Buck nodded and said, "Good mornin', all. I've been with the team in the grounds. Nothin', Matt. We took it inch by inch around the pool and worked away. Not a thing."

Matt frowned. "Thanks," he said. "We'll go into it all again later."

Buck nodded. He turned to Sarah and said, "Someone said you're a cyclist."

"Yes." Sarah looked uncertain. "Or I used to be. I don't get much chance anymore."

"Me, too," Buck said. "How about a ride? Company is good."

She cleared her throat. "That would be nice."

Aurelie smiled. Buck was quite the hunk and a nice, intelligent guy. He and Sarah could make a good pair. She looked away. If Sarah had another man in her life, Aurelie wouldn't feel so guilty over her feelings for Nick.

Three medics tromped through the kitchen carrying their equipment and left by the back door. The doctor came a few moments later and smiled at Aurelie. She'd been surprised to see Mitch Halpern again.

"How's that face?" he asked. "Apart from beautiful."

She smiled, couldn't help it. "Mending fast. You're all over the place, Doctor."

"Call it what it is, shortage of medical personnel. Not that I mind. Busy is good by me." He hesitated and said, "I'd like to have a few words with all of you before I go."

"Could it wait?" Matt asked.

"I don't think so," Mitch said. He pulled out a chair and sat sideways to the table. "I ought to check you out, Aurelie. We don't want any infection setting in. And don't forget, you need another shot in a few days."

"I won't forget," she said, feeling slightly warm. "Really, I think everything's clean and healing up—thanks to you."

He fixed her with his interesting hazel eyes. "Okay, but I'll see you at the clinic."

She smiled at him and he smiled back, slowly and with the kind of warm sincerity guaranteed to speed a woman's heart.

"What's on your mind, Doc?" Nick asked.

He was jealous of any attention she got, Aurelie thought, not without some satisfaction.

"If Sabine Webb hadn't gone out to take her husband a drink, do you think he'd have been found even now?"

"I should think so," Matt said.

"I wouldn't," Delia said. "It's a good thing she does go out to him midmorning. Poor Ed. He's gentle and quiet. Those are the people others victimize. Disgusting."

"He's got a story to tell," Mitch said. "The man who attacked him thinks he's got something that doesn't belong to him. Ed's not sure what it is except it's supposed to be worth a lot. The guy said he saw Ed with it."

Nick almost brought up the ruby but stopped in time. He wasn't about to make a fool of himself with a story he couldn't back up with anything but hearsay.

Matt had crossed his arms. "Did it strike you to make sure one of us was there while Webb was spilling his guts, Doc?"

"Call me Mitch." He looked amused. "No, it didn't. He talked while I was examining him and he's had a shock. Sometimes people talk a lot when they're shocked. I'm telling you what he said now, doesn't that work?"

"Were the medics there?"

"Yes," Mitch said.

Buck hooked his thumbs over his belt and got really interested in tubs of growing sprouts on the windowsill.

"If that's all," Matt said to the doctor, "I'll just ask you to keep what you've heard to yourself. Thanks for coming."

Mitch stood up, all expression wiped from his face. "Ed also mentioned having a bag put over his head. You've got big trouble here, Officer." He glanced at Aurelie and frowned. "Two victims of criminal attacks on the grounds of this house. Seems to me you have a pretty contained crime scene."

"Meaning?" Matt asked, bristling.

"Whatever you think it ought to mean," Mitch said. "I hope I don't see a third patient with the same story. Or worse, a third patient who can't tell the story."

"There was Baily already," Delia said, ignoring the

looks she got. "She couldn't tell her story. And that didn't happen at Place Lafource."

"No," Mitch said with a polite smile. He said, "See you in a few days," to Aurelie and left—walking through the house toward the front door.

"Thank you, Mitch," Delia said. Her mouth settled in a hard line.

"Could Baily's death have been an accident?" Aurelie asked once the doctor had left. "I don't see how we can connect it to the things that have happened here."

"It's not your job to connect anything," Matt said. "The main thing we have here is the time frame. And those labs belong to the Boards just like this house does. And unless Baily knocked herself flat on the roof of that building then got up and went over the side—hard to figure out why she'd do that—someone else did. And someone else hit the backs of her knees hard enough to send her into the parapet and over the edge."

This was the first Nick had heard about Baily having an accident on the roof before the fatal fall. "How do you know all this? About Baily falling down on the roof first?"

"Rocks embedded in the back of her head matched the ones on the roof," Matt said. "She had bruises across her sternum, consistent with a good push from spread fingers. Spread fingers of a good-size hand. We're not sure what he hit the backs of her knees with, but it did the job."

Aurelie's hand went to her own sternum, where bruises stung to the touch.

"You're sure all this couldn't have happened when she hit the ground below?" Nick asked. "Her body was twisted up and there was gravel around. Gravel shifts. It makes sense that there would be some of it in the rose beds."

"That's not what was in her scalp and hair," Matt said. "The bruises were made when her heart was still pumping good and hard. The amount of bleeding under the skin proves that. If any of them had happened within seconds of death, or after death, any bruising would be much fainter, or almost nonexistent."

"Makes sense," Nick said, wishing it didn't.

Aurelie's hand went to her throat. "Nick, that man pushed—"

"We noticed," Matt said. "You've got bruises in the same place on your chest as Baily did. So does Ed."

The way the man had jabbed his fingers into her had felt not just painful but insolent, dismissive.

"Why are you angry with us?" Aurelie asked Matt.

"Because he hasn't got anything," Nick said. "All the bruises and gravel don't mean shit without a suspect."

Matt gave him the kind of look friends didn't use on friends. "We're confident on this case, Nick. And Delia, we'll need to go over your study today, and the grounds just outside. The thief probably got in through your French doors. I hope you didn't tamper with them too much."

Delia pinched her lips together.

Buck went to the sink and poured a glass of water from the faucet. He drank it down. "It's too bad about the doc and the medics hearing what Ed had to say," he said. "Now we've got what should be private—"

"Yeah." Matt cut Buck off and gave all of his attention to the rest of them. "I'm going to impress on them what I want you people to remember. Anything you've heard, anything you know about this case doesn't get spread around."

"You don't even have to say it," Nick said.

"Good. I'd also prefer to know where I can find you. Don't leave town, please."

Delia surged to her feet.

"Leave it," Nick told her. "We're all on edge."

"I'm not on edge," Matt said. "Just doing my job. We won't need you anymore right now. When we're through with Ed we'll let ourselves out. Expect to hear from us."

23

Nick pulled the Audi into his carport. A few hours could change a lot of things, a man's mind for one thing. The confrontation with Matt had caught him off guard, but he had already rethought how he intended to handle dealing with Colin Fox. The first step would be to draw him out. Then he had to be tricked into making a mistake. When that happened, Nick would be ready.

Going into the lab that afternoon, after several days' absence, had felt spookier than he'd expected. He had looked out of his windows at the rose beds where Baily had died. Bunches of flowers had been left on the ground and several staff members stood around, apparently in silence. He thought back over his brief relationship with Baily. Outside work, music was her passion and she could be fun, but her need to cling had suffocated him.

If he'd made the parting less complete, would she still be alive?

He got out of the car and bumped into Joan Reeves.

"Excuse me," she said and stepped back. "We forgot to make a date for another meeting."

No, I didn't. "Excuse me, Joan. I can't stop now."

"You have an appointment somewhere else?"

She didn't mean any harm, he reminded himself. But she did irritate him. "We can't talk today," he said, nodding, and stepping around her.

"You're the ideal 'now' guy to write about in relation to Place LaFource," she said. "This is going to be a fun book, Nick. We hope it'll bring positive interest to this part of the country. There's no other place like it and I want to make more people want to come here. I've got good media connections and I know I can get the publicity bookings."

He noticed the roots of her hair needed a touch-up. She wore less makeup than usual and looked hastily put together in a yellow shirt with one side of the collar twisted in and a short fringed skirt that looked wintry.

"There aren't many people like you," she said. "Not that I've been able to find. But this project will be nothing but positive. Don't you think it's your responsibility to help?"

He wanted to ask when her ambitions were supposed to have become his. "This isn't a great time, Joan." He tried to go around her again but she moved to cut him off. "Look, get back to me in a few days. Then we'll see."

"Just answer a couple of questions," she said. "How long ago did the Board family move into Place Lafource? What made Delia choose Pointe Judah as a permanent home? You lived with other relatives for a few years when you were a kid. In San Francisco. Then you got together with your family in Savannah. How did you get all the way from the San Francisco area to Savannah when you didn't have much money?"

Nick gave her all of his attention. She didn't have everything quite right, but she was close. "How do you know I went to Savannah? How did you know I used to live in San Franciso? And how much money I did or didn't have? Where did all that come from?"

She looked blank, then shrugged. "I read it somewhere, I guess."

Fortunately, little had ever been written about him. "I don't think I've got anything else to say yet," he said. "People experiment—with all kinds of things. Go back to reading, hmm? Focus on what you're trying to do, then maybe we'll talk."

"Don't be like this." She caught hold of his arm. "I've sold my idea, now I need a little help. Let me take you to dinner tonight."

"Not tonight, but thanks." He smiled at her. Desperation in another embarrassed him.

She dropped her hand and nodded. "You're right." Her laugh sounded unaffected. "Forgive me. I can taste this one, and writers can get a bit desperate when they think they've got something good on the hook. That's not your problem."

"It's okay," he said. She was guilty of lousy timing, not that he knew if there would ever be a right time to delve into what he didn't understand himself. "Take care, okay?"

Joan nodded again. "I'll do that. You, too."

Nick left her in the driveway and went into his condo feeling faintly guilty. She had no way of knowing what he and the people he cared about were dealing with.

He was due to see Finn Duhon. Since he didn't want more subterfuge, he'd told Delia, who grudgingly gave her blessing.

The meeting with Finn had been postponed from late morning to midafternoon. The guy had been decent about it, reacting as if he didn't have anything else to do but wait around for Nick.

He had made a decision he didn't like and went into his bedroom. Aurelie had knocked his socks off with the casual way she'd shown up with her Glock. He couldn't afford to be unarmed, either, not now.

The Sig Sauer was also 9 mm but whereas Aurelie had described her gun as "pretty," Nick's had a blunt, businesslike elegance. He knew how to use it. He checked it out, loaded, and slid it into the back of his belt. The nylon windbreaker he put on top of his shirt was too warm, but it was also necessary.

He went into the bathroom to use the toilet. When he tried to flush, the tank ran, but little water swirled into the bowl.

Damning the extra waste of time, he took off the lid and looked inside—and laughed. He got the message. Nick Board was vulnerable and he ought to be afraid.

He wasn't.

A fatty foot, recently cut from a chicken carcass, rested between the tank ball and the valve seat.

He leaned against the wall and laughed till his stomach hurt.

An elevator behind the grand staircase in the old Oakdale Mansion rose directly to Finn Duhon's office suite. Nick got into the car swiftly, grateful that the entry hall was empty, including the reception desk. He saw Finn's hand in the deserted area and admired the man's attention to detail. Nick hit the button for the top floor.

From choice, he would have preferred this meeting to take place on his own turf but, as Finn pointed out, in his office they could control interruptions.

The elevator sucked smoothly to a halt on the top floor. The doors opened into a wide hall where an old, black mahogany console table rested its brass feet on broad wood planks, just as dark, that reflected the piece of furniture. A large, gilt-framed painting of a woman in early 1800s riding garb sat sidesaddle on a black horse, gazing out at nothing. On top of the console, fine old pieces of blue Severs and a matching pair of Masan urns begged for closer inspection.

That wasn't to be. Finn Duhon, big, dark and dynamic, strode to meet Nick. They looked eye-to-eye and Nick felt a mutual sizing up. "Good to see you," Finn said, offering a broad hand. "I hope my call to you didn't stir up a nest of snakes with Delia." One size of his mouth jerked downward.

"I assure you it did," Nick said with a short laugh. "But I think you know Delia Board well enough to expect that. I was surprised she was happy for me to come without her this afternoon."

"Come on in," Finn said. "I've got someone I want you to meet. Delia called me about an hour ago."

Nick shook his head. "I'm afraid to ask why."

"Just to make sure I wouldn't be too hard on you about interferin' with her arrangements."

They both laughed.

"How's Emma?" Nick asked of Finn's wife. "Aurelie sees her, but I can't remember the last time I did."

Finn's expression softened. "Emma's just fine," he said. "It's hard to hold her back from taking on too much but that's her way." He hesitated, then added, "We expect our first child in a few months."

Nick thumped the other man's arm. "Congratulations."

Finn broke into a huge smile.

The room they entered through an archway had walls the color of tangerines, and a mix of animal-print fabrics on big, comfortable furniture.

"Meet Angel," Finn said, and a man detached himself from the spot where he leaned on the wall near broad windows. "Christian DeAngelo. An old friend of mine."

Nick took a measure of the man in khaki shirt and pants. Impressive. Another firm handshake brought them close enough to give him a good look into expressionless gray eyes. Angel probably wasn't what his enemies called him. His shoulders and arms looked unlikely to dent if you hit them with a pick.

Angel nodded and Nick did the same.

"If you can call what's going on with you and the family good timing, then this is good timing," Finn said. "Angel's got itchy feet and he's looking for something new to keep him occupied. I'm trying to get him to stick around with me, at least for a few months. There are a lot of elements about the building industry that need someone with a strong hand—and a brain. That's Angel. I want him as my head of field operations. He's still deciding."

All interesting, Nick thought, but what did any of it have to do with him?

"Angel knows about negotiating with folks who

don't want to listen," Finn said. "But that's just one of his talents."

A fleeting thought that the guy sounded like someone in collections for the mob didn't amuse Nick. He put his hands in his pockets and tried to relax. He wished he knew what Delia had told Finn she wanted from him.

"Once I left D.C. I hadn't planned to do much of what you and your Delia may need," Angel said. He inclined his head toward Finn. "But for this guy I could be persuaded to make a brief exception." He looked steadily at Nick. "What's on your mind?"

Caught without a response, Nick said, "I was thinking I can't imagine you kicking back with the boys to knock down a few beers."

Angel's grin changed his austerely arresting face. Still arresting, but amused, he laughed a little. "You might be surprised."

"Some years in . . . special services can make it hard to relax," Finn said. "So I'm told."

Angel's grin vanished.

"According to Delia, you need a bodyguard," Finn said to Nick. "Angel's the best there is."

Nick gave the guy another good looking-over. "Special services" could be code for CIA. "I don't doubt it. What I need is someone to back me up."

He accepted a Scotch and when they were settled, he unloaded every detail of his story, including the break-in and his theory that Colin Fox was some-where around. At one point he grimaced and said,

"How do people stand going through therapy? I've got to be boring you, spilling all this stuff."

"Uh-uh," Angel said. "I'd like to know what happened to the ruby."

"Me, too," Nick agreed. "If I had it, I'd find a way to offer it to Colin Fox just to get lost."

"That wouldn't work," Finn said. "He doesn't want you around, any of you. You're too dangerous to him."

"I know that," Nick said. "I'm going to have to let Matt Boudreaux know about the chicken foot. He's frozen me out for not being quick enough to contact him."

"They need to go over your place," Angel said. "Did you check to see if anything was taken?"

"Not in detail. Nothing of value that I could see, though. The point was the severed foot—chopped, snapped, whatever."

"The amateur dramatics never quit surprising me." Angel crossed his substantial arms. "These people are arrogant. At least we've been lucky so far, though."

"Lucky?" Nick asked.

"He's leaving chicken feet rather than bodies," Angel said. "Unless he's Baily's killer."

"All true. Finn, did you tell Delia you wanted all of us at Lafource? Staying there, I mean."

"So you can be sitting ducks together?" Angel asked.

"I didn't suggest anything," Finn said. "I think you should all be in your own places."

"We're going to be," Nick said. "But I can't watch all three of them at once."

"No," Angel said. "Evidently this Ed isn't going to be much help."

"I feel a bit guilty about him," Nick said. "I think he was in the wrong place at the wrong time. Delia had felt better having him and Sabine with her, so I think they should stay. That way it doesn't look as if they were frightened off. Aurelie's setup isn't so bad. There's an alarm and she's got a dog the size of a small bear. Also, she doesn't live far from me."

"So you can handle anything she needs?" Finn asked.

"Good," Angel said without waiting for an answer. "I'll need to meet the other two so they don't start screaming if I show up."

"Right," Nick said. "Where will you be?"

Still, Angel's expression didn't change. "I'll let you know. And Finn will come in if we need him. Who watches you, Nick?"

Rarely did Nick feel like throwing a punch, but he did now. "I think I'll manage, thanks."

"I think you will, too," Angel said. "Just wanted to give you the option. Something puzzles me. Your sisters. They weren't with you when you were at that place. The Refuge. Were they already with Delia?"

"I'd appreciate it if you kept this to yourselves for now," Nick said. "Sarah and Aurelie are sisters. They are not related to me."

The other two men nodded silently.

Nick wanted to get to Poke Around in plenty of time, just in case Aurelie got it into her head to leave before he got there.

The thoughts he had about her were anything but brotherly.

24

Eileen was delighted to have Hoover at the shop. She had encouraged Aurelie to bring the dog's big bed and set it in the middle of the displays.

"Why don't you bring him every day?" Eileen asked. She'd already made the suggestion several times in the past couple of days but this was the first time Aurelie had followed through. Eileen rubbed Hoover between the ears and, not so unobtrusively, dropped a handful of dog biscuits under his nose.

"He takes up a lot of room," Aurelie pointed out.

"He also looks a lot fiercer than he is." Eileen gave Aurelie a meaningful look. "I know I'm probably silly to be nervous, but I am."

"You'd be silly not to be nervous," Aurelie told her, wondering what Eileen would say when she knew about more recent events. "I hope customers don't run away when they see Hoover."

"Ooh, he's just a little ol' bear," Eileen said.

Aurelie smiled. "Take a good look at his teeth."

Eileen peered at Hoover's mouth. "Are you going to the mayor's town meeting after work?" she asked. "He's going to talk about what's going on around here. Matt Boudreaux will have something to say, too."

Aurelie had made vague note of it. "I'm not sure." She wanted to run with Nick. And she didn't want to run with him. He seemed to have taken her on as his mission in life, to protect, comfort and become the object of his sexual fantasies and needs.

The thought made her blush.

Was that all it was? His fantasies? His needs? She couldn't know.

"The meeting's at Ona's Out Back," Eileen said. "I'm going. It's hard to sift the important comments out from the hearsay, but I think I have to be informed."

"We all should be," Aurelie agreed. That run with Nick would have to wait.

"There's Sabine," Eileen said.

Surprised, Aurelie looked up in time to see Sabine backing through the door, pulling a loaded handcart.

"How's Ed?" Aurelie asked, then glanced quickly at Eileen, who was busy looking at what Sabine had brought.

"He's good," Sabine said. "Takes more than a good shove into a tree to lay my Ed up for long."

Eileen raised her face. "What did you say?"

Sabine wiggled long, French-manicured nails. "Just joking around," she said, her eyes on Aurelie, and on her frown. "Ed took a tumble and banged himself up a bit, but he's workin' away same as usual. I sure am tickled you sold down those radios. I told you so.

Them armadillos had every gardener in town keepin' the night watch on their plants."

She was right, the pastel-colored radios had rushed from the store with grateful new owners anxious to try them out. And the positive reports had poured back.

Eileen stood up, a puzzled expression on her dramatic face. She had opened a box and removed a miniature plastic garden gnome. "I thought you were bringing more radios," she said. "Aurelie, would you find Sabine's check, please. We don't have one of that first batch left."

"These are the new ones," Sabine said. "Updated version guaranteed to make all the people who bought the first variety want a second one."

Aurelie smiled as she went to the box where Eileen kept checks for consignment items.

"Look at this," Sabine said. She took the garish gnome from Eileen and popped off the back to show off what was inside. An even smaller radio than the first batch, wired through to an on-off switch just above the base. She closed the gnome again and flipped the switch. Afro-pop filled the shop and Aurelie immediately started tapping her toes. "They just have to remember to switch over to talk radio." Sabine set the fancy radio on a counter and launched into a stomping dance, wiggling her hips, tossing her bead-clacking braids and waving her arms above her head. "C'mon," she said to Eileen. "Shake your booty."

Aurelie smiled. Eileen wasn't the "shake your booty" type.

"Whoa," Sabine cried. "Oh, woman, look at this."

And Eileen was proving Aurelie wrong in the shaking department. She copied Sabine, flipping her hips and twirling.

Hoover howled.

Aurelie didn't realize the shop door had opened again until her dog climbed from his bed and gamboled heavily to butt Nick's legs. She stood still.

Grinning, Nick shook both hands in the air and yelled, "Don't let me stop you." Promptly, he went to Aurelie and swept her into a fast sort of two-step. Despite a clapping audience, they didn't make it far before Aurelie tripped over Nick's feet and he held her up against him until she found her footing.

Sabine turned the music down. "I didn't know you could dance like that, Nick," she said.

"Probably just as well," he said, suitably humble. "What's that supposed to be?" He pointed at the noisy gnome.

"Sabine's sock-'em armadillo blockers," she said. "Improved, that is. I've moved on from plain old radios to wiring them inside pieces of garden art. Fixed every one of these up myself." She unpacked an orange toadstool, a wishing well the size of a child's sand bucket and a flamingo with short legs. The latter she plunked triumphantly on the counter beside the gnome. "The trick is you gotta play talk radio. Them critters, they hate talk radio. Sends 'em runnin'."

Nick watched the women, the relaxed grins on their faces, and resented anything that came along to get in the way of simple fun.

"You gotta have one of these for that condo of yours," Sabine announced. She put her head to one side while she studied him. "A flamingo man if ever I saw one," she said and handed him a box. "Never did give you a housewarming gift—now I have. And while we're on the subject, I've got to get in and clean that place from one end to the other." She rolled her eyes and slapped a hand over her heart. "Oh, my, I don't want to think what I'll find over there."

Once he was sure she'd finished, Nick held up the box and said, "Thank you for this. I'll have to ask you to wait a little longer before you move the bulldozers into the condo." He'd already contacted Matt, and at that moment cops were crawling over every inch of the place, hoping to find even a tiny useful clue.

He looked at his watch. "I expect you'd appreciate going home to change first, Aurelie. And getting Sucker settled in. It's too hot for him to be running out there."

"Bouviers des Flandres have a double coat," Aurelie said. "Fur and hair. The hair on the outside helps cool 'em down. That's why people make a mistake when they cut the coat short in summer. He's fine in the heat and he loves to run."

That informational message had sounded like something intended to divert him. "If you say so. I've got my stuff outside in my car. I'll bring it to your place and we'll go from there."

He noticed that the ebullience of a few minutes ago had dribbled away. Eileen and Sabine were busy with tasks.

Dropping down beside Sucker, he opened the dog's mouth and hooked out half a dozen colored glass marbles he must have lifted from an artificial-plant display nearby. "I thought I heard him crunching something," Nick said. "If we don't watch it, this guy will kill himself." He looked up at Aurelie. "What is it?" he asked quietly.

She knelt on the other side of Sucker. "He does spit the really bad things out himself," she said. "It's a game."

Nick nodded and waited for her to go on. Hanging sun catchers moved colors through her black hair. Mostly she kept her lashes lowered but when she looked at him, her eyes were almost painfully blue.

"The mayor's having a meeting at Ona's Out Back." Her voice scratched. "I think I have to go just in case someone starts talking about us. I don't see how they can avoid it, really."

Nick got up and offered her a hand. She took hold and he pulled her to her feet. When she was almost toe-to-toe with him he realized how small she was. "So you're canceling our date."

She checked to make sure they weren't overheard. "I didn't really make it, Nick."

He thought about that and couldn't argue. "You didn't turn me down."

Her quick smile helped his ego. "I didn't want to, that's why. But one of us has to be responsible."

He grabbed his belly and pretended to be hurt. "You've wounded me," he said. "What time is the meeting?"

"Eight."

"I'll take you," he told her, knowing that once again he wasn't giving her any choices unless she wanted to make a fuss, and she wouldn't do that here. "Do Sarah and Delia know?"

"I'd better call them," Aurelie said.

"They already know," Sabine piped in, with no sign of embarrassment at listening to their conversation. "They'll be there, not that I know what big-shot Mayor Damalis can say to make anything better. Unless he's figured out a way to bring people back to life."

Once they'd left the shop with Hoover, Aurelie had to deal with jumpiness again. It happened every time she was alone with Nick. "We've got a couple of hours before the meeting," she told him, cramming her hat lower over her eyes. "I can walk to Ona's from my place. We'll meet there."

"Okay," he said, but he gave her that closed-up look that turned her stomach. "I had a meeting this afternoon. I'd like to tell you about it, but not where we'll be overheard. The cops are at my place."

She glanced across at the condos and saw two cruisers in the driveway. "Why are they there? What's happened?"

"I'll tell you about it."

"Is it okay for them to be over there if you're not?"

"I asked them to come, then I didn't want to stay while they dug around."

"Come to my place," she said, knowing that's what he wanted. "You can kick back until it's time for the meeting. I've got some leftover stuff from New Orleans to deal with on the computer."

"You sure?"

She let out a slow breath. "Yes. You like sangria?"

"Sure. I can't remember the last time I had any."

"I make it sometimes." She unlocked the Hummer, and Hoover almost ran her down getting in. The dog went to his perch where he could see between the two front seats, and Nick got in on the passenger side.

They shut the doors. "I've got a big jug of sangria. I didn't know what I was going to do with it. I had a bunch of lemons that needed to be used. You know how that goes? You just get an urge to make something and you get carried away."

"All the time," he said.

Aurelie gave him a narrow-eyed stare until he looked back and grinned.

They faced each other for too long, or perhaps not long enough. She didn't want to look away and could tell he didn't, either.

Finally, Aurelie drove off. "Patrick Damalis is holding this meeting tonight," she said.

"I don't know how that guy got elected mayor," Nick said. "A lot of people don't like him."

"Yes, but he's got loads of money." Patrick owned the best, clubby hotel in town—the only clubby hotel in town. "Some say you've got to have something hc wants to get a contract in this town."

She slowed at a corner. "Sounds familiar. I've been living in the land of FBI."

"New Orleans?"

"Yeah. Friends, brothers and in-laws. You've got to have contacts to get anywhere in town. You do as well as the people you know."

Sucker licked Nick's ear. A weaker man would have fallen sideways in his seat. "Thanks," he said to the dog. "Now I won't need a shower." That got him another lick to the ear, and another up the side of his face from chin to hairline.

"Back off, Hoover," Aurelie said. "Finn should have run for mayor."

Nick smothered an explosive laugh.

"What?" She checked her mirrors and changed lanes. The town was pretty deserted.

"Can you really see Finn as mayor of Pointe Judah?"

"He'd have the place running perfectly in no time," Aurelie said.

"He'd clear the place out," Nick told her. "No-guff Duhon they call him around the construction industry. Can you see him putting up with Lobelia Forestier and her clones? Anyway, Emma's first husband was mayor here—crooked mayor. She and Finn wouldn't want anything to do with all that."

"Could be Finn would take a hard line on crime," Aurelie said.

He put a hand on her bare shoulder. "Go easy on the police. We're expecting too much, too soon. Sure, cases get solved within hours sometimes, but this one was a long time in the making. A lot of thought went into what Colin would do once he found me."

They arrived outside Frances and Lynnette's salon. Before Aurelie got out of the Hummer, she took her gun out of her purse and slid it into her skirt pocket. The salon was still open, which helped her feel less isolated. She could see people wearing floral cutting capes moving around inside the shop.

"Put the gun back in your purse," Nick said. "Now, please."

She jumped. "I forgot you were with me." She had, just for an instant. "It doesn't hurt to be in the habit of moving it to my pocket before I go upstairs."

"No, as long as you don't shoot a member of the family one day, or a friend, or even Hoover, for crying out loud."

Aurelie left the gun where it was. "Come on, Hoover, boy. Time for your dinner." She was used to making her own decisions and didn't intend to change, particularly because a man wanted to take charge, much as she cared about this one.

She let them in, locked up tight and went upstairs. Hoover rushed ahead and met them at the top.

The apartment, tiny at best, seemed minuscule with

Nick in it. Aurelie took the Glock out of her pocket and put it back in her purse. The purse went on the bottom of the bed with her hat, and when she returned to the other room, Nick was already filling Hoover's dishes. Aurelie walked into the tiny kitchen and pulled the jug of sangria from the refrigerator.

All she could feel was Nick.

They were caught in the sights of a killer yet her mind wouldn't let go of images and sensations of the two of them together one hot night.

He found glasses and took them from the cupboard. Aurelie poured the sangria. They stood with their backs to the counter and touched glasses. The drink tasted Chianti tart with a zip of lemon from the fruit Aurelie had cut in slices and dropped into the jug. Warmth flooded her veins.

There seemed little to say.

"You'll go back to the law, won't you?" Nick said. "You always said it was what you wanted."

"It was and it may be again if I can get past the bad taste left in my mouth from the post-Katrina mess in New Orleans. If and when I do go back, I'll be on the other side." She yawned.

"Tired?" Nick asked.

She shook her head. "No. This has been an incredible day, is all. Come and sit on my purple furniture, and tell me about that meeting you had this afternoon."

Nick's eyes went to the hem of her green dress, swirling around the tops of her calves. Aurelie had great legs. He liked her in high heels—which she rarely wore.

"It was with Finn Duhon and one of his friends," he said, still watching her legs. He shifted his weight. "You remember, Delia contacted him. I followed up." He told her the rest of what had happened.

"A bodyguard?" she asked. "Sounds theatrical."

"Someone trying to kill you sounds theatrical," Nick said. "On the other hand, there was nothing theatrical about what happened to Baily. She's dead."

Aurelie half turned toward him and her eyes shone too brightly. "I hate it that she is. But how will you get Sarah and Delia to accept a *bodyguard?*"

He smiled faintly. "I don't think it'll be hard in this case. He won't be creeping around corners. The man's a pro and he's an answer to my prayers. I have to make sure all three of you are safe."

"You care a lot about us," Aurelie said. "But we care about you, Nick. We're lucky people."

"Is that all you feel about me, Aurelie? That you care about me?"

Her skin prickled. "I'm not sure how to read the questions."

"I think you do. Come back here. Stand beside me."

She hesitated, then walked back slowly, the polished cotton in her dress swishing.

"Watching you move is a turn-on, lady," he said.

Aurelie looked at the floor. "Don't embarrass me."

"Sorry. It's true. Come here. All the way. I won't bite."

She stood beside him again, her back to the counter. They didn't touch but she could feel him just the same.

"I'm not pussyfooting around anymore," Nick said.

She turned her face up to his. The light was behind him and his sharply defined face was thrown in to shadows, the deep indentations at the corners of his mouth, the faint dimples that never quite left his cheeks, and his eyes, dark blue shaded by his lashes.

"You don't look at me as if you wish I'd go away," he told her.

"I'm struggling, Nick. When I went away to law school I thought I'd meet someone else and you'd remain the good friend you've always been. It didn't happen."

He turned toward her. "You're telling me you've thought about me—not just as a pseudobrother?"

The time for pretending was over. "That's what I'm saying. It's been true for a long time."

Nick took a sip of his sangria, watching her every second. He looked at her mouth, dipped his finger into her glass and touched the wine to her lips.

Aurelie licked her bottom lip and he quickly jutted his face forward and kissed her. Just as quickly, with a brief meeting of tongues, he stood straight again. "It's not going to work anymore," he said.

She felt a little sick. "What does that mean?"

"Sooner or later we have to confront the future—usually when it turns into the present. It just did for us. I want you in my life and I have for a very long time."

Was it possible he thought any problems would dissolve as long as they got what they wanted? "I'm afraid of going forward," Aurelie said.

"I'm not asking you for casual sex," he said.

Her lungs emptied then wouldn't fill. She felt shaky and her skin ached.

Nick put down his glass and used the fingertips of both hands to outline her face, to stroke to the point of her chin. His smile was mischievous. "I love that pointy chin of yours. And your pointy nose."

She laughed. "My puffy, pointy nose. I don't sound very attractive and no, I'm not fishing."

"There's nothing about you that doesn't attract me, unless it's your cheeky mouth when you're being difficult."

Aurelie prepared a verbal salvo but Nick put a forefinger on her mouth. "I'm sorry. Okay? Things are moving fast. Even if we do nothing, our real relationship, or the lack of it, will come out. It was convenient to pose as a family when we were younger. That's not necessary anymore."

She really would like to sit down. "But Delia," she said. "And Sarah." It wasn't her place to tell him she thought Sarah was in love with him. "Sarah thinks so much of you. She doesn't consider going to anyone but you when she needs something, or just wants to share what she cares about."

"I know," Nick said. "We need to tell them before someone else does. And I always intend to watch out for Sarah."

But how would Sarah react when she discovered Nick and Aurelie's new relationship?

"What do you want, Aurelie?" Nick asked quietly. He kissed her cheek and the corner of her mouth and her jaw. With his hands looped around her neck, he rested his thumbs on her chin. "Tell me. Don't hold back. And if you don't want anything from me, say that, too."

She smiled at him and arched her neck, turned her cheek into his palm. "You feel pretty safe, don't you? You know you mean so much to me."

"What do you want?" he asked again.

Aurelie closed her eyes and nuzzled his hand. "That's twice you've asked the same question. Now it's my turn. What do *you* want—apart from sex?"

He took her glass, set it down with his own, and she got the kind of kiss that backed up what she'd said about him wanting sex. He left her breathless and clinging to him. His arms, crossed behind her back, held her on tiptoe, and he rubbed his mouth along the low neck of her sundress where it met the rise of her breasts.

"I want everything," she said to him. "Then I want it again."

With his fingers hooked inside her bodice, resting on her nipples, he drew back to see her face. Then he cringed and took his hands away from her bruised skin. He grinned sheepishly. "Last night you asked me to stay."

"I did," she told him, straining closer. "This is a new night. If you still feel the same when we finish at Ona's, the offer stands."

267

25

The Roll Inn was no boutique hotel but it was clean and convenient. Joan was tired of listening to Vic Gross make snide comments about the place.

"I said I'm bored," he told her, had been telling her since he'd arrived with a tubful of fried chicken, hush puppies and a six-pack of Jax to wash it all down. That had been an hour ago. "This is taking too long." The chicken was his dinner.

He sprawled on the bed, his chest and feet bare, his blond hair mussed, and with the kind of slow blink and unfocused eyes that had nothing to do with his being tired. He took three times as many hits a day as he had even a year ago.

"I need some peace, Vic. Hours of peace and quiet. All day I've beaten on doors trying to find out what gives with the Boards. I can't get anyone to talk to me. A doctor was called to the police station last night but I can't even get a hint on the identity of the patient. These small-town people hang tight."

He yawned. "Yeah?"

"The Boards were there when the doctor was called. At least Nick and Aurelie were. I want to know if the doctor was for one of them. Nick's quit talking to me, too. I tried to get to him today but he wasn't having any."

"Maybe he doesn't have anything to tell you."

"Don't say that." She must not think about failure.

"It isn't easy playing this double game. Pretending I want one thing when I want something else. We have to get him talking. He has to let us inside or we're finished. We have to make this project work. Cooper made sure we understood what he'll do if we don't come through." She hated to speak the boss's name aloud. It made him too real. "I'll go back to Nick. It's too bad the woman chemist died just when we were getting started. He's spending too much time on that. I've got to make him concentrate on me. Trust me. I think I can get him to loosen up."

Vic snickered. "Maybe he doesn't like you. Tell Cooper to back off. What can he do about it if we don't get what he wants fast enough for him?"

Joan's heart thumped painfully. "He can send one of his contacts to *help* us. We don't want that kind of help."

"The kind that punishes?" Laughing, Vic turned onto his back. He had a hard-on.

"You're the one who's finished." Vic's slurred voice had fur on it. "If there has to be a change, it'll be you who finds out about it. I do what I do. I do what I'm told. Man, do I have it made. Have camera, will travel, that's me. Cooper knows I'm the best. He'll always have work for me."

That's what Vic thought, but he'd be easier to deal with if she didn't burst his bubble. Getting to Nick Board for Cooper was their last chance. Either they came through, or he called in what they owed. He would send in the goons.

She and Vic had been together for eight years. And all that time she'd kept him and his habit, even though few days went by when she didn't rehearse leaving him. Only, he'd find her. She'd tried to get away twice, so she knew what happened when he caught up with her.

He pointed a wavery finger. "There's a letter I'm gonna hold back from Cooper. In the pocket of my jacket. Get it."

"What letter?" She found his jacket. "Will it help us?"

"Depends on how things turn out. If Cooper gets too pissy, it'll give us some proof of what we've done so we can show him we've been working. Keep it in a safe place."

She found what he was talking about and put it at the bottom of her crowded purse.

Vic snickered again. "I'd be afraid to put a hand in that thing. Something ugly might bite me."

She didn't respond but took her cell phone from her purse and checked in case she'd missed a call.

"Give it up, babe," Vic said. "Cooper won't be calling tonight. He's probably getting laid, same as he does every night."

"If you can call that getting laid," Joan said. "I've got a headache. Be quiet, please."

"Please," he mimicked in a high voice. "So polite. Your momma must have taught you all the right things. One or two, anyway. I bet she didn't teach you how to—"

"That's enough, Vic. Sleep it off."

"Could be your momma taught you everything you know. You wouldn't be the first female to learn the game at her mother's knee."

Violence simmered in him all the time, just waiting for an excuse to break out. When he was high he could get even more physical, but Joan liked her chances better in a motel room where Vic wouldn't want to make enough noise to draw the wrong kind of attention. The sounds of pain tended to do that. "You never knew my mother," she said. "She was a good woman. Leave her out of this."

"Hoo-hoo, snooty, aren't we?" He sniffed and felt in a back pocket for the nasal spray that was his constant companion.

"Good night, Vic."

He rolled onto his belly again and propped his chin on his hands. "It isn't a good night yet, but it will be. Quit worrying. We're going to clean the slate. Cooper owes us, and since he's the one who's had Nick and the women followed pretty much since they've been here, he's responsible for making sure we know what we need to know to get the job done. I don't think he's given us enough details yet, but you do know this project is a hundred percent in the bag once you get all the material you need."

"We both need it," she told him. "And we both need money—for the day-to-day expenses, not just the big stuff. They asked me to pay for the room again today. I was promised another payment as soon as I sent in an expanded file. It's been there two days. My God,

Vic. Think, if you can. Think how much we're into Cooper for and we can't even pay for this room. He's not satisfied. I can feel it."

Vic grinned. Wobbling on one elbow, his eyelids half closed, he reached down into the front pocket of his khaki shorts and pulled out a fat roll of bills. "Why didn't you remind me before? I was in the office when the delivery came. Kid in reception doesn't know her ass from her tits. But I'm giving her lessons she'll find real useful."

Joan turned her back on him.

"You don't want to miss a word of this, Joanie," he said. "Make sure you're hearing me. I followed that chickie into the back room and her panties came off like a wrapper from hot butter. She gave me your envelope. Yep, she did that. And then she found out cashing the cashier's check was no problem. Reckon I'll be stopping back in to see her later."

"That envelope was addressed to me and the check is mine." Heat throbbed in Joan's face, and elsewhere. "You are just bad. Naughty. I don't know where you got such bad habits."

"Naughty," he repeated, falsetto. "Cut the crap, Joanie, we know who the schoolgirl act appeals to and it isn't me. Used to work pretty good in front of the camera, too. But then time rolls on and even the pigtails won't fool anyone. Too bad."

She hated him, but she needed him. "I'm going right to the front desk and we'll see who comes out on top in this one."

He vaulted from the bed, grabbed her by the waist and threw her on the mattress hard enough to make her bounce. Before she could try to move, he was on her, pushing her fringed skirt up around her hips. "Who did you say was going to be on top?" he asked, grinning down at her. "You won't go to the desk or say a word to anyone. You will never go against me because I know too much about you. All I'm going to do is look after the money for both of us. We know I'm more careful than you are."

"Give it to me." She couldn't risk what he'd do if she accused him of planning to blow the money on drugs.

"Ah, ah, ah." He caught her hand on its way into his pocket, unzipped his pants and folded her fingers around him. "I've paid for the room," he said. "And I'll pay for whatever else you need. *Need,* baby."

He slipped past her thong and buried himself deep. He pumped on and on, the coke made sure of that. For her it was all over fifteen minutes before he finished. She wasn't satisfied. "I need money now," she told him, her heart not even working a beat faster. She tried to get him to move in her again, but he slid out and lay on his back, laughing.

"Vic?" she wheedled.

"For you, anything," he said, holding up the wad of bills again and peeling off several hundreds. He flicked the edges across her mouth. "For the fastest fuck in the . . . where are we? The South. Later, baby." He climbed off the bed and stood looking down at her in the lamplighted room while he zipped his shorts.

"What a pity you're such a beautiful man," she said. "Beautiful on the outside and rotten on the inside. Cut you open and you'd stink—and foul things would crawl out."

The grin left his face. In his slitted green eyes, the ice she'd learned to fear had formed. Without a word, he slapped her face, hard, screwed up the money and dropped it on the bed beside her, and left—closing the door very quietly.

26

Ona's Out Back wasn't meant to hold a hundred people, but Nick figured about that many had squished in. The overflow filled Out Front where people listened to Mayor Damalis and Matt through a speaker Buck rigged up to the microphone setup.

Patrick Damalis didn't need a mike but took no notice of how many fingers were pressed into ears each time he bellowed.

Sarah stood between Delia and a potted philodendron. The plant climbed a long stake and made its way to the corrugated, semitransparent roof. Ona was proud of her many thriving plants.

The regular tables and chairs had been cleared in favor of folding seats set out in narrowly spaced rows. By the time Delia and Sarah arrived there wasn't a remaining place to perch and they'd had difficulty working their way along the wall to get close to Nick and Aurelie.

Sarah had given herself a pep talk about not reading things into Aurelie and Nick often being together. It was just working out that way at the moment; nothing more sinister than that.

Matt had started the presentation with an explanation of where they stood in the investigation of Baily Morris's murder. The audience hadn't seemed to move or even breathe throughout that. Then Patrick took over and repeated exactly the same facts.

The rustling and whispering started then and hadn't stopped, even though Patrick, darkly debonair and European in manner, continued to talk.

Sarah pressed Delia's arm and indicated that she wanted to squeeze past and get next to Nick. "Hey." She leaned toward his ear and rested a hand on his bare arm. "Patrick's making an idiot of himself."

Nick smiled.

"Why didn't they hold this at the town hall?"

"Something about the plumbing," Nick said.

Standing beside him comforted Sarah. He was the kind of man who inspired courage and she needed that tonight. She had a plan and very soon she'd put it into action. Her decision was to ask Nick out on a date.

"What you're sayin' then," a man shouted, "is that we've got a killer wanderin' loose and you don't know any more about him than you did when you found the body."

"Calm down, Dan," Patrick said. "We've got a lot more than you think."

Sarah tried to comfort herself with the likelihood that Baily's death could have been an accident. If not, why wouldn't Aurelie and Ed have been killed, too? Criminals followed patterns, didn't they? She shuddered but felt better when she thought about Nick's description of Angel, their new bodyguard.

"Are you cold?" Nick asked. "It's got to be a hundred degrees in here with humidity to match."

"I'm not cold," she said, "just creeped out."

He put an arm around her shoulders and spoke to Aurelie, who leaned to smile at Sarah. "We've got to hang in, sis. We can do it."

Sarah caught a woman's eyes, an older woman with a bright, interested stare. Immediately, the woman turned away, but there were others taking surreptitious glances in the Boards' direction.

"They're looking at us," Sarah said evenly.

Delia said, "That's because we're the best-looking people in the room."

Sarah giggled and passed the comment on until they all chuckled. Many more looks came their way.

"Finn Duhon's a looker," Delia whispered, inclining her head toward Sarah, who pressed a hand over her mouth. "Do you suppose the stud with him is our new bodyguard?"

"Stud?" Sarah hissed. "Very nice. Very mature. He is studly, though, isn't he?" The man standing with Finn and Emma Duhon resembled a modern-day warrior to Sarah, all toned muscle on hard bone and a face that had only improved with experience.

"Excuse me," a woman said clearly. Rosa Valenti, Betty Valenti's sister-in-law, stood up. "We all have a lot of confidence in our police department. Thank you for your efforts."

Someone nearby said, "She worked for the police for years. What else is she going to say?"

Sarah thought it a mean comment.

"Could you please tell us about all these other things the mayor says you know?" Rosa Valenti said. Her voice and manner were very firm.

The man beside her stood up and said, "I'm Rosa's husband, Bob. It does seem we're wasting time. We understand the crime and what you're doing to track the killer. What else do you have to tell us?" The couple remained standing until Matt acknowledged their questions, then sat down.

"In a way, this is the really hard part," Matt said. "I'll tell you up front that there are some confusing elements in this case. But we do have suspects. I hope that makes you all feel better."

With Buck Dupiere standing slightly behind Matt and looking in his direction, Nick didn't feel one bit better. Until now he hadn't taken Matt's prickly attitude toward him as more than frustration. If they'd settled on him as a suspect, the trouble was only getting deeper—for everyone.

"Now, I want to be able to rely on each of you to be calm and keep your eyes open," Matt said. "I don't want anything I tell you to make you panic, but there are those other developments we hinted at and they may be tough to take."

Delia caught Nick's eye and shook her head. "I like that boy," she said, "but his idea of calming the folks down could send them into hysteria."

People within hearing distance turned toward Delia and nodded significantly.

"Everything's under control," Matt continued. "There have been two more attacks but both victims survived."

"Way to go, Matt," Nick said, a general outburst making sure few heard him. "Make sure people go into shock."

Aurelie was concerned to see Frances Broussard from the salon get to her feet. On one side of her, Lynette, whose specialty was fantastic nails, chewed on her own long extensions. Sabine sat on the other side of Frances with Ed next to her. Aurelie hadn't noticed him there before, and given the bump he'd evidently taken on his head earlier, she was surprised.

Finally Matt pointed to Frances and asked, "You've got a question, Frances?"

She flipped back her intricate crystal-decorated braids. "What do you mean by attacks?" she asked, and remained standing.

"What I said," Matt told her. "Two people have been roughed up. More than that, attempts were made to scare 'em badly. We don't want to give out too much detail about our operations. I'm sure you understand why."

"So you won't tip off the maniac?" Frances asked, her dark skin shining in the humid atmosphere. "Is he stalking women until he gets them on their own? Is he raping them? Someone said that's what's happenin'."

An awkward pause followed.

"Absolutely *not,*" Patrick Damalis boomed out. "Nothing sexual at all. Any more than there was with Baily Morris, so put your minds at rest about that."

"Did he try to kill these others, then?" Frances asked.

"She won't put up with any wishy-washy excuses for information," Aurelie said. She liked both Frances and Lynette.

Questions poured in and the same answers came back. Aurelie didn't want to discuss what had happened to her but she still didn't think it wise to pretend the attacks they referred to had been little more than a poke in the back.

"Who are the victims?" Lynette asked clearly. "You shouldn't hide anything from us. We need to know how these things happened and what we can do to prevent them from happening again."

Aurelie caught Matt's eye and nodded. He looked toward the ceiling as if making a decision before he said, "Aurelie Board had an unpleasant encounter in some woods. It doesn't matter exactly where because we've got similar woods all over. My advice is to stay out of them."

"There," Lobelia Forestier announced triumphantly, rising to plant her feet as a solid base. "I knew it, but would anyone listen to me? Oh, no. It's all to do with the Boards. They're not like the rest of us, they live a different kind of life. They must know the kind of people none of us would know."

"Lobelia," Matt said.

"Don't you try to stop me from having my say," she told him. "First someone's murdered out at the Wilkes and Board lab. Then Aurelie gets attacked. Talk about all in the family. They're putting us all in danger."

Nick clamped his teeth together. Losing his cool with Lobelia Forestier would be a waste of energy, but he'd like a simple way to shut her up.

"It could be a coincidence," Frances said, surging to her feet again. Her black eyes flashed in Lobelia's direction. "And if it's not, the Boards need help from all of us." She shook back her hair and the crystals in her braids sparkled. "We've got to show this freak he's picked on the wrong people. He wants us scared and it's not going to happen."

Applause spattered across the crowd, and echoed at a pass-through from Out Front.

Aurelie elbowed Nick and said, "She's got a lot of spirit." She looked up at him and their eyes met. Desire was there, but something much more than that, a familiarity in the best way, and tenderness. With a heart that beat too hard and fast, Aurelie turned her face away.

He found her hand and pressed it. "I'm happy," he murmured. "Can't help it. I just want to catch up with our crazy friend and rip his throat out. Then we can get on with what's important."

She gave him a fake scowl but couldn't keep the laughter out of her eyes.

Order was slow to settle in again. Once again Lobelia was shushing and waving for quiet, or rather for control of the floor. When she could be heard, she said. "I never suggested we don't look after our own around here."

"No," Delia said under her breath. "Only that the Boards aren't your own."

"We all have to watch out for ourselves, is all," Lobelia went on. "That's one of the attacks you talked about, Chief. What about the other one?"

Matt frowned toward Ed. Nick studied the man and saw no reaction.

"Ed Webb got pretty shaken up, too," Matt said. "A good bump on the head, a scraped-up back and more threats, right Ed?"

Ed didn't say anything.

"Pushed him around, the guy did," Matt said.

"It was the heat," Ed said, staying in his seat. "I got heatstroke, is all, and lost my bearings. Fell into a bunch of brush and thumped my head. Thing like that can make you imagine things. I fell in the pool and scraped up my back."

"Is he kidding?" Aurelie said. She couldn't believe what she'd just heard. "Why would he say that?"

Nick's features turned hard. "Scared. Can't think of any other reason. Pretending it didn't happen won't help him or any of us now."

Things had gotten quiet.

Buck moved beside Matt and they both nailed Ed with disbelieving stares.

"You heard Ed," Sabine said. "It was the heat and he got disoriented. Did it all to himself, he did. So I guess there was just what happened to Aurelie." By the time she finished, her arms were crossed and she faced the floor.

"Right," Matt said, suddenly brusque. "Well, folks. The mayor here and I have brought you up to date. We don't want anyone bein' afraid, but lock your doors, and if you're worried about anything, contact us and we'll be right out."

Aurelie turned to Nick and waited until he bowed his head. "What about the guy asking Ed about having something that wasn't his? We've both been thinking that was the ruby. Nick, Ed's changed his story."

He drew a line with his toe. "Covering up and trying to stay safe. I still say that's what it is." For a moment he rested the back of his head against the wall, then he leaned toward her again and said, "Could be there was something completely different, something he was worried about, and he thought coming up with a fake attack connected to yours would be a good idea. Then he changed his mind when he thought about everyone asking him questions."

"What could Ed have done that he'd have to cover up?" Aurelie asked. "He wouldn't go in to Delia's safe, would he?"

"Damned if I know. But it's one explanation."

The crowd thinned quickly, amid grumbling and some worried faces.

"Time to go," Nick said.

"You're coming back to Lafource?" Delia asked.

"No," Aurelie said. "I'm safe in my place."

"You know I'm going home, too," Nick said, and Aurelie felt guilty. "But this is a good time for you to meet Angel. Outside. We don't want to bend Matt any more out of shape that he already is."

Finn, Emma and Christian DeAngelo were already on their way toward the Boards. Finn arrived first and shook Nick's hand. "The closest parking slots clear out first," he said. "Let's meet up there just for a few minutes. That way we'll have plenty of light to see who's coming and going, too."

"You've got it," Nick said.

"Hi, Aurelie," Emma Duhon said.

"Hi," Aurelie said. "Not the best reason for a gathering."

"No, I should say not," Emma said. She shook hands with Sarah and gave Delia a quick hug. "When this is all over, I'd like to have you all over. Maybe for a barbecue if Finn can light a grill without blowing himself up."

Finn's big hand ran through short, dark hair. He grinned. "She's not going to let me forget a little accident I had, are you, love?" He kissed her and they laughed together.

Emma's hair was a honey-blond version of Aurelie's dark masses of curls. Just like Aurelie's it jutted from a central part, and it suited her. Nick looked at the two of them. He preferred Aurelie's almost black hair. And was grateful she didn't wear the beige straw hat with the black brim unless she was in the sun. She'd changed into a yellow tank dress, a skimpy thing he liked a lot and would like even better if there weren't other men around.

Angel hung back, his hands in his pockets, relaxed but not noticeably engaged.

Sarah said, "Formidable," to Nick.

He almost asked what she meant, before he saw she was looking at Finn's buddy. "Maybe," he said. "But Finn has good taste, so he's a good guy."

Except for Ona and her staff, who scurried around putting the café back in order, and Matt and Buck dismantling the sound system, the room had emptied out.

"We can stay here," Angel said. He inclined his head almost imperceptibly toward the two cops. "They won't be wanting to swap jokes anytime soon. They'll be outta here. Better in here than out there in the parking lot. More casual."

Finn nodded.

Patrick Damalis approached and pressed the flesh all the way around. "Sorry you folks are having a difficult time," he said, addressing Nick. "Hang in there and we'll sort it all out."

"Thank you, Mayor," Nick said and Delia echoed, "Thank you, Mayor," with a straighter face than Nick could have managed.

"Pompous ass," Emma Duhon said unexpectedly when the man had walked far enough away. "Always was."

Matt and Buck left the equipment in one corner and made their own detour to the group. "Thanks for cooperatin'," Matt said to Aurelie.

"Ed was a surprise," she said. "What was that about?"

Buck was too busy giving Sarah a slow assessment to respond, but Matt said, "Don't worry about it. That's *our* job. I'll be talkin' to him. It could be like he said. Heatstroke. Then the bump on the head and he may have gotten confused enough to jump in the pool. Good night, all."

They watched them go before Angel stood in front of Delia and Sarah. "Okay if I call you by your first names?"

Seconds ticked away before Delia cleared her throat and said, "Absolutely. And what should we call you?"

"Angel will do," he said, straight-faced.

Nick wanted to laugh at the dazzled expressions on Delia's and Sarah's faces. "I hoped Ed was going to be the break we need," he said to Finn.

"He will be," Angel said. "He's already shown us that."

"Yes," Nick said, considering Ed's behavior. "I guess he has."

"How will we reach you if we need you, Angel?" Delia asked. "There's plenty of room at Place Lafource if—"

"No, thank you, Delia. You relax. I'll be the one doing any reaching if it's necessary."

27

Buck Dupiere scuffed up the dusty wooden steps to the tin-roofed house he'd rented by the bayou. The house stood on stilts; water slipped around them on the bayou side of the place, and on this side, the steps went up a long way to the gallery. He had already learned to avoid several loose boards up there.

A voice said, "Hi, Buck Dupiere, I've been waiting for—"

A woman emerged from shadows. He slammed her against his screen door, and knocked her arms above her head before she could get more words out. Her hands were empty. He snapped them down and wedged them behind her back. Holding her by the throat, he frisked her.

"I'm not going to be any trouble," she said. "Please, I just want to talk to you."

Buck peered closer at her face, glanced down at moonlight bouncing off the tops of a memorable pair displayed at the low neck of a tank top. "Creeping up on a cop in the dark isn't real smart," he said, loosening his grip on her throat and taking her by the shoulders instead.

"I know. I had to come. I don't have anyone else to turn to."

"You don't know anything about me . . . except my name. Why choose me?"

"I saw you." Her breasts rose and fell rapidly. "You're a strong man, honest, I could tell. And I know you don't come from around here, so you don't think like a small-town cop."

"Maybe I come from another small town."

"New Orleans?"

He didn't like the idea that she'd asked questions about him. "Yeah. You've done your homework."

"Some things aren't hard to find out."

Buck set her to one side, yanked the screen open and unlocked the door. He reached the switch and flipped on a light. He stood back. "Inside and face me."

"I'm not a criminal, I'm a writer."

"And writers can't be criminals?"

She grabbed her bag and walked across the threshold. He crowded in behind her so that when she turned around he was in her face. Her eyes widened. He noted that for a desperate woman she'd taken a lot of time with her makeup and her long, blond hair.

"We've met before haven't we?" he asked.

"I'm Joan Reeves. You asked me to dinner," she said, smiling. "Remember, I'm here because I'm working on a book about antebellum houses and the families who have lived in them. I'm using Place Lafource here in Pointe Judah, and Nick's the perfect one for me to get the facts from, but he's making things real difficult. I need to talk to you alone about how to handle him. This was the only way I knew to do that."

"How did you find out where I live? Don't answer that. I forget where I am sometimes. In this town, you probably know what I had for lunch."

"I don't know that," she said.

He looked at her, curious. The sweet, annoying little voice wouldn't bother him so much if he thought it was real. But could she be as stupid as she sounded? "That was just a figure of speech," he said.

She gave an exaggerated snort and covered her mouth. "Oh. Sorry."

"Look, I'm tired. All I want is a drink and some sleep. Come and see me at the station tomorrow."

"No!" She jiggled on the toes of shoes with thin straps that criss-crossed several times at the ankle. "Oh, please. I'm in trouble and I can't wait till tomorrow to talk to you. And it's got to be in complete privacy. Just between you and me, Buck. I promise I'll make it up to you."

That was an interesting offer. He looked at her speculatively. "It's been a long day. I'm having a beer. Want one?"

She pulled up her shoulders, then smiled. A pretty woman, a sexy woman. "Thank you very much," she said. "I know what you mean about long days. I went to the station this morning. I was hoping for a word with Matt. He was already out somewhere. The officer out front, Carly, said you were out, too. Last night I was there, as well, but I couldn't get in then, either, because the desk officer said everyone was busy with Nick and Aurelie Board. I know a doctor was called. Who got sick? Or was someone hurt? What's going on?"

He stared at her. "You're askin' me about an official meeting?"

"Aw, c'mon, questions from people like me aren't new to you. I've got a job to do and this whole town behaves like I'm trying to steal something from them."

"Ah . . . " He wagged a finger in the air. "Beer. Beer would be good. It's a nice night. We'll sit out back."

His home might be little more than a shack on stilts with a tin roof, but he had a collection of furniture big enough to furnish a much larger house. His ex-wife hadn't been interested in trying to screw him out of antiques she didn't understand, just their children.

He'd chosen the pieces of furniture he used here to keep him remembering things, lessons learned. The rest was in storage.

Mollie surely had looked good arranged on the little pink-and-silver damask chaise that had belonged to his grandmother. His habit was to look at the chaise when he came home. Mollie used to sit there holding their twin girls and he had been a happy man with his three golden-haired girls.

Times changed.

Joan slid into a chair and made herself comfortable.

There was nothing in the living room that could interest Joan Reeves. He left her there and went into his shiny clean kitchen to get a couple of beers. These he opened and he poured the one for Joan into a glass.

Matt had talked about Joan Reeves and her so-called book. She wasn't a journalist—the hated breed. He must remind himself of that regularly, Buck thought, and the obvious fact that she was very different from any reporter he'd encountered. But he needed to watch her carefully, just to make sure she didn't get into something that was none of her business. After a lot of meticulous work, he and Matt had come up empty. That did not surprise Buck one bit, or discourage him. He was patient.

This woman was too eager, too determined for the average writer working on the kind of project she talked about. He had only come in contact with a few writers but they usually took the attitude that everything they needed would eventually come to them. Not Joan Reeves. She meant business, *now,* and she was pushy, even if she did talk like a Catholic school-girl.

"C'mon out," he called, "into the kitchen." He waited until she stepped uncertainly through the door and looked around.

"Nothin' worth writin' about here," he said. "Just a bachelor pad."

"A clean and tidy bachelor," she said. "I like that. And you've got everything really nice, too. Your furniture's gorgeous."

He didn't thank her.

"May I use your bathroom?" she asked, looking coy.

Buck pointed her to the bedroom and the only bathroom in the house. She dropped her purse on a chair and swayed away from him.

Joan closed the door in the tiny bathroom and locked it. She ran water in the sink and slid open metal, mirror-fronted cabinets. They were tidy, like the kitchen, with ordinary male toiletries, aspirin, condoms, nothing interesting.

She looked around and felt stupid, and desperate. What had she expected to find, a kilo of coke under the sink?

On the back of one door, the left one, he'd taped a photo taken at a distance. Joan leaned close to see better. A funeral in the rain. A canopy with mourners clustered beneath. With pulse throbbing in her throat, she drew back and closed the door.

He was a physical man and he had action in mind. And she was ready for him. But she'd needed to take a little time and think how to use the opportunity she'd be buying.

When Joan reappeared, Buck considered asking if she'd found what she wanted in his medicine cabinet. Did she honestly think running water masked the sound those squeaky hinges made? So what. Her little attempt at sleuthing hadn't been worth the effort to her.

The back door opened onto a second gallery that jutted into gnarled cypress trees growing out of the bayou shallows. He indicated for Joan to go outside.

Curtains of Spanish moss shone silver, and mist coiled through the tree trunks, just above the water.

"Take a chair." He tilted his head, indicating for her to pass him. "Over there."

Halfway past him, she paused and looked up without smiling. "I'm not complicated," she told him. "I do have needs, though. Like being able to eat and put my head down somewhere safe." She tucked her hands into the pockets of a short, straight denim skirt and drew up her shoulders.

Her top gaped, Buck looked down on twin peaks and his automatic indicator jumped. The view she'd given him was no accident. Her message didn't need interpretation: she would enjoy paying for his cooperation in her own way if that's what it took. He was a man who liked to make up his own mind about what worked to his advantage.

He had already decided he was getting double wages.

There were four chairs, old teak weathered gray the way he liked it, and shimmed up close enough to the iron railing around the gallery to allow for foot-propping.

Joan took the second chair in and Buck sat beside her. Standing, Joan was statuesque. She must have long legs, because when she sat, he looked over the top of her head.

"You're set up for a party," she said.

He looked at her blankly.

She indicated the row of chairs. He nodded and said, "You never know how many drinking buddies will show up." The four chairs were a habit and a symbol . . . and a warning never to let anyone get too close to him again.

So far, Joan was the first person who had joined him on his gallery among the cypresses where the trees had their roots in sludgy, waterlogged ground and their branches entwined beneath the blasted skags of their crowns, victims of electrical storms.

Buck passed Joan her beer.

She thanked him and said, "How long have you lived here?"

"Not long. I heard there could be a position opening with the local police and I let them know I might be interested if they got the kind of vacancy I could take. Something came up and here I am." He'd arrived as soon as Matt let him know he understood Billy Meche would leave, but he'd kept to himself until the job came through. He liked to get to know his surroundings real well. Asking directions wasn't something he did.

"It's a lot different here from New Orleans," Joan said.

The less personal discussion, the better. "Yeah." He wasn't shedding tears over leaving the NOPD.

"I guess folks don't want to work there anymore."

New Orleans was his city. "It's a good place and it's

coming back just fine. I wanted a change, is all."

He swung his boots onto the railing.

"I'm lucky," she said. "I can work any old place."

"Are you always busy?"

"Not as busy as I'd like to be. I've had some thin times. But this is good, this thing I'm doing now. It's going to pay really well."

He doubted she had any guarantees of a good payday. Her anxiety was too obvious, too raw.

He decided to let her make all the moves, raise all the topics, and kept quiet.

"What do you know about the Boards?" she asked.

He crossed his ankles. "Nothing. Why should I?"

"I don't know. I was just hoping."

"I don't know anything about them."

She took a sip of beer. "I got the impression Nick and Matt are old friends. Doesn't Matt know stuff about the family?"

"If he does, he hasn't told me."

"I bet he would if you asked him." She looked sideways at him and the moon glinted in her eye. "And his sisters. They seem different."

Buck upended his bottle and poured the beer down his throat. If he wanted to he could wise her up to Nick, Sarah and Aurelie not being related. If he wanted to. Might make a bone to get Joan off his back if he needed to and it wasn't like everyone around here wouldn't know soon enough.

She gave his arm a playful punch. "You're a quiet one but I really like you. I haven't done so well with the Boards. I mistook Aurelie for Nick's wife once. I'm not a shining star around here."

She looked pretty shiny to Buck. He checked her over again. "Why aren't you married, with a couple of cute kids? Or maybe you are."

"No."

"You should be. Good-looking woman like you, smart. Someone's missing a bet."

He heard her take a long breath through her nose. "Thanks. I think that's the closest I've gotten to a compliment in a long time."

"It's hot," he said. There was no percentage in pretty talk with Joan Reeves. "I like it. Humid as hell. Makes me feel like takin' off all my clothes."

She didn't giggle like some women would. "You married?"

"Nope," he said.

"Lonely?"

A direct woman. "Sometimes."

"Not for long, I bet."

He smiled to himself and stroked her upper arm. "Find out anything interesting about Nick Board, anything at all? Something I might not know?"

"You looking for an exchange of information?" Joan asked.

"Just askin' a question," he said. "It doesn't hurt to offer something when you want something."

Joan said. "I found out Nick and Baily Morris had a thing. The family didn't like her."

"Which means?" His skin felt damp. There wasn't

a puff of breeze and the moss hung in gauzy, limp shrouds; black skeins over a paler sky.

"It doesn't mean anything," Joan said. "I was thinking out loud."

"Just because you don't like someone doesn't mean you kill them," Buck said.

"I didn't suggest it did."

"Sure you did. Which one of them would you pick?"

Joan fidgeted. "Who would *them* be?"

"The Boards."

"You think one of them killed Baily?" She scooted until she sat sideways in her chair with her knees pulled up. "You should have heard Rusty Barnes when I poked at the edges of that one."

Buck tipped up his chin and stared at the sky. "He thought you were brilliant, is that what you mean?"

"You're a cagey one," Joan said. "He said the Boards were some of the nicest people he's ever met and I'd better watch what I say."

"Sounds like good advice." He unbuttoned his shirt and took it off.

Joan said, "Mmm. Nice."

Buck smiled. He figured he had Joan summed up about right. A woman with a healthy appetite. Not that he was interested.

Much.

"It's not fair," she said. "A man gets hot and he takes his shirt off."

"I don't think I have to answer that," he said. "Big girls make their own rules."

Unfortunately, she didn't strip off the tank top, but she did clasp her hands behind her head and he wished she had taken it off.

"If I don't get this story . . . if it's not good enough, I'm probably in trouble. I talked my way into the project but I don't fool myself I could do it again."

"Your angle. Should be good."

"Yes." She stretched.

"You can't spend too much time here, can you?" Buck said. "You're goin' to need a lot more than one house to write about."

"One at a time will do. I've already got several."

Buck wasn't interested but it could pay off to be polite. "Good luck with it."

"I'm prepared to work as hard as it takes," Joan said. "Are you sure Matt hasn't said anything about the Board family's history?"

"Uh-uh."

"I think there's a lot more there than they want anyone to know. I checked out what I could. There's no record of Delia having any children."

Buck's interest sharpened. "That could be worth a little research." But sure as hell not now. The need that made him restless had nothing to do with the information Joan wanted. He flicked his eyes toward her again. It could, though—if it came to that.

"I'm not wrong, am I, Buck? The Boards are hiding things."

He shrugged. "Who knows. Might be worth lookin' into." It was true enough that his life would be easier if this case moved along faster. He liked to clear an issue up and move on to the next.

"Why do you think someone would kill Baily Morris?"

He shook his head.

"What if it was an accident?"

Buck crossed his ankles in the opposite direction.

"Could have been," Joan said. "Could have been that someone was asking her questions about the Boards and things went wrong."

He squinted into the night. "That's a pretty big jump."

"Probably. I'm a writer. I play a lot of what-ifs. It's a habit."

Buck weighed the odds. Either she knew nothing and she really was desperate for any lead she could get on something as boring as a house, or Joan thought she had information on the early lives of Nick, Sarah and Aurelie, and she was looking for confirmation.

She got up and leaned against the railing, looking out among the black silhouettes. The bayou didn't make a lot of noise, just the occasional pop when something alive surfaced. Even the masses of the undergrowth life seemed subdued.

Joan took long swallows of beer until it was finished. She held the glass up like a telescope and looked toward the moon.

"You see the man?" he asked, dropping his feet to the floor of the gallery and pushing himself out of his chair.

She looked at him over her shoulder. "I see him now."

"You're thinking we could help each other, aren't you?"

"We could if you wanted to."

"It's sounding like a better idea all the time. But if I don't get, I don't give."

Joan gripped the railing and braced her arms. "Sounds like a fair deal. I already gave you something."

He smiled. "What was that?"

"You didn't know about Nick and Baily until I told you."

He hadn't. And he didn't necessarily believe all things had to be equal. "I didn't. How did you?"

"I can't share that."

"Maybe it's not true."

She laughed. "Ask around."

In other words, finding out would have been easy if he'd known to be interested.

Buck stood behind her, real close, touching her. He caught hold of the bottom of the tank and waited for a signal, yes or no. He didn't get either so he pulled it up and she raised her arms so he could take the top all the way off.

He dropped it on the nearest chair.

Bouncing his hips against her bottom, he took hold of her shoulders and leaned her against him, pulled her head back on his shoulder.

Her breasts didn't need moonlight. Joan's skin was

white and there was a lot of it all the way to big nipples. He tucked his arms under hers and weighed her. She felt good, sexy enough to lock his knees. When he pulled on her nipples she rubbed her butt against his penis.

"What started this?" she asked and her voice had slid down from the little-girl pitch.

"You gave me something. It's my turn to give back."

"Weren't we talking about information?" she asked.

"You were. And I'll make good on that when I get the right stuff. Are you complaining about tonight's payment?"

She slid his hands over her belly, pressed his fingers between her legs and rolled just a little. He returned to her breasts. There was more of Joan Reeves than his big hands could accommodate. "I like my sex interesting," she said. "The necessary kind I can deal with myself."

He just bet she could.

Taking off the skirt would be a waste of time. He dipped and used his knees to spread her legs, worked his pants down his thighs and shoved up and into her with enough enthusiasm to lift her feet from the ground.

"Holy . . ." She grabbed for him, grabbed for anything to hold on to. "You'll knock me over the goddamn railing. Oh."

She'd said "interesting." He fucked her fast, used the very good muscles in his thighs to set her into a canter on him. He bucked her, all but threw her, held his hands where he could feel her breasts bounce.

The first time she came, he grimaced into her hair. The second, he was with her and grunting in time.

He held her there, panting, his own breathing a race. They had heated more than the boiling night and their skin started to cool.

She moaned and tried to slide her feet to the ground. Buck made sure she stayed where she was.

The pressure mounted again. It had been too long for him.

He gave no warning when he swung her to face him, look a long, sucking bite on each nipple and pressed her backward this time.

She screamed.

"No one to hear you," he said, pushing her some more until she couldn't reach the railing to hold on anymore.

Fear could make things tougher but the thrill was worth it. He used his mouth to loosen her up, gave her an example of a well-toned tongue in action. And when she threw her arms back and wrenched from side to side, he gave it all to her, sweated over her, watched his only piece of pale flesh play hide-and-seek with darkness.

Over.

Whimpering, she hung upside down. Her hard, sexy tush would bear railing marks for a while.

Buck pulled her up, layered her body against his and let her slip slowly down until her feet met the floor. Her big breasts, sliding on his chest, started something all over again, but not enough to tempt him to work for it.

"Do we still have a deal?" he asked.

She raised her face slowly. "A deal?"

"If we give, we get?"

"Anytime," Joan said.

28

Sabine heard rain on the windows and closed her eyes, grateful for anything to break the hot, tense silence. The torrent eased the tension humidity caused and she didn't have to see to imagine how the sky was obscured.

The sky would be obscured if it were daylight rather than two in the morning.

"Thank goodness," she said to Ed and went to a window to pull the drapes aside.

"Leave it," he said so sharply she dropped the curtain at once. "I told you we don't want anyone to know we're here."

He sat near her, in an armchair, and she could only vaguely see the shape of him. He'd kept the lights off since they got back from town hours ago. "What is it?" she asked. "I've been quiet and left you to your own thoughts, but you're frightenin' me."

"No. Don't be frightened. You don't have to be."

"Don't I? First you change your story about—"

"I didn't change my story. I remembered it

straight, is all. Thank you for backing me up, sugar."

She hugged herself in the gloom. "You've always been truthful with me," she said. "Till now." She wanted to cry.

"I'm truthful now," he shouted. "Leave it alone."

Sabine jumped. She started to rock. "Oh, my, oh, my, what happened? Ed. Tell me, hon. You don't have to hold things back with me."

"Shit," Ed said. "Let it go, will ya? Like I said, it was the heat. I must have had a turn and fallen. That's how I hit my head, then I came to and fell in the pool. Disoriented, that's the word. Disoriented, I was. Climbed up on that fountain and slipped."

"Stop it!" She'd seen the way he looked when she found him. "You couldn't have done that yourself."

"I climbed up, I tell ya. Then I slipped and caught my shirt. I'd been thinking about what happened to Aurelie, that was it. I couldn't get it out of my mind that some big schmuck pushed that little girl around the way he did and I got muddled. I thought it happened to me, too. It was the heat, I tell ya."

Sabine felt her own flesh tremble beneath her fingers. "So why are we here in the dark? Why don't you want me to go near the windows?"

Light pulsed into the room, lightning streaking and penetrating the thin draperies. When thunder came it sounded a long way off.

"There's someone out there," Ed said. "Whoever he is, he doesn't want us, but we can't risk getting in his way. And now I've got his attention by what I've said." He breathed heavily. "I've got to prove I'm no threat. I don't know anything."

"If you don't know anything, there's nothing to be afraid of. Why can't we just carry on the way we were before?"

"Just do as I tell you," he snapped. He paused. "I'm sorry, baby. All this is getting to me."

"Okay," Sabine said. "Let's be calm. I need to think."

"I'll do the thinkin'."

He sounded like a stranger. It was because he was on unfamiliar ground and trying to seem in control.

"Why does Delia still want us here in the house?" Sabine said. "It's obvious whatever's going on is too big for you and me to be any help. We should go back to our own place."

Ed worried her. She hadn't been attracted to him because she thought he was a tough guy. Sabine didn't like tough guys, but she knew a scared man and Ed was one of them. That, she didn't like, either. Especially when he wasn't opening up with her.

"It makes her feel safer to have us in the house," Ed said. "And I'd rather have you here. Our place is too quiet."

"She's just tryin' not to hurt our feelings," Sabine said.

"You think too much. I'm tellin' you to stay in this house no matter what happens."

"And you keep tellin' me not to worry? Make up your mind." She made up her mind. "I'm callin'

304

Matt. I don't care if I get him up, we need him."

"Sit down, Sabine. The police can't help. They haven't helped with anything so far. Now listen to me. I've got to go out."

"No!"

"Calm down," Ed said, but his voice grated past his throat. "You've got to do what I tell you. For both of us, go along with me and do exactly what I tell you to do."

"What will I say if someone asks where you are before you get back?" Sabine asked.

"You don't tell 'em anything. Keep your mind and your attention on your business."

"Ed," she said, finding his hand and gripping it tight. "You don't sound like yourself."

"I will. Sometimes you've got to follow your instincts. That's what I'm doing." He got up and gave her a quick hug. "I'll take the truck. You drive it sometimes. If anyone sees me leave the estate, they could think it's you."

"Ed! You think someone's after you."

"I'm just bein' careful. Damn the rain. Listen to it."

The sky was still open and a constant battering at the windows sounded like buckets of water thrown at the panes.

"Don't go," she begged.

"I've got to. Hang in here, Sabine."

"Where are you going?"

He found her purse and handed it to her. "I'd like to take whatever cash you've got."

She gripped her stomach, so sick she had to sit down. "Take anything." She gave the purse back to him. "I asked where you're going."

He came to her and kissed her cheek. "I don't know yet."

"But you'll let me know?"

Ed didn't answer.

She couldn't help crying. "When will you be back?"

He backed away, reached a door rarely used and turned the handle. "I don't know that, either. Be brave for me. And Sabine?"

"Yes," she whispered.

"There will be questions and it'll get worse. They won't believe you don't know where I've gone. But you'll manage because you won't know. You're going to thank me for that."

29

"I can't see much," Nick said, peering through the windshield of his car. "Whoopee, the sky opened up."

"It's lovely," Aurelie said while she tried to uncoil the knots in her stomach. They'd been driving and driving and she had no idea for how long, or how far they'd traveled.

"You always liked storms," he said. "Shall I find a place where we can see the bayou? It looks prehistoric in weather like this. There's a good spot somewhere along here."

She almost said they ought to go home, but why? They could go anywhere they liked and the longer they stayed away from places where other people could find them, the longer they could pretend nothing was wrong.

"Aurelie, what do you think?"

"I'd like that. We're pretty far south now, aren't we?"

"Uh-huh. There's nothing out here. That's the way I like it."

Nothing but the two of them and a carload of sexual tension. Perhaps they'd be out long enough, and get back so late they'd dodge another opportunity to sleep together.

"It's hard to see the turns," Nick said, slowing down. "Just past that ruined church there's a track. Never could figure out what the church was doing there. Nobody lives within miles."

"Maybe they did once," Aurelie said. "The place is a shell now . . . there it is."

The dark hulk of a broken building, roof timbers open to the sky, lay just ahead.

Nick slowed even more. The headlights picked out the head of a narrow track and he steered that way, mowing down a line of tall grass between overgrown tire tracks. Rain slashed diagonally, relentless, with no sign of easing.

"We're nuts," Nick said. "You know that?"

"Yeah, I do. What are we doing here?"

He laughed. "Avoiding going home."

"I already thought of that," she said and they fell silent. "We used to like to come down here when Delia first moved us to Pointe Judah. Remember how strange everything seemed?"

"We loved it. I still do."

"Me, too." The car thumped into a rut, jarring Aurelie, then bumped on again. "You do know we can't run away from ourselves, Nick?"

"Is that what we're trying to do?"

"Yes."

"At least we're doing it together." He looked at her, one corner of his mouth tipped up. "Given our choices, I'd rather be here than anywhere else tonight."

She rubbed his arm and dropped her hand again. "We're sitting ducks, aren't we?" she asked. "Waiting for another attack. He must want that ruby so badly he can taste it, and he wants all of us dead just as badly."

"He," Nick said. "We don't say his name. I hate the sound of it. I want to kill the bastard."

She looked out the side window at the sopping grass and shrubs. "Who can blame you? I'd help. I never thought I'd want someone else to die." Her stomach met her throat and the past rushed in, days and nights she had buried so deep they had rarely become even a shadow of a memory.

"What is it?" Nick asked.

"Nothing." She turned toward him. "Are we going to get through what's happening to us?"

"Which part? Being in a murderer's sights, or loving each other?"

She stared at him. They entered trees. Moss so wet it hung like seaweed slapped the windshield, then dragged away over the top of the car. The track had all but disappeared. Nick stared ahead and drove a few more feet until Bayou Nezpique came into view.

"Know what that reminded me of?" he said, frowning, pushing at his black hair. "The way the moss goes over the car."

She felt disoriented. "No."

"A car wash."

With parted lips, she stared at him. "Okay." The idea ought to seem funny.

"Okay, but I just said we love each other." He turned off the engine. "Am I taking too much for granted?"

"I think your timing is questionable," she said.

"Regardless of the timing, I'm in love with you. I've never been in love with anyone but you and that's been going on for a long time. I'm pretty sick of pretending my feelings aren't my feelings."

"We're not like other people. We can't just do what we like and not worry about who we hurt."

He faced her. "We *are* like other people. We've got the same rights to hope and to take chances. I don't want to hurt anyone, either, but I'd like to work around that. Would you?"

Aurelie took one of his hands in both of hers and traced the veins from his knuckles up a muscular forearm. "Maybe I do. But I want you to think about something. Forbidden fruit. We became brother and sister. That's how we've thought of ourselves. Has that made it more exciting somehow? More dangerous?"

When she looked at his face he was watching her eyes. He took a deep breath. "I don't think so."

"But you're not sure?"

"I'm sure how much I want to be with you."

"But you're not sure it isn't, at least partly, because it feels like . . ." Her voice had risen and she couldn't keep it down.

"Fucking my sister?" he asked through his teeth. "Is that what you're trying to ask? I thought we were past that."

"There are a lot of things we're not past," she told him, her eyes stinging.

She drove him wild. Nick turned his hand and held hers tightly. "What things? You know everything about me. Why would you hold anything back from me?"

"I'm not holding anything back," she said. "Our lives didn't suddenly turn smooth. That's what I meant. And I think it would be good if you knew everything about yourself."

She was right, but he hated her throwing it at him like that. "I will know it," he said. "I'll hunt down Colin Fox and hurt him till he tells me what I want to know."

"Then what?" she asked, shaking her hair back.

"I'll kill him," he said. "And I'll enjoy it."

"You're not thinking." She cried openly. "Go home. I don't want to be with you. All you think about is making yourself feel good for the moment."

She pulled her hand away and he didn't try to stop her.

When she opened the door and pushed out into the soaked bushes and grass, he couldn't believe it. She set off in slashing rain among trees edging the bayou.

He got out of the car and ran around to the other side. "Get back here, you little fool. You don't know what's crawling around out here."

"I know you're here," she called. "And you're dangerous."

Batting aside the underbrush, Aurelie ran on, moving faster than she should have been able in such poor light and with roots and uneven ground under her feet.

"Dammit," Nick said and went after her. "Stop right there. Aurelie—stand still."

He closed the space between them fast, but not fast enough to stop the warm rain from drenching his shirt and pants to the skin. She kept struggling on.

The eerie lime-green light off the bayou filtered to color the layer of mist.

She looked over her shoulder and let out a cry when she saw how close he was.

"That's it," he panted. "That's . . . *it.*" He closed a hand on her shoulder, shot his other arm around her waist and hauled her off her feet.

"Put me down now," she told him. When her hair was wet it reached way past her shoulders. She used both elbows to try to dislodge him.

"Vixen," he muttered, turning her to face him. "This doesn't have anything to do with being mad at me. You're mad at yourself because you can't hate me. I make you face yourself and what you feel. It takes guts to do that and you don't have them."

"The hell I don't." It took both of her hands to shove her hair out of her face. "I've got plenty of guts. I just have something extra that makes me think about the other people around us."

"And I don't? Shit, Aurelie. This is awful out here."

"You're the one who wanted to come."

He shook his head. "Come on. This is pointless." He marched back toward the car, but her steps were much shorter and she held him back. She kept trying to work her hand free but he laced their fingers together and held on tighter.

"I'm not going with you," she said in a voice he hardly heard.

Oh, great, finally the pressure had made her fall apart. "Pretend I'm someone else," he said. "I'm taking you home."

"Damn you, Nick Board. Nothing's solved and it's never going to be."

"That's what you think." Nick swung her toward him and picked her up. He carried her, complaining, in his arms and made a lot better time. "An accident forced us to play a game. It had a purpose once but it doesn't have a purpose now and I don't want to play anymore."

"You think I do?"

He smiled into the rain. "No, I guess I don't."

When they reached the car, instead of getting in, he sat her on the hood. She tried sliding to the ground, but he put himself between her knees and gripped her waist. "Do you think you're getting in my car like that?"

He'd left the headlights on. He had a new battery and prayed it would prove worth what he paid for it.

"I don't want to get in your car," she said. "I'll walk home."

"Do you know how stupid that sounds?"

She sniffed and rubbed her face hard. "Of course I do. I'm having a crisis here. That's not something you understand, is it?"

He almost laughed. "No. Wouldn't know a thing about that. Dealing with a wild woman, a wet wild woman, in the middle of nowhere is a piece of cake for me. I've told her I love her, she thinks I only want her because it turns me on that we pretended to be brother and sister for a few years. Crap!" He put his face close to hers. "Did you hear that? It's all crap. Some son of a bitch wants something we've never even seen and he's willing to kill for it. We know who he is. I said I'd like to see him dead and you decided that made me selfish, even if he is the guy who killed my mother. You're crazed, woman. And I want you so badly it hurts."

Nick leaned on the car and wrapped her in his arms.

He pushed his face into the crook of her neck and kissed her.

Slowly, her hands crept up his back. She made circles with her fingertips before she found his jaw and eased his face up until she could see him. Despite the rain on her face, he knew she still cried. She looked into his eyes, then at his mouth, and she inclined her head to bring her parted lips to his. The kiss tasted of salt and sweetness. He couldn't get close enough to her and lifted her against him. Aurelie wrapped her legs around his waist.

When she broke contact, so slowly, they breathed hard. He rubbed his nose against hers and nibbled her upper lip, and he looked down at her body. The yellow tank dress, made of knit cotton, clung to her breasts, molded her nipples. His penis, already hard, all but brought him to his knees.

She caught at the bottom of his T-shirt and worked the wet fabric up his body and over his shoulders. He had to set her back on the car and help her take the shirt all the way off.

When he moved in again, she held him back and kissed his chest, ran her fingers through the hair there, stroked it until she reached the waist of his jeans and pushed a single forefinger inside.

"Oh, God," he said and turned his face up to the water. "I want something from you. I want you to tell me something."

Aurelie licked one of his nipples, tickled the flat center with her tongue.

"Stop." He caught her by the shoulders and almost laughed when she grinned up at him. "You're wicked. Did you hear what I just said?"

"I don't know if I can choose not to love you," she said. "That's what you want to know, isn't it?"

It was good enough for now.

Aurelie pulled her scrap of a dress up, revealing full, naked breasts, and pulled it over her head. She lay back on the car hood, passive, her arms spread wide, watching his face.

Nick stroked her thighs, pressed the heel of a hand into her mound, slid his hands over her belly and ribs to push her breasts together. Bending over her, he sucked a nipple into his mouth, then kissed his way meticulously, inch by inch, downward and beneath the wisp of a thong between her legs.

The center of her swelled.

Her hips rose and fell.

Nick made love to her with his eager tongue until she convulsed, jackknifed her knees, rolled to drag open his jeans.

They came together with violence, a furious, irresistible obsession.

30

"Now you're sure you can't just tell me what's on you're mind, Miz Sabine?" Officer Sampson asked. "Chief Boudreaux likes to settle in and look at overnight reports before he starts new business in the mornin'."

Sabine swallowed an urge to shout at Officer Sampson. He'd been in the department about two years, she thought, and was still inexperienced. "You do a good job looking after your boss," she told him. "But I'm sure he'll see me. It's not so early now. Just tell him it's Sabine and it's about what happened yesterday."

"Oh," Sampson said. "What happened yesterday? Why didn't you say so. He'll want to know about anythin' to do with that. Wait here."

She waited long enough for Sampson to walk along the corridor toward Matt's office and went tentatively after him. She might as well save any time she could.

Sampson knocked on a door and opened it. By the time he began to enter, Sabine stood behind him, and Buck Dupiere, just inside the office, saw her. He looked past Sampson. "Sabine? What d'you want?"

He wasn't as kind as Matt but she supposed that's what came from working in New Orleans.

"Miz Sabine wants a word with you, Chief," Sampson said to Matt. "She says it's to do with what happened yesterday and she'd like to tell you about it herself."

Sabine heard the rumble of Matt's voice and stepped past Sampson, at whom she smiled. "Thank you," she said. "They're lucky to have you here." She had learned a lot about making sure she complimented people. Anyway, she might be glad of Officer Sampson as a friend in future.

"Mornin', Sabine," Matt Boudreax said. "Nice to see you. Coffee?"

"Aren't you nice," Sabine said. "But, no, thank you." Whatever she did, she must not appear frightened or nervous, and she must not cry. Those were the things that made a person an annoyance in situations like this.

"What can I do for you?" Matt asked.

She smiled at Buck and waited, wanting him to leave.

"A problem?" he asked.

Sabine looked at Matt again and frowned. He smiled. "Buck, why don't you go make some of those calls. We're gonna run outta day before we run outta work."

Sabine didn't look at the other policeman but he sounded okay when he said, "Gotcha," and left.

She grabbed a handful of the braids trailing forward over her shoulder and wound them together. "It's nice of you to see me. There isn't anythin' to be worried about. I just thought it might be a good thing if I came by. You know how it is."

"A social call?" Matt said helpfully.

"Well, no." Sabine fanned herself with a hand.

"Hoo-mama, it's gonna be a hot one. I reckon all that rain last night just set us up. And humid? Saints alive, I should say so. The air feels like it's steam. Don't you agree?"

"It's a warm day," Matt said. "And humid. What was it you thought you should tell me?"

"We-ell." Sabine held her tongue between her teeth and frowned. "We-ell, that's the thing. I'm not sure I should be here at all." Ed would be mad at her, and hurt.

"Let me be the judge of that." Matt got up. He pulled a chair forward and guided Sabine to sit down. He sat on the edge of his desk. "What is it, Sabine? You wouldn't be here if you didn't think you needed to be."

She didn't know how it happened, but a big bubble rose in her throat and it burned, then her nose got stuffy, and tears overflowed. Once the crying began, it wouldn't stop. Bending over, she rested her face in her hands and her hands on her knees and heard noises wrench from her throat and chest. She wasn't supposed to cry. This was a time to be strong.

Covering her ears, she pressed her face against her floral dress and sobbed. "Ed," she managed to say. "It's Ed."

She felt a hand on her back, rubbing gently. She sniffed and fought to stop crying. Hiccups forced themselves out.

"Sabine," Matt said close to her ear. "It's okay. Let me help you."

She lifted her head a little and found that he was on one knee beside her. He smiled, his dark eyes filled with sympathy, and she managed to swallow. "He's gone," she whispered. "He left in the night and he didn't come back. He wouldn't tell me where he was going or when he'd be back. Matt, I'm afraid. It's something to do with him being attacked the way he was, I know it is."

He looked away, thinking. "Last night—at Out Back—he said he hadn't been attacked. You agreed with him."

"He's my husband," she said.

Matt held her hand. "Of course." He understood she didn't think any other explanation was necessary.

The sound of voices in the corridor annoyed him and he hoped Buck or someone else would deal with whoever was out there. He didn't want to be interrupted.

A rap on the door destroyed that fragile hope. Sampson scarcely had a chance to enter before Delia Board, a green-and-yellow silk kaftan billowing behind her, walked in with both hands moving while she spoke. Her auburn hair, styled in shining, upswept waves, was a muted beacon.

Sabine moaned and went back to pressing her face into her lap. This time she folded her hands over her head.

"There you are, Sabine," Delia said. Sarah came in behind her, her eyes filled with concern. "Where's Ed? Matt Boudreaux, I don't have to tell you again that you can't question someone without making sure they've got a lawyer. You did remember to ask for a lawyer, didn't you, Sabine?"

Matt looked helplessly at Sabine, who shook her head and renewed her gales of sobbing.

Delia searched into a capacious green straw bag and produced a cell phone. This she flipped open and punched at a button.

"Sabine's here to report a problem," Matt told Sarah. "I'm not interrogating her."

Already, Delia was talking to "Sam, dear."

"Our lawyer," Sarah said. "Delia. Delia, listen to me."

Delia waved a hand at her and Sarah snatched the phone, leaving Delia with her mouth in an amazed "Oh."

"Matt's not questioning Sabine," Sarah said, then she spoke into the phone. "Hi, Sam. Yes, this is Sarah. So far there isn't any reason for you to be involved, but thank you . . . Yes, I'm sure. Delia will call you later to tell you all about it . . . Bye."

"Thanks," Matt said, and to Delia, "Sabine arrived a little while ago. She's very upset."

Delia looked from him to Sabine. "Do you honestly think I haven't noticed that? We're here because we couldn't find either of them, Ed or Sabine."

Buck came in. There was no way he hadn't over-heard everything that had taken place. "I've asked for some iced tea," he said. "Sit down, ladies. Perhaps Sabine will be calmer with you here."

"Perhaps she will," Matt said through his teeth and gave Buck a narrow look. Sometimes smooth Officer New Orleans baited Matt's hook.

More footsteps approached. "That was quick," Buck said. "Nothing like iced tea to cool things down."

"I didn't notice that things were heated up," Delia said. She remained standing and paced, showing her kaftan and jeweled sandals to advantage. "We're calm, aren't we, Sarah? Poor Sabine's been through too much." She stood still and looked around. *"What have you done with Ed?"*

Rather than iced tea, Nick came in with Aurelie. Matt gave them an appraising look. They seemed to go almost everywhere in tandem these days. Could be a flip back to childhood, he supposed. They must have stuck close together then. He was still sifting through the story of how Delia Board had ended up with three kids she'd never seen before they showed up on her doorstep. But this morning Nick and Aurelie stood side by side, and he felt something subtly different about them.

Now he was getting fanciful. "Mornin'," he said. "Come on in. Everyone else has."

Sabine's crying had ceased and she'd raised her head, but kept her hands over her face.

"Hey, Sabine," Aurelie said. "Delia called to tell us you and Ed were missing and she was coming here."

Delia called to tell us . . . As in, Nick and Aurelie had been together? Where? Matt filed the snippet away, for whatever it might be worth.

Nick didn't like the way Matt Boudreaux stared at him—and Aurelie. Like he had them on some list of suspects.

And the anxiousness, the tension Sarah exhibited paralyzed him. She stared straight into his face, occasionally flicking her gaze to Aurelie, but always returning to him. He remembered to smile, cross the room and give her a hug.

"This is getting too scary," she said, holding him tightly around the neck. "I wish it would be over."

"Me, too," he said, disturbed by the level of her emotion.

"Ed left in the night," Matt said. "He didn't return home."

Delia spread her arms. "Finally, you tell us."

"Does he have family somewhere?" Matt asked.

"No," Sabine said. "He's got me, is all."

Matt cleared his throat and glanced at the Boards. "Maybe Sabine would be more comfortable without an audience." He gave Delia a hard-eyed stare. "And before you start yellin' about lawyers, she can have one anytime she likes, but she's the one who came to ask me for help. No crime's been committed, as far as we know."

"Oh!" Sabine shed more tears and Delia rushed to hug her.

Nick turned away from Sarah, gave an exasperated shrug and then caught Matt looking at the ceiling.

"As I was saying," Matt continued, "this is just a chat between Sabine and me. Anytime she wants to quit talkin' to me, that's her prerogative."

"I don't want to quit," Sabine said. "But Miz Delia and all are welcome to stay." She cast them glances that suggested she hoped they would.

"So be it," Matt said. "Some things we just have to ask. They don't mean a thing. Routine stuff."

"So ask," Delia said.

Nick had to smile. The expression on Matt's face suggested he'd like to gag Delia. He said, "Sabine, did you and Ed have a fight last night?"

She blinked. "No. No, not the way you mean."

"If you had a fight in a way you mean, what happened?"

"You're pushing her," Delia said.

"Sabine's supposed to be answering the questions," Nick said, wishing he could suggest Delia go home without causing a bigger ruckus.

"Nothing happened," Sabine said.

Nick saw a flicker in her expression and figured Matt must have noticed, too.

Sabine's eyes moved rapidly from Matt to Nick. She threw some of her braids over her shoulder. "He decided to go out for a drive, is all."

"Does he do that a lot?" Matt asked.

"Now you're being impertinent," Delia said.

Matt gave Delia all of his attention. "No," he said, "I'm not. I'm asking routine questions and hoping we can figure out how to find Ed and bring him home just as soon as we can. That's what Sabine wants."

"It surely is," Sabine said. "Ed doesn't go out at night. Me, that's why I'm so upset. He had that bump on his head and I don't think he was himself. I'm afraid he could have gotten into an accident."

Someone knocked on the door once and Matt said, "Come in."

Christian DeAngelo entered and Nick could tell Matt remembered the man from somewhere. Matt snapped his fingers, "You were at Ona's Out Back last night. You were with Finn and Emma Duhon."

"Good morning," Angel said. A big son-of-a-gator. No attitude except complete confidence. "Christian DeAngelo. Angel." He put out a very large hand.

"Mornin'," Matt said and shook hands. "I'm Chief Boudreaux. Matt. This is my second-in-command, Buck Dupiere." Buck also shook hands. Matt raised his chin in silent question.

Nick figured they'd all find out what Angel wanted when he was ready to tell them.

"I spoke with Mrs. Valenti at Place Lafource and she told me I'd find all of you here. Convenient. I'd have been coming to the station anyway," Angel said. "I understand you're looking for Ed Webb."

Sabine jumped up and went to him. "You know where he is?"

He put his hands on his hips. "Not exactly, Mrs. Webb."

It sounded as if Angel had a flair for names. He'd probably learned a bunch the previous night.

"Angel," Nick said. He had a few questions he'd like to ask himself, such as what exactly being a bodyguard meant to Finn's buddy. "How do you know Ed's missing?" *And who's been watching Delia and Sarah while you got your fingers into Ed and Sabine's business?*

"Mrs. Valenti told me," Angel said with a smile that showed fine, straight teeth but didn't warm his eyes a notch from instant freeze. "She said Mrs. Board had mentioned why she and Sarah were coming here."

Predictably, Delia said, "Call me Delia," in her best smoky voice and extended a long, smooth, perfectly manicured hand.

Angel shook hands with visible care.

Since he'd introduced the two himself the previous night, the charade amused Nick. He admired Sarah's blank face. Talented actors on every side. That wasn't such a comfortable idea.

"You must have been coming to see us today," Delia said, thrusting her head forward and emphasizing each word. "Just the way you said you would at Ona's. I do like a man who keeps his word. I apologize for not being there to greet you."

She was hiding Angel's tracks! Nick grinned. Delia didn't want her bodyguard to blow his cover in front of the cops.

The bodyguard gave Delia a million-watt smile and she took a breath deep enough to be heard. She let her appreciation of the big man, his curly, dark blond hair and much darker brows show, and actually touched a white scar along the right side of his jaw. "My," she said, "that must have been painful."

"Not really," Angel said, still flashing his killer smile.

Nick noticed a rhythmic tapping and traced it to the toe of Sabine's left shoe. Her feelings showed. She didn't give a rat's ass about any of the small talk, she wanted her Ed back.

"What do you know about Ed Webb?" Nick asked Angel. "About where he is?"

"Ed drives a red pickup some of the time, doesn't he, Mrs. Webb?" Angel asked, ignoring Nick. "A Ford?"

Delia sucked in a sharp breath. Her hands went to her face.

"Yes," Sabine said very softly. "Was there an accident? Did you see the truck?"

"Did you?" Delia asked.

"I saw the truck," Angel told her. "Outside Buzzard's Wet Bar."

"Last night?" Sabine crossed her arms tightly. "Why would it be there? Ed hardly ever drinks. He doesn't like taverns and places like that. It probably wasn't his truck."

"It's his," Angel said. "He was in Buzzard's early this morning, with a man Buzz didn't know. The two of them left, but Ed didn't drive away in his own vehicle. It's still there."

31

Nick's temper rose. He didn't want to be at the lab; it was too far away from Aurelie and the others, and having Angel splayed in a chair he'd moved where he could see through the window of Nick's office wasn't helping a thing.

Angel had been silent a long time when he said, "He's a night mover."

It only took an instant for Nick to follow the other man's thought process. "Except for when he got to Ed," he said. "That was late in the morning."

"If our man was responsible for that." Angel had a stillness about him. "Ed could have been telling the truth when he backed away from his original story."

This wasn't a new idea to Nick. "Yeah, but this time he went missing in the night."

"If he's gone missing."

Nick thought about that comment. "Rather than what? Taking off on his own for some reason? He didn't take his truck, so he left on his own—we don't know how."

"Could have been on foot. At first, anyway."

"Could have been," Nick agreed, pushing away from his desk and standing up. "Was there anything else on your mind?" If not, Nick needed to check in with Matt and he didn't want an audience.

"Yes. They're following up on ID found in the grave."

"In California?" Angel had his attention now. "How do you know that?"

Angel shrugged.

"What's that going to accomplish? Colin made sure his ID was there with the others. Are they sure none of his bones are down there? In a different spot, or dragged off by something?"

"Yes," Angel said. The sky was darkening again and he leaned to peer upward. "He wasn't there. There went our sun."

"So he changed his identity. But we already figured that out. Damn. Matt and crew have got to get someone for Baily's murder soon so I can put some time in looking for Colin. Whoever he's supposed to be now."

"Matt won't want you to do that. Neither will the California cops—when they find out about you."

Nick heard the first sharp pings of rain hitting the windows. "What would you do if someone murdered your mother?"

"I'd go after him. If I'd ever known my mother."

"Sorry," Nick said, although Angel's expression hadn't changed. "How did you get your information?"

"I asked for it."

"I don't suppose it would do any good to ask who you talked to?" Nick said.

Angel shook his head, no. Once.

"There's something else I have to do," Nick said. He didn't know why, but he trusted this man. "I want to know more about my mother, her history. And how Colin got his hands on her." But he didn't trust Angel enough to talk about wanting to identify the father of Mary Chance's son.

"Whatever you do," Angel said, "don't tip your hand on those plans. They'll find a way to stop you, at least till they get what they want, or give up."

"How the hell would they do that?" Every way he moved, he hit a wall. "The law doesn't manhandle peaceful citizens and I don't intend to do something they could arrest me for."

Angel turned from the window and got up. They stood, eye to eye over the desk, and Nick saw the slightest change in Angel's expression. Sympathy? Or a warning?

"The *they* I'm talking about aren't cops."

32

"I'm gonna turn down the air-conditioning," Eileen Moggeridge said. Poke Around felt cooler than usual. "It's pretty cruddy outside but it's still hot. Not that it should make a difference to us in here one way or the other."

Aurelie said, "Hmm," and dropped an embroidered tablecloth on top of Hoover. He rolled over in the cushy dog bed Eileen had bought for him to use at the shop and let all four feet flop in the air.

At lunchtime, Aurelie had gone home and brought her mail back to the shop with her. An envelope from her former employers in New Orleans interested her, but made her nervous, too. It reminded her that she couldn't ignore her career forever. So far she hadn't opened the envelope.

There were plenty of reasons for her to stay put in Pointe Judah in the near future. She tried not to think Nick's name, or drift off into seeing his face—or anything else about him.

"I haven't seen so much of Matt lately," Eileen said. "Maybe he isn't interested anymore."

Aurelie studied her friend's face.

After doggedly insisting her friendship with Matt was no big deal, Eileen's frequently wistful manner, her frowns when she spoke of him, proved what Aurelie had already believed: Eileen wanted Matt. If Aurelie could make just one guess about what was going on, she'd say Matt was too tied up with trying to control big crime in a small town to have time left over for a love life.

Eileen gave a long sigh.

"He's busy," Aurelie said. "There's too much on his plate and he doesn't have enough staff."

"That's true." Eileen smiled at her and some of the tension in the shop released.

Three customers, two women and a man, made piles of intended purchases on the counter. They were strangers who said they were from Indiana. One blonde who said, "Call me Suzanne," had cleaned out the shop's collection of colored glass frogs and was considering a toothpick holder shaped like a sarcophagus. None of the shoppers seemed interested in Eileen and Aurelie's conversation.

Aurelie sat at one of the tiny tables near the espresso station, opened the envelope from the Caring Company and swiftly read the contents. She looked up to find Eileen watching her. "From my old employers," she said. "Just people doing a job that gets dirty sometimes. They want me to consider working for them again. When I go back to the law, I'm starting over in another field."

"When will that be?" Eileen didn't try to hide an anxious look. She didn't want Aurelie to leave.

"Not yet," Aurelie said, smiling. "D'you think you can put up with me for a while?"

Eileen turned on the very high heel of one shoe and said, "I'll do my best," over her shoulder.

She could open an office in Pointe Judah, Aurelie thought. There were a couple of lawyers in town but they were entrenched with the old school, the Patrick Damalis types in the area, and a lot of folks didn't hesitate to say they needed someone "with their feet on the floor who could do business without wanting lunch thrown in."

It probably wouldn't work for Aurelie. There were stormy family times ahead. She couldn't see how they'd be avoided, and she didn't want to think about the chance that some really special relationships might not come through in one piece.

Sarah opened the shop door and Aurelie felt as if she'd conjured them up—Sabine came in with Sarah and exuded misery.

"Have they found Ed?" Aurelie asked, then wished she hadn't.

It was Sarah who answered, "No," in a flat voice. She was growing her hair a little longer and it flipped up in soft curls all over. Aurelie liked it. She liked Sarah's out-of-character chocolate-colored silk pants and tank top, too.

What had influenced the sudden, more feminine appearance, Aurelie had no idea.

Sure she did.

This was in anticipation of running into Nick.

Very soon she and Sarah needed to have a talk, about the present and future complications facing them. "You're looking sexy, Sarah," Aurelie said. "That color is super on you."

Sarah cracked a smile and said, "Thank you. You don't look so bad yourself."

Sabine presented Aurelie with her profile and the set of her features was grim.

Bending over Aurelie, Sarah asked quietly, "Can you come out to my car? I'm worried about Sabine."

Aurelie nodded. She got up. "I'm going to pop out for a few minutes, Eileen, okay?"

Eileen nodded.

Sabine all but ran from the shop, with Sarah and Aurelie hurrying behind. Before they could get into the car, Sabine faced Aurelie. "I don't believe a word of it," she said. "And I don't like that Buck Dupiere. Real sure of himself, that one is. He doesn't smile when he gives you the bad news, but me, I can feel how he enjoys himself."

"We're getting wet," Sarah said, grimacing at wet spots on her silk outfit. "Please get in the car."

Sabine immediately scrambled into the cramped backseat of the red Miata. Aurelie and Sarah got into the front and swiveled around to look at Sabine. "What's up?" Aurelie asked.

Sarah squeezed her hand, communicating for her to give Sabine time.

Tears ran freely from Sabine's dark eyes. Her burnished skin hid most of the bluish marks under her eyes, but not all. The woman didn't look at all like her usual sunny self.

"They're lying," Sabine said. "They're trying to frighten me into giving something away and it won't work because I don't know anything."

Aurelie waited. She smiled encouragement at Sabine.

"Buck called me not an hour after I got back to Place Lafource this morning." She gulped. "He said Ed's got a record. For awful things. Armed robbery. Dealing drugs. So many things. Now Buck says he thinks Ed's got something to do with the assaults here and he deliberately pretended he'd been attacked at Place Lafource to cover for himself." Her voice trailed away. "He said Ed changed his story because he didn't want the police looking around too close."

"Oh, Sabine." Aurelie couldn't bear what this was doing to a good friend. "Just because Ed went out of town, the police can't pin anything on him. I think

Buck was fishing, that's all. He was testing you to see if you were hiding something about Ed." Buck would have run a check before saying such things to Sabine, but Aurelie wanted to console her.

"If I knew anything, I wouldn't tell them," Sabine said in a loud, choking voice. "If all those horrible things Buck said are true, I wish Ed had told me. I love him anyway. He's a good husband to me and he hasn't done anything wrong since we've been together. I'd know if he had. We don't have any family. I don't know what to do. That's why I went to Sarah."

"You've always got us," Sarah said at once. "Stay there. I'm taking you back to Delia. We're going to deal with this and it'll turn out okay." She opened her door and indicated for Aurelie to join her in the parking lot.

Sarah made a run through the warm, steaming rain to stand beneath an awning on the new pastry shop next to Poke Around. When she got there, Aurelie waved at the shop owner, Felice, through the window.

"What are we going to do?" Sarah asked. "Should we go to the police station and ask Buck to tell us exactly what he knows?"

"It doesn't work like that," Aurelie told her. "He'd say it's none of our business. He doesn't have to share information with us."

Sarah screwed up her face. "That pisses me off, sis. Why would he accuse Ed of things like that?"

Aurelie turned to look out through rain pouring

from the edge of the canvas awning. "He wouldn't if he didn't have proof. They've done a check on Ed and he's got a record. Pretty colorful record from the sound of it."

"I don't believe it."

"Believe it, Sarah. No cop is going to make up things like that, not if he wants to keep his job."

"So there's been a felon living in Place Lafource, with Delia?"

"People do reform," Aurelie remarked. "I'm not afraid for Delia or for Sabine."

"I want Nick's opinion," Sarah said. "We have to tell him."

"Sure. But I do think I can make my own decisions. So can you. We don't need permission from Nick."

Sarah got a faraway look in her bright blue eyes. "I just feel better when I know what he thinks. He thinks so clearly. I'll trust whatever he decides."

"Right," Aurelie said. She didn't dare say what she really thought. And if she was worried about Sarah's feelings for Nick before, now she felt frantic—and guilty. "Take Sabine home. She needs comfort and Delia will make sure she gets it."

"You think it's okay to have her at Lafource with Delia?" It was obvious that concern for Delia was the only reason for Sarah's concern.

"I do think it's okay," Aurelie told her. "Get her home. I'll see if I can find Nick so we can talk to him." She almost said that he would know what to do but stopped herself and almost laughed.

"You're right. He'll know what to do." Sarah shot away to the car, got in and drove off with Sabine.

Aurelie smiled to herself. She stood on the sidewalk, rubbing at her forehead. Too bad she couldn't rub herself a fresh supply of energy. The knot she'd started carrying around in her stomach drained her.

She returned to Poke Around, just in time to pass the same group of shoppers who had been there when she left.

"You don't look so good," Eileen said when she saw Aurelie. "How about some coffee?"

"In other words I look as crappy as I feel. Coffee's a good idea." She went to the bright red espresso machine and picked up a mug. "You want something?"

"No, thanks. Aurelie, what's going on?"

Muscles in Aurelie's shoulders were so tight, they hurt. She couldn't give Eileen a straight answer. "There aren't any breaks in the case."

"I understand," Eileen said. "Make your coffee. I'm hoping we get a busload or two through today. Business is good but it can always be better. Do you think I should call Matt? Just to let him know he's on my mind?"

Aurelie smiled while she poured steamed milk on top of the coffee in her mug. "That's what I would do, but some people tell me I should think longer before I follow my instincts. Hoover! What's in your mouth? Come here. *Now.*"

"I'm going to do it," Eileen said. "Seems like

everyone's mad at him. I'm going to invite him to dinner."

"Do it. Great idea. Oh, no." She knelt beside Hoover and lifted his head. A piece of biscotti stuck out of his mouth and he sucked and drooled over it. "Darn it, boy, you're naughty. Where did that come from?"

The dog worked his lips, drawing in the big cookie, and Aurelie saw where he'd found it. A large box of assorted biscotti had been put down on its side. Hoover had taken advantage of a loosened piece of tape and burrowed inside.

"You're a rotten dog," Aurelie said. "Give me that." She attempted to wrestle the slimy biscuit out of his mouth, and lost the contest.

"Don't you be mean to him," Eileen said, laughing. "That must have fallen out of the box and he was trying to help by cleaning up. Here, darlin'. Have a fresh one." She peeled the crackling paper away and set a fresh biscotti in the dog's bed.

"Oh, look," Aurelie said, baring her teeth in disgust. "Half-chewed jelly beans in his bed." She began scooping the sticky mess from beneath Hoover and pulled out pieces stuck to his fur. At the same time she removed the new treat Eileen had given him. "You're going to get sick, silly boy."

The sound of screeching tires grabbed Aurelie's attention and she looked out to see two police cars hit loose surface grit in front of the condos where Nick lived. Nick was just climbing out of the Audi and slammed the door with enough force for the noise to travel as far as Aurelie.

"Looks like more upset," Eileen said. "They're all so mad all the time."

"It's frustration," Aurelie said, but she was tired of posturing males throwing testosterone around. "I'm going over there."

"No, you're not." Eileen hurried to Aurelie's side. "You think the police wouldn't send you on your way? You'd feel like a fool. And how about Nick? He doesn't want his little sister muscling in to protect him against the big bad policemen."

Along the sidewalk outside came Joan Reeves and the photographer, Vic. Joan was put together like a model ready for the runway—all in shades of brown and cream. Vic was his usual casual self, not that he needed sexy clothes to make him a standout.

Smarting from Eileen's dart to the heart about acting like Nick's protective little sister, Aurelie didn't feel like facing this duo, but in they came. Joan's makeup was expertly applied and it showed just how beautiful she could look.

"Hi, Joan," Eileen said. She sent a sheepish glance in Aurelie's direction. "You lookin' for that special gift, folks. You surely do look great, Joan. Going to a party?"

Joan blinked at Eileen and said, "No. We came to see Aurelie. Vic's going to take a picture or two in here if it's okay with you."

"It's not my shop," Aurelie said.

"We want you in the shots," Joan said to Aurelie. "You know about my book on antebellum houses and the people who live in them. You may not be in one now, but you qualify. I hope you'll let me interview you shortly."

Eileen said, "I'm sure it's okay to take photographs in here if Aurelie wants you to."

Vic unloaded his equipment without waiting for permission. Aurelie saw a Band-Aid on his cheek and redness turning to bruising just below. She said, "What did you do to your face?" and jumped when he straightened up fast and glared at Joan.

"He cut himself shaving," Joan said quickly, but she covered her own Band-Aid, one stuck over the end of a finger on her right hand. She didn't cover it before Aurelie noted how long the woman's nails were—all but the broken one she'd obviously hidden.

Joan seemed a gentle, almost bumbling soul. The idea of her beating up on a man cast her in a different light. But Aurelie had to suspect Joan had thumped Vic's face.

"Let's get this done," Vic said, his voice harsh. "Where d'you want her?"

Joan didn't look at him. "The bird feeders would be nice in the background. I want to show your life today, Aurelie."

Vic grunted and said, "Too busy."

"Then why ask me in the first place?" Joan asked, sounding furious. "You don't need me."

"How right you are," he said and waved Aurelie to the right, in front of a handmade quilt.

Aurelie didn't move. "Let's back up," she said. "I didn't say you could take my picture. You haven't even asked if you can."

Joan's attention had wandered. She looked across the street toward the two police cars outside Nick's condo. "Are they pestering that lovely man now?"

"Just routine stuff," Aurelie said, and she'd back up what she'd said if she had to. "After all, Baily Morris did die at our lab and they don't even have a suspect."

"Are you sure?" Joan asked. "They wouldn't think Nick was a suspect, would they?"

"They would not," Eileen said sharply. "Nick wasn't even out there when it happened."

"How do you know that for sure?" Joan asked.

"We're busy," said Aurelie, grateful that the shop was empty of customers. "It's time to get on." Hoover decided to exercise his growl just a little.

"I'm sorry," Joan said, and looked it. "I don't think sometimes."

"You can say that again," Vic told her.

Joan began the rapid blinking again. "Forgive me. If we could just get a couple of good shots we'll leave you alone."

"Why do you want them?" Aurelie asked.

"Oh." Joan's expression turned blank. "I told you. Past and present generations. I want to know every little thing about you."

33

"Make sure I don't have to go lookin' for you," Matt Boudreaux said. "I want you right here where I can find you."

Nick locked his hands behind his head, leaned back in his chair and stared at Matt.

"I want an assurance," Matt said.

"I'd like you all to leave now," Nick said, his eyes flicking to Buck. "Unless you're charging me with something." Young Sampson and another officer whose name hadn't registered with Nick, stood looking awkward with four brown paper bags of so-called evidence between them.

"We'll be going," Matt said and Nick thought his old friend didn't look so happy. "I'm doing what I have to do. Thanks for lettin' us take a look around."

Nick had seen no reason for a warrant just for Matt and his people to make a superficial search. The chicken foot had raised the most interest. Matt had subjected Nick to a lot of questioning about the entry being made without break-in. Did he lock his doors? Who had a key to the condo? Nick came close to telling Matt that he, Nick, must have made the whole thing up, planted the foot himself. For once he'd managed to keep his mouth shut, but he couldn't shake the conviction that Matt really did suspect him in the case.

"It's too bad you didn't call us in yesterday," Buck

said. "They've dusted for prints but we don't expect much luck. You've been all over here for twenty-four hours."

"I've had a lot on my mind," Nick said, but he knew he'd been wrong to take so long to report the intrusion. "The only reason was to leave the foot. And I was supposed to find it. Delia told you about the legend or what little she can remember."

Matt grunted.

Nick shrugged. "It's getting hard to take some of this stuff seriously. A friggin' chicken foot and some crap about a vulture."

"I suggest you take it very seriously," Matt said. "Did I mention we went over the study at Lafource and came up empty-handed. That's another case of any evidence being tampered with. The tape on that bag of sand came from a roll on Delia's desk. Nada. Not a mark on it."

"I regret we didn't come right to you on these things," Nick said.

"I know it's hard for you not to be in charge," Matt said to him. "But hold it back, okay? Don't get in the way. You don't have the training to help and you could make it harder for the people who do."

Fury immobilized Nick. Fury and common sense. He didn't dare move, didn't dare let himself follow his instincts. He'd like to put a fist in Matt's face and tell him he, Nick, would decide what was best for him to do.

Buck opened the door and the two younger officers

stepped outside, bumping into each other in their hurry to escape. Matt made to follow Buck but turned back. "Just a last question before I go," he said. "Is there anything else you'd like to tell us?" Buck had stopped and stood in the doorway, observing.

Like what? How I've been running around town attacking and killing people? "Can't think of anything, Matt," Nick said.

"Why did you decide to take Baily Morris's briefcase away from the lab after she'd been killed?"

Nick ground his fingers together behind his back. "I already told you. The reason hasn't changed. It was automatic. It seemed as if I should look after it because it belonged to her."

Matt snorted. "Were there some parts of an experiment she was running in the briefcase?"

"Who told you about that?"

"A friend of mine," Matt said. "The stuff she was working on wasn't hers, was it? It was your invention. Your baby. See you around. Soon."

The two men followed each other out.

"Shit!" Nick let his arms hang between his knees. He bowed his head and closed his eyes. That Matt would even think Nick had something to do with Baily's death, or the attacks that had followed, showed no progress had been made. To hell with them. He didn't have proof that Colin was behind the crimes, but if he was, Nick intended to get the evidence needed to back up his theory.

Could be time to lawyer-up. Aurelie would know.

Nick put his elbows on his knees and wrapped his hands and forearms over his head. He was tired. Apart from the times he'd spent in Aurelie's arms, he hadn't known a moment's peace since the news broke in California.

"Don't jump."

He did jump, but Aurelie's voice was the best thing he'd heard since the last time they'd been together. She had opened the door without making a sound, and she closed it softly.

"Hi," he said, not lifting his head. "Did my visitors see you coming here?"

"No." She rubbed his forearms and the backs of his hands. "I waited for them to drive off. They were in a hurry to get away."

"They've told me not to leave town and this time it wasn't so much a suggestion."

She knelt down in front of him and rested her head on his thighs. "Matt doesn't have any leads," she said. "Everything's fragmented." She told him that Joan Reeves and her buddy Vic had stopped by the shop, and by the time she'd finished her story he was mad all over again.

He stroked her hair, and her back, exposed between thin straps on a coffee-colored sundress.

"I think I need a lawyer," he said. "And Delia's family lawyer isn't what I have in mind. Sam's a good man, but he's never done any criminal stuff."

"I want to scream," Aurelie said. She slid her face higher up his thighs and put her arms around his waist. "I don't like to hear *criminal* used in the same sentence with a reference to you."

He bent to kiss her back. "It's showtime, sweetheart. They want someone's head on a plate and mine looks tasty. Know a good lawyer?"

"Joe Gable in Toussaint. He's one of those guys who does everything well. If I could do it myself, I would, but it wouldn't be appropriate."

"You know how to contact the man?"

"Finn and Emma know him. So does Eileen."

"Divorce? Is that what he does?"

"Not solely. He's done some pretty big cases for a small-town lawyer. You could make an appointment to see him. If you wanted me to, I could come with you. Or we could ask him to come here. He might go for that."

"I've got to think some more first," Nick said. "Someone told Matt what was in Baily's briefcase. The stolen formula."

"I thought you already told him about it," Aurelie said.

"I didn't. It didn't seem that important and frankly, I didn't want to sound malicious."

"Because that could make you look guilty?"

"No, damn it." He pushed to his feet and Aurelie lost her balance. She fell back on Nick's blue Oriental carpet, slammed her elbows down for balance and said, "Ouch, Nick!"

"Sorry," Nick said, his back to her. "Not a lot of people around here could give Matt that information.

So I guess I'm going to have to weed out the worm."

"I kind of think that's one of the things Matt's going to do."

"Think, Aurelie! Matt already knows who told him, that's the problem. It was probably a Wilkes and Board employee. I suppose I shouldn't be upset about that. They wouldn't have volunteered the information."

She smiled up at him and he felt like an overgrown, badly behaved kid. Leaning over, he scooped her off the floor and set her in his favorite, ugly, blue corduroy recliner. "I'm a pig," he said. "But I didn't knock you over on purpose."

"I know. If I didn't, I'd be downtown applying for a restraining order."

He stared into her lovely, currently snapping, blue eyes and grinned. "What do we do about Joan Reeves prying into our business?"

"I'm not going to be in her book," Aurelie said. "I don't like the idea of people making money on other people's lives, and she could run across something that would take her right to the middle of the time we spent at The Refuge. We have to freeze her out of town."

"She's already shown she won't be easy to get rid of," Nick said. "We'll manage. We'll get together with Sarah—and Delia—and work out a plan."

"Are you okay?" Aurelie asked.

"Not at all," he said and flopped into another chair again, trailed his hands over the sides. "I'm in terrible shape. I don't think it would be a good idea to leave me alone."

Aurelie crossed her arms. "Well, I know it looks like our kind of weather, but I'm still a bit bruised from the last time you attacked me in the rain. In case you've forgotten, that was only yesterday. I've got to go."

"Yesterday?" He widened his eyes. "Of course I'm dying here. *Yesterday?* This is today. You can't expect me to go a whole day without—"

"*Nick.* I'm leaving."

"Too bad," he said. "You don't know what you're missing."

"I've got to get back to work."

"Of course."

Aurelie couldn't ignore what she felt, or what she'd really like to do right now, but she still had control of her actions. She waved and approached the door.

Nick got there first, falling against the wall in his crazy dash to cut her off.

"What are you doing?" she said. "You're mad."

He shook his head. "No, I'm not." He locked the door and put on the dead bolt. "We're not here."

"Your car's outside and Eileen knows I'm here."

His attention didn't leave her mouth. He watched her talk and gradually brought his face closer to hers.

"Nick, not now."

"Now," he murmured and pressed their lips together, slipped his tongue into her mouth. Very easily, he turned her back to the wall and braced a hand on either side of her head. For a second he raised his face and looked down at her, but only for a second. The next kiss felt like a softly dangerous attack laced with some sort of drug. Aurelie began to lose control. Her bones turned soft and useless, her legs weak.

You are a spineless woman. She dodged under his arm and whirled away from him, held up her hands to ward him off. "We can't keep doing this," she said. "It feels sneaky."

"You couldn't be more wrong," he told her. "There's nothing sneaky about the fact that we're locked in here and we're going to make love. It's open season, Rellie. If you run, I'll hunt you down."

Excitement, a rush of tumult, sent her running anyway. She ran for the kitchen, but he got there neck and neck with her. She sprang around, set her eyes on the door, and escape.

Nick shot an arm around her, spread his hand over her back and slammed her against him.

"Nick," she cried. "What's gotten into you?"

He caught her mouth with his again, kissed her breathless again. Trapping her against the counter, he undid the buttons on her bodice and slipped the straps from her shoulders. She tried to hold the front of the dress over her breasts but failed. Nick spread his hands over her and kissed her from brow to waist, over and over.

His eyes turned wild and he panted, held the tip of his tongue between his teeth. And he lost any battle

348

for patience. She heard fabric tear and grimaced. The dress fell around her feet and he pulled her from the puddle of coffee-colored fabric.

"Mmm," he said while she crossed her arms and covered her breasts. Wearing only a thong and high-heeled sandals, she felt wanton. She landed on the counter, the granite cold under her bottom, and Nick got himself out of his clothes. He kept a hand on her because he thought, correctly, that she might flee if he let her go. Wriggling and tearing, he ended up naked, his skin gleaming all over.

And he was so ready for her.

He pulled her arms from her chest and let his head fall back. "If I keep on looking at you, one of us is going to be frustrated because I won't be able to hold on."

A thrill, something too close to fear to call, engulfed Aurelie. She stared at him, all of him, and wondered how she coped with a man like him. He ought to break her in two just entering her body.

"Why doesn't it feel weird when we're together?" she asked. "Anymore?"

He closed her mouth with his own, then mumbled, "This was always going to happen."

She pulled her feet onto the counter, wrapped her arms around her knees and scooted sideways.

Nick laughed deep in his throat, a rumbling that spread to his chest. And he bent, pulled her ankles far apart, and gave her a forceful tongue sampling of what he intended to do to her next.

Aurelie was the one who didn't last, she started to slump onto the counter, but he put an arm around her back and held on, anchoring his grip by holding a breast. She bumped her bottom up and down and her knees flopped open. When the rage of pulsing started, and spread, she felt slick all over, drowning in self-made moisture and the film of sweat on Nick's body.

Her climax still raged when he pulled her to the end of the counter and pushed into her.

Far away, she heard hammering at the door.

Nick either didn't hear or didn't care—or both.

He exploded into her, his face between her breasts, his mouth wide open and teasing her flesh.

Loud knocking sounded again.

Nick said, "Drop off and die, suckers," and carried Aurelie to the bedroom. He paused long enough to close and lock that door, too.

34

Nick picked up his phone and switched it on. "I don't want to do this but I'd better reconnect with the world."

"Yes," Aurelie said. She sat on the bed beside him, comfortable in her nakedness, and stretched, ran her fingers through crazy curls and yawned. "I've got to go back to the shop and explain why I've been gone for two hours."

"Easy," he said. "I needed you."

She dropped her arms. "Very funny."

"No. You know I wouldn't be flip at a time like this. I did—do—need you. In fact, you can't go back to the shop today."

"Oh, yes, I can." She hopped from the bed but he captured her hand before she could get away. "C'mon, Nick. You're needed at the lab, too."

"No, I'm not. Absolutely not."

She kissed him quickly. "You're impossible." How she wished she could let go and just play with him and forget everything else.

"Aurelie, we have to talk."

"And we will," she said, afraid to meet his eyes, afraid of what he might say. "Later, when we've got more time."

"What I want to say won't take much time."

She put a hand over his mouth. Her heart began to bump. "I think we should take a little time before we go any farther."

He tipped her over him. "I'd have said we've gone about as far as we can go. But you can prove me wrong if you like." She felt him grow still. "I was afraid to hope this would happen for us," he said.

His phone rang.

"I'm not answering that," he said. "I shouldn't have turned it on."

"Turn it off," Aurelie said, jarred by the sound.

Nick picked up the phone and glanced at the readout. He turned it off and lay quiet.

Aurelie sat up. "Who is it?"

He propped his head. "Delia."

She hopped off the bed and started gathering her clothes.

"What are you doing?"

"You can see what I'm doing."

"Yes. You're panicking. Stand still and take some breaths. And think. Delia's trying to get hold of me. She does that several times a day. We're in the same business, I'm her assistant and general advice counsel, and she needs to talk to me sometimes." He sat up and threw off the covers.

Aurelie didn't look away. "I feel as if I'm lying to Delia, and to Sarah. We're hiding things from them. How would you feel in their position?"

He thought about it. "Like a fool. And probably angry."

"Help me figure out how to get around that. Unless . . ."

"Unless what?" he asked, with an uncomfortable notion he knew what she'd almost said.

"If this is just a fling, why worry them with it?"

Nick shot from the bed and pulled her against him. "If you wanted someone to have a fling with, would you choose me?"

She laughed a little. "I don't think so. Too complicated."

"Good. I think you're right. We'd better get back to business, at least until this evening. We're going to dinner at Damalis's." Sometimes it worked to use bulldozer tactics with Aurelie. "It'll be a good way to start letting people see us together—as a couple."

352

Aurelie averted her face from him.

"I expected you to overreact," Nick said. "I'm not doing this in an impetuous way. I want to make a reservation for the four of us. I'll see if we can get one of the small private rooms."

"Why not just meet at home? I'll cook," she said. He meant to let Delia and Sarah know about them, then anyone else who was interested. She shivered and pushed open the door to the bathroom.

"No," Nick said. "No home-cooked meal. This time we're not having a family powwow. This is about us as grown-ups and what we want to do with our lives. We're going to ask them to encourage us. And we're going to have to make it public that we're not related."

Aurelie sorted through arguments for why they shouldn't go out for the express purpose of making an announcement that could be taken very badly by at least one of them.

"I'll invite the other two."

She felt wobbly. "Don't do that."

"You're not going to stop me. Humor me and go along this time. We can deal with it and not hurt anyone."

She hoped he was right but didn't think so.

In the distance, she heard voices, droning voices. "D'you hear that?" she asked. "It's outside. Sounds like someone talking."

Nick stood still and concentrated, then laughed. "It's nothing. Catching armadillos with my lovely flamingo radio, is all. The thing's faulty. It comes on when it feels like it."

"They work," Aurelie said. "And the best thing is that you don't end up with dead animals in your yard, they just run away."

She took a shower, blew her hair semidry and dressed, just a tiny bit disappointed that Nick hadn't come into the bathroom. Control was no longer in her hands—if it ever had been.

A small tear at the waist of her dress didn't show when the bodice was buttoned. She borrowed a comb and went through the painful process of working the tangles from her hair.

A tap on the door startled her. She opened up and smiled at Nick.

"Can I get in the shower?" he asked and she noted he wasn't grinning anymore.

"Of course," she said as she returned to working on her hair. She couldn't keep her eyes off him in the mirror. He turned on the shower and tossed a white towel over a hook.

Running on instinct, she went to him and put her arms around him, buried her face in his chest and hung on convulsively. He was solid, and felt so good under her hands.

Nick held her hard and rested his cheek on top of her head. "You're scared to just go along and be with me," he said. "I'm going to have to cure you of that. Honey?" He waited for her to look up at him. "The phone rang again when you were in the shower. It was Delia. She's coming here. She doesn't know about us yet, remember."

Aurelie pulled away from him. "When is she coming?" She had used a new toothbrush she found under the sink. She waved it in the air. "I'll replace this. How long before she gets here?"

"Any moment."

Aurelie twirled around, checking for any possessions. "I wish you'd put her off a bit longer."

"You know how Delia is when she wants something. Just get out of her way."

Cold darted up her arms. "At least the Hummer is over at Poke Around. As soon as Delia gets here, I'll go out the back way and cut around the block."

Nick stepped into the shower. The glass doors were clear and she saw him lather his hair, hold his face up to the stream of water, flatten his hands on his chest while soap poured off him. He scrubbed water from his eyes and stuck his head out the door again. "Delia does know you're here," he said, and closed the door again. He started to sing, and soap himself all over.

Aurelie couldn't stay in one place. She went to the door, changed her mind and returned to the sinks. Then she stood next to the shower and rapped on the door. It vibrated, making an unholy racket.

Nick's face was covered with soap again while he washed other parts.

She actually felt herself turn red. Then she hammered on the door again.

He sang both parts of the main aria from

Turandot—very badly. His voice soared, falsetto, and broke long before the top note, and bellowed forth in a tenor that also broke long before the top note.

Aurelie marched back and forth.

Stop it.

She sat on the toilet lid. *Fight or flight. Run away or stay and be a grown-up.* At least Delia didn't know the truth.

But Nick wanted to tell her! Tonight. With Sarah there.

The next noise from the shower sounded like a horse clearing its ears. Nick turned off the shower, located her on the toilet and gave her a huge smile. He swiped away a patch of steam, pressed his face to the glass, crossed his eyes and stuck out his tongue.

And Aurelie laughed. She laughed, shook her head hard and shook her hands like a primo Italian chef who'd just presented a masterpiece.

She stood up and held the sides of her head. "I'm losing it," she said and by the wicked expression on his face he'd obviously heard. "My mind isn't strong. You've told me that often enough. Well, you're right and I think I'm having a nervous breakdown."

"No time," he called. "Delia's going to—"

The intercom, with a convenient panel in the bathroom, chimed three times. Nick leaned out of the shower and punched a button. "'Lo?"

"Wait till I get out there," Aurelie said and slapped a hand over her mouth.

Nick covered the speaker and said, "Ouch. Just go

out now and stop worrying. We're grown-ups and so is Delia."

"She can't be this grown-up," Aurelie said, and left. "She must have heard me. She's going to know."

Any cover-up would be pointless. She went to the front door and opened it wide. But she couldn't make herself smile at Delia.

Delia wasn't smiling, either.

Fascination, that was the reaction on Delia's face. She stepped inside carefully, as if afraid to make any noise.

"Come in," Aurelie said unnecessarily. "It's still raining." Lightning cut the sky in the distance and Aurelie was grateful. Anything, rather than focus on Nick and herself. "Lightning," she said.

"Close the door, please, Aurelie," Delia said, but gave it a hard enough push to slam it herself. Pointedly, she avoided looking toward the bedrooms and went directly to a chair at the small dining-room table. A chair facing the wall. "Where's Nick?" she said.

"Um. Nick is—in—getting out of—he's in the bathroom."

"That's what I thought."

She'd forgotten to put her shoes on, Aurelie realized. And her hair wasn't dry yet. And she wore no makeup at all. And her dress was damp in places from putting it on over moist skin.

"Sit down, please," Delia said. She gave her head a shake and ran her fingers through her hair. She kept her eyes wherever they didn't have to see Aurelie's.

Aurelie sat down.

"You two have the worst timing I've ever seen," Delia said quietly, examining the backs of her hands.

There wasn't even a way to protest, to deny, to say Delia was jumping to conclusions. "Pretty bad," Aurelie said.

"Delay the summit," Nick said. In jeans, an unbuttoned white shirt—and no shoes—he joined them, careful to sit at the end of the table with one of them on either side of him. "How're you doing, sweet Delia?"

She narrowed her green eyes to teeny, tiny slits. "Don't you even try that on me. When did you get so sneaky? You weren't a sneaky teenager when I expected you to be. And neither were you." A long finger leveled at Aurelie. *"Nick's just getting out of the shower?* Was that what you were going to say a while back?"

Aurelie nodded.

"How very cozy and comfortable you two are together."

This was when he was supposed to be masterful, to take charge, Nick decided. "Everything here is perfectly natural," he said. "Would you like some coffee, Delia?"

He got another flinty look. "Do you know how to pour gin into a glass?"

This wasn't good. "You don't drink gin."

"I didn't ask you to remind me about my habits."

"Gin. Yep, one gin coming up. What will you take with that?" He went to a cabinet under a corner wet bar in the living room.

"Nothing," Delia said. "If you can manage it, you can say *vermouth* extremely quietly over the glass."

Nick didn't dare look at Aurelie. He went right and got that gin.

"If I wanted a thimbleful of gin, I'd say so," Delia said. Her pale peach linen suit gleamed, and so did the diamonds around her neck and at her ears.

Nick splashed more gin into the glass.

"Yuck," Aurelie said.

Delia's head snapped in her direction. "What did you say?"

Aurelie shrugged. "I said, yuck. I think gin is horrible."

"Give her some white wine," Delia said to Nick. "That's about all she can handle. And you'd better have something yourself."

Nick knew better than to argue. He poured the wine and had Scotch himself. "It's a bit early," he said, mostly under his breath.

"It's a bit early for a lot of things," Delia said. "I imagine some people are even still working." She looked at her watch.

Nick couldn't manage to feel chastened. There was something funny about a man in his thirties being taken to task for . . . well, just being taken to task. He put Aurelie's glass in front of her and smiled into her eyes.

She turned the corners of her mouth up.

"Whoa," he said. "Listen to that thunder." He sat down.

"I never knew you two were so obsessed with the weather," Delia said. "It's hard for me. Thinking of the two of you . . . doing . . . that."

Aurelie set her glass aside and put her forehead on top of her hands on the table. But she wasn't quick enough to conceal the pulsing glow on her face.

Delia turned to Nick. "You can understand, can't you? Just like children never think their parents . . . do it. Parents don't think their children do it." She took a large swallow of gin, coughed and shuddered.

"I think most parents think their children do it," Nick said, wiping the bottom of his glass on his cuff. He'd forgotten the napkins. "Usually they think they do it all the time. Every moment they can't see them, they think their children are doing it."

"Nicholas."

"It's true. And I know you've done it, Delia. I wouldn't be surprised if—"

"Enough."

"Nick," Aurelie said mildly, but her grin was naughty.

"I'd like us to go out for dinner this evening," Nick said to Delia. "You and Sarah and the two of us. It's time we had a nice family dinner."

He winced, and so did both Aurelie and Delia.

"We'll go to Damalis's. I haven't been there for

ages but the food's good. I'm getting a private room."

"A soundproof private room," Delia said. The gin was going down much more easily.

"Soundproof?" Aurelie said.

Delia gave Nick a sideways glance. "In case Sarah gets carried away."

Aghast, Nick leaned closer to her. "What do you mean?"

Both women pinned him with stares.

"You know, don't you, Aurelie?" Delia asked.

"Yes, but I didn't think you did."

"I know everything," she said, raising her chin. "Everything. I always have. Not one of you could or can make a move I don't know about. You think about doing something, and I get a telegram delivered right here." She poked her forehead. "I've got to go and talk to Sarah. What time's dinner?"

Nick did a fish-out-of-water imitation while he tried to think. "Seven? Eight?"

"Seven," Delia said, getting up. "Where's that sweet dog, Aurelie? Don't you neglect him because your affections are elsewhere."

"No," Aurelie said. "He's over with Eileen."

"Convenient," Delia said.

"Stop a minute, both of you," Aurelie said. She knew what she had to do. "I'm going to talk to Sarah myself. That's the way it should be."

"Darling," Delia said. "That would be so hard—"

"She's my sister. We've been through everything together. I'll talk to her. Nick, I'd like to put dinner off until tomorrow—if Sarah feels comfortable about doing it then."

His disquiet showed. "If that's what you think's best, that's what we'll do." He cleared his throat. "Should I come with you?"

Aurelie smiled at him and shook her head. "No, Nick."

"Oh, I can't pretend anymore," Delia said. She tossed back the rest of the gin, slapped down her glass and opened her arms wide. "I always knew you were perfect for each other. What took you so long? Come and kiss me, right now."

35

"Hoover's been ignored all day," Aurelie said. She pushed the words past a throat that felt paralyzed. "It seemed cruel to leave him alone again. I'll put him in the garden. It's not raining anymore and he loves it out there."

Sarah let them into the guesthouse. She smiled and looked directly into Aurelie's eyes. "The sun's out again. I had the covers on the furniture. Why don't we go out there, too. We haven't done that for a long time."

"Yes," Aurelie said. She felt like an assassin softening up her victim. "I like to look at all the vines." The garden was walled and the creepers old with thick, tortuous trunks.

She followed Sarah through the kitchen toward the

single door to the outside. As they passed the counters, Sarah picked up two tall glasses of freshly poured iced tea. In the quiet, the ice clinked. Aurelie opened the door and Hoover pushed his way out in front of Sarah.

"Rude dog," Aurelie said. Her jaw didn't move quite right and she could scarcely breathe. How would she move from empty small talk to telling her sister about Nick? Nick and her, Aurelie?

"Glad you've got your hat on," Sarah said. "Wouldn't want the sun to touch that skin." She laughed.

"Mmm, the flowers smell wonderful." Aurelie pulled off striped covers, waited for Sarah to put the glasses on top of a wooden table aged to silver-gray, and sat on one of four chairs. "You should have a hat on, too," she said. "You're as fair as I am."

"Northern European heritage," Sarah said and sat beside, rather than opposite, Aurelie. "At least, I guess that's what it is."

That was a subject they dodged, who they were and where they came from. Aurelie looked at her pale arms. "I guess so. As far as we know. The light eyes don't help."

"I like your eyes," Sarah said. She wasn't smiling anymore. "You're a good sister. You've always been there for me. Thanks for that. And I think you're interesting to look at—you show you're an individual, as well as being gorgeous. And, for the record, I like your old hat."

Aurelie parted her lips. She couldn't speak.

"Come here, boy," Sarah said to Hoover. She patted the thigh of her white jeans. "Do you like my hair a bit longer, Rellie?"

Hoover swayed his way to Sarah's side and nudged her with his head.

"I really do," Aurelie said in a rush. "It's softer with a little more length." There were so many things she'd like to tell Sarah, so many good things.

"The garden is as great as ever this year," Sarah said.

Wisteria loaded an ironwork frame around the back door and bougainvillea covered the old garden walls. Sarah's favorite colors were purple and orange and they were so bright they made Aurelie squint. "It's lovely. Your passion flower is doing so well. I didn't think it would make it."

"You came to tell me something," Sarah said. She rubbed Aurelie's upper arm. "Didn't you?"

The garden felt smaller, as if the walls moved closer to Aurelie. Sarah reached into a pocket and pulled out a fistful of beef jerky chips. "Okay?" she asked Aurelie, who nodded. Hoover snuffled up his windfall and sat where he could gaze at Sarah.

"I should have said something ages ago." Sarah's bright eyes glittered with tears. "How stupid could I be? I told myself I could have what I want because I'd wanted it for so long."

Aurelie bounced a shaky fist against her mouth. She saw her sister's face through a film. "You know why I came?" Did she, or was this something else?

"I've been watching you and Nick for several days, really watching," Sarah said. "It isn't that I didn't guess the truth before, but I wouldn't face it." She got up and walked away. The dog thudded along behind.

"Sarah," Aurelie said. "You're in love with Nick. You want him so badly it hurts."

"Yes," Sara said, her voice louder. "Yes, I do. And I have. And I hate him, too, because he doesn't love me."

"He does," Aurelie whispered.

"Don't pity me," Sarah said. "Don't hand out stupid little platitudes. You're sleeping with him, aren't you? You're sleeping with the only man I've ever loved." Her voice disappeared in a hoarse whisper.

"I didn't know," Aurelie said. "Not when it first started to happen between Nick and me. And when I did notice . . . Sarah, I can't stand hurting you."

Sarah shook her head and wiped the back of a hand over first one, then the other eye. Then she returned and sat down again. She let her head hang. "This is killing me. And I'm angry at you. You saw, you must have, you said you did. Why didn't you get out of the picture? Why didn't you go back to New Orleans?"

Aurelie felt full. Above all she longed to take her sister in her arms. If she could, she'd offer to leave now, but it was too late.

"Answer me!" Sarah cried.

"I didn't expect this to happen and if I went now it

would be too late. Sarah, don't hate me, please. I can't bear it if you hate me."

"I'm such a fool," Sarah said. "You went to New Orleans, you were the lawyer with the big career. You never showed any interest in Nick. Not that way. It was awkward and I couldn't tell him how I felt."

"No," Aurelie said.

Sarah looked at her. "But if he'd cared about me in that way he'd have made a move, wouldn't he? He'd have come to me instead of you." Her chest rose with her next huge breath. "You tempted him, you must have. The night you stayed at his house, is that when it happened? Did you crawl into his bed when he was—"

"Stop it!" Aurelie shook. Tears ran unchecked down her hot cheeks. "You're not yourself. I'll go. I'll go now. Leave Pointe Judah and never come back. I won't tell anyone where I've gone."

Sarah clapped her hands over her ears and waved her head from side to side. "And would he love me then? Is that what you're thinking? He'd detest me because he'd blame me for you going. Then I wouldn't even have his friendship."

Trembling, her teeth clamped together, Aurelie stared at Sarah. "I didn't plan it. Please believe that."

"Does it matter?" Sarah jerked her chair closer to Aurelie's and sat there with her hands clamped between her knees. "He never saw me that way and I feel like such a fool."

Aurelie moved her chair all the way beside Sarah's.

366

"We haven't just been like sisters." She settled a hand on Sarah's cheek. "We've had so much happen to us. And we kept going because we were together. You've been like my other self, like I wasn't complete without you. I don't think I could have gotten through on my own."

"I know I couldn't," Sarah said. She covered Aurelie's hand on her face. "You love Nick, don't you?"

"Oh, Sarah. We both love Nick. We've loved him for years."

"But not the way you love him now, or the way I love him now." Sarah sniffed and swallowed. "Not the way he loves you."

The ache Aurelie felt made her heavy. She felt Sarah's hurt. "I knew you'd fallen in love with him," she said, resting her head on top of Sarah's. "I started to see the signs right after I came home. All I worried about was how it would work out. I could *see* it in you, but I thought I was hiding what I felt."

"You did, mostly."

"I hoped going away would cure me, but I never stopped wanting him."

"This is the pits," Sarah said, crying freely. "Darn it, why doesn't he have a twin or something?"

Aurelie gave a croak of a laugh. "So we could fall in love with the same twin, or the wrong twin, you mean?"

They were babbling. But they were trying to keep what they shared intact.

"I'm afraid," Sarah said. "Us—you, Nick, Delia and I have something too good to lose. But this feels like grief, like I can't still be part of Nick's life at all."

"That would hurt him as much as you." But Aurelie couldn't let herself imagine how Sarah must feel.

"There isn't a way to make this go away, is there?" Sarah said. She straightened and looked at Aurelie. "I hate what I feel. There are going to be so many times when I want to tear your hair out, or fly at Nick, but I'm not letting either of you go."

36

"**W**hy now?" Joan asked. "We're going to get everything we want soon. Trust me. I'm starting to get their confidence. But if you drop out now and the old man calls looking for you, all hell's gonna break loose. Vic, listen. Please don't leave me."

He sat behind the wheel in her truck and wouldn't look at her. All of his gear was piled in the back.

"Tell me where you're going," she said. "At least do that for me. And let me know how I can get hold of you."

"We've already been together for too long," he said. "Look, we've had a good run but it's over. If this job hadn't been a pain from day one I'd have kept going, at least a bit longer, but it isn't working. You saw that bitch's—Aurelie's—reaction to both of us. You won't get anywhere with her, any more than you have with Nick."

Her hands shook. She turned sideways and held his arm. "I love you, Vic."

He laughed.

"Don't be like that. It's been too long for you to treat me like that."

"Damn it." He half turned his face toward her. "Don't try to turn us into Cinderella and the fucking prince. We were great together on film. You could take it and I could give it."

"We can still do that."

He laughed again. "I've still got the biggest cock around, you don't still have the youngest pussy. You should have known as soon as the old man moved us on to what he calls his 'special projects' that it was over for you."

Anger straightened her back and sparked her pride. "I haven't seen you being passed along to some nubile chick."

He slapped her across the mouth with the back of his hand. The sharp, coppery taste of blood ran between Joan's cracked lips.

They were on the outskirts of town. Vic had said he wanted them to have a chance to talk where they wouldn't be interrupted.

Tears ran silently. She touched her mouth and blood trickled onto her fingers.

"Shit," Vic said. "I didn't mean to do that. You make me so goddamn mad sometimes. You don't know when to shut up."

"Don't leave me here," she said. Her nose ran and

she wiped it on the back of her hand. She was really bleeding.

"Don't you have something to clean that up with?" Vic said.

She found tissues in a pocket and pressed them to her lips. When she ran her tongue over her teeth they didn't seem harmed.

"Please, Vic. If you go, I won't have any choice but to go back. I don't know what he'll do to me."

"What he'll make you do, you mean?" Vic said. "That's what scares you most. Relax, enjoy one of the benefits of old age. Making fake snuff is way out of your range now. So what's the worst that can happen?"

She cried harder. Blood mixed with water and mucus. She was so hot, so scared. No, she wasn't going back. Not ever. She'd die first. "I'll die before I'll do that again," she said. "What have I done to you, Vic? I've looked out for you. I've come up with money when you had one foot in a concrete bath. And I've done things for that money no one should have to do."

"You sure have," he said, expressionless again. "Look, I've got a plan. Fuck the book bit. I should have let you in on the truth from the beginning."

Joan licked her lips. "What do you mean?" She only got more scared. "He wants to get a movie out of what we're doing. He said so. We're supposed to help him make a killing on this. He said it would be a dark film and the background would be perfect."

"There isn't going to be any book or movie. That was just the cover Cooper came up with for us being here. I want you to stay here and pretend you're still working on it. Anyone asks, I had to report to the publisher but I'll be back. Keep your eyes and ears open."

He looked at her sharply. "Can you do that?"

"Yes. Oh, yes, Vic. Anything."

"I hit you too hard." He tilted up her chin and looked at her mouth. "We've never had much of a chance, you and me. We started out up to our necks in shit and never could climb out."

She nodded.

"You're okay," he said. "You think I don't appreciate anything but I do."

Joan didn't dare overreact but she grew a little warmer and little more hopeful. "You're okay, too," she said, and attempted a laugh. "Just tell me what to do, and I'm your girl."

"Yeah. Okay. Cooper owes us more information. He's got it all, the whole enchilada, but he kept too much to himself. That's because he's paranoid. Old fucker. Go do it, he said, but don't ask any more questions. That's his way of giving instructions." He ran the palms of his hands around the steering wheel. "I wasn't going to tell you, but I'm going back to San Francisco."

"Oh, my God," Joan said. "You're not going to ask him to explain, are you? You're not going to try getting tough with him? Vic, don't. He's got people. You

371

know it. We're just supposed to do as we're told."

Vic snorted. "Things are going to change. From here on in, I'm in charge and you're my insurance."

She gave a little cry. "I don't know what you mean."

"Piece of cake. You lay low here and become what Cooper fears most. The unknown quantity. Because if something happens to me, you'll turn him in. That's what I'll tell him. And I'll tell him there won't be time to stop you, so he'd better treat me easy."

She shrank back. "I couldn't turn him in. Everything would come out. The kids—"

He took her by the shoulders, shook her hard. "We're not responsible for what he's done."

"We hung with him. We helped. If we turned him in he'd have us picked up, too."

"Stupid," Vic said. "I'm only going to threaten him with that. You're never going to do it, but with me there and you not with me, he'll get scared."

"He's never been scared of anything."

"Things change." Vic reached behind the seat and pulled a small duffel onto his lap. From inside he took a videotape in a scratched case. "Take this and hide it. I don't mean under a bed. Put it where no one will think to look. Just till I get to you with more instructions."

She began to feel better. "Yes," she told him, taking the tape from him. "What is it?"

"Don't ask and don't look. I don't want you messing anything up. Just use your imagination. Get it out of sight as soon as you get back to the motel. I'll need this pickup. If I pull over out of town and sleep for a couple of hours, I can make it all the way there in thirty hours. I'll use the same route we came by. It's the shortest."

"I won't have a way to get around," she said.

"You'll figure something out. And I also think you can get the Boards to talk to you."

"How?" Her nerve began to crack again. "You just told me to forget about that. Why would I try getting to them now?"

She got another shove. "Because I'm telling you to. You've got to have some cover for being here. Go ahead and tell them I did that to you." He indicated her face. "Don't whine, just let it be seen. Give them the loyal, it's-nothing routine. Make them sorry for you. Then let it out that I've left you. Make 'em work for it but let them get it out of you that we're broke and if you don't get the money from the book, you could be in trouble with collections. Make it seem like I'm out of the picture, and make sure they draw you into their circle. I'll call you every evening to see what you've got."

"I'll do it," she told him. "Vic, I'm sorry I've disappointed you so often."

He sniffed. "You've got to work with what you've got. You can't help it." He looked ahead. It was getting dark and the rain still drove straight at the windshield. "I hate the fucking weather here. Either it's hot and wet, or hot and wet. The only thing that varies is how hot."

Joan loved the climate but she knew better than to say so. She nodded.

"You know what you've got to do," Vic said. "Take advantage of the sympathy. They're soft, all of these people. I've left a camera for you. We don't want them to start looking for some other reason you might be here. You're writing a book and you want to feature Place Lafource, past and present families, because it's so friggin' interesting. Period. Make them trust you, want to help you—just long enough for me to deal with Cooper."

"Yes," she said. She couldn't even go to Buck looking like this. He'd ask too many questions—he already had. "I may need to talk to you. Can I call if I need to?"

"Shit." He locked his arms, then slowly relaxed them. "Yeah, of course you can. Just don't do it because you're feeling lonely. The only reason to call is because you think trouble is coming my way. Misuse the privilege and I'll toss the phone, and, as far as you're concerned, disappear. You won't be able to reach me at all."

"Why can't I just come with you?"

"I've explained, damn it. Get out. I need to get going and find somewhere to pull off and catch some sleep."

Slowly, Joan started opening the door. She was only a mile or so from the motel. "I've got to ask you something," she said.

"Not now."

"Yes, *now.*" She looked at him over her shoulder. "You killed that Baily Morris, didn't you?"

He bared his teeth and chords stood out in his neck. "You don't know when to shut up."

"You did kill her, then?"

"I didn't say that. But just you remember, all we came here with were the so-called facts we were given. It wasn't my fault Cooper's incredible tails failed to notice that Sarah wasn't the only one who worked some nights at the lab. They also didn't make sure to tell him the other chemist also had short, bleached hair and wore a ton of makeup. What I got on Sarah Board seemed watertight. She should have been at the lab that night—on her own. All I intended to do was scare her. We wanted them to make a move, didn't we? It wasn't my fault if the other one got in the way."

"I don't know what you're saying," Joan said. "What kind of move? All we wanted to do was get them talking."

He sneered at her. "You are such a gullible fool."

"You killed Baily," she repeated stubbornly.

"Yes, I killed her," he shouted. "I couldn't leave her around, could I? She'd have gone screaming to the cops and they'd have been bound to look at us."

"At you," she said and started sliding out of the vehicle.

"Wait." He pulled her purse from her hands and took every last dollar she had in her wallet. "Work out the rent with the motel manager. I've seen the way he looks at you. Go. Now. I'll make sure you get more money soon, and Joan . . ."

"Yes," she whispered.

"You've arrived at your last chance. Make a mess of this, and I won't be able to help you out again."

37

Until today, Aurelie had never been closer to the Roll Inn than the street that passed a wide stretch of crispy yellow grass with a single sign standing tall enough to be seen for miles around. Not read, just seen.

The Superior Diner stood next to a single, long group of units with an office at one end.

"This is the first time I've really looked at this place," she said. Nick hadn't said a word since a call came in from Joan Reeves while he was driving Aurelie home after a late meal. He had tried to drop her off but Aurelie insisted that since Joan apparently sounded very upset, it could be a good idea to have a woman along.

He remained silent.

"She said to meet her in the diner?" Aurelie asked. She should just shut up and let him stew on his own.

He nodded, yes.

"Why don't you want me along?" Aurelie asked. "You said Joan was crying. You know you hate that sort of thing."

Nick looked sideways at her, his blue eyes intense.

"I'm not sure what I think about her. I don't know if I believe her story."

"And that means you don't want company when you deal with her?"

"So I'm protective of you." He stuck out his chin. "Make something of it. I'm not going to change."

They both laughed, then Aurelie said, "I'm pretty independent, Nick. I like it that way."

He turned in at the entrance to the motel and drove slowly toward the diner. "I don't see Joan's truck, do you?"

She studied a straggle of vehicles in front of the motel, one by one. "No. Maybe she left."

"I hope you're right." He waved a hand. "I can't be blamed for wanting to avoid more drama."

He'd become withdrawn after she told him Sarah's reaction when the two sisters got together. She realized he'd had no idea how deeply Sarah cared for him. Far from being flattered, he seemed devastated and preoccupied with making sure there was something left of the family after the dust settled.

He parked, nose in, by the diner.

"I see her," Aurelie said. Joan had pulled her hair back into the ponytail she favored. "Looks like she's the only customer."

"That's good and bad," Nick said. "Sometimes it's nice to have other conversations around. More private that way."

Despite the hour, heat blasted Aurelie when she opened the car door. Her sandals stuck to the patchy blacktop. She reached back inside the Audi and grabbed her hat.

In the act of jamming it down to her ears, she looked at Nick over the car and he grinned. "I like your hat," he said. "I don't know if it makes you look mysterious or ridiculously young."

This was yet another day for analyzing The Hat. Aurelie smacked the top of the crown and said, "Mysteriously youthful. I'll take it. C'mon, Hoover. You can't stay in there."

The dog climbed awkwardly between the seats and slithered out.

"Let's find him a cool spot," Nick said. "Hoover! Come here, boy. I'll get you some water."

Moving like a greyhound with the lure in his sights, more or less, Hoover barreled into Nick and snuffled at his pockets. When Nick took out a plastic bag with pieces of white chicken meat inside, Aurelie rolled her eyes.

Nick used the diversion of letting Hoover slurp at the bag to take an assessing look through the diner window at Joan.

Instead of doing the same, Aurelie watched Nick's reaction. "Is she okay?" she asked, already knowing the answer.

"I don't think so. She's got her head down."

"Maybe she's tired. She could be resting," Aurelie said.

"This shouldn't be our problem," Nick said.

Aurelie put her hands into the pockets of her full,

red skirt. "I think you and I attract people with problems. Let's see what we can do."

"That's your problem," Nick said. "You think—let's see what we can do. I think—let's get this over with."

"You're mean and hard." As long as they bantered, she didn't have to fixate on what Sarah was going through.

"She's seen us." He took Aurelie by the elbow and steered her toward the doors. "We can put Hoover between the two sets of doors. It's too hot out here."

Before Aurelie could think of an appropriate opening comment for her, they stood in front of a table where Joan Reeves continued to study her hands, folded in her lap.

"Hi, Joan," Nick said.

Too simple. Aurelie didn't figure a reasonable approach would accomplish much. "It's Aurelie and Nick," she said. "We came as soon as Nick got your call."

"Sit down, please," Joan said, her voice muffled. "I'm sorry to bother you. I need help and I can't think of anyone else who might do it. I need money."

Aurelie and Nick looked at one another.

"Tell me about it," Nick said.

Joan said, "I don't have any money, not even the price of a cup of coffee."

Aurelie noticed Joan had nothing in front of her on the yellow plastic-topped table. She swiveled around and waved to the only waitress in sight. When the woman hurried over, Aurelie said, "We'd like coffee, please." She looked at Joan's slumped shoulders. "Did you have dinner, Joan?"

"I'm not hungry."

"What soup do you have?" Aurelie persisted to the waitress.

"Red bean," the woman said, and her round face brightened. "You never had red bean soup till you've had ours. It's famous."

The soup's fame hadn't reached Aurelie but she said, "In that case, please bring us three bowls. I hate to miss great opportunities. And corn bread, please."

She and Nick had eaten Ona's party dish, stewed duck with turnips cooked in a rich onion roux, and although they hadn't thought they were hungry, they had cleaned their plates. But they would manage red bean soup, too, if it helped this situation.

The waitress returned quickly with the coffee. Joan poured in a hefty amount of cream and picked up the mug in both hands the moment the three of them were on their own again.

And Joan's face was fully revealed.

Nick leaned forward. "Who did that?" He had never been one to tiptoe around a point.

Joan shook her head, kept her eyes on the coffee and drank.

"Your eyes are turning black," Aurelie said, shaken. "And your poor mouth. Oh, Joan, what's happened?"

Tears pooled in the corners of Joan's battered eyes. "If I could borrow some money to get away, I promise you I'll pay it back. I don't know when because I've got to go a long way away and start over. But I will pay you."

Nick put a restraining hand on Aurelie's wrist. He hated what had happened to Joan but he also knew she needed more help than just money. "We'll help you," he said quietly. She needed some guarantee of safety until she made a new place for herself. "Please tell us everything. You need to trust someone and you can trust us. We've both known enough trouble to understand."

Aurelie's smile at him, her approval, felt like winning first prize for something.

The bean soup arrived.

Steam rose from fresh, deep yellow corn bread.

Nick picked up a spoon and waited until Joan did the same. She ate, a bean at a time, then two, and finally a spoonful. Rich butter melted on the bread and all three of them made satisfied noises with the first bite.

He let a few minutes pass. Some color had returned to Joan's cheeks.

"I want to be sure you're going to be safe," he said.

"I've been a fool for so long, I just hope I can change," Joan said. "If there was a bad choice to make, I made it."

Now, *there* was a conversation stopper.

"Today I found out the whole thing about the book was a lie. Our boss sent us so . . . so Vic could do something completely different. I was just the main decoy."

Nick was grateful Aurelie seemed to sense it was best to let Joan talk for as long as she would without interruption.

Joan dabbed at her mouth with a napkin. "He lost his temper and hit me."

Picking up his coffee, then setting it down again without drinking, Nick continued to wait.

"You wouldn't understand about lives like mine. I must just seem dirty to you. Maybe I am, but that's not what I'd hoped for. What time is it?"

Aurelie said, "Almost ten."

Joan looked momentarily disoriented. She stood up and said, "Please excuse me. I'll be right back."

She walked outside, stopping to pat Hoover on the way.

"What do you think?" Aurelie said.

"I want to know what the book thing was a supposed cover for. I'm afraid she'll change her mind about talking to us and run before we can get anything out of her."

Joan dialed Vic's cell number. She didn't want to say she was angry with him, but although he had only wounded her mouth, he'd set her up for the pair of black eyes, and other, bigger bruises and cuts covered by her clothes. The motel manager liked his sex rough and when she'd begged him to stop hitting her, he'd found even more violence to heap on her. And afterward, he told her she only had until morning to clear out of the motel.

So now she was asking more strangers for money.

They would probably bring up the police before too long and she couldn't go there.

Vic's number rang and rang and she checked what she'd dialed. It should be right. Then a voice said, "This is no longer a working number."

Driving a fist into her stomach, she dialed again, and got the same message.

He'd dumped her, taken her car and every penny she had in the world and left her, knowing that even if she could find a way, she wouldn't follow him, not back to Cooper. Vic would make sure Cooper blamed her for the failure of whatever he'd sent Vic to do. She had nowhere to go back, and nowhere to go to.

She looked through the diner windows.

Nick and Aurelie sat with their backs to her. She looked toward the road. There wasn't even much truck traffic down here. She'd have to make her way to a freeway ramp if she wanted to take her chances on a ride.

Tiredness, heavy, muscle-numbing exhaustion, weighed her down. Another strange man who wanted sex, that was the best she could expect up on the road, or it was the reasonable thing to expect. She couldn't go on. There was only one chance for any kind of way out that she could think of, and with a lot of luck, it was inside the diner.

"Okay?" Nick said when Joan slid back into her seat.

She looked from him to Aurelie and shook her head. "I don't see how." He could see her deciding what to say next. "Vic's gone back to California—San Francisco. That's where we're from. The man we work for is there. He's evil."

Aurelie sucked in a breath. "Why do you work for an evil man?"

"I don't anymore. I don't work for anyone."

"We're going to help you stay safe," Nick said. A jumpy excitement started in the pit of his stomach. Vic had gone back to some creep in San Francisco. Could there be a connection to his own story? Regardless, he couldn't ignore any leads. "What's the boss's name?"

Joan's eyes slid away but Nick didn't prompt her. He did look at Aurelie, who shook her head a little.

"Cooper," Joan said at last. "That's all I know."

"What would you like us to do now?" Aurelie said. "I don't think running without knowing where you're going is a good answer."

"I don't know."

Nick had put off the next question. "It makes sense to bring the police in, Joan. What Vic did to you is a crime."

"No police," Joan said at once. Nick could feel her fear. "I can't talk about it now, but give me a chance and some time and I will."

Nick wanted one thing—he wanted to get his hands on Vic, and on Cooper, whoever he was.

"He took my truck," Joan said. "And my money."

"Is he coming back for you?"

"No. I don't want to believe it but I know he's not."

"But you're going to protect him anyway," Nick said. "That makes you a victim by choice. If you want out, you've got to deal with him."

"How?" she whispered.

The waitress arrived and Nick was glad for a few moments to think. She refilled the coffee and left.

"When did he leave?" Nick asked Joan.

"Just a couple of hours ago. He was going to pull off and sleep as soon as he got to a good rest area. Then he'll head out. He's got his route all mapped out—the shortest way to where he's got to go."

Nick held his breath. "Would it hurt if I caught up with him and asked him to reconsider what he's decided to do?"

He heard Aurelie's indrawn breath.

"No!" Joan's face had paled again and it shone with a film of sweat.

"Okay. It was just an idea."

Joan picked pieces of corn out of her bread and chewed them one by one. She cast frequent glances at Nick and at Aurelie. "I know the route he'll take," she said. From her bag she took a folded piece of computer paper. "He left this on the screen and I printed out a copy. We came that way. It's fast."

Nick took the paper from her and nodded over it. "I-10. Yeah, that would be the fastest way."

"Vic needs his sleep," Joan said. Her hands shook. "He sleeps in a rest stop so he can use the bathroom and wash. He likes to be near a gas station, too."

"What are you saying?" Nick said. He hoped he

knew, but pushing her could make her back off.

"If you went after him, he might try to do something to you," she said, her despair showing. "No, forget I said anything."

"You're rethinking my idea to go after him?"

"Forget it."

"Okay." *Give her more time.* "How long did you work for this Cooper?"

She averted her face. "Too long. Around fifteen years."

Aurelie spread a hand on the table. "How did you meet him?" she asked.

"I was a stupid kid who thought she could make it in the movies. I was going to Los Angeles but I met Cooper. He was charming and kind and seemed sophisticated. He knew stuff about movies and he offered to help me get a start." Joan lolled her head back. "I was so stupid." She closed her mouth tightly.

"You aren't the only one who ever bought a convincing story," Aurelie said. "One of these days I'll tell you about my sister and me. We got lucky, but we probably came close to being in a similar situation to the one you're in now."

Joan looked at her intently. "You did?"

"Yes. A man tried to suck us into really bad stuff. Someone stopped him."

"If Vic wants to go back to Cooper, good luck to him," Joan said. "But he didn't have any right to take my truck and my money."

Nick heard the start of real anger in her voice and

his hopes rose again. "He also didn't have a right to hit you," he said. "No man should take out his anger on a woman."

"I want my truck and my money," Joan said.

Nick sat back in his chair and made sure he looked as if he was trying to make a decision.

"What?" Joan asked.

"I'll do it," Nick said. "I'll go after him. You want him brought back here?"

She shook her head. "No. I don't want to see him ever again. Don't do anything."

"I insist," Nick said. "I couldn't live with myself if I didn't help out. I'll leave tonight. Just as soon as we get you situated." He'd figure out where to stash Joan. Finn could be enlisted again. "Believe I can do this for you. I know where you'll be staying tonight, and who you'll be with."

He still had the map, which he folded and put into his shirt pocket.

"I don't know," Joan said.

Aurelie gripped the woman's hand on the table. "You could be in danger just being on your own. I know about these things. What choice do you have but to take help from someone?"

"None."

"Do you think you can trust us?"

Joan nodded, yes.

"Let's move," Nick said.

38

"**I**'m not getting out," Aurelie said. "And the longer you stand there trying to push me around, the farther away that man gets."

"This isn't a joke, damn it." Nick moved to haul open the driver's door on the dark blue Honda that Finn Duhon had insisted be used for the trip. Both Finn and Angel said the car handled well and would blend in on the highway. They thought the Hummer Aurelie had offered would have every advantage except for being impossible to miss. And Vic had seen Nick's Audi a number of times.

The car was gassed up and standing in front of Aurelie's apartment. Hoover had run inside as soon as Nick opened the front door. But Aurelie had slipped into the driver's seat while Nick's back was turned. She would stay in the car by whatever means it took

"C'mon," Nick said. "I want you where I know you're okay. I've got to get going. Every minute counts now."

"Yes, it does. Lock my front door. I'll call Frances at the salon first thing. She'll take care of Hoover. You intend to follow Vic all the way to San Francisco, don't you? You think Cooper is Colin and you want to be the one to get to him first."

"I never said that."

Aurelie noted the tone of his voice. She'd told it the way it was. "But that is what you intend. I don't blame you, but I'm not letting you go on your own. Get in."

He threw up his hands. "First I have to insist Angel and Finn are needed more here than chasing along behind me—never mind how far I may be going. Now there's you holding me up."

"Let's get on with it. We'll talk about it while we get some miles under the wheels. You need me. Believe it. Who do you think's going to be sharper—even if he does start out with some sleep grabbed at a rest stop or wherever? We are, because we can trade off the driving and one of us can get some extra rest in between. Also, one of us has to be awake all the time if we're going to make sure he doesn't get away from one of his *naps* without being seen."

"Get out and get in the passenger seat," Nick said.

Promptly, Aurelie climbed over the console and into the passenger seat. She strapped herself in. "You won't regret your decision," she said. *Even if he had just tried to get her out of the car so he could drive off without her.* She heard his heavy sigh.

"Aurelie," he said quietly. "You could slow me down and also, if something goes wrong, you could be in danger. If I have to call the police for any reason, they'll get in the way of me trying to see if this Cooper guy is actually Colin."

"Now you admit what you're hoping for," Aurelie said.

Nick said, "Please stay here."

"No," she said. "Let's go. Don't you think I want to confront Colin, too?"

He looked at the ground for a moment, then went to lock her front door.

Three hours from Pointe Judah, at a big rest stop off I-10 in the vicinity of Houston, Aurelie grabbed Nick's arm.

He managed not to swerve. "What?"

"Over there." They were cruising through the parking lot with a view of vehicles parked on the other side of restrooms, vending machines and a display of lighted maps. The night was dark but the area well lit. "I think that's Joan's truck, between the Airstream and that white SUV."

Nick checked behind him and backed up, away from the bright lights. He pulled beneath a tree and took binoculars from the glove compartment. For about ten seconds, he focused on the vehicle Aurelie had pointed out, then he handed the glasses to her. "That's it," he said. "I didn't expect him to go this far before stopping. I thought we might have passed him already."

"Me, too," Aurelie said.

Nick looked hard at the truck. "I don't see him in it."

"He's probably sleeping in the back."

He figured the same thing but wanted to be sure. "I don't want to sit here for hours then find out he managed to leave in another vehicle. If he is in there, he's been here for several hours. He could drive off at any moment. We've got to know whether or not he's there."

"We can't check that out, Nick," Aurelie said.

He said, "Show a little faith. And do not get out of this car, please."

"Nick—"

Standing straight and walking normally, Nick left the Honda and strode left, putting the rest-stop buildings between him and Joan's pickup.

He didn't stop moving. A circle around and he strolled behind the Airstream, then the truck. A single turn of the head and Nick made out an occupied sleeping bag in the bed of the truck, protected by the canopy.

"He's moving."

Nick heard Aurelie's voice and smiled. His neck hurt but he didn't care. He liked waking up with her beside him.

"Nick!" The engine turned over. Aurelie had been keeping watch while he snatched some sleep.

He sat up as the Honda started to roll and stared around. Darkness still pressed in around the car. He scrunched up scratchy eyes and focused. Joan's truck was gone from its former spot.

"He's going to get on the freeway," Aurelie said. "He's headed there now. I looked at the map while you were asleep. The exits are pretty close together, so we could lose him fast. I'm going to give him two minutes, then follow. You think that's okay?"

He nodded. "Yeah. Let me drive."

"I'm perfectly capable of driving." She said it sharply and glared at him.

Nick sighed. "I know you are. I thought we agreed we'd take it in turns getting some sleep. It's your turn to sleep. Stay, or switch right now. There isn't time for discussion."

"Right," Aurelie said. "Sorry about that. Let's switch."

San Antonio, Fredericksburg, Fort Stockton, followed by a load of forgettable burgs, then through El Paso. For a third time Vic had pulled off for gas. Nick and Aurelie hung back at the station, then filled up, too, hoping they wouldn't lose him.

The sun had taken a hike and the sky turned an unnatural shade of green. The air was heavy with pollution and Aurelie figured they needed a good rain to wash down the muck.

"That's it," Nick said, dropping into the passenger seat this time.

Aurelie peeled out of the forecourt and onto the freeway entrance, swept down and started searching for the dirty cream-colored pickup.

"Just concentrate on the road and making ground," Nick said. "Leave the looking to me."

She did as she was told, going faster than she ought and checking her mirrors frequently for any sign of cops.

Nick laughed suddenly. "Don't worry too much, everyone on the road is exceeding the limit. Thank God I taught you to drive."

"Arrogant ass," she said, not taking her eyes off the task. "I was a natural."

"I see him," Nick said. "Fast lane but too blocked in to really move. You're fine the way you are for now."

Aurelie turned west on I-10 at the junction where I-25 took off to the north.

They were silent for several miles then Aurelie asked, "Do you think Joan will stay put at Finn and Emma's? She was so scared."

"She's got good reason," Nick said. "Joan knows she's probably going to be arrested."

"So why wouldn't she run?"

Nick puffed up his cheeks. "This is just my gut. I think she's whipped—completely. And she knows if she does take off, she'll be tracked down."

"I like her," Aurelie said.

"You'd like to fix her . . . watch it! He's coming over a lane."

She watched. The pickup was still forced by the vehicles around it to keep a steady pace.

"Do you think he could have seen us by now?" Aurelie asked and her heart gave an involuntary thud.

"No." Nick shifted in his seat. "Aw, hell, we can't fool ourselves. He might have but I just don't think so. Half the cars around could be interchanged with this one."

The day swept by; night came fast. Phoenix, Blythe and Palm Springs were just famous places they had no time to think about before making the loop around Los Angeles and eventually getting onto I-5.

On the other side of Los Angeles, Vic pulled into

another rest stop. This time he went from the restroom to a coffee stand run by some local club. He took coffee and a heap of cookies back to the truck, by which time Nick and Aurelie were already backed into a slot with plenty of room between the two vehicles, but not so much that they wouldn't see the next time Vic moved.

"He's having a picnic," Nick said. He frowned at the windshield where raindrops had started splattering. "Run to the bathroom if you have to. Grab coffee and head back. I'll go for the restroom a couple of minutes after you leave."

She hopped out, walked around the back of the car and moved along behind the entire row before cutting up to the buildings. By the time she came out of the bathroom, a glance at the Honda showed that Nick had followed his plan. She bought coffee and some cereal bars and arrived back at the car a couple of minutes behind Nick.

"Damn, I was hungry," he said, downing three cereal bars, one after the other, in about two bites apiece. He inhaled the coffee.

Aurelie drank her coffee first. The bars tasted like shredded cardboard held together with dry peanut butter, but she ate one anyway.

"Shoot," Nick said suddenly. "I thought he'd rest. There he goes."

Aurelie groaned and strapped in.

The car was already moving.

It was dawn. They'd kept moving throughout a second night when Vic finally drove from the road again and into a gas station. Aurelie was driving and she followed. She really needed sleep, or even to close her eyes until they stopped burning.

She knew it would be harder to keep Vic in sight from here on.

Before long they would cut from I-5, making a turn to the west on 580.

The entrances and exits would come even faster and the traffic would soon be congested.

Vic got back into the truck and drove, not back to the freeway but around the corner of the building.

Seconds passed while Aurelie and Nick watched. Then Vic appeared. "He's going inside," Nick said. "I'll put a few gallons in."

"Time to switch again," Aurelie said. "I'll run to the bathroom." She'd seen another woman take the key from the convenience mart at the station and intercepted her before she could get back to the minimart. The woman gave up the key without any sign of surprise.

Aurelie rushed inside the bathroom. On her way out she caught sight of herself in a cloudy mirror and almost laughed.

She whipped open the door.

Vic grabbed her before she could scream and bundled her into the truck.

Watching for Aurelie to return, Nick grew restless and slammed back the gas hose. He looked to the right and his stomach turned. The truck had gone. He turned back to the other side of the building, where Aurelie had gone to use the bathroom—too long ago.

The truck appeared, driving slowly.

Nick took several steps.

Vic put on the breaks and looked quickly around as if checking the area. That's when Nick saw Aurelie sitting beside him.

From his lap, Vic raised his left hand. He shook his head a little, smiled at Nick and let him see the gun in that left hand.

39

"**P**ut your head on your knees."

Aurelie breathed through her mouth. The sky grew lighter. Vic had driven so fast she had started to pray the police would chase the truck down, or even that they would have an accident.

"Put your head on your knees and your arms behind your back."

She looked at him, then looked behind, searching for the Honda.

"Face the fucking front, bitch!"

Aurelie faced forward. Ahead was a sign for the turn onto 580. The miles shot beneath the wheels. Soon they would head north again and after that, across the Bay Bridge.

"Just let me out," she said, and folded her arms. She leaned against the seat. "I'm not afraid of you. I don't have to do anything you tell me to do. Pull over to the side and let me out. You'll get away and I won't be able to do anything about it."

He laughed. "You'd like that." He grabbed her behind the neck and slammed her face down on her knees. They must both have heard the crack as her nose hit because he said, "Owie. That's going to hurt."

It already did and when she moved her face a little she saw blood. "Bastard," she muttered.

He reached behind her, held her right wrist and jerked it behind her and up her back until she screamed.

"Still not afraid of me?"

"Stop it. You'll break my arm." Unbelievable pain and throbbing heaviness radiated from her shoulder.

"You can put your other hand behind you or I'll do it for you," he said, his voice flat, completely without expression. "She sent you after me, didn't she?"

Aurelie put her other hand behind her. She knew he meant Joan. "We came because we found out about you. About your history. And what you've been doing in Pointe Judah."

Seconds passed before he said, "What have I been doing in Pointe Judah, other than taking photographs? That's my job."

She should have kept her mouth shut.

"I'm going to throw up," she said and made retching sounds.

"Go ahead," he said. "Knock yourself out. What am I supposed to have done?"

"Stop the car!" Aurelie shouted. "Let me out." She moved her arms.

A blow smashed into the base of her skull. She heard the thud and felt black agony melt her mind.

Nick settled in behind the truck. He couldn't let anything get between the two vehicles, not again. If there was a way to force Vic off the road, Nick would do it.

He flipped open his cell phone and, with difficulty, dialed 911.

A dispatcher answered and Nick said, "Take down this license plate number. You've got to stop the vehicle. There's a hostage." He shook his head while the woman on the other end asked for his name and location. "Just take down this number. The vehicle is going toward the Bay Bridge and San Francisco—"

"What kind of emergency is this, sir?"

He lowered his head to peer through the truck canopy to the cab. Vic's head and shoulders were visible. Only the top of Aurelie's head had been visible . . . He couldn't see her at all.

"You shouldn't have come, damn it!" He pounded the wheel with a fist, then tried to move toward the center of the road. If he could, he'd sideswipe the pickup. A massive truck, headlights flashing, horn blaring, headed for him and Nick pulled quickly back.

The dispatcher asked another question but Nick didn't listen. He closed the phone and threw it on the passenger seat.

The pickup rode in the fast lane. Moving streams jammed the other lanes. Nick followed as close as he dared, to the bridge.

Traffic on the Bay Bridge thundered. Rush hour lasted most of the day but at this time of the morning it resembled an inbound tsunami of metal and mankind.

Once over the bridge, the pickup shot off the Freemont exit and Nick followed on Market Street, keeping up until a delivery van pushed in and cut him off.

He looked over his shoulder, swung the wheel left and shot beside the van, in time to see Vic run a light, leaving Nick with a blockade of vehicles at a standstill in front of him. Ahead, everything slowed down and he leaned forward, willing the lights to change. "Come *on*. Come *on*."

The light switched to green. But the traffic in the next block also moved. They were on Market Street.

Two blocks ahead, the pickup swerved in front of a motorcycle, turned a corner and disappeared between buildings.

Nick pressed his foot to the floor and immediately braked. The Honda shuddered and slewed sideways. He stared at a row of vast wheels on a truck and fought to straighten out again.

Moments he needed lost, he took the right turn where the pickup had gone and drove, searching ahead and side to side.

Nothing.

At the end of the first block, he dithered, sweating, breathing through his mouth. Another block and he was in Union Square. Panic hammered in his throat. Fighting the crammed, sluggish traffic, he drove a circle back to where he'd started, then drove the next one until he approached Market Street again.

There he was!

If Vic had walked and mixed in with the crowd quietly, Nick wouldn't have seen him, but Vic ran, the loose tails of a white shirt flapping, his elbows pumping.

A car pulled out in front of Nick, who slid into the space, leaving his right rear bumper stuck out in the nearest lane. So what. He grabbed his phone and rushed in pursuit. He'd never catch the man now.

The white shirt saved Nick. The shirt and the movement. He tore across Market, dodging honking traffic, slamming his hands onto the hood of a cab and jumping out of its way.

Powell Street BART Station.

Nick registered the shift in Vic's motions. He leaped down a staircase into the station. Nick's throat burned, he swallowed and coughed, and reached the staircase Vic had taken.

Down he went, bringing curses from others making their way.

He marked time, feet moving, staring around.

Vic left a ticket machine and headed for a turnstile.

Nick stuck money into the nearest machine and took the ticket without looking to see what he'd bought.

An employee yelled, "Watch out," but Nick didn't. The station was very deep. Already his quarry had made too much headway on the escalator.

Nick hit the platform in time to see Vic pelting along the platform to a train's open door.

Nick followed, threw himself through the closing doors and landed at the feet of a crowd of commuters who turned their heads away from him. He stood slowly, peering between bodies.

Vic's white shirt and the back of his blond hair appeared in glimpses, moving farther along the car. He never looked behind him. Because he didn't think he was still being followed, Nick thought. But that hadn't stopped Vic from moving fast, wildly even. He pressed himself against the door, peered through the window. The train traveled beneath Market Street, heading toward Civic Center.

They slid into the station, the doors opened and the people behind him hurried Nick onto the platform.

The white shirt and Vic's dishwater-blond hair were already on their way up the staircase. Pelting along, flinging himself forward, Nick dared to hope. But he had to cool it, to make sure he wasn't seen.

Nick wasn't ready for Vic's next move. He took a leap onto the wide black marble coping that rose beside the handrails on the stairs.

Shouts went up.

People jogging upward paused to watch.

Vic bent his knees and took a jump, grabbing vertical metal banisters and hauling himself, hand over hand, until he could ram the toes of his sneakers between bars to steal a foothold on the platform above. The MUNI platform.

Go, don't think. If the cops don't stop him, pray they don't stop you, either.

In no more than thirty seconds, Nick sucker-stepped himself up banisters intended for no such purpose. *Up, hook a knee over the top and drop to the platform.*

He didn't believe it when he saw Vic hopping onto the first car of a waiting train.

Nick couldn't risk getting into the same car a second time. He skirted a bank of billboards and made it to the second car in time to get on—still vertical. He slid into a seat and kept still.

One stop, Van Ness, and there was Vic sprinting for the exit.

Losing him was out of the question. Now it was Aurelie that drove Nick, and getting his hands on Vic to force him to reveal where she was. Tied up in the pickup was Nick's best bet.

God, he hoped she wasn't dead.

Once out of the station, Nick hung back as far as he dared, kept himself close to walls and windows.

Workers massed the sidewalk, sometimes slowed by delivery trucks pulling into alleyways or delivery entrances.

Aurelie, where was she? What had Vic done to her? Nick kept an eye on the white shirt and worked to melt in with the crowd. He pulled out his cell phone, and it rang.

He jumped and kept moving, looking at the readout between strides. The number meant nothing to him. He frowned and flipped on. "Yes?" he said quietly.

"It's Aurelie." She sounded odd. "I'm okay. He knocked me out and shoved me under the dashboard. Where are you?"

"On Haight. Heading toward Buena Vista Park. I was just going to try calling you. He's a madman."

"Tell me about it. And I don't have my cell phone. I'm calling from a restaurant."

He winced. "Aurelie, are you okay?"

"No. But I will be. I want you to give up on this. We're dealing with dangerous people."

"To quote you," Nick said, " 'tell me about it.' I can't stop now. This isn't just for you and me and Sarah, but for my mother and all the others. If I walk into what I think I will, it's going to be up to me to make what we've done count. I wasn't ready before. Now I am. I want you to go to an emergency room. Then check into the Fairmont. I'll find you there. I'll call the cops myself."

"Where's the car?"

He had let Vic cross the road and waited a few seconds before crossing himself.

"Why do you want the car?" he said.

"My purse is in it, Nick. And my cell phone. And it might be nice to drive where I need to go."

"Of course." At least she was more or less okay. He told her where to find the car. They had both decided on a spot to hide a spare key in a magnetic case. "See a doctor, then go to the Fairmont. Put your cell on. Mine will have to go off now."

40

From the upper windows of the house you must be able to look at Buena Vista Park between the buildings opposite.

A house on Haight Street, within spitting distance of Asbury. If Cooper was Colin, would he live on the street where he'd met Mary Chance?

He wouldn't care, he'd shown that in the ultimate way.

Nick had ducked just inside a convenience store to let Vic get a bit farther ahead, and watched from a window when he ran up the brick front steps and through the unlocked front door of a four-story Victorian. The facade was painted deep green and white with plaster chevrons picked out in gold.

A lovely, if typical, San Francisco Victorian.

Normal people lived in houses like that. Didn't they? Normal people with deep pockets. These properties were valuable.

Nick had to get into that house and find out who lived there. He put his hand over the left side of his waist, where he felt his gun through the baggy black T-shirt he wore.

Each of the double front doors had insets of dark stained glass. They were set deep inside a porch with a small second-floor window in the wall above. The roof over the porch could block the view of the immediate approach from up there—as long as that approach was made from the left side of the house which butted up against the next building and where there was no room for a window.

The only danger came from a bay window on the ground floor, but the draperies were closed.

As long as his quarries weren't hanging around just inside the house, he had a chance to sneak up on them.

Nick stood in a surprisingly bright front hallway. Light through the stained glass threw colors across yellow silk-covered walls and up banisters freshly painted white.

He stood, his hand still on the doorknob, and listened.

Not a sound, not even a creak came to him.

Straight up the first flight he could see a furnished open gallery, the back of a piano with a vase of flowers on top. Across from the stairs, the room with closed drapes made a dim focus, a contrast to the rest.

Then there was a sound. Nick didn't recognize the sibilant thud, or the slight zinging that followed, but it came from below, from the basement.

Leaving the front doors cracked open, he edged along a wall until he saw behind the staircase. The area was permanently open and reached through an archway. A ramp led down.

Nick took two long strides across and stood to one side, just out of sight of anyone looking up that ramp.

The sound came again, a little louder this time.

And a raised voice. Nick couldn't make out what it said.

He pulled his gun and took one step on the ramp, sucked in a breath at the squeaking from his tennis shoe and carefully removed both of them. His feet were bare, so at least he wouldn't slip.

All the light was upstairs. The basement consisted of a gloomy corridor with doors on either side.

Nick crept forward on dull brown carpet. At some time the walls had been badly paneled. He made it all the way to the end of the corridor, listening, but not picking up the voice again. The last door on the left, a room facing the back of the house, stood open. He went forward; one foot, waited, then the other foot.

"You've had time to think, now you can answer my questions and maybe we'll talk about keeping you alive," a grating voice announced. It sounded as if the owner smoked heavily. He burst into spasms of coughing and spitting.

"I went to Pointe Judah with Joan." This was Vic's voice. "She gave the story about writing a book. I worked on finding your item. I tried to follow your instructions to the letter but there was a slip."

Nick noted that Vic didn't sound afraid.

"And I want to know about the slip?"

"I shouldn't have mentioned it. It was nothing."

Once more the odd, breathy, singing sound issued.

Then the thump and more rapidly paced zinging . . . or whining. The sound reminded Nick of someone playing a saw.

"Goddammit," Vic said, but not as vehemently as Nick might have expected.

"I want you against the wall," the stranger's voice said. "Put your arms out where I can see them and spread your legs."

"No way," Vic said. "Without me, you wouldn't be getting anything from this effort we've made. You're the one who made a mistake by choosing Joan to be my cover."

"I never told her exactly what was going down."

"She worked it out. She's a pain in the ass."

Another zinging and thump.

Vic cried out. "Shit, Cooper. Shit. You're irrational."

"Joan did whatever I told her to do. Always. Except get in too deep with you. Women are fools that way. Tell me what went wrong."

"A woman died. Her name was Baily Morris."

"I know," Cooper said. "I know everything, I've known everything that happened around the Boards, as they call themselves, in Pointe Judah since the day they arrived there. I first caught up with them in Portland. You can always buy information and I bought lots of it. P.I.s are a dime a dozen, maybe cheaper. I've had those three pains-in-the-ass followed every step of the way, just in case a time came when I needed to deal with them. Like now, you asshole."

"So why didn't you go after your fucking due years ago?" Vic said. "Why wait until it turned desperate?"

Cooper coughed, hacked and Nick heard him spit. "I'm not desperate. I've never been desperate. As long as the grave stayed closed, the way I expected it to forever, I didn't want to draw any attention to myself. I had my new life so I just kept tabs on those three and made sure I stayed out of the way. Now all that's changed. I want to make sure there's no one left who can identify me, and I want what's mine. I don't need it, but I don't want those friggin' little thieves to have it."

"My ass," Vic said, a violent urgency in his voice. "You need money. You're broke."

"Shut the fuck up or say bye-bye," Cooper said. "I wondered how long it would take you to come clean about the other chemist, you ass. I told you to avoid collateral violence. Makes things messy."

"It was your fault for not making sure your informants did a complete job. He got the bleach job right and that Sarah worked some nights. Only she wasn't the only one and it wasn't her that night. It was this Baily Morris and she had bleached hair, too, and the same sort of long build as Sarah. And the thick makeup job. The description matched. How was I to know for sure when I hadn't seen Sarah yet? I knew I needed to work fast. The very first night I went out to the lab and I thought the woman there was Sarah. I took her up to the roof. I wanted to frighten her into telling me what she knew about your goods. She said she wasn't Sarah and didn't know anything. In the end I had to believe her. Only I couldn't leave her alive. Sarah has a history she wants to forget. That would silence her, but I had no guarantees this other one would keep her mouth shut."

"So you killed her."

"And got away with it. They're no closer to finding her murderer than they were when they found her."

"Among the broken roses," Cooper said. "I didn't know how poetic you are. When I read that I almost cried. What else?"

"Nothing else. I left Joan and came to you. She's too scared to be a threat."

Laughter followed. "That I believe. But we will have to get her back here and see if she can be useful and kept under control. Otherwise . . . " The man left his words hanging.

Nick fought for patience, for the sense to wait for what sounded like the right moment to enter. He'd give anything for a look inside the room.

"Why did you come back?" the man asked suddenly.

"Because I said I would. You've been good to me."

"You hate my guts."

"No—"

"But you know I have people who would deal with you if you tried to drop out." He coughed. "So you didn't pull it off and get what I sent you for. I need it, Vic—and it's mine. I like to keep what's mine."

"Didn't you expect it to have been fenced by now? A long time ago probably?"

"If it had, I'd have known about that. A perfect Burmese pigeon's blood ruby the size of that one isn't easy to sell. It's probably the biggest in the world."

41

Aurelie lay down across the backseat in the Honda.

A parking ticket, flapping behind a windshield wiper, was too much action for her aching head.

She squinted at her cell phone, her thumb hovering over the keypad. If she made the call she wanted to make, she might solve the most dangerous situation she had ever faced. Or she might regret what she'd done for the rest of her life.

Aurelie placed the call.

42

Aurelie took a last quick look at the paper on which she'd written the address on Haight Street and crushed it into her palm. With the strap of her shoulder bag crisscrossing her body, zipped open to allow easy access to the gun, Aurelie lifted her inconvenient red skirt and rushed up the brick front steps.

Double front doors with stained-glass insets stood slightly open. She stopped and gave one door a slight push.

Yelling voices came from somewhere deep in the house.

Aurelie pulled out the gun and stiffened her wrist against shakiness that attacked her all over.

Following the noise was easy. The place felt empty, like a museum after closing, with exhibits waiting for the next crowd to arrive. The shouting sounded obscene.

She found a ramp leading to the basement. That's where the voices were. Stepping carefully—her sandals weren't ideal stalking shoes—she took deep breaths that didn't calm her down and jammed her right elbow to her side. She could do this. She had to, for Nick. He'd walked right in here, right into what must have become an ambush. Who could know how many people were down there? He'd told her he was following Vic. There was one man with a gun for a start. And unless the bang on her head had knocked her senseless, she had to expect more armed people down there.

And she must take them on—no, that should be take them out, all by herself.

Nick's voice snapped, "Keep your hand out of that bag."

"Where's your respect?" another man asked. "What would your dear mother say?"

Aurelie gritted her teeth and moved quickly, reached the bottom of the ramp and turned in to a corridor. All the ruckus came from a room at the end. She could see the door was open.

She wiped the gun grip on her skirt, then her palm, and stood tall.

"Put your hands up," she said loudly, stepping into the doorway and sweeping the gun from side to side. "Not you, Nick. Get over here by me."

Nick, his gun drawn, stood behind a wheelchair where a gnarled man sat, staring at her—and smiling. His emaciated body looked fragile in the chair, his back grotesquely curved over. Vic, to the right of the man, held out a hand with a big lump of ugly red glass balanced there like a genie's lamp.

"We've got them," she told Nick. "It's exactly what they deserve. If he—" she nodded at Vic "—had tied me up, I couldn't have gotten out of that truck when I came around. Now look at him. If he wasn't holding that dumb thing, he could have a gun, too. Or did you lose your gun, Vic? Did you call the police, Nick?"

Nick didn't look at all well. And she thought he was really angry.

"Which one are you?" the man in the chair said. "Muriel or Ena?"

She gaped at him, got close enough to see his face clearly and recoiled. "It is him," she whispered. The face seemed strangely young in comparison with the withered body, and Colin's eyes were still the color of faded green glass.

"Hi, there," he said. "Sarah or Aurelie, of course. I forgot the new names for a moment."

"Old people do that sometimes," she said, barely able to move her mouth.

"Aurelie," Nick said, "I want you to leave this room and go outside as fast as you can."

"Why?"

"Because I don't want you here right now."

Her stomach turned. "You don't want me to watch you kill them?"

"Aurelie." He piled warning into her name.

"If they put him on trial, he'll suffer more," she pointed out. "It'll be really ugly for him, take it from me. And Vic's going somewhere not quite lonely enough, too. They don't like his kind of murderer inside."

"How do you know he killed someone and how did you get here?" Colin asked, not smiling anymore. "Who else knows?"

"Shut up," she told him. "I've already called the police. I just wanted to see if Nick had, too. Nick, I'll take Colin, you watch Vic."

Someone very large grabbed her from behind. He held her with an arm around her waist and one hand entirely encircling her neck. "You over there, you will drop the gun," he said and gave a shake that rattled the ache back into Aurelie's head.

"He's Nick," Vic said helpfully. "He's trying to kill the boss and me."

"I thought that might be so," the rumbling voice behind Aurelie said. "My name is Vasilly. I look after Mr. Cooper. I don't want you to have that gun, *Nick*. If you don't do what I've asked—politely—I will break your friend's neck."

"Don't listen," Aurelie said. "He'd need two hands for that."

Vasilly tightened his hand ever so slightly.

"Let her go," Nick said. He hovered. She could see him trying to decide what to do. And she could feel the hand, like a band of steel, around her neck.

"This is very good," Colin said. "I should like them both to suffocate. It'll be appropriate since they missed their first opportunity. Vic, let Vasilly see the ruby. The two of us have talked about it so often."

"Drop the gun," Vasilly said, and the steel band grew tighter. He looked at the ruby. "The biggest I have ever seen. Hold it to the light—as best you can, please."

Vic held up the red lump. Aurelie supposed uncut rubies always looked like that.

She caught Nick's eye, looked at his gun, then remembered what she had in her own hand, the one wrapped tightly around her waist. Everyone seemed to have forgotten or never to have noticed she had a gun.

Without having to move more than her finger, she pulled the trigger. The report vibrated through her body, blasted her ears, and Vasilly released her.

On her knees—she couldn't keep her footing—she stared, horrified, at the big block of a man who lay bleeding. He grasped a fleshy handful at his left side. Blood rushed through his fingers.

Aurelie heard approaching sirens, heard them get

louder and louder until they screeched in the street outside.

Vasilly gasped, "I knew I should have gone myself. That is no ruby. That is a fake."

43

I had it good. I had it better than anything's ever been for me. But I've blown it. Even if I get out of here alive, the cops will have done a background check and when they fill her in, Sabine won't forgive me for being a liar.

If I'd told her everything and let her make up her mind, she would have said we could put the past behind us. "Where it belongs," she'd say. I can hear her voice now.

Help me out here. Don't let me blubber or beg. You don't get anything that way. I should know.

If I puke I'll be living with it inside this bag. I'll choke on it.

Let me out. Please let me out. I've gone straight for years now. I'll never go back. I'll never slip up again. Just don't let him kill me.

Ed's guts twisted tight, and if he weren't tied in a chair he'd double up to ease the pain. He needed to distract his thinking, put himself somewhere else.

How long had he been there?

Two days?

When they arrived early in the morning, the day

before yesterday, the rain had been falling like it did all the previous night. Yesterday, another day of fighting his bladder between supervised trips to a dirty bathroom, the temperature had gone up. But the night cooled off, like the first one had. Now he felt the sun warming up on the back of his neck again.

When he'd been brought here, and from a distance against a still-dark sky, Ed had thought he was looking at a smokestack and decided the structure they were headed for must be a mill of some kind, but once they got a bit closer he recognized his mistake. The building had been a detention center. It said so on a bleached-out placard hanging from a single anchor on heavy chain-link fencing that still had barbed wire along the top. They drove on parking lights but the old letters showed just the same. The gates sagged open and the tower overlooked the yard and dilapidated prison buildings.

That's where he had been taken, to the tower's upper platform, and where he'd been knocked down and kept down with a foot in the middle of his back while the bearded man secured the bag at Ed's neck. That was before he got taped in the chair.

The view should be something if he didn't have a scratchy hemp bag over his head, and if the sides of the lookout platform weren't so high with him sitting down. The stranger, the swarthy one who dropped him when he was getting into the truck at Buzzard's Wet Bar, had driven him out of town, to the north, to the long building with a lookout tower at one end.

He clung to the hope that a man, who stopped his car the night he went to Buzzard's to check on him after he pulled off the road not far from Place Lafource, would hear Ed was missing and decide to go to the police. The man, who stopped because he thought Ed was dead over the wheel, had talked him into going to Buzzard's for a drink. He had left the tavern at about the same time as Ed, and might have seen him get punched out and stuffed into an old gray Impala with no shine left on the paint. Did the man know Ed's name? He thought about it. Sure he did. He'd given Ed the bearer bond he'd hoped to surprise Sabine with, but Ed couldn't recall the guy saying anything personal. He couldn't even remember what the guy looked like. There had been more, many more drinks than Ed was used to. He couldn't even recall exactly why he'd told the man about the ruby.

Rum and Cokes with tequila shots. Darn it, he'd drunk too much that night. And that man had the ruby. He wouldn't be calling anyone about Ed.

Sweat broke out all over him, soaked his T-shirt and turned the waist of his jeans cold and damp. More than anything, he wished Sabine didn't have to deal with what he was doing. She didn't deserve this. Tears prickled in his eyes. Even if the bond hadn't been taken from him, he wouldn't keep it—if he got a chance to decide.

The guy with the beard had left again hours ago, saying, "I need some tools."

What kind of tools did he need and why?

Another spasm gripped Ed's belly.

The pain faded and he caught his breath. Then he heard footsteps climbing from the stripped control room at the bottom of the tower, toward the top and Ed.

As the person climbed, he hit the metal steps with something that clanged.

Ed felt the moment when he wasn't alone anymore. The guy brought odors with him, sweat, and oil.

Was he going to set fire to the place? A deep breath didn't slow Ed's heart down. If fire was what the man had decided on, he could set it at the base of the watchtower and the whole thing would go up.

A punch to the side of the head knocked Ed and his chair over. His elbow and forearm, his bony wrist, smacked into the floor. He cried out. With the whole weight of his body, and the chair, pressed on the arm, a sickening snap sounded and he figured the bone in his elbow was wasted.

"Up you come," the anonymous voice said, and he was swung up until the chair legs connected with a hard base again and Ed screwed up his face against the torment in his elbow.

He sweated harder, barely held back the need to throwup.

A laugh from the guy hurt Ed's brain.

"Just wanted to make sure you're wide awake," the man said. "You gotta be able to think clearly."

Ed grimaced and let his eyes close.

"You've been jerking me around," he was told.

"That stone isn't in any gnome-covered radio or tape recorder. There's gotta be a dozen of those things at Lafource. It's taken me two days to get through 'em all, and come up empty. You think that's funny? You think it's funny to send me to a place where there's a bodyguard hanging around so I have to take risks I don't want to take?" He cuffed Ed.

"I don't know," Ed said, terrified.

"I'm going to be patient and start over at the beginning," he was told. "It's all about a ruby. Do you like being told stories? I don't care if you do or don't. You've heard it once, now you can hear it again. It's about a big, beautiful, Burmese pigeon's blood ruby. According to what I've been told, it could be the biggest flawless example of its kind. You know the one I mean?"

Ed shook his head once and a hot ache seared the backs of his eyes.

"Sure you do."

Ed shook his head again and a fist landed on his breastbone, winded him so bad he couldn't drag in any air. The feeling must be like having a heart attack. He almost laughed. That would be justice if he just up and died on this piece of shit.

"You laughing, sucker?" the man asked. "Why's that? You find it hilarious when you get hurt?"

"No," Ed managed to say.

"I'm bored with this." The man dragged something that sounded like nylon across the floor. A zip opened. "Time we finished up and moved on. A little bird told me you know all about the ruby with the dumb name. Yama Dharma, the Vulture Ruby, or some fool thing. The little bird reckoned you took it out of Delia's office and hid it somewhere so you could fence it later. That makes you one stupid man. What were you going to do, walk into a pawnbroker's with it? Yeah, that's what you must have had in mind. Mr. Pawnbroker, see this perfect ruby? Just give me two or three million and it's yours."

The laugh that followed got higher until it sounded like it belonged to a teenage boy whose voice just broke.

Ed kept quiet.

"Maybe you know all about fencing a beauty like that to the right people. You know what I mean? Collectors. Collectors' agents. It's a complicated world, but a few know all about it and maybe you're one of them."

"I don't know anything about anything," Ed said. "I only said the thing about the gnomes 'cause you wouldn't let up. I'm sorry I made it up. I never saw your ruby and I wouldn't know what to do with one if I had it. If you let me go home, I'll stay where I am till you're away and I won't send anyone after you. I can just go back and say I got drunk and lost my way for a couple of days."

Again the laugh skated up the scale.

"Honest. That's what I'll do." Ed's eyes hurt, and they stung. He couldn't cry. "If I knew where your ruby was, I'd tell you that, too."

"So tell me."

"I told you I don't know," Ed said, raising his voice. "You gotta know I'd tell you if I did."

A big fist drove into his belly, right below his ribs, and his throat closed. He began to choke.

"Just you think about where that ruby is while you get your wind back."

This wasn't a random bad guy. He'd worked people over before and he enjoyed it. Ed could feel the other man's excitement.

"Coming to you, is it? What have you done with that stone, Ed?"

"Nothing." He hated the thin sound of his voice. "I haven't done anything with it. I never had it."

"You don't want to try that, Eddie boy. You want to help me so you can go home. Just tell me where you hid it—for real—and you'll be a free man."

Ed couldn't hold his head up. It lolled forward. "No. I don't know. Why do you think I do?"

"You told someone you did. You were seen with it."

"That was you?" Ed said, choking down saliva. "At Lafource. You hit me on the head, but you didn't see me with the stone." He had already slid the ruby inside on the window ledge in the breakfast room, ready to put it back in the safe, when the guy dropped him. Afterward, when Ed went back for the stone, he could hardly believe it was still there. And he'd changed his mind about putting it back where it came from. That was too dangerous.

The man had turned quiet, and still.

"It was you, wasn't it?" Ed asked. "You pushed me around and hung me in the pool."

"Nah. You already admitted you made that story up."

"But—"

"Maybe you should save your brain. You may need it."

"Okay, I give up," Ed said. "Take this thing off my head and I'll tell you. You gotta give me a guarantee you're gonna let me go."

"You've got it," the voice almost sang out.

Steady fingers dragged at the string around his neck, burned his skin with the stiff twine and jerked the bag off his head.

Ed looked up and his heart lightened. A stocking, with eye and mouth holes, covered the man's head. You couldn't tell what he looked like, but the beard was still obvious. He did intend to let Ed go—and he knew he wouldn't remember his face from the darkness outside Buzzard's, not when Ed had been scared shitless, or from the drive, despite the gradual lightening of the sky.

Sunlight hit his eyes, then faded with the shadow of a cloud.

The man turned his hand palm up and beckoned with all of the fingers. "Give me what I want," he said. "Where is it?"

"It's gonna be hard for you to get it," Ed said.

Eyes stared at him through the mask. Ed looked away, and on the floor he saw a dark blue duffel bag, its open zipper gaping. A drill poked out, a long, thin bit in place.

Ed turned icy. His wet clothes stuck to his skin. He didn't think his companion planned any woodworking jobs.

"Where did you put it?" The voice came at Ed in a harsh whisper. "Really, this time."

"I . . . I'm afraid to say. You're going to kill me anyway." Maybe there would be a chance to call Sabine and get her to have the police arrest this guy when he showed up.

"I said I wouldn't kill you. Are you calling me a liar?"

"No," Ed said. "No, I'm not. You're gonna let me go, right?" He couldn't think anymore.

"Yeah."

He didn't believe it but there weren't any choices. "It's out back of Nick Board's place." He didn't want this guy anywhere near homes, his own, the Boards' or anyone else's, but he didn't see any way to avoid it. "There's a flamingo there, in a new flower bed. The ruby's inside."

He got another unflinching stare. "Why there?"

"I planted the bed. It wouldn't surprise anyone to see me messin' around out there. You can't miss the flamingo."

Once more the scaling laugh burst into silent air. "Good," the man said. "Really good. It's too bad I can't just have you go get it for me."

"I'd do that," Ed said. "I surely would. And I'd do

it without givin' a thing away. That's a good idea. You wouldn't have to worry about someone seeing you."

The drill thumped the floor, sent an echo into the space below.

Ed said, "What's that for?"

"I like to play around with tools. It's creative." He emptied the bag and hauled a small chain saw from the bottom. "This is my favorite. I might go into business making those wooden animals you can sell along the road."

When Ed swallowed he made a clicking sound, and coughed. He kept his mouth open and took short breaths. "Don't do it," he said when he could speak. "God, don't do it."

The other man fired up the gas saw and held the blade up to the sun. Shards of light shot from the clean steel with its rotating teeth.

Ed made meaningless sounds. No words would come out. Pushing with his feet, he tried to scoot the chair backward. It started to tip. With the saw vibrating in his right hand, the man pulled Ed's hair with the other and held him steady.

A grinding bounce against the inside of Ed's thigh started him screaming. Screaming and watching blood pump through the leg of his pants.

"Please," he yelled, and screamed again. "I told you what you asked."

"You told me you think I'm a fool. Gnomes, then a flamingo? You don't know where the thing is, do you?"

424

Held aloft, cocked with an elbow on the hip like a shotgun, the blade shone in the light some more, this time streaked with blood.

Ed saw black filling in the edges of his eyes.

The man was there, his eyes narrowed inside the slits in the stocking. Slowly, he began to lower the saw again.

Ed took in a great breath and threw himself, chair and all, at the arm with the saw.

The saw slipped, jerked from the man's fingers, and the rotating blade snatched at his free wrist.

Blood spurted. It felt like it washed over Ed's eyeballs.

He heard the other one bellow.

That was all.

44

Two boys stood beside the track. Matt slowed down to take a good look at them. Wild-eyed with sweat running down the sides of their dusty black faces, they were maybe ten apiece and scared out of their jeans.

"This is it," he said to Simon Vasseur, a transplant from Lake Charles to the Pointe Judah force. "Let me take it."

"Yes, Chief."

Vasseur had two years' experience and Matt figured the guy would turn into a real asset. He knew the people and had a nice way with them. And he could be one cold son of a bitch when he needed to be.

Matt got out of the car. "Hey, boys. You two call into the station?"

"Yes, sir, Chief Boudreaux," one of the boys said. They had both smiled at the sight of Matt, who knew most people around. The smiles had gone now.

Matt stood with his thumbs hooked into his belt. "You would be Marvin Jasper's boy, Ted," he said to the slightly taller one who wore a red T-shirt that said, Make My Day. Try It, on the front. "And you're Soccer Brown," he said to the other. He'd never asked him where he got his first name but the kid didn't look too athletic.

"Yes, sir," they said in unison.

"Gettin' late," Matt said. "You want a ride back to town?"

The light was still full but it wouldn't be for much longer and the boys had around an hour's walk out to the main highway again.

"We found somethin'," Soccer said. "That's why we called." He pulled a cell phone out of a small backpack on the ground near his feet to prove his point.

Matt bent to get closer to the kids and raised his brows. They didn't look so good. "What's up?"

"Back there," Ted Jasper said. "In the old penitentiary."

"It was just a detention center," Matt said gently. He looked at the place, a hundred or so yards ahead and desolate looking. "What did you see?"

426

"Blood," Soccer said promptly.

"Blood," Matt repeated. "You want to take me there?"

"No" he got in another chorus.

"Who do you think did the bleeding? Did you see 'em?"

"Nope, just the blood." Ted kicked at the ground and dust rose in a nose-twitching cloud from flattened, dry white grass. "It come through the roof, we think."

Matt stared off in the direction of the old building again. "You two playin' around in there?"

Both heads hung.

"You know the kind of stuff went on in there. I reckon a lot of folks did some bleeding from time to time. They fought, like happens when there's tempers and mean minds around. Don't you worry. Just stay away in future, hmm?"

"We saw blood," Ted said, squinting up at Matt, his mouth set in a stubborn line. "A lot of it."

"Old blood?" Matt asked. He'd have to take a look, but this pair didn't need to lose sleep having nightmares about stuff they imagined.

"New blood," Soccer said. He was a slightly built, handsome boy with greenish eyes and a straight nose. "You gotta see."

Vasseur had been listening through the open window on the cruiser. Matt turned and called, "Let's take a run to the old facility here with the boys." Vasseur nodded and unlocked the back doors.

With Matt back behind the wheel they drove past the mostly torn-off gates of the place and parked close to the building.

A call came in and Carly at the station said, "Chief, just heard from Nick Board. He and Aurelie got back from San Francisco and he says he knows you'll want to talk to them."

Matt slammed on the brakes. "You bet your—" Furious, as he had been about Nick and Aurelie since they left town without a word, he collected himself. "Are they there now?"

"They're at Place Lafource. Nick says do you want him to meet you at the station, or—"

"Tell him to stay put. I've got something to do first, then I'll go over there."

"Yes, Chief." Carly sounded unusually formal and Matt figured he wasn't doing a good job of hiding his feelings.

The call ended and he said, "The Boards think they can do what they like. If the San Francisco police hadn't called for information, I still wouldn't know where they'd've been." He was off base talking to Vasseur like that, but he doubted the man would repeat a word. He was too ambitious.

On top of having Ed Webb missing for days, now they were searching for Joan Reeves, as well. And he wanted the photographer, Vic Gross, extradited back to Louisiana where he could charge him for the murder of Baily Morris. Nothing was going his way. Yes, he would be going to Lafource the moment he was through here.

428

"Where to now, boys?" he said, as evenly as he could manage.

"Over there," young Ted said. "In the tower."

Matt and Simon gave one another a long-suffering glance. "The tower, it is," Matt said. "Let's walk over."

Simon Vasseur went with them but the closer they got to the watchtower, the slower the boys walked.

"You stay here," Matt said when they were about at a standstill. "Where's the blood?"

"On the floor," Soccer said. "And way up overhead. You can see it up there."

"Under the floor of the lookout platform?" Matt asked.

"I guess," Soccer said. "We didn't do it."

Matt almost laughed. "Just you wait here with Officer Vasseur." He decided the kids had scared themselves silly and didn't want to leave them alone.

He jogged the rest of the way to the base of the tower, where a door stood open, and went inside. He flipped a switch on the wall and was surprised when light flooded the place.

Light wasn't the only thing causing a flood in there.

On the floor, a little to one side of metal steps going straight up to the lookout area, dark red blood shone in a slick pool. Congealed blood that would gum up like jelly if you touched it.

Matt rubbed a hand over his face. One thing was for sure, the blood wasn't so old. He looked up and saw a stain on the wooden ceiling way above his head. He stepped back, half expecting drips to hit him.

He stepped back outside. "Simon. Why don't you lock the boys in the back—just for safety's sake—and give me a hand here." He gave the kids a reassuring grin but his stomach tightened, not because of the blood but because he didn't know what he'd face at the top of the stairs.

Simon did as he was asked at a trot and joined Matt. He narrowed his eyes at his chief. "There's blood, right? And it isn't old?"

"You've got it," Matt said quietly. "We're going to have to go up a flight of stairs in there to a trapdoor at the top. Looks like it pushes up, which is somethin'. Probably locks from above. We don't know if there's someone waitin' for us to put our heads through that floor. I bet the guards used to like the idea of that advantage, just in case some yahoo sneaked up."

"Do we call in?" Simon asked.

"You bet we do. Buck's off but ask for backup out here. I'll go first, you cover me." Not that backup would help if he got his head blown off.

Simon began speaking quietly into his radio. When he finished, he followed Matt into the tower. The expression on Simon's face didn't change when he saw the blood. He just raised his chin to look up.

Softly, Matt put a foot on the stairs. Too bad about the metal—the danger of making too much noise increased with that. But at least the flight was still in good shape.

With the top of his head several inches below the

level of the trapdoor, Matt stopped and listened. He glanced down at Simon, whose face remained impassive. The man held his gun.

Not a sound came from the watchtower platform.

Spreading the fingers of his left hand, Matt braced the tips against the panel and pushed, held the muscles in his hand and wrist rigid and hoped the thing wouldn't rattle. It didn't budge.

He stopped and pressed his lips together. Breath through the mouth could be too loud sometimes. The trapdoor had probably rusted in since it hadn't been used in years.

Applying more pressure, he pushed again, and the trap raised a little at one side. Again he pressed, but gently, and the gap between the opening in the ceiling and the edge of the trapdoor continued to widen. There was no handle on the lower side, which made sense, and Matt was certain it locked tight from above. In case of trouble when the place was a prison, the guards couldn't be easily stormed.

Damn, he needed absolute concentration.

Inch by inch he lifted until he had to take another step to continue.

No sound.

He'd left his hat below. If he wanted to, he could see over the rim now.

No sound.

Matt stretched up until his eyes were above the level of the platform.

Straight ahead, taped into a chair that lay on its side

he saw a man, his neck and the underside of his jaw arched, so his face wasn't visible.

The man and his chair rested in a lake of blood.

Behind him, sitting propped in a corner with his left arm held up on a crate, was another man, this one with a stocking over his head and eyes that seemed to glint from deep holes. "Couldn't open the goddamn trap," he whispered.

The raised arm bore a makeshift tourniquet. It had no hand.

45

"How much farther?" Aurelie asked. "We're almost there, aren't we?"

Nick gave her a quick glance. "Just a few miles."

At least it was a dry night, so driving too fast for almost any conditions was a small measure safer.

"Matt seemed different," Aurelie said, looking at the beginning straggle of the Lafayette outskirts. "I didn't expect him to call back to us so fast after he came to talk to Sabine."

A weary Matt Boudreaux had come to Place Lafource and closeted himself with Sabine and Delia. Then he'd left again, after Mitch Halpern had come to help Sabine, saying Nick and Aurelie would have to wait for him to talk to them.

"We're going to get through this, y'know," Nick said. "Every one of us will, even Sabine. Damn, I hate that this happened to her."

Aurelie let her eyes wander up to where the moon touched the purple-black sky behind the pitch crowns of trees. "She's one of the best people I can think of. Ed wanted to make her life better. You could see how much he loved her."

"I hope Matt's going to come out with more details," Nick said.

"Yes," Aurelie said. "He could have said why he wants us in Lafayette—at the hospital."

Nick let the car slow suddenly.

"What?" Aurelie said.

"Nothing, sorry." He continued at a steady rate again.

"What, Nick? Don't do that to me."

"It was silly. I wondered if he wanted one of us to identify Ed, but that wouldn't make sense."

"No, it wouldn't," she said promptly. "He doesn't need us for that."

"We're about to find out what's up," he said. "I've run through everything I can think of. I don't know of anyone missing or sick."

Police presence at the hospital was impossible to ignore. Cars outside, officers inside. Carly Gibson stood in the all but deserted reception area and came toward them.

"I've been waiting for you," she said. "Matt said to take you along but I'm to call him." This she did promptly and when they stepped off an elevator, Matt met them.

He nodded to Carly, who left at once, her blond braid flipping from side to side.

"We're looking for Joan Reeves," Matt said. "Any ideas where she might go?"

This was the reason for bringing them here? Nick shook his head. "You must have talked to Finn—"

"I did. She went out a window at their place about an hour ago as far as he and Emma can figure. We'll get her."

Matt put his hands behind his back. He looked hard at Nick, who felt Aurelie shift at his side.

"You two going to get married?"

Nick opened his mouth but didn't quite have the right comeback.

"You didn't bring us here to ask us that," Aurelie said. She pinched the back of Nick's arm.

He didn't know if he was supposed to back her up but he said, "When we're ready to talk about that, we will."

"Just thought I'd try to catch you off guard so you'd say yes before you had a chance to think."

Nick smiled but everything about this moment and this place was ominous. "We didn't much like leaving Place Lafource. We're needed there."

"I know you are, but this is unfinished business. I owe it to you to bring you up to speed, and to apologize. Sorry I've been a jackass."

Nick fixed on the shiny top of the reception desk, "Well—"

"No need to say any more," Matt said. "I've done it now."

"Right," Nick said. "Is that it? You needed Aurelie here for that?"

"It's just a start. And I'm the one who let some of the snakes out in the first place."

Aurelie put her hand into Nick's and he squeezed her fingers. "I find it's easier to get things said fast."

"I shouldn't have decided you were the enemy," Matt said.

"Why would you do that?" Aurelie said. "Nick's been your best friend for years."

"I listened to the wrong people and got some convincing stuff pointed out to me. I didn't think you were a criminal, not deep down, but . . . aw, hell." The strain in his face ate at Nick. "Come on."

The corridors were quiet, and apart from the slight noise from Matt's rubber-soled shoes, nothing interrupted the silence. The hospital was battening down for the night.

After making another turn, two more officers came into view, one on either side of a door. The lights were brighter in the area. A nursing station, monitors blipping on three sides, was opposite a room with half-glass walls where the police officers stood.

Aurelie hung back.

"It's okay," Matt said. "Let's just get this over with. He had a bad history."

"Ed?" Nick said.

"No," Matt said. "I should have done more homework."

They reached the room and looked through the windows.

On a bed, hooked up to multiple leads, lay Buck

Dupiere, his sleeping, or unconscious, face the same color as the sheets.

"Oh, God," Nick said. "What happened to his hand?"

"It was too late to reattach it."

They gathered in a private waiting room where Sampson appeared with mugs of steaming coffee and plates of sandwiches. Just looking at the food turned Aurelie's stomach.

"Why did you hire him?" Nick asked Matt.

"He came to me first, months ago, and let me know he wanted out of the NOPD. Word was already going around that Billy Meche might be retiring. Dupiere doesn't have a record of anything but bad relations with fellow officers and a marriage that broke up because . . . I think he was pretty much absent and when he wasn't, he could get mean. Twin daughters. His ex-wife's been told and she actually seems upset for him."

"Has he said anything?" Nick asked.

"Some. He comes and goes. He's lucky he didn't manage to get away from where it happened. He used a tourniquet but he might not have made it back alive. Eventually he'll probably wish he hadn't made it anyway."

Matt filled them in on the details of the scene in the watchtower and Aurelie shuddered. "You mean someone suddenly turns into a monster like that? There's got to be more."

"Yeah," Matt said, worrying his bottom lip with his teeth. "We're waiting for a report from the army. He didn't get an honorable discharge. That may turn something up. Not that it matters anymore. He's already said Ed had it coming." Matt hung his head. "Ed was doing great. He just had that one opportunity to get into Delia's safe and he couldn't let it pass. Vic saw him take the ruby and worked out his own plan for getting it back, but Buck saw Ed, too—later. Vic did get his hands on the letter, which Ed didn't bother to take. Ed stuffed the package with Delia's sand and Vic replaced your letter with a bill from the drawer, Nick. Later, Vic gave the letter to Joan for safe-keeping and forgot to get it back before he skipped. The police in California passed along the details on Vic. He's been full of useful chatter. A lot of what he's said only backs up what you told us, Nick, but it's good to have.

"We think Ed tried to put the stone back and that's when Buck saw him. We'll probably never know for sure now unless Buck tells us, and as he gets his feet under him, he'll stop talking. It makes most sense that Buck took Ed down at Place Lafource that day, and roughed him up, copying what Vic had done to Aurelie to make it look like the same perp. When he didn't find anything on him, he left him in the pool. Ed must have changed his mind about returning the stone and hidden it somewhere instead, then collected it again later.

"Buck may have given up on it then, but he got the

letter to Nick—he took it from Joan's bag—and Ed's one slip to Mitch Halpern about something valuable started Buck on the trail again. He surely had the right cover to be watching Ed's moves."

"Vic got the so-called ruby, Matt," Nick said.

"I know that. But Buck didn't. He thought Ed still had it. Vic Gross is saying anything he thinks will buy him some lesser charges. He came on Ed beside the road and got him to go to Buzzards. Gave him some phony bearer bond for the lump of glass. Buck must have been waiting for Ed when he came out of the tavern. When we found him Buck had on a beard and mask."

"He must have gone mad when he found out Ed didn't have the stone, so he killed him," Aurelie said.

Nick said in a low voice, "Buck would have killed him anyway. He couldn't afford to have him alive. The same reason Colin had for wanting to get rid of us." He sat down and took a mug of coffee. "You've got the letter, Matt?"

"As soon as we can, you'll have it," Matt said. "For now it's evidence."

This was what helpless felt like, Aurelie decided. Disaster in every direction, not that anything mattered as much to her as how Nick would cope.

Nick smiled at her, kept on smiling at her, though the set of his jaw was hard. He looked steadily at her and she felt their connection.

"Chief," Sampson opened the door, "a word?"

Matt went into the corridor and they listened to the rumble of conversation, but not for long. Matt returned, with Joan. Her face remained a mess but she held her head high and met Nick's then Aurelie's eyes.

"Joan's showed at the hospital," Matt said. "Reckons she's giving herself up. But she's got something she wants to share in front of Nick and Aurelie before we take her in."

Nick stood up.

"They said I could play a video in here," she said. "I owe it to you two to let you see it."

"Who said you could play a video?" Matt said rapidly. "What video?"

"I haven't hurt anyone," Joan said, flashing a glare at Matt. "Not the way you're thinking. I want to show this—"

"Whoa." Matt stopped her. "I'm gonna read you your rights," he said and read the Revised Miranda to her. "You understand?"

"Yeah, yeah," Joan said. "I'm tired. Look at this and it's up to you what you do with it—and me."

"Buck told us he got an envelope from you," Matt said. "You know what I'm talking about."

She ignored him and pushed a video into the player under a TV provided for waiting families.

After setting the machine to play, she stepped back, her mouth turned down and jerking. "There was an envelope in my purse. Vic gave it to me for safekeeping. I lost it somewhere."

"Could Buck have taken it from your purse?" Matt asked.

She stared at him, and finally shrugged. "He had the opportunity."

The screen came to life.

Nick slowly let his hands fall to his sides. Colin Fox, younger and fitter, sitting behind a big, black desk, looked directly at the camera. "We have our latest selection for you," he said. "You'll find plenty to interest you. The usual arrangements will apply."

One after another, images moved across the screen. From time to time Joan, also much younger, was present, interacting with a girl or boy to keep them quiet and make sure they turned to show all sides.

Once she said, "Look at Vic, he always makes sure everyone can see how pretty you are."

Abruptly, Matt crossed the room and stopped the video. Sampson had reentered the room and he stood beside Joan, holding her elbow.

"What is that?" Aurelie said.

"Vic brought the wrong video to give to me," Joan said with a slight smirk. "He must have intended it to be one that showed me, but he couldn't have known he was mentioned on it, too. It was his insurance against me, to keep me quiet. But it wouldn't have done him any good by now. That video is a sales catalog."

46

"My place or yours?" Nick braced for Aurelie's comeback.

"I have a dog waiting for me," she said.

"So your place." He deserved whatever he got. His mouth was out of control.

Aurelie rubbed his thigh, pressed her fingers into the muscle.

"Does that mean yes?" Nick asked.

She slid sideways and rested her head on his shoulder. "You can have the purple couch."

"Huh?"

Aurelie smiled. "Propriety must be observed. We have new status to consider."

He thought about that. "What kind of new status?"

"You know. Everyone knows I'm not your sister."

Nick grinned and kept his eyes on the road. "Of course. Sleeping in the same bed was okay before."

"I don't think that's exactly how I meant it."

"No?" He was grateful to drive into Pointe Judah. "Are we engaged?"

Aurelie tutted. "How old-fashioned, Nick. Yes, we are. And I like surprises, like diamond rings. Last time I was in New Orleans I saw a nice canary-yellow one in M.S. Rau."

"How old-fashioned," he said. "I'm glad we've made up our minds, though."

"So romantically," Aurelie said.

"That comes shortly," Nick said. "It's about time you decided to do the honorable thing. I've been worried about Hoover's self-image. Being a bastard can mess with your mind. Just ask me. He deserves to have both of his parents around."

She chuckled and moved her hand to his groin.

"Whoa," he said. "I'm driving."

The Letter

The Refuge

Dear Nicholas:

By now you know why I had to send you away. There's no need to be sad because I'm already grateful that I can keep you safe, and if you read this, I'll be at peace.

My parents are good people but they couldn't accept my child if I wasn't married. That meant I had to leave them, too. Their name is Chance, like mine, and they live in San Francisco. I want you to know this because it's your right. I am their only child.

Your father never knew about you. He left for college on the East Coast before *I* knew about you. Don't blame him for anything. He married the girl he broke up with before his high-school prom. I was the thrilled replacement for the ball, all starry-eyed to be invited by a senior. This sounds tawdry but it wasn't. I had loved him in that intense, teenage-girl way for a long time. He's an honorable person and he apologized afterward because he felt he'd led me astray. I wouldn't change a thing about having you.

You think you look like me, but you haven't seen your father!

When I left my parents' home I worked in a shop in the city. One day I saw Delia Board, who graduated a year ahead of me. Her family was very wealthy and she had an apartment and went to USF even though she could have gone to any school in the country. She saw me one day and ran after me till she caught me. It wasn't hard. You were born a few weeks later.

I expect you know what I mean about Delia's strong will. She wouldn't leave me alone until I'd told her everything, then she moved me into her apartment and she's the only person I have, apart from you, who has always loved me for myself.

Delia knows about Colin although I don't suppose she's ever said his name to you. She begged me not to have anything to do with him, but I hated her feeling responsible for me and I thought I was in love with Colin then. He was good with you and that was something I longed for, a man around my son. We met in a bookshop, and met there again and again and eventually I told him I would stay with him. Three months later we left with a group of people who wanted to make a quiet, simple life.

Colin found the place and he called it The Refuge.

I've liked it here, except for seeing Colin change. He's been changing for a long time and I'm frightened. I'm frightened for you and all the young people, and I'm very afraid for these children he has brought here. He says he unites them with their families, but no family has ever come for one of them. They're just taken away, supposedly to a meeting place.

I don't believe any of it, but I haven't found out otherwise. Muriel and Ena won't go that way—whatever it is. At least we'll save them. Ena told me they don't have a family but I'm scared what Colin might do if I pressed him about it.

The ruby? Colin's obsessed with the thing but he doesn't tell me how he got it. Sometimes he takes it out and shows it to me, and tells me it'll make sure we have everything we ever need. This isn't the Colin I met, the simple man who wanted a peaceful life.

I'm sending the ruby with you to Delia so it can be sold to pay for bringing you up, and Muriel and Ena. Colin will lose his mind when he finds out it's gone and he'll know it went with you. He'll blame me but I won't tell him where you are. And none of that will matter when you're reading this letter.

The ruby is very old. He said it passed from hand to hand until the true owner wasn't known anymore. That's why he said he had just as much right to it as anyone else, but he didn't. I'm sure it was in payment for something awful.

According to Colin's story, a king was once saved by the ruby. He used it to buy his life back from assassins. And there was a legend that the ruby had been stolen a number of times but always the thief ended up being staked out in the sun and eaten alive by vultures. There's a nice bedtime story for a mother to tell her son! Colin was vague about what happens to whoever has the ruby now but I haven't seen any vultures around.

So please help Delia get the stone sold, Nicholas. Delia won't know how to handle something like that, but you are so resourceful. You'll find out. If Colin's stories are right, there should be enough money to keep you—and the girls—until you can make your own way—with plenty left over to help get you started in life.

I'm sorry, Nicholas. I made bad choices. You should never have been in this place, especially when we all know what's being grown here. The adults are breaking the law. But we did come here looking for a refuge and I made an excuse to stay by telling myself how hard it would be to get away. And Colin warned me never to try. I don't love him. I never have, really.

My love goes with you, all of it. Live and love and be happy, then everything that's happened will have had a purpose.

Mom

Center Point Publishing
600 Brooks Road ● PO Box 1
Thorndike ME 04986-0001 USA

(207) 568-3717

US & Canada:
1 800 929-9108
www.centerpointlargeprint.com